CONQUEROR'S BLOOD

ZAMIL AKHTAR

Cover by Miblart

Edited by Fiona McClaren

Special thanks to Salik and Robert

This book is a work of fiction. Names, characters, places, and incidents are the product of the author's imagination or are used fictitiously. Any resemblance to actual events, locales, or persons, living or dead, is coincidental.

Copyright © 2021 by Zamil Akhtar

All rights reserved. No part of this publication may be reproduced, distributed, or transmitted in any form or by any means, including photocopying, recording, or other electronic or mechanical methods, without prior written permission of the publisher, except in the case of brief quotations embodied in critical reviews and certain other noncommercial uses permitted by copyright law. For permission requests, write to the publisher, addressed "Attention: Permissions," at the email address below.

Zamil@ZamilAkhtar.com

FREE BOOK

Get *Death Rider*, a prequel novella to Gunmetal Gods, for FREE by joining my mailing list at ZamilAkhtar.com!

*In loving memory of my big brother Jon, who introduced me to fantasy
and inspired those near him to reach for the stars.*

CONTENTS

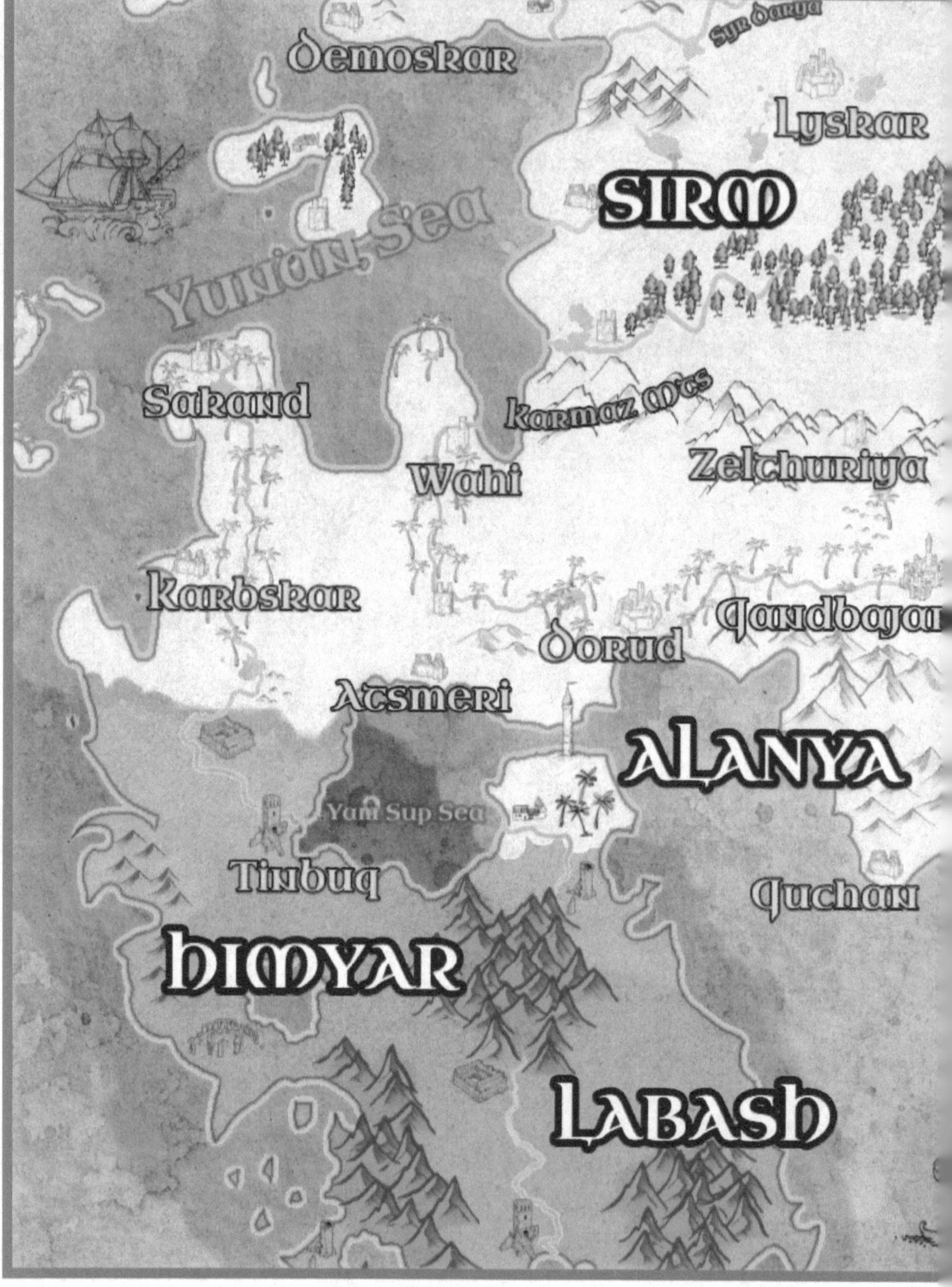

Demoskar
Syr darya
Lyskar
SIRM
Yunan Sea
Sakand
Karmaz M'ts
Zelchuriya
Wahi
Karbskar
Qandbajan
Dorud
Atsmeri
ALANYA
Yam Sup Sea
Tinbuq
Quchan
HIMYAR
LABASH

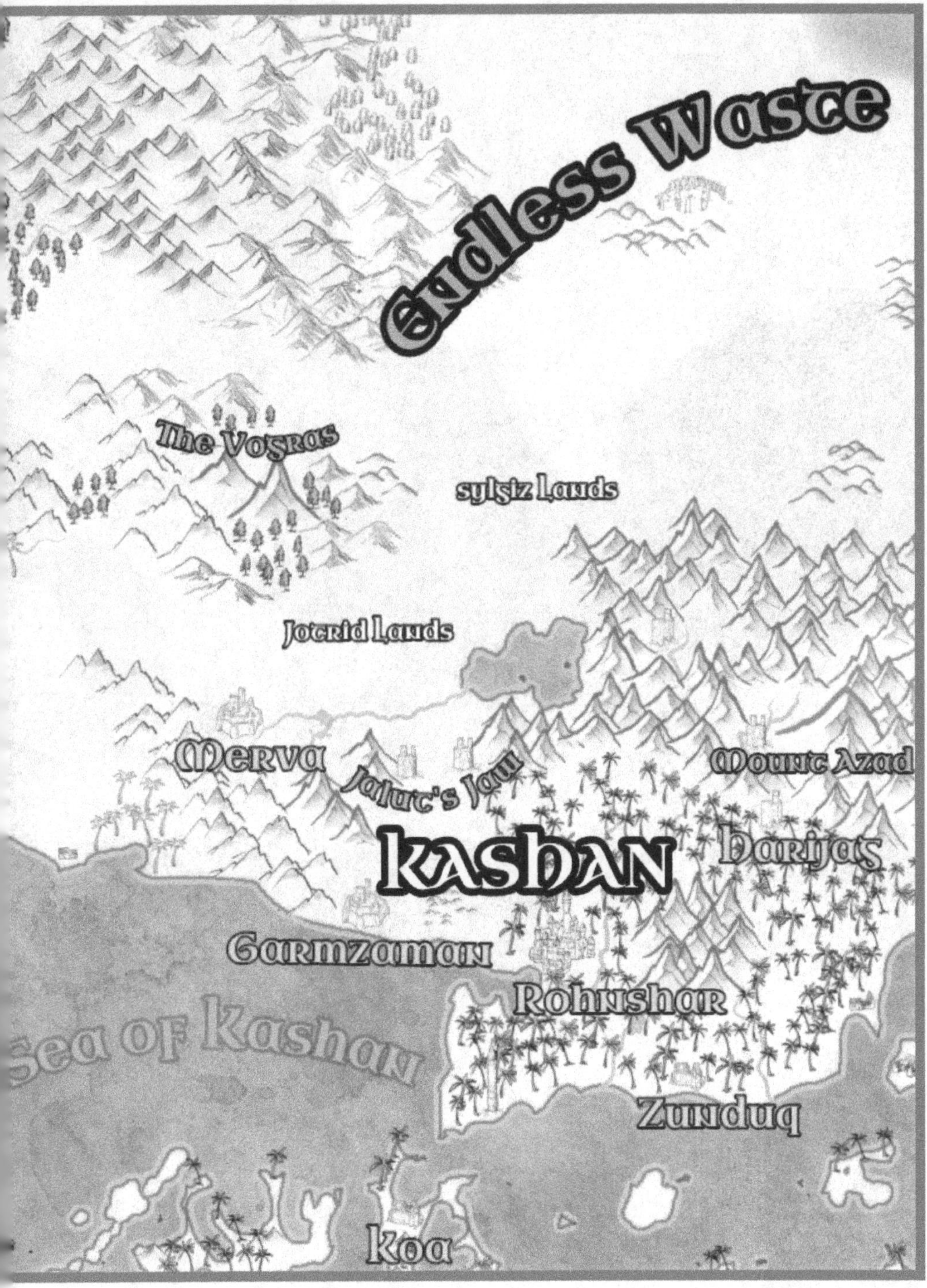

Endless Waste
The Vosras
Sylsiz Lands
Jotrid Lands
Merva
Jalut's Jaw
Mount Azad
Kashan
Dorijas
Garmzaman
Rohnshar
Sea of Kashan
Zunduq
Koa

1

CYRA

The sand tribes claim that a jinn with eleven fiery horns, born before time began its flow, climbed a ring in the seventh heaven and — overcome by some mysterious, primordial rage — hurled a thousand and one pearls at the earth. A thousand of those pearls burned as they surged toward the ground, becoming the stars that still blaze. Only one pearl landed, and it created this city: Qandbajar.

Which was, at this moment, besieged. By my brother. From high on the palace balcony, I stared beyond the sand-colored city walls at the colorful yurts dotting the desert and shrubland. Our besiegers would find their yurts too warm in the Qandbajari summer — ovens heated by the sun's gaze. Though fertile, the pastures by the river and its canals couldn't support them and the tens of thousands of warhorses they'd brought. But that wouldn't deter them. Little could deter the warriors of the Sylgiz when they'd set their arrowheads upon something; little bother it happened to be the capital of the richest and most powerful kingdom in the east.

Like Qandbajar, I have a fanciful origin story. It begins with my brother and me huddling in a yurt, covered by a harsh, moth-holed blanket. I'd let him have the last bits of horseflesh, knowing Father would lament his death more than mine, him being the heir of a line of khagans that stretched to the time of Temur, and me being an ungainly daughter; my belly ached from the rotten broth I'd scarfed down instead. We held hands and resisted the Waste's deadly winter as best we could. Then, as we inched closer, his bony knee jutted into my belly, worsening the ache. Still, I welcomed any warmth as my flesh numbed.

A screaming wind beat against the eight walls, and soon my brother would have to rush outside to hammer the nails lest our yurt collapse, despite his toes almost having frozen yesterday, rescued only by the heat of our stove's final embers. So, to save us, as well as our baby brother in his bone-built crib, I shut my eyes and prayed.

The memory unnerved me. Had that really been my life before coming to the *paradise* that was Qandbajar?

"Today is not for reminiscence," Shah Tamaz had instructed when he debriefed me an hour ago in the great hall. *"You're the sand-brick bridge connecting us and the Sylgiz,"* he'd said, sitting straight-backed on his golden divan, his usual kind smile stretched across his face.

I bent my neck and replied, *"I'm more of a…bridge-left-in-disre-pair-for-eight-years-because-the-treasurer-didn't-care-about-the-people-on-the-other-side…but I see your meaning, Your Glory."*

So I took a carriage to the city gate. As I'd requested, a warhorse waited there. The saddle was sheepskin, the stirrups almost wire-thin iron. I patted its head — it huffed and snorted. A typical mare from the Waste: slightly bigger than a pony, with slender legs and light hooves that barely disturbed the grass. She didn't belong in this city, surrounded by marble palaces, cobbled streets, and heaped-up mud houses. But perhaps the Sylgiz would regard me as one of their own if I trotted over on a worthy steed.

The glittering, golden gholam warriors on guard raised the portcullis, and I galloped toward the Sylgiz camp. Though it'd been years since I'd ridden a horse, I'd learned to ride one before learning to walk, so said the stories. Judging by how swiftly I bolted against the wind and how natural it felt to sit so high, I almost believed them.

As I galloped into the forest of yurts, Sylgiz men and women gazed upon me. The Sylgiz were, on average, smaller than the Alanyans. They fit their mares well and drank deeply of the milk, whereas the Alanyans drank from camels, some as large as elephants. I think I'd grown a few inches after coming to Qandbajar, despite being fifteen at the time.

Around me, men hauled water in horsehide sacks, while others tempered steel over fire pits, the *clank-clank* of their hammers a perfect beat for the throaty and harsh Sylgiz tongue. Their sheep, goats, cows, and camels devoured the fruits, crops, and even the reeds that grew by the canals that snaked from the Vogras River. I imagined what followed such rapid consumption: cold, bones, and despair.

Hardy, though short men clutching matchlocks guarded the imposing sun-colored yurt at the camp's center. I climbed off my horse, dusted my silk caftan, and readjusted my plumed hat. A million thoughts raced: who waited in that yurt? What would they think of me? And most crucial, would they tell me what they wanted?

"I am Cyra, daughter of Khagan Yamar," I said in Sylgiz to a guard with thin eyes and a wing-like mustache. I didn't recognize him — the tribe had grown since I'd been taken, so most here were new faces. "I've come to entreat on behalf of the Seluqal House of Alanya and His Glory, Shah Tamaz of Alanya."

He looked up at me, then gestured his head toward the entrance flap.

Inside, the simple ways of the Sylgiz prevailed. In the center, an ice-filled stove barely provided relief from the swelter. Around it, men and women sat upon sheepskin blankets and passed around a tree branch molded into a crude pipe. The stench of opium weighed heavier than air. Opium and mushrooms were oft used in our rituals, to see beyond the Gate into the realm where the Guided waited.

A familiar face stared back from the dais at the far end. Warm, wolf-like yellow pupils. Looking upon my brother, after eight years apart, he seemed both a stranger and the boy I knew. Tears bubbled behind my eyes, and I strained to keep them there. I wanted to hug him. I wanted to cry in his arms and ask about Father and Mother and baby Betil. But when he got to his feet, he towered and cast a cold gaze upon me.

"Cihan," I said.

"Cyra," he replied, as if my name had been boiling in his belly.

I trembled as he approached. He put a hard hand on my shoulder, then pulled me in. I barely reached his chest as we embraced and could no longer hold my tears. When I'd left, my big brother had been skinnier than a goat, and now he looked like he could rip a goat apart. The warmth and cold from so many memories flowed through me.

"Is it true that…Father died running from battle, an arrow in his back?" I asked. The Alanyans had rejoiced that day, relieved of a thorn in their side, though a worse one grew in its place.

He clasped my cheeks and studied me, as if he were as surprised by my appearance as I was by his. "Alanyan and Jotrid lies. Father fell honorably in battle. It's true, the arrows were in his back, but he was feigning retreat and luring the enemy into a trap. Since then, Mother hasn't left her bed, and I'm told her soul will have gone by the time I return. As for baby Betil…I wish there were more to it, but he caught the pox and returned to Lat."

I choked on my sorrow and cried out. Betil was dead, too? Mother bedridden? There were others I wanted to ask about — aunts and uncles and cousins — but what did it matter? They'd all been dead to me, anyway, because I was certain I'd never see them again. But now, my brother stood before me, twice the width of his image in my memories. A man, fully grown. A khagan, like our father. A besieger of the city where I'd been a hostage for eight years.

"Why are you here?" I asked, struggling to shut out my tears. Though we'd hugged and talked of our loved ones, there was still an icy air between us, and the Shah had asked me to be quick and leave recollecting for later.

"Beloved sister, I think you know well the crimes your captors have committed upon your tribe, upon the Sylgiz."

"But Shah Tamaz assured me he hasn't been raiding Sylgiz land."

"Raiding?" Cihan chuckled and shook his head.

Laughter bubbled from the men and women in the room, who still passed around that tree-branch pipe. That's when I recognized the one laughing loudest: Gokberk, a cruel cousin who'd once stomped on a puppy's neck for fun. Now he had a scar down his cheek, which created an ugly gap in his beard, and he was missing an ear, too.

Cihan said, "We are no longer sheep to be milked and sheared and slaughtered, like when our father was khagan."

Of course, I'd heard about the battles my brother had won and the lands he'd captured. He'd brought the Sylgiz a new dawn, but to be so bold as to siege Qandbajar, the crown jewel of Alanya...

"Then what crimes do you speak of?" I asked.

A balding oaf of a man grabbed a woolen sack and handed it to my brother. He emptied it on the floor. Heads sloshed around my feet. Heads!

A twisted, half-decayed face brushed my ankle. I gasped. A shard of cranium stuck out where the eyebrow ought to be. A worm crawled out of the skull. I backed away toward the entrance flap and only just stopped myself from running.

Cihan said, "This is how Shah Tamaz paid three of our riders, whom I'd sent to trade spices and furs."

"This can't be!" I shook my head and slowed my breathing to

inhale less death stench. "The Shah is a good man. A faithful Latian. He would never kill without cause."

Cihan handed me a parchment. The simurgh seal of Alanya blazed at the top in wax, the Shah's stamp.

Payment for your sins was all it said in Paramic. Perfect flourishes at the ends of the letters with deep, bold strokes — a royal scribe wrote this, or perhaps an imitator of one.

"Surely, a falsification," I said after swallowing whatever shot up from my stomach. "I've lived under the Shah's protection for eight years. He wouldn't recompense sins with sins. Heads with heads."

Red boiled in Cihan's cheeks as dimples formed. I used to tease him for being so adorable when angry. But the ferocious, towering warrior glaring at me was anything but cute.

"Those men did not sin," he said. "To even claim—"

"I didn't mean it like that!" I took his calloused hands, remembering that in the Waste, you had to watch your words, unlike in Alanya, where they flowed freely. "You've come here for revenge, that I understand."

"Not revenge. Each had wives and children, who now weep through the night. You think I wanted to come here? I came to silence that weeping with one thing — justice."

"I understand. You must believe me. Shah Tamaz is a good man. He couldn't have ordered this. It must be a deception."

He huffed, then nodded slowly. When he stared into me, he was looking at something else: a memory, perhaps. "Seeing you again takes me back to happier times. Simpler times, like when Father caught a red squirrel, and you wanted to keep it as a pet rather than skin and eat it." He chuckled. That was a plentiful time when it seemed we'd never run out of rabbits and yaks and goats and especially horses. But ten moons of drought changed everything.

Cihan pulled on his beard. "When I heard they were sending you, I feared the worst. Feared I'd find a girl with no teeth and wrists as thin as reeds. But you...with your tanned skin and curled hair, you look like an Alanyan, and I mean that in a good way. They've treated you well, and for that, I'll give them time to explain this." He pointed at the decaying heads.

A heckle sounded from the back. Gokberk glared at me, his upper lip pushing against his nose in obvious disapproval.

I ignored him and nodded, pleased that I'd laid the first brick for what would hopefully be a bridge between the two sides. "Thank you, Cihan. I'd always smile when news reached that you'd won a battle. And yet, it never sounded real, as if it were some other Cihan winning that acclaim. But now...seeing you...I finally understand."

His chuckle trailed off into a melancholic sigh. "Tell me, Cyra, are you happy here, amid all this sand and clay and mud?"

A memory burst through my mind: Cihan and I sharing a bone, shattering our teeth on it because we were that hungry. "I'm content," I said, "and grateful. Shah Tamaz treats me as a daughter. I couldn't ask for anything more." That last part wasn't entirely true. I always wanted more. But the things I wanted, my brother couldn't give.

As I approached the flap to leave, a big-bellied warrior blocked it.

Cihan said, "He may have treated you like a daughter, but Tamaz isn't your father. Here, in this yurt, you're in the Endless Waste. We brought it to you. And yet...you'd just walk away. Back to your captors. Back to our enemy."

I froze upon realizing what he meant. The chills of the Waste's winters ran across my spine. "If you don't let me go back, it'll be bad. Shah Tamaz will assume the worst." I turned in Cihan's direction so he could see my pleading eyes.

"Perhaps that's truly why I came, little sister. To take you back. We'll ride away, to the Endless," the tribes who called it home chose to shorten it to *the Endless* whereas others chose *the Waste*, "and be done with this country and its lies and cruelty. But I won't go against your will. Taking you back — that's recompense enough for those heads." He paused, peering deeply into me, trying to see beyond whatever facade I was putting up. "What say you? Ready to go home?"

I turned away, went toward the exit flap, and said, "Qandbajar is my home, now."

BACK WITHIN THE outer walls of the Sand Palace, gholam in shimmering bronze and gold plate surrounded Shah Tamaz, though I wasn't sure which was him. His two body doubles wore the same dirt-colored caftans and thin chainmail, stood lanky, and slacked their jaws to the right. They even had the precise shade of gray hair and imitated his limp.

That voice, though, wasn't so easy to imitate. Whenever Tamaz spoke, it was as if earthy syrup melted down your ears and cheeks.

"What did he say?" The real Tamaz wasted no time, huddling close to me with his gholam forming a wall of armor around us. Turned out, he was wearing the golden armor of the gholam, only his walnut pupils visible through his helmet.

"Your Glory." I bent my neck, then whispered what happened in his ear so no onlookers could hear.

"A pretext to attack us?" he said with wide eyes.

I shook my head. "I don't believe my brother to be lying."

"But who would try to sow such calamity?"

"If we can prove we took no part in the beheadings, I think Cihan will turn around."

Shah Tamaz put his anxious breaths to my ear and whispered, "Whoever did this timed it perfectly. A mere week after I'd sent most of the gholam to retake our sea forts, leaving this city under-defended. But anyway, you've done your job and done it well. Leave the rest to me, sweet one."

I nodded, then turned toward the palace, which glimmered like golden sand beneath the rising sun. Before I walked out of earshot, the Shah said, "Seems your brother still trusts you. Be ready — I'll needs call on you again."

Stepping on the silk carpet in the palace hall, I cringed. I thought of those putrid heads rolling at my feet and yearned for another bath. I climbed the winding stairs toward the harem wing, then greeted the braided eunuchs guarding the bath chamber with a polite nod. Once inside, amid the blue, star-patterned tile, I stripped and entered the steam chamber. It was busy this morning, as usual, with a few eunuchs tending to their duties and more than a few concubines tending to themselves.

As I sat against the moist walls, the soothing humidity calmed my insides. Sorrowful memories played as I drifted between alertness and dozing.

Father, dead. Betil, dead. Mother, about to be dead. The saddest part of me wanted to steal the fastest Kashanese horse from among the Shah's racing steeds and ride to the Waste, just to hold her hand. But I was no longer her daughter, truly. This palace was my mother now. Its walls were all the embrace I needed.

That day when the Jotrids raided us, their khagan had forced my father to make humiliating concessions, me among them. How terrible the moment when their warriors pulled me from my mother's arms. The Jotrids were blood enemies to our tribe. They prayed to the saints, like the Alanyans, whereas we prayed only to the Children. *Lat hears our prayers because the Children live beneath her throne while the saints roast within a chasm of flame in the thousandth hell for their falsehoods.* That was what I'd been taught, though I didn't believe it anymore.

The Jotrid khagan, who had even lived with us for a time and was barely older than my brother, *gifted* me to the Alanyans. Though it took me far from home, in the end, it was for the best. Now here I sat, in a bath chamber fit for the sultana of the world, my belly full. And yet, my heart still ached from all that had been severed.

The steam pressed against my chest, oppressive, so I soaked in the lukewarm pool in the center of the bath chamber. I always avoided the ice bath. Being so cold that I felt my veins freezing reminded me of those frigid, starving days in the Sylgiz lands. While I shivered just thinking about that time, concubines flowed in and out of the bath chamber — the ones that didn't hate me smiled with polite greetings. The rest were careful to avoid my drifting eyes. To think, after all I'd been through, I'd end up *here*.

Zedra entered. Her black curls fell past her breasts as she removed her hair towel and joined me in the lukewarm water. I sat up, smiled, and mumbled a greeting — hopeful not to have bothered her with my lack of attention, though she'd always been kind to me. Kind to everyone.

"I'm so jealous," she said, giggling. Her reddened cheeks made it plain that she'd been drinking. "You're an ambassador, now. Nay, Grand Vizier!"

"Nothing of the sort. It's just, the man at the head of that horde happens to be my brother by blood."

"You've the blood of conquerors," she said. "Another reason to be jealous."

"You've no reason to ever be jealous of me."

"Humble too, yet another thing to be jealous of."

"Stop it."

I splashed water on her face. She didn't even flinch and took it with a grin. I remembered when she first arrived in the palace, barely a year ago; she wouldn't even bathe. She refused to get in the pools, despite the pleading of the eunuchs, and would instead sit on the floor and dump water over her head with a pail. She told me that was how they bathed in the Vogras, where she was from, but the other Vograsian concubines didn't do that. Sometimes I'd catch her staring at the pool water in a daze. Strange woman, to say the least.

Though I was, by law, a free woman and Zedra a slave, her status towered over mine. After all, she was the beloved of the Crown Prince, a man loved by the people as much as his father,

Shah Tamaz. And, out of all his concubines, she was the only one who'd given him a son.

Eunuchs wearing maroon robes placed fresh incense in the corner burners — a zesty scent with earthy tones, probably aloeswood with musk.

"So what was it like seeing your brother after all this time?"

What did it feel like? As if I'd been smashed by a hammer, hugged by a bear, and trampled by a horde; I tried to find measured words instead. "He felt like my brother...and yet, he didn't. It was like he was the boy I knew and a complete stranger at the same time."

Zedra nodded. "Time and distance make strangers, yet blood bonds are forever. I'm sure he felt the same as you." She was so wise for a nineteen-year-old. Her expression tensed. "So...tell me, what's going to happen now? Should we worry?"

I hadn't noticed bombards in Cihan's camp, so they couldn't easily get inside the walls. If it came to it, the gholam who'd been sent westward could be recalled to deal with them. But despite reassurances, ants still crawled through my veins; I didn't want war between two peoples I cared for.

"I think we're going to solve it, in peace."

Zedra bit her lip. "Can't lift the veil, can you? What ever will I gossip about at supper?"

I chuckled. "Don't gossip about this, all right?" Secrets always spilled in the Sand Palace, but I trusted Zedra and needed to pour out my worries.

She zipped up her lips.

"Someone beheaded three Sylgiz traders and framed Shah Tamaz. We need to prove it wasn't him."

She gasped, holding her hand to her mouth, her ruby rings dripping. "Who could...who would ever do such a thing?"

I said the first thing on my mind: "The Jotrids. I mean, I don't know if it was them, but they've every reason to foment war between us and the Sylgiz. Their khagan, Pashang, is as cruel as a broken slipper."

Zedra chuckled, then splashed water on me. "By Lat, what is that saying?"

How embarrassing — my cheeks tightened. "Just something my mother would say. Us Sylgiz have the dumbest sayings." I'd always tried to avoid showing where I came from. My tribe was not liked in Alanya — we followed a different path toward Lat, our language was bitter, our ways violent, and our customs savage.

The lukewarm water began to bore me, and I yearned once more for steam. I pushed out and wrapped myself in a star-patterned towel.

"Let's go into the city later," Zedra said, "just you and me. It's been a bit dull around here. Oh, apart from the siege and all." She laughed.

I was planning to go anyway, to tend to a certain scheme I was part of, so I nodded and went toward the coals.

STRANGE WHAT A SIEGE does to a thriving city. The food bazaars were bursting with haggling and desperation. Stall sellers had raised prices, a precaution if a long siege would choke their supplies. City folk sought to stock up on whatever they could: dried fruits, vats of well water, teeth twigs, lye. As for Zedra and myself, we rode together in a carriage surrounded by mounted gholam and watched the crowds from our windows. As we neared Laughter Square, the air of wealthier folk seeking a good time replaced the panicked atmosphere of the food bazaar.

Upon getting out, Zedra raised her hands and twirled like a Vograsian dancer — how carefree and fluid. The Vogras, where she was from, was a mountainous part of the Waste and a different world from that of the Sylgiz, Jotrids, and other lowland tribes, so I didn't know too much about it. Strange that, until today, it had all seemed so unimportant. Though I'd learned about the world since coming to this city, the Philosophers who'd tutored me focused little on the Waste, its tribes, and its geography.

Today, Laughter Square lived up to its name. Men and women lined up before an array of poets, each poet standing upon a richly tapestried dais. The treasure chests at their feet overflowed with all manner of coin: Alanyan, mostly, but I noticed coins with the soaring falcon emblem of Kashan, the aggressive peacock of Sirm, and even some with blocky western letters.

Of course, Zedra and I went to the front of the line, ignoring the glares and foot-stomping of those we'd cut past. Her favorite poet, a man draped in so much green silk he resembled a pig covered in grass, glowed with an eager delight. "The moon has just risen," he turned to me, "and with it the sun."

"Ooh!" Zedra clapped. She tossed a silver coin into the treasure chest below his dais. It made a satisfying clank as it landed. "I hope that was merely a taste."

I looked behind. Too many were staring, either upset we'd cut in front, or perhaps enraptured by the sight of women from the palace. Uneasy, I wrapped my veil over my face and turned back toward the poet.

The poet glowered. "The sun has just gone out, leaving us bereft! Oh lady of the sky, do not deprive us of your light!"

Clever. Begrudgingly, I loosened the veil.

Zedra said, "Hmph!" and shook her head. "I paid you to praise me. The moon needs adoration, too." She grinned impishly.

"Radiance leaps from your sandstone cheeks — ancient eyes full of love — a spirit that sails, piercing the mists with its bow…"

While the poet flung flowers at her from his tongue, I studied the square. Snaking lines stood before all the favorites: Babar of Zunduq, from a city deep in the jungles of Kashan, positioned himself near what I believed was a pleasure house and sat high upon a mechanical elephant. He rained warlike songs upon the gholam, pashas, and khazis who lined up before him. At the entrance to a coffeehouse, a beardless boy named Jilqees composed rhyming verses, mostly about magical, faraway places, which he'd learned about from the pirates and sailors who frequented his *nighttime* job. But the longest line belonged to a man I'd never seen before, who sat upon a brass throne studded with fake emeralds and rubies. A Himyarite, judging by his skin, which was the color of deep soil. Unlike the gholam around us, who were mostly Himyarites too, this man seemed frail of build. And he wasn't shouting his verses, like the other poets, but writing them on parchment with a rather fat brush. Why was he so favored?

I interrupted some syrupy nonsense about how Zedra was a *lioness on a mountain peak* to ask, "Who's he?"

The poet in green silk squinted at the Himyarite and said, "Oh, that fool. Been here a week and everyone is falling over his verse." The venom in his voice could kill a snake.

"What's so special about it?"

The poet huffed. "Toss a silver at his feet and he'll spew the vilest insults — truly unholy, vulgar."

"Insults? About whom?"

"About you, my dear. Whoever pays him."

Zedra gasped. "You mean to say people pay him to be degraded?"

"Indeed!" the poet said with a growl. "It's despicable and should be forbidden! What is this country coming to?"

"Sorry." I touched Zedra's arm with both my hands. "I've just remembered, I'm to meet someone at the Grand Bazaar. Briefly. Do you mind?"

"Of course, dear," she said. "Go flutter about wherever you may. I'll be here, wasting my time and money."

I fingered the scroll in my pocket and let out a tense breath. I'd joined this scheme by choice, days before my brother arrived, and couldn't back out now.

With an escort of four gholam, I proceeded on foot across the Bridge of Saint Jorga toward the Grand Bazaar. How much it'd changed in the eight years I'd lived in Qandbajar. When I'd first come to the city, it was an overstuffed series of lanes and stalls that sat stinking in the city center. Now it stood as a hollow, open-air stone pyramid with nine levels. Nine! A Philosopher had designed it, and it dwarfed even the Sand Palace. The only taller building in the city was the Tower of Wisdom.

At the first level of the Grand Bazaar, cloth, sheepskin, and leather merchants draped their wares across wooden stalls, which were arranged like a maze. Barely room to walk, but everyone stepped out of the way of the gholam and myself. I'd not regularly worn such common materials since moving here, so stared straight as we ascended the stairs to the next level.

Fruits. As we walked through the slightly less crowded area, fruit sellers lowered their gazes, their hands outstretched with whatever ripe perfections they'd reserved for the palace that day. Before handing over the treats, a gholam would pick off a piece with a gold-hilted knife and test the taste. Soon, tangy grapes, spicy dates, and sweet oranges were falling into my hands.

I devoured a date. The spices danced on my tongue and burned down my throat — a rather *Kashanese* taste. Considering I could barely fit into this pearl-studded caftan Grand Vizier Barkam had gifted me last year, I declined the other delights.

The third floor was nothing like the others. In perfect rows, spices of every color — even sky blue — sat piled in polished glass cauldrons. Cinnamon, turmeric, ginger, saffron, sumac, cumin, caraway, coriander, cloves, cardamom — to name the ones I was familiar with. Every food smell imaginable invaded my nose, as if an army of kababs, lamb shanks, and mutton balls were on the march. And it was all the work of one man. He controlled Qandbajar's — nay, Alanya's — spice trade, and upon seeing me, he smiled with warmth. He bent his neck, despite his rank exceeding mine: he was a pasha, after all. And he looked like one; down the middle of his caftan, purple pearls twinkled as if stars burned within.

"When I awoke this morning," he said, "I prayed Lat would

bless my eyes. And by the sight of you, a humble man's prayer is answered."

"A *humble* man?" I looked around. "Has he run off?"

Ozar chuckled, a good-natured grin seizing his pastry-filled cheeks. "*Sultana*," he said, granting me a title I did not possess nor deserve. "The clouds part when you arrive. The breezes burn with fire. The mystics fall over themselves, drunk and debased."

"Keep your day job, pasha. You'll be laughed out of Laughter Square with verse like that."

He wagged a thick, ring-covered finger. "Not my words, sultana. The wise Eshkal himself breathed them to life."

My ignorance of poetry laid bare. How embarrassing. "You need not call me that, pasha. I've not attained such rank."

His face twisted. "Are you not the daughter of a Sylgiz khagan? Considering the men at our gates, I'd wager your rank on the ascent."

"Yours may be, too." I reached into my caftan pocket and took out the parchment, then handed it to Ozar.

"What's this?" He snapped his fingers; one of his retainers brought him a spectacle. Ozar squinted through it as he unrolled the parchment and read its contents.

"Dear Lat," he said, his eye enlarged and bulging through the spectacle. "I've been begging the Majlis for months. By the thou-sandth heaven — by the saints beneath the glorious throne — how on earth did you get this?"

So bombastic. "I have my ways," I said with a curt grin, knowing it would drive him mad.

"My dear, do you not realize how valuable this piece of paper is? Barkam has been hounding me for years. 'Ozar's monopoly on spices must be broken!' is the first thing he says when waking up, and his final prayer before sleeping. 'Ozar's price wars are against the laws of the Shah and the Fount!' is what the Grand Vizier whis-pers in his wife's ear when making love." Ozar covered his mouth. "Excuse my crudeness, but I can scarcely contain myself. *How* did you get him to stamp a paper granting me exclusive rights to the Koa spice lane?"

Now he really was prodding me to bare myself. "The more important question is — *what* do I want in return?"

"I'll give you half the world, and the other half too."

"Wonderful. I like being owed favors by rich and powerful men."

He raised an eyebrow in surprise. Perhaps he thought I'd ask for my return now. But, like any debt, it's better to call it later — with interest.

"You know, sultana, you're nothing like that girl they dragged from the Waste, eight years hence. Thin-wristed, stinking of horse manure, barely a legible word on your tongue. You're truly a woman of the city, now. To see you climb so high has been a pleasure."

To have the richest merchant in the land owing me a favor — that was the real pleasure. Or it would've been had this exchange been genuine. I couldn't ignore the shudder in my bones when I thought about the parchment I'd just given him, and who had given it to me.

ZEDRA CLAPPED as the little monkey danced on the red-tusked elephant's back. She tossed a gold coin — how excessive — at it; the monkey caught it with its hard, red cap and then flipped it toward its owner, who beamed beneath his gray mustache.

"Our sultana is as generous as Saint Kali," he said.

A deadpan expression seized Zedra's face, as if she were insulted. Slowly, a smile spread across her cheeks, but her eyes remained sour. Strange. "That's too much praise for a paltry gold. You've trained the creature so well — you deserve a thousand more."

I gave the owner a polite nod, then said to Zedra, "Feeling a bit faint. Would you mind if I went home?"

"Been a long day for you, dear. Of course, go and rest."

Wonderful, she'd bought my excuse. But the four gholam escorting me would be harder to trick. As we traveled by carriage toward the Sand Palace, we passed by the Shrine of Saint Rizva. Barely anyone beneath its sandstone arches — an almost-forgotten relic. Shouts and clamor from the adjacent coffeehouse assured worshippers would get no peace, anyway.

I ordered the carriage driver to stop and stepped outside.

"I would pray, for a moment," I said to the gold-clad gholam captain sitting high upon his horse.

"Mistress," he said. Ah, at least someone knew my proper title. "This shrine is known as a gathering place for degenerates. You can pray at Saint Jamshid's, up ahead."

I shook my head. "Saint Rizva was a peacemaker. I would seek her intercession, so my diplomacy with the Sylgiz bears fruit."

"We'll come with you, then," the captain said.

"Into the women's section? That would be scandalous." I raised my eyebrow. "I think I can survive five minutes in a shrine."

The gholam captain nodded begrudgingly.

Elderly women sat on the faded sandstone in the women's section, reciting holy words and flicking prayer beads. They ignored the tall and frankly stunning man standing behind them. Hadrith stood with his arms crossed; he'd cut his curly hair short, but his combed beard grew longer each day, now reaching his chest.

"You kept me waiting," he said, obviously unamused, "and I only wait for good news and god."

"He bought it," I said. "Didn't question me. Ozar truly believes the Koa spice lane is his."

"Well done, little fawn."

I made a fist. "I told you not to call me that."

"My *beloved*. How's that?" His false grin revealed perfect, glossy teeth. He'd once pontificated about how I ought to use teeth-cleaning twigs from the arak tree at least three times a day. Seemed they did work.

"What kind of man uses his *beloved* for his illicit schemes?"

He stepped closer — I barely reached his chest, which was broader than mirror armor. He'd clearly been out in the sun; his perfume-mixed sweat was at once overwhelming and intoxicating.

"If you're to be my wife, we'll be scheming illicitly till the dust of the earth washes over us. The foremost lesson I learned from my mother and father, so best get used to it."

I didn't know if I could. The thought of Ozar being arrested because of me made me feel so…unclean.

"Did you really use your father's stamp? When they arrest Ozar, he's going to tell your father that I gave him that parchment!"

"No one expects a little fawn to bare teeth, so you'll be seen as an unwitting accomplice, at worst. Besides, I've been dealing with my father for twenty-five years. Very successfully, might I add."

"The Grand Vizier isn't known for his clemency — far from it. Can't you see I'm worried?"

The praying women turned to look. I'd been too loud in this hallowed place.

Hadrith came to my ear with sweet and heavy breaths. "O' little fa…my beloved. Trust is the bedrock upon which love grows. Ours will bloom into a wondrous cypress, stretching toward heaven itself." His tongue was almost in my ear when he said, "I'll have another task for you soon, my loveliest."

At that, he left me. After doing something so wrong, I wanted to take another bath. And yet, I burned to know what he wanted me to do next. Whatever it was, I couldn't stop now.

I DID TAKE ANOTHER BATH, my third one today. This time, I made sure no one was around, so I could cry. The eunuchs at the door must've heard, but a woman bawling in the harem bath was nothing new.

I even prayed. First, to Saint Rizva, begging her to forgive me for using her shrine for such sordid business. But the child within, awoken after so long because of my brother's arrival, felt *sinful* for praying to a saint, so I prayed to Father Chisti. Or was he Saint Chisti? Ugh, what did it matter? He was the founder of our faith, regardless of which path you walked. The straight path or the path of heretics — which was which?

Mother, baby Betil, Father, Cihan — the child in me ached. Memories played. Why always these painful ones? Like the time my father didn't return after a battle with an infidel Rubadi tribe — I would sit on his bed, smelling his sheets, even drinking his awful salt tea. My mother was almost forced into remarrying the *new* khagan, whom my father promptly decapitated when he returned, eight moons later. In all that time, I never ceased praying to Father Chisti and the Children so we could be a family again.

As I remembered such things, tears burned down my cheeks, heated by the steam that smothered the air. But the memories always left me cold and shivering. I needed more heat. More fire.

I fetched more coals for the steam from a bag in the back of the chamber. While piling the coals on the burning tray, one tumbled off the edge and fell on the damp floor behind the tray. Black water ran toward my feet. Sickening. I pushed the tray to the side to pick up the coal.

Across the wall, behind the tray, was a red handprint. No, a *blood* handprint. What the hell?

I brushed my wet hand against it, but it didn't drip. The blood was caked onto the tile. Ugh, were the eunuchs not taking care of this place? Well, someone ought to. I grabbed my towel, wet it from the puddle on the floor, and rubbed the handprint. Harder and rougher, as if I were cleaning my horse. But when I pulled the towel away, the fabric was perfectly yellow and star-patterned, and the bloodstain remained undisturbed.

As I stared at it, whispers floated into the steamy air. But as far as I knew, I was alone in the bath. I pushed my hand toward the blood print. It fit…perfectly, as if it were my own hand that bled it onto the warm tile.

What the fuck?

Whispers. Just outside my steam room. I peeked outside — no one there. Was I going mad?

I pushed the coal tray back, blocking the blood print from sight. Had someone…bled in this room?

Died in this room?

2

ZEDRA

EXTINCTION. FRACTURES WITHIN FRACTURES, BREAKING THE WHOLE. A river dilutes into streams that lead into an ocean. Salt and seaweed muddle the sweet water, erasing its purity. A firm root and a tall stem decay into wispy branches, and then—

"My dear, you haven't touched your eggplant soup." Tamaz's butter-oil voice broke my anxious thoughts.

My gaze returned outward. Just Tamaz and I, at a low table in his supper chamber, surrounded by serving girls, beardless boys, and braided eunuchs. I'd only been here once before; with its bare, sand-brick walls and floor covered with the square-patterned rugs of some sand tribe, it seemed the dining room of an ascetic sheikh, not the *glorious* Shah of Alanya.

"Apologies, Your Glory," I said, bending my neck. "Truth is, I haven't lost all the heft from carrying the child."

Now he glared at me, nostrils flaring and mouth hanging. The king of the land looked like an irate farmer — no turban, hair unkempt, caftan a mud-brown. "Zedra, you are as lovely as a red tulip plucked from the holy soil of Zelthuriya."

How *classical*. Perhaps he ought to drag his dais to Laughter Square. "I'm afraid younger eyes are a bit more...discerning."

"Had Kyars said something unkind before he departed?" Thunder rang in his voice. "That lout. I thought war would make him a man and—"

I shook my head. "No, Your Glory. The Crown Prince has been nothing but kind. Some of his other women, though...oh, I shouldn't gossip."

"Hmph. Jealousy. Not much else to it. Let them say what they will. The truth is, you are the mother of the future shah. You could be bulging as a laden camel or thin as prayer beads, and you'd still be the sultana of this harem."

A beardless boy placed more softbread onto our floor table. The irony: neither I nor the Shah ate much. Every day, servants carted the palace leftovers to the poor living in the Alleys of Mud. I imagined a rag-wearing family sitting within mud walls, gorging on the eggplant soup and softbread. Good — they deserved it more than we.

"I fasted today, in honor of Saint Nora's ascension," the Shah said, "and strangely, I've no appetite. You know, my father passed at my age — peace be upon his soul. The dreaded gout. Nothing better than fasting, the Philosophers say, to keep gout away."

I'd seen men die from gout — all oafs who could devour a lamb in a single sitting. No, Tamaz would not die that way.

"I heard a rumor," I said, broaching the topic that really mattered. Even the mother of the shah-to-be had to ask weeks ago for this intimate supper. I feared the Shah would disdain to meet, given the Sylgiz arrival — who'd come days earlier than I'd wanted — though thankfully, the Shah kept true to his schedule. "Is it true someone beheaded three Sylgiz traders and that their khagan seethes for vengeance?"

Tamaz sipped his water and stared straight in silence, then said, "I supposed, with the entire Majlis apprised of the happenings, that everyone would find out eventually — but news has spread faster than I expected. Believe me, I've dealt with all manner of khagans — they come for one raging reason or another, but always leave with their horses dragging chests of gold. And in that, we're not lacking."

"But I also heard they blame you. That there was a royal message, stamped by you, with the heads of the dead. This year, there's already been an attempt on your life. That assassin was Path of the Children, too, was he not? I fear what these heretics are plotting for you…Father."

Tamaz loved when I called him that. He told me once that he'd sorely desired a daughter, and Lat had blessed him with three, though all had been cursed to die in childhood. Well, that wasn't entirely true — he didn't tell me. I overheard him lamenting with the gholam commander, Pasha Kato.

"We all must die, dear Zedra. I pray Lat forgive me for what my hands have wrought. When I became Shah, I believed I would be better than my father. That I'd follow the Recitals of Chisti — word and spirit — in all I did. But only Saint Chisti carried both holiness and kingship with equal weight. For the rest of us, forgiveness is the only salvation, so we must not cease begging for it. 'Forgive if you wish to be forgiven,' a recital that I live by."

That was why the people loved him. How many death sentences had he commuted this year alone? Dramatic moments: just when the executioner was about to swing, the Shah would appear and hold up his hand. Cheers and ululating and thigh-clapping followed — true, the people desired justice, but they loved mercy. The Shah was as clever as he was pious, for certain. You didn't rule for two decades, otherwise. Of all three reigning House Seluqal shahs from the kingdoms of Sirm, Kashan, and Alanya, Tamaz's was the longest, most peaceful, and richest reign.

And that only made my task harder. "You are so wise, Father."

"Comes with the gray hair, my dear."

Oh, I knew that well enough. "Will you recall the gholam?"

He huffed — seemed he didn't want politics at dinner. But I had to press.

"Are you so keen to see Kyars?" he asked.

"I miss him dearly and worry what those Ethosian pirates may do." Tamaz would be more pliable with that framing, surely.

"My dear, never forget that Kyars smashed a fully stocked and armored Crucian army at the Syr Darya last year. If not for him, Micah the Metal and Imperator Heraclius would've wiped our ungrateful cousins up north from history. What is a smattering of infidel pirates, compared to that?"

Meaning: *I will not be recalling the gholam.* Perfect. "You're right. Of course. He'll be back before the cold winds blow down from the End…from the Waste."

"We can't let pirates winter in our seaside towns and forts, cutting off trade with Ejaz, Sirm, Dycondi. Kyars and twenty thousand gholam will show them an Alanyan recompense for their crimes. By the coming of the desert chill, you and Kyars will be cuddling amid a coal-burning fire, surely."

A sickening thought, for which I suppressed a shudder. Nonetheless, winter remained moons away, and so my window seemed wide enough. "A wonderful thought."

I kept silent after that, allowing the Shah to grab a morsel of softbread. He chewed it for an eternity and gulped deep. Then he tossed the remaining piece of bread on a brass plate. His saliva moistened the part where he'd bitten.

"It's been a wonderful supper," he said, "but with age comes an early rise and an even earlier bedtime. And before I sleep, I would stand in vigil before Lat and her saints, so that this kingdom I tend may remain blessed and at peace."

"I, too, will pray. For your good health, for peace, and for my beloved Kyars' victory."

As Tamaz stood and stretched, I reached over and grabbed the piece of bread he'd bitten, then slipped it into my sleeve. I looked around at the beardless boys, serving girls, and eunuchs, hoping none had noticed. They all stared straight in silence. Good.

As I WALKED toward my room, I thought about the Philosopher who'd engineered the Sand Palace. Last week, I borrowed his biography from the Tower of Wisdom so I could break from my serious reading with something pleasurable. He lived about five hundred years ago, just after Temur the Wrathful carved a blood trail through half the earth. Born in Tinbuq, the seat of the once Golden Kingdom of Himyar to the southwest, the man came to Alanya with nothing but a dream. He imagined a vast construct, made of baked clay and mud and sand, that stretched the breadth and width of the highest hill in the city.

And he imagined it to be opulent: today, encrusted jewels lined the walls of the halls. Hanging lamps encased in platinum, carpets of angora silk so soft you could safely wrap a baby in them, lenses that caught the moonlight so that entire rooms would glow silver — I could go on and on. Tamaz's sanctimonious asceticism hadn't poisoned the other Seluqals, who outweighed his simplicity with their indulgence. My *beloved* Kyars being the worst among them.

"Make way for Sultana Mirima!" a eunuch called.

I stood to the side in the hallway, bowed my head, and hoped the Shah's sister wouldn't notice me. Unfortunately, I'd worn a stunning blue and gold dress for my supper with the Shah, which resembled sunrays striking a river. The woman adored fashion. More than that, she loved to show her superiority over us concubines.

As expected, Mirima stopped her prance in front of me. She gazed at my dress, then caressed the brocade on my forearm with the back of her ring-studded hand.

"Who made this?" she said in a lofty tone.

I raised my head. "Sultana, it was a gift from His Eminence, Grand Vizier Barkam."

She opened her mouth as if to retch. "He buys a size too small on purpose. A walking scandal, that man."

True, and ironically, Barkam was one of the few men whose words I could stomach. Something about his obvious perversity rang sincere.

I kept silent, hoping Mirima would move on. But her gaze stayed on me like the midday sun.

"What do you do all day, Zedra?"

Oh dear, not an open question. Bait, coming from this woman. The black dye in her hair disguised the gray so well, and whatever soaps and creams she lathered hid wrinkles and pockmarks. A decent mask that gave her back ten years. But mine was better.

"Today, I went into the city," I said, hoping to escape whatever trap she was setting, "with Cyra, my dearest friend." Mirima loved Cyra. The older men and women here seemed to. "We inquired as to the feelings of the people concerning the siege." I'd given my best answer, though I expected her to smell the lie.

"And what do the *people* say about the siege?" How bitterly she intoned *people*. Her disdain for them blinded her to my obvious deception. Good.

"Like here in the palace, opinion is divided. Some see it as serious and others as a trifle." Everyone knew that, though. Better to give obvious answers and reassure them that I'm dull.

"Fools. It is whatever we make of it. If we wanted it done, we'd end it today. Obviously, there's some benefit to having these Sylgiz savages on our side." By Lat, she used *we* and *our* so confidently. A trait I respected somewhat.

"I agree." I glanced up and down her thick, flowery gown. How to end this agonizing conversation? "To be truthful, I was so scared. When I looked out from the balcony at the yurts and horsemen filling the horizon, I so wanted Kyars to be here to hold me."

Sympathy glimmered in Mirima's gaze as she put her hand on my shoulder. "My dear, you are like an unplucked flower that knows not the vagaries of the wind." Decent verse. Another thing to respect, despite how wrong it was. "So young. So fragile. But you need not fear a thing. My brother is the greatest king alive." She thrust her fist in the air. "Unshakable, unbreakable. A khagan from the Waste is but a fly on an elephant's ass."

I giggled. Didn't expect such language from her. "You're right, dear sultana. Thank you for reassuring me. I hope the years will make me braver."

She finally went on her way. To be honest, that conversation wasn't as terrible as I'd expected. Still, best to keep them short; Mirima was more perceptive than her brother, and I worried one day she'd see through me.

Back in my room, I took my son from the wet nurse and cradled him close. A sweet warmth flowed through me, as if I were one with the world.

"He's feeding joyously," the wet nurse, a dark-skinned woman from Himyar, said. I smiled and thanked her.

I gushed as Seluq fidgeted. Yes, that was what the Shah named him. Apparently, Seluq the Dawn had come to him in a dream the night my baby was born. I didn't recall the details, but there was some nonsense about the sun and birds and fish. Kyars loved the name, too. As for myself, I couldn't imagine a worse man to name my son after, but I had no say.

"You may go," I said to the wet nurse.

I kissed my son's scalp and inhaled his fresh, life-giving scent. He giggled. I laid him in his crib and marveled at his beauty. But the beauty of a baby to his mother can't be described. It is like *fanaa,* like unity with god herself.

Words once spoken by my uncle and father-in-law echoed in my mind: *"Don't raise your children the way your parents raised you. They were born for a different time."* It couldn't be truer with my son and me; I'd have to raise him for this time, this place, this mission.

I moved toward the balcony, which gave me an encompassing view of Qandbajar, its ancient quarters, the double-layered walls, and the yurts beyond. A stillness ruled the night — no breeze, barely any birds chirping.

A comfort to just stare at the world and not have to think. Grind and grind your mind toward whatever purpose you sought. A comfort I couldn't claim because too much remained to be done. And only I was left to do it: carrying the truth on my shoulders, the survival of Lat's beloved Children, and, ultimately, the fate of mankind. The world held up by one old woman.

"Father Chisti," I prayed, "bless your daughter with your strength, your righteousness, your victory."

I wiped a tear from my cheek. Holding up the world hurt. Carrying the pain of the lost, the dead, the annihilated only numbed me so much. It was these silent moments that I couldn't endure, that I'd rather fill with anything: banal poetry, tawdry gossip, strolls through the pleasure gardens.

Or, best of all, my mission.

I often obsessed over one question: who was the most powerful man in Alanya? The obvious answer was Shah Tamaz, but thrones veil those behind them. A more astute answer was Grand Vizier Barkam because his hands plucked the strings. But that too was wrong. Neither Barkam nor the Shah held the minds of the people, and without them, a kingdom was nothing but ordered mud and stone. Then it was Grand Mufti of Alanya and Grand Sheikh of the Order of Saint Jamshid, Khizr Khaz, who tended the souls of all Alanyans...but if forced to choose one man to save my life, it wouldn't be him.

So after dawn, I went to the man I would choose. An empty barrack is rather dull. Finches and sparrows — a rare sight these days — sang in its central garden, which didn't deserve the name. More like an uneven and stony mess of plants and flowers. Beneath the shade of a bent cypress sat the most powerful man in Alanya: a slave named Kato. Or rather, Pasha Kato.

Grand title for a slave, but mine was better, and I wasn't free either. He held an entire branch of dates in his chiseled forearm. Upon my arrival, he stood, said "Sultana," then sat back against the tree bark in one careless motion. He had the coal-dark skin of the Himyarites and still spoke with their accent, which I always found melodic.

"Go away," I told my gholam escorts, not of mind to say more. Of course, Kato was the greatest of the gholam, so leaving me with him wasn't supposed to be a danger. But the gholam guarding me were loyal to Kyars, not Kato. Still, they gave us space, standing near the arched entrance, out of earshot, though within eyesight.

Kato looked up with a date-speckled grin. "Would you whip me too with that firm tongue?"

"Here you sit, sulking." I shook my head in disgust. "It's despicable. Pick yourself up. There are enemies at the gates. Maybe it's a blessing Kyars left you behind."

He stared at me, tongue out. "Just the lashing I needed to feel better."

I wanted to grab a stone and crack his bald head. But he was the one man my plan couldn't do without, and so I suffered his obscenity. "You're pathetic. Tamaz will notice your absence. You'll lose your command."

"Already lost it. My soldiers march west to fight the infidel without me. And I'd just been given the post after the death of my dear friend. You see, Barkam — and his shit son Hadrith, as well as a dozen or so viziers, I can name them all — detest me, all because I refused to do their bidding. Barkam, or perhaps Hadrith — if I'm really as weak as I think I am — will have me killed or sent to some metal mine to die, soon enough."

No, he didn't sound like the most powerful man in Alanya. Because he wasn't…yet. I'd have to build him up.

"Oh? Would Kichak have sulked about it like a little girl?"

Now he pointed a finger at me, as if to stab my chest. "Don't act like you ever met the man. He was a hero to us all. Saw his end at the hands of some debased sorcerer in Sirm."

"And how will you die? Given it a thought? Because if you had, you wouldn't be wasting today stuffing yourself."

He stood and didn't even wipe the grass off his caftan. "Nor would I be sparring with a little girl who looks a lot like my first," he closed the distance, breath stinking of a bitter southern brew, "all those years ago, in a cottage overlooking the breathless Yam Sup Sea. How sumptuous were her moans," he licked his lips, "I'd so like to hear them again before they kill me."

I'd slap him, but only a fool slaps a cornered lion. "You do know I am the Crown Prince's consort and mother of the shah-to-be. How dare you spew such filth?"

He laughed. "Want me to *sultana* you every time you break wind — shouldn't have told them to leave," he pointed at the gholam waiting near the entrance, "you'll get only truth from me when no one is listening. Looking for flowers? You're in the wrong square."

Just why I liked him. Kato seemed loyal, but I wagered he'd take anything — everything — if he could get away with it. I counted on that.

"When you're done feeling sorry for yourself, here's what I suggest you do. There's a man hiding in a sordid little reed-roofed hut in the Alleys of Mud. I'll tell you precisely where he is. Arrest this man and bring him to the Shah. Do so, and you'll be a hero once more," I snapped my fingers, "just like that."

Kato spat a date pit. "What man? Who is he? Why would I—"

"Do it," I said firmly. "The last time I gave you a hint, the Shah promoted you to Grand Commander of the Alanyan gholam. Forgot already?"

"Some good it did me, when it was your beloved who fell prey to the whisperings of my enemies and ordered me to stay. Think soldiers follow titles? Soldiers follow those who bleed with them, kill with them, shit in a ditch with them."

Another thing I was counting on.

"I know a thing or two about men and what they'll follow."

"Not men — soldiers."

I sighed. Kato was a blood-stained dagger, but I wore armor that shattered most edges. "All men are soldiers when enough is at stake. There's one thing they'll follow above even their brothers, their fathers, their kings, their god. Know what it is?"

"Hah, what are you, nineteen? At that age you think you know everything."

I grabbed the date branch from his hand and flung it to the side. "They'll follow the winner. And that's what you'll be, if you take my advice."

Kato grinned, revealing date stains on his lovely whites.

As I walked toward the exit, I kicked at one of the date pits Kato had spat. Then I bent down to brush my shoe and picked it up in one smooth motion. Surely, no one noticed.

For breakfast, I bit a peach and enjoyed sips of ayran: too salty, and it left me with a yogurt mustache. After bathing and wearing my brownest brocade, I got to work.

Before all this began, before I was ripped from my world and brought here, I was unfamiliar with the seductive lure of something so simple: privacy. Aloneness. With baby Seluq asleep and my room devoid of handmaidens, eunuchs, and wet nurses, I locked the door and crawled into the closet. The silk of my hanging clothes brushed against my face and hair. Sunlight beamed through the single hole I'd made, which also provided me with air to breathe.

Darkness, stillness, peace.

I shut my eyes and strained to hear it: the call of the black drongo.

Chirp-peep-peep-chirp. The call remained faint, but its flapping wings beat like a storm against my mind. *Chirp-peep-peep-chirp.*

I opened my eyes. And ears. At first, it was difficult to tell which was sound and which was sight. Both mapped the world. Both wrestled for that commanding spot among my senses. I saw and heard a sky so bright and endless. A city, tiny and mysterious. A desert, which seemed like a thin layer of sand on the back of a god. The river snaking through the desert and city, though a quarter-mile wide, seemed like a string I could pull and tangle around a god-sized finger. The cultivation at the riverbank blazed green and brown with rich, canal-irrigated soil growing the rice, millet, couscous, wheat, figs, and grapes that fed the city. But now, the warhorses of the Sylgiz trampled it. And those horses sprawled a great distance, roaming the thornbush-ridden grasslands to the south and even the scrub to the west, which was dotted with acacia trees, palms, and gazelle.

And everything was upside down. Above me, the city surged, a wart amid the sand upon the god's back. I wanted to fall into the clouds below, but I was frozen in place. Instead, the city fell upon me, raging to smash me to pieces. But as it neared, it was as if I'd entered a bubble, and I now breathed air mixed with trees and sand and dust. An earthy taste.

The screech of a holy song scathed my ears, as if a wolf howled in my brain. I fluttered in trepidation, then landed on whatever was beneath me. My talons scratched at something solid. I looked down — hardstone. I looked around — Qandbajar's skyline. Chanting and prayers and holy words rang. *To Lat we belong...I beseech those beneath her throne...do what is beautiful...lay not upon us burdens we cannot bear...take us not to task for our error...bestow us your mercy, lest we be lost...*

I flew off the yellow dome of Jamshid's shrine and soared toward a palace by the river. Air rushed against the bottom of my wings, keeping me in flight. And yet, it always seemed like the world was moving, not me. Like a giant had tossed the city in my precise direction.

I flapped to slow my descent and landed on the flat roof. Already, voices sounded and bounced off the interior walls, forming a map of the inside. Divans, shelves filled with scrolls and books, hanging carpets, oil lamps flickering in the corner niches — so much sight from only sound. I dipped down to the windowsill; my left eye watched the men inside: Hadrith, Grand Vizier Barkam's son, and Ozar, the spice master of Alanya. A man who, the rumors say, sacrificed a baby daughter for the blessing, or perhaps curse, of unending wealth.

Hadrith poured date wine into a crystal glass and said, "It's fateful that Kyars is not here. Something of a wonder, perhaps, how the stars could align like this."

Ozar nodded, his plump form wrapped in thin, sky-colored silks. "Oh yes. But be honest — it's your father's absence that you treasure."

They sat together at a glass floor table, maroon cushions softening their asses. Hadrith was so tall, he seemed to tower even when sitting. I never understood why he didn't trim that unruly beard — was anyone buying the warrior facade? "I'll tell you this — it's too advantageous. Why would Kyars suddenly agree to leave Kato behind and bring my father instead? It's not his style. Kyars didn't win a thing by himself but rather on the backs of men like Kato. Everyone knows this — Kyars most of all."

"You're saying the idea didn't come from Kato?"

"Someone *closer* is playing the flute and Kyars dancing to the tune."

Ozar caressed his chin hairs. "Who?"

"I don't know, but before proceeding, we ought to find out."

"Oh, you're just getting sweaty feet. Lat has given us an auspicious gift, something she doesn't do often. My fleet is just beyond the river bend, ready and waiting. You have your father's stamp. The Majlis won't go against you because you are your father's son. Give the order. Open the way."

Hadrith eyed me through the window. He grabbed his glass and flung it at my face. I fluttered upward as the crystal arced and shattered on the grass below.

"Fucking drongos," he said as I repositioned to the head of the window, just out of sight, "one pecked my cat to death last week."

"A bird…killing a cat? Oh dear, what is the world coming to?"

"They don't belong here. Ever heard of a place called Talitos?"

Ozar drew in a shocked breath. "Of course, the land beyond the sea mists."

"I was in court the day an ambassador came, claiming to be from there. The woman wore bizarre clothes that changed color as you stared, the way a waterfall flows. She also brought a cage full of black drongos as a gift. In the sky above, you used to see hawks and eagles and doves. Now you see black."

"Foreign plagues seem to be our bane these days."

"Precisely. Foreigners. How many have the Crown Prince's ear? His concubines from the Waste, his gholam from Himyar, none are truly Alanyans. What interests have they? What agendas?"

Ozar squeaked a sound of approval from high in his throat. "The great Eshkal once said, 'your heart is with whom you share the battlefield and bed.'"

Hadrith, it seemed, had stronger suspicions than Ozar. I hoped none led to me.

"Eshkal — a eunuch who'd never thrust a spear, of any kind. I don't share your admiration."

"Wisdom has two founts — doing and observing." How true.

The sun's gaze heated the window head to a discomforting sizzle, but I clung on with my talons, hoping to learn something I could use.

"Anyway," Hadrith said, voice ringing with impatience, "I'll task my beloved little fawn with scouring the harem for enemies. There's nothing she won't do," a perverse laugh bellowed from his chest, "nothing."

"She's a lovely girl, Hadrith. And more than that, her brother is at our gates, with a horde. Don't even think of dishonoring her. You'd endanger us all."

They'd brought Cyra into their schemes? Why would she work for Hadrith? How curious…and annoying.

"I don't shit where I herd sheep, Ozar. Something you never learned."

"I became the spice master of Alanya so I could shit wherever I wanted."

SULTANAAAAAAAAA—

A crack formed in my consciousness and shattered it into a billion pieces. Back in the closet, sweating, eyes wide, staring up at the eunuch Sambal, his braids reaching his shoulders.

"Sultana! Oh, fetch the healer at once!"

Slobber moistened my left cheek. I blinked what must've been a thousand times, sat up, and heaved. Heaved every speck of air I could. It felt as if a barrel crushed my chest and heart, which beat a thousand times a second.

"I'm all right," I muttered, unsure if I'd even made a sound.

Sambal slapped his own cheek. "Oh, she's awake! Thank Lat!"

He and another eunuch pulled me up and onto the bed. Numbness and pain alternated through my bones and flesh, as if tossing me on waves. But worse than that, a nauseating rage built up inside. I'd been severed from the drongo, at the worst moment, just when I was about to learn their plan.

O' Lat, heap your curses upon the saints.

3

CYRA

Some days, I'd rather not wake. Some days are so laden I'd rather drop off the world. Why the dread? Because last night Hadrith explained his plan.

"Ozar and I have come to a wonderful accommodation," he'd said as we shared glasses of tamarind sherbet on the floor of his palace's solar. "Koa spice lane is his, but it's a nasty sailing route. The old-timers even claim sea dragons prowl those waters. So Ozar has agreed to use my crews, who haven't seen much action since the Ethosians took our entire western coastline. No doubt my men are expert at sailing turbulent seas, and a twenty percent cut is quite fair."

I sat there sipping the spicy ice in disquiet. Disbelief. "You said he was corrupt. That his monopoly was making the city sick, that the people were poorer for it. And now you've gone and joined him?"

"Oh Cyra, I'll pay you your share too. Once Ozar accepted that paper with my father's stamp, there was no walking away. You made it happen, and I'm a fair man."

"Aren't you people rich enough?"

"No such thing."

What would I do with more money? The palace already gave me enough. How would I explain it to Tamaz, to Mirima? Would I hide my ill-gotten gains in my underthings? "I don't want it."

Hadrith smiled pridefully at me. "I'll put it aside for you anyway. Perhaps once you've wizened up to the nature of things, you'll learn that no gain is too tainted to refuse. You may one day find that the tower you've been building all your life is missing a foundation. It comes crashing down, crushing everything you love, and you've to pick up the pieces and rebuild with whatever you can — ill-gotten or not."

Oddly particular. His smile turned to a scowl, as if he swallowed bitter memories from his frothing ice cup.

"When will you tell your father about us?" I asked, preferring a topic closer to my needs.

"The moment he steps through the gate, hopefully with a bag of infidel heads. You have my word."

Heads! I felt them rolling around my feet again. What became of the Shah's deliberations with my brother? I'd have to find out.

"Think about what I can buy you!" Hadrith exclaimed with a wry smile. "Half the world, perhaps? And the other half!" What? Ozar had said that phrase to me. Was this all some big jest? "Oh, by the way, there's another little thing I'd love your help with."

I slurped the sherbet. To be true, I wanted nothing more than to be useful. Whether it was Tamaz asking me to negotiate with my brother, or Hadrith's underhanded schemes, at least I wasn't idle like I'd been for the past eight years. Nothing but an ornament for the Seluqals to show they'd a Sylgiz khagan's daughter in their keep. But in Qandbajar, if you were clever enough, you could be more than what others saw you as.

Still, a dark, sickly feeling had begun to make heavy my body. A part of me wanted to run from it, and another to take it in, bear it until I no longer noticed.

"So, please don't let this startle you," Hadrith began, "but I intend to gift His Highness Crown Prince Kyars something fitting once he returns victorious. And, knowing the good man's proclivities, I feel he would love a rather…how should I say it…exotic fruit? See where I'm going with this?"

"I'm not an idiot. You want to gift him a woman." But how the hell could I help him with *that*?

"Not just any woman." Hadrith twirled his beard hairs. "An exceptional one. You see, he has so many concubines that look like…that look like you and Zedra. Sand-colored skin, black hair that curls endlessly, big noses — typical features of Sylgiz and Vograsian girls."

"*Big* noses?" I shouted, poking at mine. It certainly wasn't small…

"I love your nose. One day I hope to lick my sherbet off it." As if that made me feel better. "Don't take what I say the wrong way, but I'd like Kyars to have…something he's never tasted."

It wasn't just me who'd been changing; Hadrith was far from what I remembered. He'd lost that boyishness that made him sweet; there was a time when he'd stutter when talking to me. Now he was more calculated and purposeful in his interactions, much like his father, the Grand Vizier. It made me want to peel away that layer, though it hardened by the day.

I knocked my fist on the table. "You do realize I've never bought a slave before. How could I possibly help?"

Hadrith beamed. "I love seeing you ready and willing. Here's how…" And on he went.

So that was why I didn't want to wake this morning. I would have preferred to be talking with my brother or Shah Tamaz, helping them resolve the impasse that held Qandbajar in its jaw, but I'd promised to help Hadrith and began the day with that intention.

Into the city I went — on foot, for the sake of my shape — as the sun's glaze rimmed the morning clouds. Barely any birds chirping about, which was the trend lately, aside from a few red-eyed, black-feathered drongos perched here and there. Along with my gholam escort, I descended near the river's edge toward the northern wall, which, though clay-colored, had these pleasing deep-blue merlons.

It wasn't long before I arrived at the harbor, which was built on an inlet of the Vogras River. The pungent stench of dried fish replaced the usual sweet air by the riverside. I passed by wooden and reed-built boats, seafood stalls, and hawkers selling everything from palm oil to fake artifacts from the ruins on the Pedang Isles, toward the slave market. Or rather, the Stables, as the city folk called it. A herding place for men, women, and children. I loved horses, as my Sylgiz blood demanded, and I'd never think to keep a horse the way they herded slaves at the Stables. But there was no place better to find a gift for Crown Prince Kyars.

From any vantage, the Stables resembled a massive, open-air prison. Wooden cages covered a length of the embankment in perfect rows and columns. Reed matting shaded those herded within.

Upon entering the premises, my gholam kept the touts at bay by brandishing their gilded batons. But the touts shouted their wares at me anyway.

"Muscular workers from Himyar, the Sultan's best! Can carry loads all day!"

"Serving girls from the Waste, easy on the eyes and ears!"

"I've singing girls, my lady, from distant Sargosa!"

"Northmen! Ruthenians! Perfect for the metal mines!"

"I've a Crucian princess for sale!"

That last one — I found the man who'd said it. He wore the turban-wrapped red hat of the Sirmian zabadar and a floral caftan.

"You're an attention grabber," I said to him. "Is it true?"

He laughed from his round belly. "Of course not, but she likes to think it."

"Hmpf. Crucian slave girls are as rare as sea foam." I was ready to move on.

"Her skin is like snow, *unkissed* by the sun. Come, see for yourself." Oh, then she wasn't *sand-colored* like me and Zedra — probably had a slight nose and straight locks too. Fucking Hadrith. Might as well see her and get this over with.

As we followed the man, I tried to ignore the human sea around me. Dusty-faced children stood in cages, wailing for my attention as I walked. They wanted to sell themselves because anywhere was better than here. Or so they assumed. I wasn't so sure, given how many perished in the mines and plantations throughout Alanya. But the fates of the free often weren't much better — a pasha's boot crushed all beneath, and sometimes those pashas were slaves themselves. One thing was true about Alanya: anyone could climb high or die in a ditch — it was what you made of it, and I had to climb as far from that ditch as possible.

Finally, we stopped at a rusted metal cage at the end of a row. A single girl sat inside against the bars, light brown hair draped over her forehead. I'd call her pale — not fair — and rather short and plump, though *my* opinion of her beauty didn't matter.

The zabadar man whistled; the girl pushed her hair off her face, dusted sand from her rags, then stood and raced toward the bars in front of me.

She stared into my eyes with her mellow, hazel pupils. "You look like a sunshine lady," she said in Sylgiz, pronouncing each word at an odd angle, as if they'd fallen off a cliff. "Please aid my soul. I don't settle here." Strange word choice. It took me a second to realize she was speaking Sirmian, which was a cousin language, though not entirely similar.

"What's your name?" I asked in Sylgiz.

She stared at me as if I'd just cursed her mother. The zabadar repeated my question in proper Sirmian. I guess the word for *name* wasn't the same.

"Celene Saturnus," she said. "My father is Imperator Josias of holy Crucis. Please, you must aid my soul."

The zabadar man laughed and slapped his thigh. "She does that routine so well."

But something in her voice rang sincere.

"How did you end up here?" I asked.

She seemed to understand my Sylgiz this time. "I escaped from the Shah of Sirm, then I was caged by the zabadar, then..." the rest I couldn't understand too well, but I gleaned it amounted to her being brought here.

I looked her up and down. *Shapely* was a word men would use. Innocent demeanor, too. But good enough for Crown Prince Kyars? A snow-skinned Crucian girl who spoke Sirmian and seemed to believe, earnestly, that she was a princess...I could do worse.

I tossed the bag of gold Hadrith had given me at the zabadar man. He opened it; his eyes almost fell from their sockets.

"Thank you, my lady," he said, wind in his mouth. "May Lat bless you a thousand and one times. May the saints chant your name beneath her glorious throne. May Ahriyya never—"

"Just get her out," I said, feeling the sudden urge to retch.

"Chains or no chains?"

"Are you jesting?"

"She likes to run, this one."

"She won't be running." I pointed to the four gholam warriors, each holding a glimmering baton.

The zabadar man released *Celene Saturnus* and gave her a pair of wooden sandals. Off we went.

NOT FIVE MINUTES LATER, as we ascended the sandstone stairs toward the central thoroughfare, Celene grabbed my shoulder and begged, "Sunshine lady, please, put me on a ship for Hyperion. I want to go to the resting place." *Resting place...*probably meant *home*. The bags and rings around her eyes were obvious imprints of tears and sorrow.

"You're going to the palace. You'll be much safer and more comfortable there."

She shook her head, hazel locks waving over her face. "Please. I don't belong here. I haven't seen my family in over a year."

I'd felt the same eight years ago when I was brought to the Sand Palace for the first time. But today was not for sympathy. In any case, she'd be better off in the harem than whatever pleasure house she was about to end up in.

"You'll have a new family soon. Best get used to it."

"That's what they keep telling me, but I never will! I'm not carved flesh to be tossed about a land. I'm the princess of an empire that once ruled the world, and will again, one era."

Conversing with her made me understand the distinct Sirmian words better. And her eyes...so sincere, so pleading. If I really wanted to, I could escort her to a ship, though none would sail for Crucis. After all, Ethosian pirates controlled the fort city where the river met the Yunan Sea, so no ships would sail that way until Kyars rooted the pirates out.

Celene didn't look like a Crucian princess; she looked like a Crucian slave girl. But did it matter? If she really was a princess, all the better for Kyars. I wouldn't let her go after paying so much — in Hadrith's gold and my pride.

I brushed her locks off her face. "Calm yourself and listen. You're going somewhere so plentiful that you'll never want for anything again. And in that place, no one will ever hurt you. I promise."

"That's what they told me in Sirm. And then they did hurt me. This is all a nightmare. A nightmare within a nightmare within a nightmare."

I supposed her prior masters had mistreated her, and she feared the same here. But for all his faults, Kyars was kind to his women. He showered them with rapturous attention, extravagant gifts, and didn't restrict their movements. As long as his loyal gholam were their escort, they could go wherever they pleased and thus enjoy every delight Qandbajar had to offer. It truly wasn't that bad, but this girl wouldn't know it yet.

The earthy smell of lentil soup wafted as we passed the yellow-domed shrine of Saint Jamshid. Outside, lines snaked around the colorful stone arches of the shrine's plaza: men, women, and children stood in rough-spun wools and rags, some with dirt caked on their faces. Meanwhile, the men and women of the Order stewed soup in massive stone cauldrons.

"Cyra," a voice called.

I stopped and stared at the man who'd uttered my name. He wore carded wool and a hood. No turban because the Order of Saint Jamshid didn't permit themselves soft fabrics.

Khizr Khaz, the Grand Sheikh, mixed a cauldron across the lane. I'd met him before only in passing; how did he even remember my name? He fixed his deep-set eyes on me; his beard was whiter than the clouds above.

"Sheikh?" I said.

"Follow the straight path, Cyra."

"What?"

"The straight path." Though he merely whispered it, his voice boomed through the surrounding clamor.

All I could do was nod; a chill ran through my back, as if a jinn had pricked me.

"What did he say?" Celene asked, her slender nose raised in curiosity. Clearly, she didn't understand Paramic.

"Nothing," I replied. "Let's keep moving."

CELENE and I stood in the main hall of the harem as the chief eunuch Sambal and the Shah's sister Mirima glared at us with their hands covering their mouths.

"Whose idea was this?" Mirima finally said.

"Mine," I lied. "I was browsing the Stables when I noticed her. Thought she'd be a fine gift for your nephew."

Sambal made a sizzling sound with his tongue, as if he were a boiling pot.

Mirima moved her hand across her eyes, as if — by some miracle — that would make Celene disappear. "My dear, I am more than capable of selecting the Crown Prince's nightly entertainment. As sultana of this harem, only I choose who's allowed within it."

I bent my neck. "Apologies, sultana. But last year, His Highness gifted me a handmaiden of my own. A lovely, young Ruthenian girl. I thought it only fit to repay the gift in kind."

"Gifts do not need repayment, Cyra. They are given from those who have to those who don't." She let out an old woman's sigh. "But I see you are well-intentioned. I won't punish you. However, this...this...ill-blooded creature cannot stay. Send her back to the Stables."

Quite the barb; Mirima was expert at those. Good thing Celene couldn't understand Paramic.

"Ill-blooded? Whatever do you mean?" I asked, hoping not to strain Mirima's tolerance.

"Look at her," Mirima commanded.

I looked at Celene, who stared at the floor, hands clasped politely across her belly.

"I see nothing wrong," I answered. "A perfectly good woman, with wide, child-bearing hips. Perhaps she'll give Crown Prince Kyars another son."

"That's precisely what we don't want," Mirima said. "Another son to challenge Seluq, with the blood of some western swine herders. Weak blood that will see him a puppet of the gholam and viziers. Why do you think the Seluqal House of Alanya has remained strong for hundreds of years while our cousins to the north and east flounder from invasions and civil war? Because we are careful with whom we breed. Our blood comes from the Waste, just like yours. And that blood must be renewed from the source, not mixed with Lat-knows-what."

If I messed this up, Hadrith would be furious. But what could I say to Mirima? Not all Kyars' women were from the Waste, but the ones that weren't at least had status.

I blurted out a dumb thing, "She's the daughter of Imperator Josias."

Sambal squeaked, then laughed with thigh slaps. "Is that so? Then her Crucian must be perfect — heavenly, even." He said something to Celene in Crucian.

Of course, Sambal hailed from Crucis too — it had slipped my mind. Though I forgot which part.

Celene said something back at him; his bottom lip hung, and he turned away, nose pushing between his brows.

"What did you say?" I whispered to Celene.

"Nothing." Seemed she didn't trust me.

Now Sambal whispered something to Mirima. I felt like a child left out of a fun game. What the fuck was going on?

Mirima snapped her fingers at one of the other eunuchs waiting compactly at the doorway. "Get her a room," she ordered. "Bathe her and call the tailor to take her measurements. Call the healer, too."

Whatever Celene had said, it'd changed everything.

"What did you say?" I asked with just enough fierceness to show her I was serious, though not too much to scare her.

"Why should I tell you? You were tested on the path. The Archangel saw you. You had the chance to do a good, to help me go home. But you chose the path of evil, and now I'm here and have to fight the wolves for myself. I don't want to be in your sight ever again." She sounded like a sheikha who'd once berated me for stealing a jelly sweet when she wasn't looking.

"I live here too, idiot. You're going to be seeing a lot of me. Don't even think of getting on my bad side. Now tell me what you said, or I'll devote my days to making your life hell."

"Eat a slipper," she said. A Sylgiz taunt for children. Didn't know the Sirmians said the same.

"Only children say that!"

"Go away, you giraffe!"

Sambal pulled us apart. "Girls, girls. We don't allow fighting in the sublime harem. Celene, first thing to remember — always keep your voice at a whisper. Cyra, run along now. Wonderful find, truly, but we'll take over from here."

BACK IN MY ROOM, I flung a crystal cup at the wall. It didn't shatter and just bounced off. How unsatisfying. I grabbed a brass plate, threw the red grapes to the side, and banged it on the closet door. It chipped the wood and bounced across the room, clattering to the floor.

Hadrith had told me, "Whoever you choose, become her best friend. From her, you must learn everything about Kyars that you can."

And I'd told him, "But I'm friends with Zedra. She already knows everything about him."

"And has she ever given you details? Intimate details?"

I thought about it and answered, "No, never. She's a very private person."

Hadrith raised his brows in a smug, satisfied expression, then said, "Private people oft have much to hide. And Zedra is not beholden to you, the way a fresh slave would be. We need to learn everything about the shah-to-be and his affairs — worldly, spiritual, nocturnal. You get me?"

I sat on my low bed and dug my head into my knees. Hadrith, Hadrith, fucking Hadrith. He was all I'd been thinking about the last few moons, like a sickness I couldn't cure. But did he really feel a thing for his *little fawn*?

"Obviously not," I said out loud as a trickle formed in my eyes. "I'm such a fool." I thought about all my moments with him. Eight years ago, when I saw him for the first time, laughing at a low table with Prince Faris, Kyars' younger brother. We bumped into each other in the hallway, and Hadrith smiled, scratched his head, and said, "You're pretty." Or how about last year, after he'd returned from a trade mission to Kashan and put a little mechanical horse in my hands. "It's from the Silklands," he said, as if he'd conquered it. "It made me think of you."

How many mechanical horses had he bought for how many gullible girls? Could I expect him to be so different from Kyars, the man he looked up to most?

The door squeaked open. Vera, my young Ruthenian handmaiden, stepped inside, gaze low. Kyars gifted her to me a few moons ago, though she'd been in his service far longer. She locked the door behind her.

"Mistress." She bent down near the edge of the bed and put a warm hand on my knee. "Half the hall heard a clamor. What happened?"

"I'm fucking worthless."

She shuffled closer and touched both my knees. "Is it him again?"

"Why can't I do anything right?"

She tousled her yellow hair, then sat her lithe form next to me. "You're frustrated."

"Of course I'm frustrated. I've been frustrated my whole life. Nothing I do ever gets me anywhere. I'm almost twenty-four, I'm not married, and all I do all day is walk in a garden, pay some poet to fill my head, spend someone else's money buying trinkets in the bazaar."

"And you think Hadrith will save you from that?"

"Someone must. My brother offered to take me away, you know. I told him I have no other home but here in the Sand Palace. And yet, sometimes, I feel these walls are just a prettier prison."

Vera pushed her shoulder against mine. "You want things when you already have things."

Is that what passed for wisdom in Ruthenia? But I couldn't blame Vera for not being wise. Kyars didn't buy her for her words.

"Everything I have is on the outside. Within, I'm bereft. Hollower than a wispy cloud."

"I disagree. When Kyars told me he was giving me to someone

else — I swear, it was the most awful thing I'd ever heard. Half the ladies here beat their handmaidens, the other half consider us too base to even touch. But when I learned it was you, I was so joyous. Because you're kind. And good." She put a hand on my thigh.

"Stop," I said. "I don't want to do that."

Follow the straight path. Khizr Khaz's words bounced through my head.

She slid her hand up — it felt good just to be touched — then whispered, "You're frustrated."

I shook my head, but didn't have the resolve to push her hand away. "It's wrong."

"Everything is," she whispered hot in my ear.

As she slid her fingers closer, I shut my eyes and put my hand in her shirt.

I CRIED in the bath again. *The straight path.* That was what the Recitals of Chisti taught us, the most important precept being to worship only Lat, and to never worship another god or ascribe to her a partner. Second, to tend your own soul, not to dirty it with sin, impurities, and vulgar thoughts. The sheikhs and sheikhas had planted these seeds in me, but the roots never took hold, blown away like thin topsoil upon salted land. I feared I was forever bent. Unclean, in mind, body, and spirit. No steam or water could purify me, make me good again, so might as well go all in.

I had to succeed at whatever game I was playing. Celene had talked tough, but beneath that, I sensed a terrified little girl. I'd have to teach her respect and make her beholden so she could be useful to Hadrith and me.

As I scrubbed myself with twice my normal vigor, I realized I was in the same steam room as the other day. I pushed the coal tray aside, and to my surprise, the bloody print was still there. But because I'd pushed the coal tray further, I noticed something else: a picture, of some sort, drawn in blood. I crouched to get a better view; it looked like three eyes around a star.

I could understand if some clumsy girl fell, hit her head, and put a bloody print on the wall. But how badly did you have to hurt your head to draw a picture with your own blood?

Strange and alarming, but what wasn't these days? I'd enough on my plate, anyway. People hit their heads and died all the time, so best to shrug it off and get on with things.

I needed a break, so went into the city with an escort of two gholam. Less than usual, but I didn't want a crowd around me. Part of me wanted to head outside the gate to see my brother, but what would I say to him? More reminiscence? No, I wanted to bring something of substance, something that would solve his standoff with Tamaz, next we met.

The sun glared at its annoying afternoon angle. Sunshine bounced into my eyes from every shimmering surface. At Laughter Square, the lines were thinning — usually by afternoon, the poets' fresh morning verses decayed into easily plucked cliches and banalities. I moved to the front of the grass-covered pig's line, hoping he could cheer me up with clever praise.

"Mistress!" he said upon eyeing me. "The sun has broken through the clouds—"

I turned and walked away before he could finish. Fuck the sun and the moon and the stars and the rivers and the oceans and pomegranates and cypress trees and love and death and resurrection and the light and the dark. Enough with that trite nonsense.

The Himyarite sat upon his brass throne, just across the square. By the time I'd walked to him, he was up and stretching and yawning, as if weary from a long day. He kicked his coin-filled treasure chest shut.

"Closed," he said.

I dug my hands in my coin pouch and jingled the gold and silver.

"I've made enough money to fill my stomach, buy a good vintage date wine, and more," he scoffed. "Come back tomorrow."

"I'm straight from the palace. You'll make verses for me."

The Himyarite chuckled. "*From* the palace. If you were a Seluqal or the woman of one, you would have said it. But you're *from* the palace — the canteen barmaid, perhaps?"

My fists formed instinctually as the young, dark-skinned man grinned.

He continued, "Pissed because the princes don't grab your ass when you serve their drinks? You need to have one for that to happen, my dear."

My eyebrows flared. Then it dawned: these were his verses. This was what people paid him for.

He pointed at my chest. "I've known grapes that are more fondleable." Was *fondleable* even a word?

"Is that all you do?" I said, unimpressed. "Insult appearances? Ever go any deeper?"

"Deeper? You're as deep as a eunuch's thrust."

I nodded. "Better. What else?"

He waved me away. "That was a taste. Come back tomorrow for more."

"Tell me who I am, Himyarite."

He sighed and sat upon his brass throne, then picked at the fake ruby on its armrest. "I happen to have a name." He put a hand through his utterly curly, though short head of hair. "Eshe."

"I'll forget it by morning."

He stared into me and tilted his head, then relaxed into a sincere, almost sympathetic gaze. "Want to know who you are? You're here three times a week, with your more voluptuous friend. You hang off her like a leech, without a purpose of your own. You wouldn't be here if you knew what you wanted, but you don't, and you fill the chasm with whatever you can — because, at the end of the day, you're a quivering little girl, the cold fingers of despair wrapping your neck like a noose."

I felt those cold fingers now as I shivered, despite standing amid the declining sun's warmth.

"Have you been watching me?" I asked. "Do you know who I am?"

Eshe shook his head, got off the throne, and stepped off his dais. Face to face, we were the same height, and I could see patches in his beard.

He held out an open hand. "You know the going rate. Pay me and go back to your palace, lady. Tomorrow is a new day. And don't even think of jumping my line. In front of this throne," he pointed to his cheap brass chair, "all are equally worthless."

4

ZEDRA

One thing you didn't do in Qandbajar: forget to return books. Specifically, books borrowed from the Tower of Wisdom.

For failing to return a book, the punishment was ten lashes for each day late. And, unless you were a Seluqal, the palace wouldn't save you. Sultanas, pashas, and peasants — all had endured the Philosophers' whip. The Tower even had an executioner on retainer, and believing the more outlandish tales, he wasn't all that bored. According to the Order of Philosophers, losing knowledge was worse than losing life because *ink is weightier than blood*.

Why so punitive over heaps of ink and paper? Because some tomes in the Tower were among the only copies in the world, and the printing presses couldn't reproduce them fast enough. A true wonder, those presses — among many inventions that dazzled me since arriving here. I could hate them all I wanted, but by allying with the Philosophers, the Seluqals had not only amassed knowl-edge — they'd purposed it.

Thankfully, I was in good standing with the Tower, and as a sultana, only the top two floors of twelve were forbidden. Today, I climbed the winding stairs to the eighth floor.

Looking down upon Qandbajar from the stairwell windows reminded me of the black drongo. What a feeling to fly freely, to be but feathers on air. These bodies of skin and meat and bones that we dragged and clothed and armored now seemed a curse from the star that created us. How sad — even if mankind staved off the Great Terror, we were doomed never to fly.

Defeatist thoughts weakened my already weary knees — climbing seven flights left me huffing and aching and feeling like an old woman again. I took a break and peeked into the seventh-floor reading room: full of brightly turbaned men with serious mustaches and flowing robes, some crowding around book niches, others lying on their sides upon wooden divans while resting their elbows on pillows the color of lapis lazuli. This entire floor was for military tactics, so they must've been khazis and gholam and order men.

I recognized someone: gholam commander Kato, in a golden turban and bronze caftan. He lay on a divan, book in hand; the cover read *Subduing Mounted Archers: Gunpowder Tactics to Counter Feint Retreats and Lightning Flanks — Volume Five*. Did such a specific topic really require five volumes? A stack of books lay next to him, probably with similarly hefty titles. Well, you didn't become a gholam commander by being an ignorant fool. But if he was here reading, had he done what I'd asked?

He put the book down and stretched his arms. I stepped back so he wouldn't notice me. Best he not see another of my many sides, lest he discover the whole. I climbed to the eighth floor.

Shelves covered the circular room. Each shelf was divided into square sections in a three-by-four grid. Within each section, three or four books lay flat in a pile. A Philosopher had told me that this arrangement allowed *"each book to breathe, relax, and luxuriate."* They really did value them more than lives.

Flavors of Blood Volume Two by Aligar of Zunduq ought to be on shelf seven, column two, row three. I circled around the room until

I found shelf seven. But, curiously and concerning, only dust sat in column two, row three.

I made my way to the librarian standing behind a giant ledger. He wore the tower-like felt hat of the Philosophers and a blue silk robe with a black trim.

"Checked out," he said when I mentioned the book.

"By whom?"

"We do not share that information." Not a hint of courtesy on his dull, old, pockmarked face.

The words *I am beloved of the Crown Prince* almost came out of my mouth. But I realized the librarian hadn't even referred to me as *sultana*. He simply didn't care for my title.

"When will it be back?" I asked.

"One week."

So the usual term, which meant it had been checked out this morning. But who else in this city was interested in an old, outdated medical tome? Should I be worried?

For now, I could make do without it. The first volume had refreshed my knowledge of blood: it came in flavors, like sherbet. Each flavor had its own unique recipes — though some recipes could be written with more than one flavor. The second volume supposedly described the tastes of the rarest flavors, which could help me identify them if ever I came across more.

Disappointed, I left the Tower of Wisdom and returned to my room. At midday, I proceeded to the great hall of the Sand Palace. The simurgh guarded the palace entrance, its wolf head gazing down above the ornate, sandstone arches. Its eagle wings spread out across the garden, providing more shade than the surrounding palm trees. The Seluqals were too proud of their bird standards. It was said two hundred artisans labored to create this single statue, and it took them six years, such was the detail, though hyperbole bloated most stories in this city.

Sunshine streamed through the great hall's glass dome. The Sylgiz khagan stood at the head of twenty warriors, each wearing hard, maroon laminar, as if coming to a battle. Opposite them, Tamaz sat upon his golden divan and glared fire at the chained, shriveled man who trembled beneath his dais.

"Let the world bear witness," Tamaz said, "say it again."

The trim-bearded man wore a dirty caftan and stunk even from this distance. The tips of his hands were cut like half-sausages. He couldn't hold a pen, not anymore.

"An emissary of the Jotrid khagan ordered me to write it," he said.

"You are…*were* my scribe," Tamaz said with disgust, "not Khagan Pashang's. So why did you?"

The scribe stared at the floor, lips trembling yet silent. Good.

"Seems we'll need to do more to get the truth out of him." Tamaz waved his hand; two gholam approached the scribe, golden batons in their brawny hands.

"I've a question," boomed someone in the crowd. A hardwood voice that seemed to echo on its own.

"Approach, Grand Mufti," Tamaz said.

Khizr Khaz pulled down his hood: his cropped white hair and rough brown robe seemed out of place amid this Seluqal majesty.

"What *sins* were they punished for?" he asked. Of course, the letter the scribe had written simply said *payment for your sins*.

The poor scribe continued to shiver on the floor. Then he looked up at the Grand Mufti and said, "They burned all the flowers." Hmm? What was he talking about?

"Flowers? Where?" Khizr pressed.

The scribe sobbed as he stared into the sheikh's eyes, then muttered, "An emissary of the Jotrid khagan ordered me to write it."

He could say little else. Good.

Shah Tamaz said, "Khagan Cihan, you may take this man into your custody. Do what you will to arrive at the truth and find those who unjustly beheaded your men."

Cihan stepped forward and gazed with ice on the trembling

scribe. He really did resemble Cyra — both were tall, though while Cyra's height made her rather lanky, Cihan was broad enough to intimidate. His long hair curled less than hers, though wasn't it disrespectful for men to sport long hair in the Shah's presence? Perhaps he didn't care. "This scribe is ready to shit himself," he said in Sylgiz, which was similar enough to a dialect I knew, spoken by a tribe that neighbored mine. "And yet, he didn't kill anyone. He merely did his job — he scribed. Justice demands killers, not this empty, fingerless fool."

"Perhaps Khagan Pashang can tell you more," Tamaz said, now speaking Sirmian, which was also similar enough to Sylgiz.

Cihan shook his head. "Pashang and I were once friends, believe it or not. Bosom friends, even. Couldn't get enough of each other. One day while we were wrestling, he hit his head on a rock. Has been a bit light up here," he tapped his head, "ever since. It's true, he'd love for the Sylgiz and Alanya to be at war...but clever ploys are not his thing."

"Someone else could have come up with the idea," Tamaz insisted, "and he merely gave the order."

"*Someone else*. That's what you so want it to be."

Tamaz raised his hands, palms up. "Do I look like I care what Sylgiz traders are doing at the market?"

"*Spice* traders," Cihan said. "Since I took over, we Sylgiz have secured the land routes to several spice-bearing kingdoms. Who else here is a spice trader and stands to lose, I wonder?"

A gasp spread throughout the crowd. I eyed Ozar somewhere in the middle, dabbing his sweaty, pink face with a golden cloth. Everything was progressing as I'd hoped.

Tamaz sighed. The old man had clearly digested enough intrigue for one day. "You don't want to accept the confession. You don't want blood money. What else can I do for you, Khagan?"

"Seems you'd rather not clean your house. Are you so ready to accept murderers in your court?" Considering Ozar was married to his sister, Tamaz had little choice.

"And what are you?" Tamaz sniggered. "Don't pretend your hands are bloodless. Driving a hard bargain, I can respect, but your *love* of justice is wearing thin. What do you want, Cihan son of Yamar? Speak plain or go in peace."

My gaze caught on Cyra, who stood against a calligraphy-covered pillar near the front while fidgeting and biting her lips. Too much to lose for her if this negotiation soured. As for myself, I had a reserve plan — several, actually. Foolish to rely on one outcome in a world birthed by chaos.

Cihan whistled and pointed toward the exit. He and his warriors walked out with an even march. As they left, chatter erupted among those remaining. Tamaz grabbed his cane and limped toward the exit, a gholam escort surrounding him.

"I'm being framed!" Ozar exclaimed to a fellow vizier. "I'm being framed!"

As I made for the exit, I eyed Kato leaning against the wall, holding a sack of what must've been gold. He noticed me, nodded, and smiled. I nodded back, satisfied.

WHILE WALKING the palace halls on the way to my room, I thought about blood: specifically, the seventeen flavors of blood that ran through the veins of mankind. But almost all alive possessed one of four flavors: seeker, sower, settler, or soldier.

While Aligar believed there was a medical significance, in my opinion, these names were nomenclature and didn't describe any qualities of those possessing them. Not that the actual distinctions between the four common flavors — their magical uses — interested me much; I was far more concerned with the rarer flavors. One flavor, in particular: conqueror's blood.

But, as I'd gleaned from my studies, conqueror's blood was becoming impossible to find. At the time of Seluq, it was widespread in the Endless — which was why Aligar gave it that name — with about ten in a hundred there possessing it, compared to one in a thousand Alanyans. But now it was in decline everywhere — supposedly a hundred times rarer than when Aligar lived — and I needed it to write my special runes.

I opened my room door to see the chief eunuch Sambal standing barefoot on my bed and thrusting a broom from the wrong end as if it were a spear.

"What are you doing!?" How dare he intrude upon my chamber without permission? I wanted to grab that broom and break it over his head.

He bent his neck. I was no Seluqal, so it wasn't appropriate, but *who cares*. "My apologies, sultana. A rat inspired by Ahriyya ran into your room — I had to give chase, so I could finally kill it and end its pantry-raiding spree."

Oh no, he'd seen my rat. Stupid thing was always getting into trouble. What else had he seen? "Get out!"

I slammed and locked the door behind him; they'd put in a fresh lock after the last one broke at the worst time. I looked into the crib — empty. My heart almost beat out of my chest. Then it flickered into my mind — obviously, Mirima was looking after baby Seluq today. I sighed in relief; the fear that it was all happening again eased.

I pulled off the false wall behind my bed and took out my wares: a box of tiny, blood-filled bottles, various wooden containers with bits of chewed food, and my notes.

The food I ought to probably throw out. By tasting someone's spit, I could also taste their blood flavor, so now knew that Tamaz and Kato were both seekers. I, too, was a seeker, making their blood worthless to me. Our first kiss told me Crown Prince Kyars was a sower — among other things — a similarly worthless flavor, since most runes that could be written with sower's blood could also be written with seeker's blood. The four common flavors overlapped too much for anyone possessing them to be useful, which made almost everyone worthless.

I put the bottle of conqueror's blood to the reddening, midday sunlight streaming from my balcony; mere drops of watered-down blood remained. But a replenishment would, I hoped, be forthcoming.

I slid onto my bed, the weight of the world pushing me into my silk sheets. Sniffed the red tulips in the emerald-studded vase by my bedside — knowing how much I liked them, the eunuchs daily brought me fresh ones from the pleasure garden. They smelled oddly like home, though they didn't grow when and where I'd lived.

The gate to fanaa is nothingness. God is only drawn on a blank slate. Father Chisti had spoken these words, though you wouldn't find them in the Recitals of Chisti. If I could burn every copy of that falsehood, I'd even burn myself. How saddening that rage shattered my *fanaa* so easily. Anger was why I was weak, but something had to fuel me.

An hour later, a gentle knock sounded on the door. I arose with a stretch and opened it. Vera, the adorable, strawberry-cheeked handmaiden I'd made Kyars gift to Cyra, greeted me and came inside. From her dress pocket, she pulled a blood-tinged silk kerchief and presented it to me with a grin.

"This is unexpectedly quick," I said. "How are you so good?"

"I do as my sultana commands."

"No, really, how did you get that? I hope you didn't hurt the girl."

"I would never hurt her." Said with such sincere, smitten eyes. "She's as lovely as a lily in the thaw."

I didn't need much blood. On the silk was perhaps a nosebleed's worth. I brought the kerchief to my mouth and licked. A storm of spice and metal, like a coin doused in tamarind. Unpleasant on my tongue, but Vera wasn't lying. This was conqueror's blood.

I'd only tasked her this morning with getting more. How had she delivered so fast?

"Which part of her bled?" I asked.

Vera fingered her bottom lip. "Right here."

I'd noticed Cyra biting her lips in the great hall. Could be nerves got to her, and she bit down too hard.

But Vera's cheeks had turned from strawberry to pomegranate. Why was she blushing?

"You seem a bit too happy about this," I said as I followed her avoidant eyes.

"I'm just pleased to have served you, Sultana of Sultanas." Said so musically.

Perhaps her methods were better kept secret, like mine. I couldn't begrudge that — secrets often were our survival. "You've served me well, dear. I won't forget it." I gestured with my head toward the door.

After she'd left, I soaked the handkerchief in water for a minute, then rung the reddish liquid into a cup. Good thing about blood: it's mostly water, so adding more water, up to a limit, was a handy trick that allowed you to write more runes with less blood.

If only conqueror's blood flowed in my veins. How sad that I possessed the blood of seekers, considering my ancestors were of god's blood, among the thirteen rare flavors. Perhaps the rarest, but all thirteen were nearly impossible to find now; the baser flavors diluted them into extinction.

Once I'd poured Cyra's blood into a tiny perfume bottle, off I went.

I would place this rune in the wine cellar, a few minutes' walk from my room. No concubines went down there, but eunuchs and handmaids did all the time. It was a cool, damp, sour-smelling place full of stacked barrels and bottles. No one would notice it, surely.

Once there, I dabbed my finger in the bottle, as if it were ink, then wrote the pattern of souls as delicately as I could in a crevice behind a barrel stack that smelled of fermented barley. It resembled an eye within an eye. I whispered the incantation, "O' Morning Star, give it life, as you gave life to us." The bloodrune glowed for the briefest moment, as if the Morning Star were saying *I have heard and I have given.*

I BUMPED into Cyra on the way back. A tooth-sized gash ran across her bottom lip — it looked deeper than a nervous bite. I pointed to my own lip and said, "What happened?"

She darted her eyes and said in a single breath, "Oh, uh, I was slurping stew and bit myself. How careless. So shameful."

Bit yourself…while slurping? Well, it was from the horse's mouth, so I supposed that mystery was solved. "I was just about to have coffee. Care to join?"

She nodded. The bulging bags beneath her eyes made plain her sleeplessness and worry. She also seemed oddly demure as we sat at a low table in the harem's dancing hall. Cyra kept her back toward the dancers and flute players — she'd seemed uninterested lately with the usual entertainment.

I said what was on my mind, "That was nice of you, returning a gift in kind."

With a half-smile, she replied, "That's how I was raised."

"Lovely Crucian girl. So young. Kyars will be overjoyed." Should I have pretended to be jealous? I couldn't care less whom Kyars fucked, since the man's seed was as bereft as the Zelthuriyan Desert. Rather, it was Cyra's motives that concerned me. Or, more specifically, the motives of her taskmaster.

"I hope so," Cyra said, eyes distant.

"What's wrong, dear?" I put my hand on hers.

She pouted and said, "I'm worried about my brother. And Shah Tamaz." Her voice cracked. "It seemed like it would come to blows earlier. I just want their standoff to end."

"You're the one thing they have in common. Surely you could bridge the divide." Although that was the last thing I wanted.

She shook her head. "Me? What do I know about politics, about justice, about any of it? I'm just an ignorant girl from the Waste."

Several of my daughters suffered from similar self-doubt. Hadrith clearly understood how to take advantage of a girl's weakness, which made him annoying, if not dangerous. Not only did Cyra possess conqueror's blood, making her useful to me, she'd been tutored by the same Philosophers as Kyars for the past eight years. And yet, unlike the Seluqals, she didn't have these luxuries at birth and so would, naturally, have unsatisfied yearnings. It seemed Hadrith knew how to tug at her hungers. I was neither towering, bearded, nor brimming with gold, so couldn't compete.

Now a dilemma presented itself: encourage her weaknesses, or reassure her strengths? Build her up or break her down? I didn't need the competition. Hadrith was already a pest, and with Cyra bolstering his agenda, it could endanger everything I'd suffered for. Everything I cared for: bringing back the Children, staving off the Great Terror, my fiery aches for vengeance — it all barreled through my mind during this one, hesitant, painful, bitter gulp.

"Cyra, dear, you're like a diamond that thinks it's quartz. A baby lion that, only because it's small, believes itself to be a street cat. You're not ignorant, nor are you weak. You're everything you need to be. I'm sure if you speak with your brother, speak with the Shah, we'll all be better for it. You don't know your own strength until you try." I squeezed her hand. If only I'd said such things to my daughters and granddaughters and great-granddaughters while they still breathed.

She shut her eyes as tears streamed. I'd touched her heart, it seemed. "You really think so?"

"I know it, dear." I wanted to ask her about Hadrith and her feelings for him. But how without revealing that I'd been spying on them? Hadrith and Cyra rarely met in the open, so I wasn't supposed to know. Could I coax it out?

"Cyra, ever thought of finding a husband?" You'd think, given our friendship, we would've already discussed this topic. But both Cyra and I kept private about that sort of thing. Me, for obvious reasons. I wasn't sure why she'd never brought it up, though.

"Of course I have. I'm almost twenty-four. But no one's made an offer."

That, I found hard to believe. Hundreds of viziers and pashas would want the hand of a khagan's sister for their sons or themselves. Alanya was full of wealthy merchants, Philosophers, sheikhs — all who would've noticed a girl like her.

"Have you ever asked Shah Tamaz if someone has made an offer? He's your guardian so it would be directed to him."

"Wouldn't he have told me?"

"Not necessarily, if he didn't consider it appropriate. You ought to ask him." I raised a playful eyebrow. "Unless…you yourself have someone in mind?"

Dimples formed on her pinkening cheeks as she smiled. "Well, maybe. I mean, I don't know."

"For Lat's sake — who is it? You can't keep it from me!"

She sat straight and brushed stray hairs off her forehead, a rosy vigor in her expression. "All right — it's Hadrith."

Now…what ought I do. Encourage this awful union, or lace it with doubt? A friend would encourage it, but Hadrith was sniffing around and had the power to destroy everything I'd built. What would I say if Cyra were my daughter?

"If that works out, we'll be seeing even more of each other," I said. "He and Kyars are such good friends. Best friends, even. And so…very similar. In good ways…and some not-so-good ways."

A frown snapped onto her face. "Like what?"

"Well, like, last week…umm, you know, I shouldn't say. Never mind."

She craned forward. "Tell me."

I clasped my hands. "I was on my way from the Grand Bazaar and saw Hadrith coming out of…"

"Coming out of what?"

"You know."

"A pleasure house?"

I nodded.

Cyra glanced away, from sorrow more than surprise. "He meets all kinds of folks, Hadrith does. Sometimes he has to take viziers or ambassadors to those places, to make deals and such."

"You're right. Although, there was also…"

Cyra thudded her elbows onto the table. "Also what?"

"The other day, I saw him with the Grand Admiral's daughter — you know, the girl with fire-red hair. Half Karmazi. They seemed…"

"Affectionate?" Dread drenched her voice.

"I'd use…a stronger word."

There. Her pupils enlarged with sharp rage as she slouched again. Seemed I'd succeeded.

"You're trying to dissuade me," she said. "Why?" Or perhaps I hadn't…

"No dear, I'm not—"

"Are you jealous?"

I could see her fist under the table.

"What? No, I'm just looking out for you."

"No you're not. I think you know how powerful Hadrith is, and you don't want me anywhere near that kind of power. Because then it would rival yours."

Ugh. Frustration welled in my tightening chest. I'd miscalculated. Perhaps I underestimated her raw ambition, and now a conversation that had started so well was going all wrong.

"Cyra, I just want you to be happy."

"Tell me this — are you happy?"

I shook my head in a moment of honesty. If only she knew the depths of my despair.

"Happiness is for fools," she said. "For drunks. For pleasure-seekers. I'm not after happiness. I grew up in a place where entire tribes would fight to eat rats. Then I was brought here and given everything one could imagine." We were more similar than she'd ever believe. "Want to know why Shah Tamaz hasn't found me a match, despite my age? Because, at the end of the day, I'm his hostage. And what is a hostage for, if not a bargaining piece to be sacrificed when needed? Do you think I'm not aware that if the Sylgiz do attack, he would use my life to buy time for your *beloved* and his gholam to return? Do you think I'm not aware I could be strung up in a noose?"

"My dear, I didn't—"

"Hadrith — for all his terrible failings and flaws — can save me from that. Will save me from that."

"Don't you know he's using you!?" I blurted out. So rash of me to reveal what I wasn't supposed to know. "You talk about being a bargaining piece, but what are you to him? Just a pawn, to be sacrificed all the same."

"That's what you think of me?" She sniggered, colder than ice. "The way you seduced Kyars — think I can't do the same to Hadrith? You really do believe you're better, don't you?"

"I didn't seduce Kyars! I'm nothing. I'm a slave, for Lat's sake!"

Cyra shook her head and chuckled. Then she swallowed hard and said, "Right, but you're the mother of his only son. Your status will never be questioned, from now until little Seluq dies of old age, and by then you'll already be long in the grave. Your life is secure — how nice for you. Don't get in the way of me securing mine."

Curse the saints! She'd completely misunderstood my concern. Not unlike my own daughters, to be fair.

"What did you just say?" she said, eyebrows high in surprise.

"Huh? I didn't say anything."

"You just said 'curse the saints.'"

Oh Lat, I'd said what I was thinking out loud, hadn't I? "No, you misheard me."

"I heard you quite clearly. 'Curse the saints.' Are you...Path of the Children?"

I shook my head a bit too fast. "No, of course not, that's heresy."

"And yet, I heard it from your lips."

I had to think of something. Anything. "My mother was. She used to say it all the time. 'Curse the saints.' Sometimes when I'm stressed, her words just…come out of me. I don't know why." Not a complete lie, actually.

Silence lingered. Then Cyra nodded. "My mother was…is, too. My whole family, in fact."

No. The Sylgiz were not truly Path of the Children. They cursed the saints and revered the Children, but in all the wrong ways. Because the right ways had been eradicated. How disappointed I was to learn that one of the few tribes that claimed to walk the straight path was also far astray.

"Do you still believe it?" Cyra asked.

"No, of course not. The sheikhas made clear how absolutely heretical it all is."

"But you've only been here a year or so. Surely, in your heart, you must still believe some of it."

"It's forbidden in Alanya."

"I didn't ask if it was forbidden. I asked if *you* believed it. Are you waiting for the Guided to come out of occultation? For the Gate to open, and all that?"

Those were the *wrong* beliefs. The Children never spoke of a gate or of someone called the Guided. Inventions ascribed to us by people who were trying but didn't know better. Still, those who called themselves Path of the Children today were better than these saint worshippers by their intentions alone. If I succeeded in restoring the true Path of the Children, I prayed they — and everyone — would flock to it.

"No!" I said. "It's all nonsense. I pray to the saints, like everyone else."

She sighed, almost disappointed. Then she bit her lip — where that gash was — and nodded. "I have an idea."

She pushed up and rushed toward the double doors.

"Where're you going?" I asked.

She turned around, reinvigorated and rosy. "Outside the city. To talk with my brother. Please, forgive my rude outburst. Thank you for the coffee, and the conversation, dear friend. I'll see you soon, all right?"

Perhaps sooner than she realized.

WHAT HAD I DONE? What was Cyra going to do? In order to learn just how badly I'd messed things up, I sat in my closet and forced my soul into the drongo. Glided from what must've been the second heaven — where the sky was bleak and cloudless — to the clouds and below. I drank deep of the air and witnessed the world in its endlessness. And then, with a straight-down dive and a flutter, I landed atop a yellow yurt at the outskirts of Qandbajar.

Around me, the Sylgiz went about their late afternoon tasks. How they lived reminded me so much of home — relaxing, working, and bathing beneath the sky, lambs roasting on spits, four times more horses than humans. But I couldn't enjoy the nostalgia. Voices sounded, showing Cyra and her brother alone in the yurt below.

That she was allowed to leave the city and visit her brother any time showed how much Tamaz trusted her. Perhaps I could exploit that trust for my own end, but that was a thought for another time.

I peeked through the hole at the top, where the stove's chimney would be if this weren't such a hot season. The pair sat beside each other, on the floor, like a brother and sister ought to.

"Why should I even let you walk back into that mud heap?" Cihan said. "You belong with us, Cyra. I don't blame you for how they changed you. I blame Father for being weak and letting them take you."

"You want the truth?" she said. "I won't ever come back. Not because I don't love you, not because I don't love my people. I miss Mother. I miss…almost everything." Her voice trembled. Was she targeting his sympathy with her tears? "But one thing I don't miss — the cold. I don't ever want to be cold again."

"You're staying here because you hate the winter?"

She nodded. "Isn't that why you're here, too? Winter is three moons away. I know what you want, Cihan. Father always talked about it. 'We ought to be like the songbirds,' he'd say, 'and find a way south, singing all the while.' But the Alanyans would never allow it. You've come for land, not justice, and you're trying to see just how far Tamaz will bend."

Clever girl. But there was no chance Tamaz would give the Sylgiz land. She needed a better strategy to counter what I'd set in motion.

Cihan said, "It's not just the cold. A year ago, the deep tribes started migrating south, bringing their heathen ways with them. Some eat their dead. Others ride mammoths into battle. The Endless was always dangerous, but now we can scarcely spare a night in peace. Though the Sylgiz are stronger than before, we've more enemies than before, too. With the deep tribes uniting against us, I don't think it will hold."

How ominous. One khagan or another was always trying to unite the tribes to push south. Knowing the people of the Endless, you'd have better luck uniting the fish in the sea, though Seluq the Betrayer had united all the fish and sharks and dolphins and even the corals, to stretch that analogy.

"I don't claim to know everything," Cyra said, "or much at all, really. But I know that in Alanya, everything has a price. Whether its verses, spices, slaves, or land."

"We don't have nearly enough gold to pay for the land we need. I was hoping to set up trade here so we could earn more, but someone beheaded our trade delegation, as you know."

Cyra shook her head. "When has gold ever been our currency, brother? We have something that the Alanyans would pay half the world for. And the other half, too." She was smiling, wasn't she? Too bad I could barely see her face at this overhead angle. "As you well know, Alanya doesn't have a coastline anymore on the Yunan Sea. Ethosian pirates, remnants of the same army that Kyars defeated last year in Sirm, have taken every seaside fort and city.

Winter is three moons away. There's no way the Crown Prince and his gholam can take all that coastline back. At best, one or two forts, which the enemy could reoccupy once they leave." This girl had more knowledge than she let on. Skill with the tongue, as well.

"You're saying we help them?"

"No. I'm saying you agree to drive the pirates out, and as your reward, the Shah gives you the coastline to protect on his behalf."

Now that was an idea — farfetched, but I respected the tenacity. Tamaz would never agree, though.

Cihan grunted. "Tamaz will spit on that. We're too different from the Alanyans. He might give us some bereft mountain if we drive a hard bargain, but the western coastline? The moon will split before that happens."

"I believe he'd rather you have it than the Ethosians. But you'll have to do one more thing for him. A big thing."

He sniggered. "Kill his enemies for him, and...?"

Cyra stood and looked down upon her brother, curly locks still blocking her face from my view. "Go to the Shrine of Saint Jamshid, get on your knees before Khizr Khaz, and, in the sight of the entire kingdom, renounce the Path of the Children and embrace the Path of the Saints — effectively, for the whole tribe."

"You're serious?" Cihan held his hands up, as if in disbelief. *"This* is your idea?"

"You want Alanyan land, and yet you don't want to become like them. You can't have it both ways, brother. You said earlier that you don't blame me for the way I am, but I chose this way of life with my whole heart. I am Alanyan — I am not one of you, not anymore. Want to be warm in the winter? Want to escape the frightful tribes up north? You can't come to a new land clinging to old ways. You better practice your Paramic, too, because I recall you were never very good with it. Now, if you agree, I'll go present the offer to Shah Tamaz."

Impressive. I'd learned long ago that a good tongue-lashing was all many men needed to move mountains. Her raw confidence jittered my nerves, making me twitch my wings.

"Well…" Cihan scratched his beard. "Converting would undermine that unending thorn in my backside, Gokberk and his saint-cursers. The fool thinks he'll be khagan if I'm dead — well, surely not if we change paths. Perhaps be a good reason to even—"

Knock-knock sounded on my bedroom door. I was back in the closet, shrouded in darkness, a dismal beam of setting sunshine streaming through the small hole. Whoever was knocking on my door had pulled me from the drongo, though unlike before when I'd been pulled in the middle of a cycle, this cycle was nearly done, so the severing wasn't painful.

In any case, it seemed like Cyra was about to speak with Tamaz, so I had to switch to the rat shortly. Not something I enjoyed like I did the bird: being a rat chittering about within soaking-hot walls wasn't as fun as it sounded.

I got out of the closet and opened my bedroom door to Sultana Mirima's beaming face. She held baby Seluq in her arms. "He's been such a good boy. A wonder. Not at all fussy like his father was."

I took the warm bundle that was my son and kissed his cheek. "Thank you, sultana. You've cared for him so well. He's truly blessed to have a grandaunt like you."

"I'll look after him anytime, dear. Your son is the treasure of my eye, and my purpose for — may Lat provide — hopefully living another fifty years."

Poor Mirima was as barren as the winters of the Endless, just like Kyars. That was why her husband had left her, and she never remarried. But to be true, she seemed the type that would be a good mother: usually strict, yet soft when appropriate.

After she left, I put Seluq in his crib and rocked it gently. "One day, you'll be the Shah of Alanya. And then you'll be the Shah of Sirm, and then the Shah of Kashan. The Master of Shahs, they'll call you. *Padishah.*"

How ironic. Seluq the Dawn had been called *Padishah*, and then Temur a hundred years later. None before and none after attained the title. But unlike them, my Seluq was no Seluqal. Not a drop of that wicked blood ran in his veins, thank Lat.

I took him in my arms again, desiring his warmth on my cheek. His gentle cooing made me giggle. If only this happiness could be eternal, but given whom we were, that was impossible. Destiny would carry us in its storm. "You are the Children," I whispered in his ear. "You are god's blood."

5

CYRA

Upon hearing that I'd negotiated with my brother, Shah Tamaz admitted me into his office. He sat at a low desk and threaded a pair of diamond-encrusted rubies through a golden chain. That and the jewelry shimmering in the flower-patterned chest to his side seemed so out of place amid the plain carpets and unadorned sandstone walls. I peered into the chest: rings of coiled platinum, eightfold diamonds, pearl-studded bracelets, diadems with impossibly specific etchings, earrings of lapis lazuli and sapphire — that chest was worth more than the Sylgiz tribe. A simpler orange cat sat on his low desk, licking its paws and mewing while Tamaz crafted.

"A woman's affection is hard work," the Shah said, beaming. "But nothing earns it like jewelry, especially crafted with your own hands. It's the same with poetry, really. An original verse earns more than a borrowed one."

If only someone would gift me rubies and verses. I bent my neck. "My mother's favorite was a horn made from a red-antlered deer. Took my father twelve hours to track the animal."

"True love is rare, so that which displays it ought to be, too. If it rained gold, it would be as worthless as sand."

73

"But you have everything, my Shah. What could one possibly gift to you?"

He chuckled. "A moment of peace, perhaps. The chance to sit in the sand, beneath a starry sky." I could hear the nostalgia in his sigh. "I'm not unlike you. My mother hailed from a fierce desert tribe not far from Holy Zelthuriya. When I was born, my father sent me to live with them so that I wouldn't grow to be soft. You think the Waste is bare, but we survived weeks on sips of water. I didn't see Qandbajar until I was twelve." He smiled as if dreaming happy memories. "Want to show your love? Send me back to that place, that time."

"You ask a bit too much of me," I said with a chuckle. "I think I can manage a nice pair of shoes, though."

He gestured for me to sit on a floor pillow. "You sell yourself short, Cyra. Obviously you have something more, otherwise you wouldn't be here. So tell me, what did your brother say?"

I sat and crossed my legs. It had taken a heap of pleading to get my brother to agree. I wasn't a good negotiator, clearly, because my first offer to Cihan was my best one. I'd watched the common folk haggle in the bazaars, and they always asked for more to start, then negotiated toward a compromise. I resolved to be as clever with Tamaz.

"My brother said he won't be leaving. Either you give them what they want, or they'll take it by force."

"If only I knew what they wanted."

"Ten thousand hectares in the fertile fields east of Qandbajar."

Tamaz stroked his funnel-shaped beard. "I understand the winters have been getting harsher each year. My agents in the Waste tell me that one of ten didn't survive the last one, and I'm only talking about the southern part. Speaking of which, the khagans in the north are fighting to get south, and the khagans in the south are fighting to get here. Your brother's desperation is plain. But let's skip the fanciful demands and get to something more reasonable. You know your brother. What would he accept?"

I rubbed my chin as if I had a beard too and pretended to think deeply. "Knowing my brother, he wouldn't want charity. That's why he's framed this whole thing as a recompense for those dead traders. Sylgiz don't like to be given. They like to trade…or take. Let them make a fair trade."

"What kind of trade?"

"It doesn't rain gold in the Waste, like it does here. But they have warhorses and warriors to ride them. Let them fight for Alanya. Let them take back what was taken from us."

Tamaz straightened his back and nodded. "Send them to fight the Ethosians? In exchange for what?"

"What do you think would be fair, my Shah?"

He sighed, sharp and weary. "They could protect what they retake in my name. But putting the Sylgiz beside the gholam and khazis would be like putting a barrel of gunpowder in the path of a flaming arrow. The moment a khazi hears 'curse the saints' come out of a Sylgiz rider's mouth, they'll be slaughtering each other, not the enemy."

I nodded, finding it hard to subdue my satisfied smile. "They won't be cursing the saints anymore. As part of the deal and on behalf of the whole tribe, my brother has agreed to renounce the Path of the Children and embrace the Path of the Saints."

Tamaz snickered. "Do you know how many missionaries we've sent up there? I'm sure you're aware how strange your tribe's customs are. Not only do they pray to the Children, but they combine the faith of Lat with all kinds of heterodox ideas from the Waste that the Fount have deemed entirely unacceptable. They're as stubborn as a barreling ox. Something more is needed."

The orange cat jumped off the desk and purred around my legs. I gave it a pat and realized that perhaps I ought to try a more thoughtful tact.

"Look at me," I said. "What do you see, Your Glory?"

He groaned. "Don't play games, Cyra. You've tried your best to make a deal, I know. The sincerity and earnestness you've shown, it makes me proud to have raised you these past eight years. But I'm the Shah of Alanya, and I must protect Alanyans. That's the job Lat gave me. And there's nothing…absolutely nothing I wouldn't do to protect my people."

"Am I one of your people? Or one of them?" My voice quavered. "What do you see when you look at me, Your Glory?"

"You're the daughter of Khagan Yamar — that's why I took you in. For this purpose, this very moment, to be a reason for them not to attack us." He gazed into my wetting eyes. "But…that was then, and this is now. I could never hurt you, Cyra. No matter what happens, I would protect you as if you were my own, because you…" now his voice quavered too, "you are as a daughter to me."

Was I? The shaking part of me wasn't so sure. If he wouldn't find me a husband because I was his hostage, would he protect me when truly desperate to win? When it was his final and only card to play? And, if so, would my brother relent to spare me? Perhaps I was as worthless as sand…to both of them.

"The truth is, my Shah…the truth is I don't belong here. Nor do I belong there. I'm not cherished here, nor am I cherished there." Ugh. Fuck me. Always, tears gushed and my voice cracked when speaking heavy and honest words. "I'm an ornament, like one of your jewels."

"Cyra—"

"My Shah," I interrupted, hardly concerned with propriety. "I have one more proposal. And if I'm as precious as you claim, you'll at least consider it." I had to ask for something he wouldn't give, so we'd settle on what I really wanted. I also had to test him, to know if he truly considered me family. "I'm almost twenty-four. I need a husband, lest I fall into temptation." I gulped. "Marry me to your son, to Prince Faris."

While I bared my heart, the cat distracted Tamaz by pawing at the wall and growling.

"Faris is only fifteen." Tamaz *tss'd* his cat, and it looked back at him with a *mew*. "You've a few too many years on him." He shot me down, as expected. "But, as I stated, I'm impressed with you, Cyra. Until now, I'd assumed you were like every other girl in the harem, content with prancing about the bazaars all day. But it's clear that higher yearnings have awakened in you. Therefore, I have a better idea." Shah Tamaz cleared his throat.

I needed to suggest Hadrith, now, before he proposed some lowly vizier's son. "I have another suggest—"

"You'll marry the Crown Prince."

What?

"Pardon?"

"Crown Prince Kyars needs a wife. He needs someone who will inspire…stability. Loyalty. Simplicity. You've a khagan's blood. You grew up knowing the value of a sip of water, a bite of food, like I did. That's what that fool needs to make him a better man. And speaking of food…prices are soaring in the markets because your brother's horde is devouring all the crops and grazing grass. I can only supply so much grain from the palace reserves. I'm of the mind to compromise, and to seal that compromise with a marriage. So, I ask you, why not? Do you accept?"

Only now did I notice my whole body was shaking. My heart quaking. All I could do was nod.

"Wonderful. Tomorrow," Tamaz said while scratching his cat's chin, "I will invite your brother to the palace. We'll sign an agreement. I will give him whatever forts he retakes on the coastline to govern in my name. Khizr Khaz and the Order of Saint Jamshid will accompany them to ensure that they practice the *true* faith of Lat, with all the proper precepts and acts as set down in the Recitals of Chisti. And, finally, you will marry Kyars. I'll stand in for him in absentia — I'm not giving him the chance to say no."

"T-Tomorrow?"

As the orange cat jumped in his lap, Tamaz picked up the golden chain with the diamond-encrusted rubies and handed it to me. "Tomorrow."

• • •

I PINCHED myself on the way to my room. No, this wasn't a dream. This was like wrecking your ship in a storm and waking up on an island, only to find trees that grew emeralds.

As thoughts raced like chariots through my mind, a fat, black cat sprang in front of me. I stared at it, aghast. A slithering tail, hand-like feet, flappy ears — that was no cat, it was a rat! A rat with bulging, angry eyes…as if I'd killed its brother.

Before I could scream, the eunuch Sambal jumped out from behind a pillar and smacked the rat with a broom. I ducked as it flew over my head, smashed into the wall, and landed on its side. Its ugly feet jittered in the air, then its twitching slowed, and it laid limp.

"I…I did it!" Sambal cheered. "Finally, that Ahriyya-spawn is no more!" Sambal took my hand and shifted his head back and forth, shaking his hips, then twirled me twice. He let go, tip-toed while waving his arms like water, then danced his way down the hall, skipping steps and singing in some strange language. But it was melodic and joyful enough.

It seemed many of us had a reason to sing today…save for that rat. Poor thing died with tormented eyes.

I returned to my room and ransacked my closet. None of the dresses inspired joy, so I headed to the Grand Bazaar. While walking through the garden toward the gate, I spotted the last person I wanted to see: Hadrith, sporting a checker-patterned maroon sash tied loosely around his brocade.

I kept my gaze low, trying to pretend I didn't notice him. But he diverted onto my path and said, "I've been looking for you, dearest. Where've you been?"

I avoided his eyes, which were always so penetrating. "Had a toilsome day."

"Oh, I know. Riding back and forth between here and your brother's camp. You're better at my father's job than I am, it seems. You could be the first woman Grand Vizier." Hadrith's snigger turned into a chuckle. He could mock all he wanted, but I'd be something even greater tomorrow.

"I'm busy right now," I said. "It was nice talking and all, but if you don't mind, I'll be on my way."

He lifted my chin with his finger while gazing down with those diamond-hard pupils. "Come by my house before the sunset prayer."

"I really can't today—"

"It's very important. Very, very important."

"Hadrith, I would but—"

"Did I not say 'very'? Am I not your *beloved*? Why would you refuse?" He folded his arms.

"All right, I'll stop by. But I can't stay long."

"See? Obstinance never works with me. In the future, save your breath and my time."

I wanted to call him the son of a slipper, as we would in the Sylgiz lands, but decided to swallow my irritation and get on with my tasks.

On the brocade floor of the Grand Bazaar — found at the end of a wearisome climb — the tailor measured me and promised something splendid by mid-morning. The sheer number of fabrics, jewels, and styles overwhelmed my already strained mind, so I let him choose. Since this event was tomorrow, there wouldn't be a big wedding, just a signing ceremony, but I still wanted to look better than ever. The festivities would take place once Kyars returned and learned that the girl he'd once called a *"dull, reed-limbed savage"* was now his wife. Although, that wasn't the worst thing he'd said: *"I could have you anytime, you know. I just don't want you."* He'd lost that mean streak with age, thankfully.

After leaving the Grand Bazaar, I went to Laughter Square to get verses from Eshe — I needed some humbling after what had transpired — but his brass throne sat empty upon its dais. The flowery nonsense of the other poets didn't interest me, so as the sun declined and streaked red across the clouds — and being a woman of my word — I made my way to Hadrith's palace. My gholam escorts waited at the entrance while I went inside.

Sitting around the living room on plush floor cushions was a motley collection: Hadrith, a hookah pipe in his mouth, Ozar, also smoking, the rat-slaying eunuch Sambal, who was chewing sesame seeds, and, most surprising, the master of insults himself — Eshe.

"What is this?" I asked.

"Sit." Hadrith snapped his fingers, and a serving boy approached. "Get her whatever she wants. What do you want?"

"To know what's going on."

"Oh, you'll know soon enough. Don't smoke, do you, Cyra?"

I shook my head and fixed my gaze on Eshe, who was reclining on a pillow and eating green grapes. "Why are *you* here?"

"I have no idea," Eshe replied. "But I never refuse hospitality, especially from on high."

"Cyra likes sherbet," Hadrith said to the serving boy. "Raspberry is her favorite."

"I hate raspberry." I made a disgusted face.

Hadrith looked like he'd just stubbed his toe. "Oh, ah, masala then?"

"Have you misplaced where I come from, too? Just get me orange or tamarind."

I sat on a sequin-covered cushion beside Eshe, eager and wary about this gathering.

"Now that we're all here," Hadrith said, "I can start. But...by Lat...where to start? It's hard to even form the words, so I'll just come out and say it. I believe — and I've the evidence to back it up — that at this very moment, there is a faction in the palace plotting to overthrow the Shah, and — and I can't believe I'm saying this — that this faction is led by a sorcerer."

Holy...that was unexpected. And not something I wanted to hear the day before my marriage ceremony.

But why was I the only one surprised? Eshe kept popping in

grapes. Ozar bubbled his hookah. Sambal chewed his seeds so loud, it grated.

"Well, most of you already know this," Hadrith said, "except for Cyra…and Eshe. So really, that speech was just for you two. I hope it was plain."

"What directed you to this conclusion?" I asked while staring at a wall carpet with a picture of a dragon breathing fire on its own tail. Hadrith had mentioned it was a gift the Sultan of Abistra bestowed on him during a trade mission.

"Mistress." Sambal swallowed his seeds. "I have seen the blood-runes in the palace. Well-hidden, but they're everywhere."

Bloodrunes? "I've seen one too," I blurted out. "In the bath!"

"That's not all," Ozar chimed. "Someone is trying to make it look like I want war with your brother and his tribe. The man who stamped and wrote the *payment for your sins* letter was a former scribe of mine, whom I recommended to the royal office. And while I've been known to crush my competitors in the spice trade, I didn't kill those Sylgiz traders."

"Why?" I asked. "How would blaming you help them overthrow the Shah?"

Hadrith said, "That's the final piece. Right now, the Sylgiz tribe is camped outside the wall. But what if, one night whilst we sleep, the gate was to suddenly open? Do you know who controls the defense of Qandbajar's walls?"

"It would be the gholam, of course."

Hadrith nodded. "One person connects all these events. One sinister, scheming upstart who has been rising in power and presence for the past year. That's right, I'm talking about none other than Pasha Kato — commander of the Alanyan gholam by day, schemer and sorcerer by night."

Honestly, I struggled to sew the holes. "So if it's Kato, why did you have me place a new slave in Kyars' harem?"

Ozar blew smoke strands and said, "Kato has help. In the harem. How else is he able to sneak in and write his runes there?"

"And what do these runes do?" I asked.

Eshe cleared his throat. "So now I see I wasn't invited merely to sample your fruit and wine." He sat up, chin high. "I assumed you were just another schemer making pomegranate juice without pomegranates. But now I realize you're slightly more intelligent than you look, Hadrith."

"It's Pasha Hadrith to you. And I think my looks and intelligence a good match. Now, Eshe, what exactly do bloodrunes do?"

"What a bloodrune does depends on the kind of blood used. Without knowing that, I can't say."

"Kind of blood?" I asked. "You mean whether it comes from a human or animal?"

Eshe shook his head. "No. You can't make bloodrunes with animal blood. Humans have different *flavors* of blood, each flavor only able to write certain runes, though some runes can be written with different flavors. But I'd have to see the runes to know what they do."

"How is it some vulgar poet is our foremost expert on sorcery?" I asked.

"Poet?" Hadrith said. "My dear, you're talking to a Disciple of Chisti, the protectors of Holy Zelthuriya itself."

"Former disciple," Eshe said, his voice muffled and somber. "But yes, in my former life, I studied all manner of sorcery, blood-writing included."

Blood…writing? How spine-chilling. "So what are we to do?" I raised my hands, palms up. "Tell the Shah?"

Ozar shook his head. "Oh no, absolutely not. Shah Tamaz does not trust a single one of us. Hadrith has never been in his good graces. And though I'm married to the man's sister, Grand Vizier Barkam has made sure I'm no beloved of his either." He turned toward Sambal. "A eunuch isn't exactly…you know." Then toward me. "You, my dear, are someone he cares for genuinely but might not trust in matters as extreme as this." Well, that I didn't agree with; the Shah trusted me plenty, but perhaps we needed more evidence before telling him.

"So here's what we're going to do," Hadrith said. "Beyond the river bend, our good man here," he gestured at Ozar, "has docked a small fleet, since they aren't able to sail west anymore. What no one else knows is that waiting onboard this fleet are a thousand khazis, of Kashanese birth. They believe they're being sent west to help free our shoreline from the infidel. But we're going to sail those ships into the city and, with their help, arrest Pasha Kato."

An unbelievably dramatic plan, surely. Resting on shaky evidence, too. Further, I'd heard Hadrith and Ozar mention their dislike for Kato long before. Was all this a convenient pretext, then, to lop off the head of someone who rivaled their power? If so, I wanted none of it. "When are you planning this lunacy?"

"Tomorrow," Hadrith said, cheeks wide and satisfied. Precisely what I didn't want to hear. "I'm telling you this, Cyra, because though we may arrest Kato, for the Shah and his family to truly be safe, we'll also need to catch his agent in the harem. And you and that Crucian you purchased are well-placed to do that...for obvious reasons, obviously."

Obvious reasons. Was this why Hadrith had included me in his intrigues all along? "So, wait, when you asked me to give him that paper," I gestured with my head at Ozar, who was enjoying a lengthy puff, "you were—"

"Testing you," Hadrith completed. "To see if I could trust you. And you passed. Oh, my father may despise Ozar, but I'm a more... practical man than he is."

More practical than Barkam? Was that even possible? To be true, I wasn't surprised at the deeper layer to Hadrith's requests. And yet, I couldn't sew these dreaded holes. Something underlying this conspiracy didn't add up. "Why would Kato do this? He's rich, powerful, and close to the Shah. He already has everything and more."

Ozar snickered. "Somehow, you think that being rich and powerful makes you *less* ambitious? More satisfied with life? But it's entirely the opposite, I assure you from my own experience. Power has gone to Kato's head. He convinced Kyars to let him stay in the city, so he could strike while the heir and the army were away. He killed those Sylgiz traders and put a spell on that scribe, which is why the poor fellow can't mumble more than a few words. He's going to raise the gate, allow the Sylgiz to ransack the city, and then seize the throne during the chaos, probably with Kyars' son as a puppet."

Hadrith punched his palm. "We all have the same purpose here — to protect Alanya. To protect the Shah, who is father to all Alanyans. And to protect Crown Prince Kyars, a man as dear to me as my own flesh."

How poetic. The pieces of this conspiracy started to resemble a whole. But I believed I had a better plan than putting a thousand khazis in the city. "What if I told you that peace with the Sylgiz was imminent? That it was already agreed upon?"

"It wouldn't change everything," Hadrith said. A serving boy handed him a teeth-cleaning twig, which he put in his pocket. Seemed he trusted his servants. "Kato wouldn't rest his entire plan on the Sylgiz — he must have a backup. But if there is peace with your brother — certain peace — it would delay things, at least. He won't risk taking over the palace without a pretext."

Eshe said, "Wait a minute. Wait just a minute." He wagged his finger. "You're all making a very ill-informed and dangerous assumption about this Kato fellow."

"Which is?" Ozar asked.

"That he's also the sorcerer. From your description, he sounds like a military man. Sorcerers tend to be experts at only one thing — sorcery. Now, you said there were bloodrunes in the harem. What if the sorcerer is someone else? What if the sorcerer *is* his agent in the harem…a eunuch, perhaps? Then, even if you arrest Kato, the far more dangerous party will still be free…and worse, you'll have exposed yourselves to him."

Sambal made that satisfied hissing sound he always liked to make. "This fellow is very wise. But there are over sixty women in the harem and hundreds of us caretakers. Where to start?"

"He's right," I said. "If you arrest Kato but not the sorcerer, who knows what he...or she will do. Let me find out who's helping Kato before we take serious action."

"And I need to see those runes," Eshe said, "or rather, taste them."

"Taste?" Ozar's flat nose almost reached his eyebrows.

"They don't call them *flavors* of blood for nothing. I'm going to have to...you know..." Eshe licked the air.

Ozar shuddered, then bubbled his hookah with a deep inhale.

"One recently appeared in the wine cellar," Sambal said, "I can take you there."

"So we'll delay," Hadrith concluded. "But I fear the longer we wait, the stronger Kato becomes. Cyra, you must find the traitor in the harem. Sambal, you must help her, no matter what it takes. Eshe, go...lick these runes and find out what they do. This country and its survival rests on each of us doing our jobs. Doing what's right."

I nodded. Watching Hadrith take charge like this, seeing how sincere he was to protect his country and shah, I can't lie about the butterflies that fluttered through me.

I said, "I love Alanya, the Shah, and his family as much as anyone. I won't let them be harmed. No matter what it takes — on pain of death — I'll find this traitor, and then we can hang them together."

EsHE and I left Hadrith's palace at the same time. As we walked together on the sandy road that led to the thoroughfare, we spoke of idle matters — last month's heatwave, the dearth of birds in the sky, the year-long demolition and rebuilding of the Garden District. I didn't want my gholam escorts to become wise to any topic covered during the meeting, so I asked my question with a whisper, "You're not Alanyan, are you? Why help us?"

He whispered back, "I'm curious about the bloodrunes, that's all."

"I thought being a Disciple of Chisti was a lifetime thing. Why'd you leave?"

"I didn't leave. I was…removed."

"What? How come?"

"Not your concern, lady."

I stopped in the middle of the road and said, "But how can we trust you if we don't know who you are?"

I envied his carefree smirk. "Listen — like I said, I just want to taste those runes. I'll tell you what they do, and then I'll go back to my brass throne. I'm not made for palace intrigues, petty wars, and what-have-you."

"From a Disciple of Chisti to a vulgar poet." I folded my arms. "Quite a fall."

"From a starving girl to the jewel of the harem. Lat raises and debases as she wills."

"How did you know I was once a starving girl? How would you even know a thing about me?"

He tapped his head. "Why do you think hundreds line up at my throne each morning? Insight is a powerful thing, lady."

"My title is *mistress*, actually." Tomorrow, it would be *sultana*, the second-highest station a woman could reach in Alanya. And when Kyars ascended the throne, it would be the highest: *Sultana of Sultanas*.

Eshe chuckled. "I had a title, once. A grand one. The people of Holy Zelthuriya envied me, and I basked in that glow. But I soon learned that titles are not who you are — they are given and can be taken. Remember that, Cyra."

At the end of the sandy road, we parted ways. What a day this was turning out to be. Whether this whole thing was a power play or a genuine conspiracy, I hoped it wouldn't get in the way of tomorrow. Once I became Kyars' wife, I would have more authority and could help discern the truth. I hoped I could help everyone — the whole country — in ways only afforded to the Sultana of Sultanas.

Back in the harem, healers, eunuchs, concubines, and handmaidens crowded outside the large room at the end of the hall. Zedra's room.

"What happened?" I asked Sambal, who too had recently returned.

He covered his mouth and said, "The sultana…she's been hurt!"

"You mean Zedra?"

He nodded with a tremble. Oh no. This day was heavy enough!

I pushed through the crowd and slipped into the room. Zedra lay on the bed, surrounded by white-cloaked healers. Mirima glanced at me, sweat thick on her forehead. I approached my friend, my heart jumping.

"What happened?" I asked.

Mirima shook her head and softened her eyes.

"Is she…" I swallowed worry and tears.

"Her breathing is fine," a healer said, a miniature water clock in his hand. "Her heartbeat is normal. No obvious wounds."

"Why won't she wake?" Mirima asked.

"It will require further investigation."

Mirima took a deep breath. "Cyra, you'd spoken to her earlier. Was she feeling all right?"

I thought back on our conversation in the dancing hall. Zedra had seemed…somewhat angsty, though nothing unordinary. "She was fine."

"I'd prefer if you cleared out this rabble," the healer said, motioning with his hand at the crowd as if swiping at a fly.

"Everyone, out!" Mirima pointed to Sambal and me. "You two stay."

Zedra's complexion seemed…dull. Her mouth was open slightly, in a pained expression, as if she were screaming.

"Lat heal her," I prayed.

Mirima ran her hand through my hair. "Dear, you have quite a day tomorrow. I don't want this terrible incident to burden you further. Rest assured that we'll do everything for your dear friend's well-being."

I nodded. Terrifying thoughts ran through my head. What if the sorcerer had hurt Zedra? What if he would hurt me next? This harem was no longer safe.

"Sambal." Mirima turned to the eunuch. "My brother has tasked me with preparing our dearest Cyra for her ceremony tomorrow, so I'm tasking you with Zedra's care."

"Ceremony?" Sambal said with a bewildered smile.

"Cyra is to be wed."

Sambal's jaw dropped as he turned to me. "Mistress, I'm so happy for you. I pray this dark cloud not rain upon your most auspicious day."

"You won't be calling her *mistress* anymore. She's a *sultana*, now."

Sambal clapped like the little monkeys in Laughter Square. "By Lat, this is an extraordinary day. I'm so excited for you, *sul-ta-na*! Who is this most fortunate and blessed man?"

Mirima caressed my cheek. "This lovely one will wed the Crown Prince."

Sambal shrieked. "The Crown Prince!" He covered his mouth to hide his shock. "I would jump for joy. I would fly to the moon itself. I would grab the stars and shower them upon all in sight." He turned to Zedra, his joy suddenly vanishing. None of us, it seemed, knew whether to laugh or sob. Mirima smiled somberly. And in my mind, the weight crushed me. I wanted to cry and pray for Zedra, and also to try on every jewel and dress Mirima was no doubt picturing on me. How to juggle two opposing emotions that have been thrust upon you?

"I'd like…to rest for a while," I said, my head heavy.

"Of course, my dear." Mirima hugged me. Though a cold

woman at times, whenever she was caring, it so made me miss my mother. "Take all the time you need. I'll come see you later, all right?"

I went to my room. Vera was there, sitting on my bed. A bit too familiar for my liking, as that bed was a rather intimate space. She stood when I entered, then said, "Sorry, mistress." Her eyes were red and leaking. "I just…the sultana was so kind to me. I can't bear the thought of her hurt."

She stood there crying, head down and shoulders slumped.

"Could you please leave?" I said. "I want to be alone."

Instead, she charged and put her arms around me, then bawled into my armpit. "I found her like that, in the closet, her eyes stuck in terror. Someone hurt her!"

Oh Lat. *Someone* could only be the sorcerer. But I had to be strong. "I'm sure she'll be fine." I patted Vera on the back a few times, though I was as unsure and rattled. "Mirima will be coming to see me later. You can join her, all right?"

Vera looked up with the eyes of a lost stray, then thrust her lips toward mine. I backed away.

"Not now. I told you I want to be alone."

But she kept crying, then pushed against me even harder.

"Stop!" I didn't want to be firm, but how else to make her leave? "Please leave!" As if I were scolding a clingy stray.

She rushed out, tears trailing across her cheeks. Scolding her added to the pile that weighed on me, and made my eyes water. But I could apologize later.

I crashed onto my bed, barely able to think. More had happened in one day than in the last eight years. I hoped — I prayed — that tomorrow would be better.

6

ZEDRA

THE CLIFF AT THE EDGE OF TIME. THAT WAS WHAT HE CALLED THIS mountain. It was as if you'd climbed the tallest peak and arrived at a sad, barren vision of heaven. An endlessness persisted in all directions; below the cliff's edge, there was nothing but black. Above, a band of light lit the sky, as if a cut made by a god-sized sword on the drape that covered the world. *"It's a ring,"* he'd told me. *"We can only see one side of it. That's why it seems flat."*

No cold or warmth here. No wind. Just a stillness, a silence, a lifelessness.

A man stood at the cliff's edge. He'd been standing there a thousand years. Waiting. Watching. Hearing.

"I.." as soon as I spoke, I gasped. Such a crumbling voice, as if a thousand holes covered my throat. I felt my face — creviced and rock-hard. Hair so wispy and white, I wasn't certain if it was real. As I walked toward the man, the weight of my body burdened my worn knees.

"Father," I said.

He kept his back to me, refusing to even look in my direction.

"Father." I dropped to my knees. How they cracked.

"No, Zedra." His voice came from the sky. "You don't have the right to call me that."

My hands would not cease trembling, as if a sudden frost found life in my veins. "What happened to me?"

"Do you know how sad it makes me that our survival depends on you? I'm not at all surprised you failed."

"I...failed? But how? I don't...I don't remember."

"I told you to bind your emotions. *Fanaa.* To work from a cold, careful plan. But, sadly for us, for everyone, you weren't capable. How terrible is this fate — my holy Children, ended by your inadequacy. Your weakness."

No. How could that be? "I...did everything...I could." My heaving made it hard to talk. "I...did...follow a plan. My...emotions—"

"Grovel, cry, scream, pray — all futile, now. It was unlikely to begin with. If only one of my sons had survived instead, there would be hope. But you...it was a curse to even watch you try."

"Father Chisti!" I called out. "I didn't spare a moment for myself. Not even a drop of happiness. All I did was further the plan, from wake to sleep." That wasn't true, though. I'd sought pleasantries, pleasures. Gotten fat on good food. Grown lazy lying upon silk sheets. But in my heart, I never let go of our cause.

"Shush now. Your best was never going to be enough. The horror that I feel, you can never know. Because you haven't experienced what's coming for us. If only you'd sipped that terror, become one with it for the briefest increment, perhaps even you could have succeeded...if only from utter desperation." He was always going on about how he'd sipped *it*. But to me, it was merely a fear brought to life by prophecy, not experience, and perhaps that was why I'd been so careless.

I crawled to his feet. I kissed the back of his cold, hard shin. "Then let me sip it."

"Do you know what you ask? The Great Terror is surging

toward us, coming to remake us all in fire. Are you so sure you want a sip?"

"I'll do whatever it takes to stop it, Father. I will carry the mission of the Children on my back until I'm dust and bones."

"Not enough!"

"What else have I?"

"You think dying is a sacrifice? A life is not a thing. There exist fates of eternal suffering that words cannot encompass. Imagine your skin boiling until it's liquid, then you're given a new skin to boil again — forever. Does that sound terrifying? It's bliss compared to what will happen. It's paradise to what's out there." He pointed to a patch of utter black in the ring-lit sky. "To what's coming."

"I'll stop it. I'll save us all. I will."

He turned to face me. He touched my head with a single, chill finger. I dared not look up. I dared not look upon his face, to see those disappointed, deadened eyes.

"You will sip the Great Terror? Then, in your vigorous desperation, you will save us all from it?" His laughter — it shook with sadness, with despair. "You? You who already failed!"

My tears moistened his toes. I clung to his ankles. "If I'm dead… is this…where souls go? Is this Barzakh?"

He chuckled. "You're not dead. And no, I won't let you sip. Because, despite your failings, I still love you. To see you cry — do you not think it hurts my heart? That's all the suffering I'd have you taste. The suffering of your own disappointment. The suffering of a single life…it's a drop compared to the ocean that will drown us. A hundred years, a thousand, ten thousand, a hundred thousand. It doesn't matter how long we delay. Unless my righteous Children are brought back to rule, as Lat intended, *it* comes — more assuredly than death."

Father pulled me up by the hair. I screamed. I felt like a plant being ripped from its root. Then I saw his eyes: sad, dead, and as terrified as mine.

He plunged two fingers into my sockets.

I AWOKE SCREAMING. The sunshine's high angle through the open balcony door told me it was midday. When I lived with the Children, we had no water clocks, so told time by shadows and rays. Ah, the *nightmare* faded, and present concerns replaced its terror. A day had passed with me asleep. Was I too late?

I tried to move my hands and legs...nothing budged. I was a brick. And alone in my room — where was everyone?

The ceremony, Cyra's marriage to Kyars, the peace accord with the Sylgiz...all things I didn't want. All things I had to stop. For the sake of the Children. For the sake of mankind.

But what could a brick lying on a bed do? Perhaps it was as Father had said...I'd failed. I couldn't save us. The Great Terror would envelop the world, and we'd be remade in fire. Without the Children to stop it, without the restoration of our righteous rule, there was no escape.

The door creaked open. A youthful girl with delightful hazel locks entered. She set a tray of incense on my bedside while staring into my eyes. "You're awake?" she asked in strangely accented Sirmian. "They told me to fetch the healers if you woke."

"No, don't," I croaked. "Celene is your name, right?"

She nodded.

"I'm glad we could meet. Please, stay with me for a moment. Sit, if you would."

With some hesitation, she sat on the edge of my bed and stared at the floor.

"I know how you feel," I said, my throat dryer than a dune. "To be ripped from your home and brought to a strange place. It hurts, doesn't it?"

She remained silent. I gestured with my eyes at the water cup at my bedside. She fed me sips, easing my throat pain.

"On the outside, we make it look like we're fine," I said. "But within, the storm never stops raging. Even if that storm shrinks and slows, it's always there, in the center of your heart, ready to rage again."

She remained silent.

"They tell me you're a Crucian princess. I was…sort of a princess, too, you know."

"It sounds like you want me to do you a favor."

"Pardon?"

"Whenever someone tries to get to know me, it means they want something. It was the same in Crucis, and it's the same here." Said so dryly. "So, what do you want?"

She wasn't wrong, as sad as that was. I did want something. I gestured with my eyes at the closet. "Carry me in there."

She chuckled. Good. First emotion I'd gotten out of her. "I'm not strong. I don't think I could lift you."

"You don't know your strength until you try. You might surprise yourself."

She looked at the closet, then back at me. "Do you feel safer in there? Because that I can understand…I suppose."

Soulshifting required one to be relaxed, comfortable, and unstimulated. In the Vogras, I would soulshift from a cave that overlooked our tribe's land.

"Something like that." It hurt even to smile, but I did for her.

Celene pulled me up. I barely felt her wrap her arms around my waist and her tug. She dragged me, huffing all the while, into the closet. Panted on her knees after letting me go.

"You did it, dear," I said. "See?"

She actually smiled, and it was as sweet as halva. "Want me to close the door?"

I nodded, surprised I could move my head so much.

THAT POOR RAT had died a rather ignoble death — unfortunate, as it had taken hours to catch it and write the bloodrune on its belly —

so I shifted into the drongo. I landed on the roof of the Sand Palace, shedding a feather somehow, then fluttered about until I settled atop the great hall's glass dome.

A feast was taking place below. Kashanese men blowing into long, reed flutes and gyrating girls wearing sequin-sown silk performed upon a platform in the center of the room. Around them sat the Sylgiz and the Alanyans, intermixed and jovial. At the head, on the dais, sat Khagan Cihan, Cyra, and Shah Tamaz, joking and giggling and sipping rose water. Her wedding dress...by Lat, the crimson silk suited her, as did the airy shawl and the fat, ruby-encrusted diamond around her neck. A part of me was joyous for her, as I'd been when my own daughters married, though none had ever looked so radiant.

No. Like Father had said, I wasn't desperate enough because I hadn't *sipped.* I'd wasted time making friends, listening to poetry, enjoying dances. That had to end; I'd never get a chance like this and couldn't let a tender thought distract me.

I eyed Grand Mufti Khizr Khaz laughing in the back with a man wearing thin, desert-appropriate Abyadi garb. Given the atmosphere, the ceremony had obviously ended, and I was too late to stop it.

I flapped my wings and fanned my tail, yearning to peck out all their eyes. Cyra's marriage to Kyars would seal the peace between the Sylgiz and Alanya. She could bed Kyars all she wanted, his seed wouldn't put a child in her, but my child would now be hers. Seluq would be hers — she'd have more authority over him than me. Authority to twist and turn him into whatever she wanted, whereas I had to guide him to be the restorer of the Children. The shield against the Great Terror. Not just Shah of Alanya, but Padishah of everywhere Lat was worshipped.

The peace accord I'd have to undermine. There were ways to cause chaos that didn't involve the Sylgiz sacking Qandbajar. I'd worked hard to make that happen, plotted and planned for months, but it's impossible to consider everything. I hadn't considered Cyra

— my blind spot. Her sudden cleverness had come from nowhere, and her desire to make peace and wed had somehow overcome my careful plan.

Curse the saints. I had to do what I had to do. Set things right before it all slipped away. Turn this sordid twist into an opportunity. No weakness. No mercy. Because to show mercy to anyone down there would imperil mankind itself. Destroy all that I'd toiled for, for the sake of the Children, for the sake of all.

It was time to act. It was time to activate the bloodrune.

7

CYRA

ABSENT THE TENSION OF WAR, THE SHAH AND MY BROTHER GOT ALONG like songbirds. After all, both were tribal folk at heart, preferring the rugged countryside to a city's comforts. Good that my husband was the opposite, like me. So while I enjoyed the dancing girls and flute players, they conversed about hunting, fishing, and archery. Both also claimed to have sighted simurgh carrying off camels, or in my brother's story, a mammoth. They'd even wandered upon jinn tribes in the guise of humans, walking with backward-facing feet.

"I was barely seventeen when this happened," Shah Tamaz said to my brother, "but I caught a bizarre fish. Its scales were like glass — you could see through it, to the bone. And its insides glowed, as if it had swallowed stars. Didn't care — I was hungry. But when I began cooking it, within minutes I fainted from inhaling the smoke of its flesh. Then I had the strangest dream. I was on an island — in the sky were twelve lights of red and green, and they danced around each other in the most peculiar orbits. Felt so real. And then I saw my great-great-grandfather Ismaid. He'd driven out the Sirmians when they sacked Qandbajar almost a century ago. He

97

told me I'd go through the same as him and emerge victorious, like he did."

My brother barely blinked as he listened — the best audience of one Tamaz could have. Though he actually had an audience of two: I pretended not to hear. Better they bond without me getting in the way. Men's stories become circumspect when their sisters or wives or daughters are around.

"I wrestled a wave lizard once," my brother said. "Bit me twenty-seven times. The bites make you see things. For six days afterward, I thought I was a blade of grass, bending in the wind. And that's not poetry — I did believe I was a blade of grass."

"A poet — I think it was Ravoes — once said 'bend like grass, and you'll never know suffering.'"

"He obviously never experienced actually being grass." Cihan and Tamaz laughed together. "Tell me, you ever fight?"

"Of course," Tamaz said. "How do you think I got this limp? Almost twenty-five, thirty years ago now — the last time I saw battle. The Sirmians crossed south of Zelthuriya, violating our treaty. Shah Jalal wanted to make himself a *padishah*, it seemed. But my father was not having it. We lined up against them in the desert. A plucky, muscular man stepped forward from their line and challenged our best to a duel. So naturally, I stepped up.

"I don't recall the details of the fight, but it was over rather quickly. The man was good at getting low — he cut into my thigh and left me writhing in the sand faster than I could swing. I was certain those would be my final prayers, but for some reason, instead of finishing me off, he simply backed away and returned to their line while his army cheered his name — 'Murad! Murad!'"

"The Sirmian shah!" My brother looked on, entranced. "Did he tell you later why he spared you?"

The Shah shook his head. "I haven't spoken to him since. We've had good relations, though — strong trade, especially. When the Crucians seized Kostany, the Majlis debated whether we should help Sirm fight back, or finish them off." Tamaz paused to breathe.

"I'm not a man of war, Cihan. Though we could have taken their land, eventually we'd find our borders at Crucis. And then the wars would never end. Better the Sirmians deal with them than us, so we can enjoy the fruits of peace. That's why I overruled the Majlis and sent my son to help them. And now, with our aid, Sirm is strong once more."

"Most khagans would conquer whatever they could," Cihan said, "not concerned about overextending or creating a buffer with the enemy. You are a wise shah, Tamaz. I thought my own father weak, all those times he didn't attack. Perhaps it wasn't weakness that led to his end but rather a lack of foresight." Wonderful how they were bonding.

I looked out at the guests. Oh Lat, I made the briefest eye contact with Hadrith, who was sitting with his sisters and glaring at me. He hadn't even touched his plate of bone marrow pilau, piled like a mountain. Perhaps he was jealous. Wonderful — he had his chance and let it slip away. We'd still have to work together to find the sorcerer, but in a purely proper way.

I wondered how Zedra would feel if she were here. Perhaps she'd be jealous too, or perhaps she'd dance for me. Tamaz's wife and concubines seemed to get along, in the rare instances when I saw them. Tamaz's harem was separate from Kyars' and much smaller, and the Shah rarely let them leave, as was the custom among most Seluqals, so I didn't really know how well they got along.

I eyed Pasha Kato talking to a Sylgiz warrior — that son of a slipper Gokberk, who had to lean in with his only remaining ear. Whenever I saw his scarred face, I remembered the puppy whose neck he crushed; it took him seven stomps to silence its dying screeches. By Lat, we were both only eight or nine years old at the time; he must've been born cruel. Now, he seemed rather jovial for a man my brother had supposedly undermined with this marriage and conversion to the Path of the Saints, though the latter would happen tomorrow at the Shrine of Saint Jamshid.

Anyway, the way Kato gesticulated, it seemed his hands did half the talking. I could tell he was recounting a battle from how he darted his fingers, as if they were a horse's hooves stomping on the ground. Was *this* man really conspiring to take over Alanya?

Hadrith had some evidence on Kato. After all, Kato had suspiciously remained in the city while his forces went with Kyars, and he'd also *found* the scribe who wrote the letter which brought the Sylgiz here. But...the man didn't strike me as a cold, considerate schemer. Hadrith, Ozar, Barkam — they never liked Kato to begin with. Perhaps he was less pliable than Kichak, the former gholam commander who had died in Sirm, so they reached for any reason to topple him.

A thought struck: what if the sorcerer was the one conspiring to take over, and Kato merely a distraction? A piece on the board?

Just then, Sambal walked into the great hall, his wimpy-looking fists at his shoulders. Behind him was Eshe, looking absolutely wretched in that eunuch disguise: a green, fur-lined robe over floral brocade and a pillow-like hat — just not his style. They both went to Hadrith and whispered in his ear. Then Hadrith gazed up at me with a wide, terror-filled gape.

Hadrith got up, dusted his brocade, and waded through the crowd. He bent his neck before the Shah, just below the dais.

"Your Glory," he said with a quaver that made him difficult to understand. "I...I believe there is about to be...an attempt on your life."

Dear Lat, what had Eshe learned?

The Shah straightened and said, "Hadrith, say that again."

"My Shah, there is—"

Eshe pushed past him and said, "First of all, I'm not actually a eunuch. I'm a Disciple of Chisti and an expert in bloodrunes. You must get away from these two at once!" He pointed to Cihan and me. What the hell?

Gold-clad gholam approached and surrounded us, as if instinctually sensing danger.

The Shah shook his head. "Slow down. What exactly is the danger from my new daughter and son?"

"The bloodrunes are of conqueror's blood," Eshe said. "A flavor found almost entirely among the tribes of the Waste."

"I don't follow," the Shah said sternly, as if losing patience. I didn't either. What was he trying to say about Cihan and me?

Eshe took a heavy breath. "Excuse me, but my eloquence has departed in this moment. I saw the runes all over your palace, and I know what they do. We're not dealing with just any sorcerer. Any Sylgiz in this room with conqueror's blood could, at this very moment, be under the control of something far worse. A soulshifter."

Oh Lat. Conqueror's blood — one of the flavors? Perhaps my brother possessed it, or someone in the crowd. And *soulshifter* sounded far more terrifying than *sorcerer*.

The Shah turned to Hadrith and said, "Do you vouch for this man, on your life and the lives of your household?"

Hadrith nodded rapidly. "My Shah, I do. You can ask her as well." He gestured toward me.

"Cyra?" The Shah turned to me. "You know about this?"

"I'm not fully grasping what this has to do with me," I said, "but I've seen a bloodrune in the bath."

My brother, who'd been silent, now stood and said, "It would be best if the Sylgiz and I returned to camp until your matter is sorted. We'd not have our peace poisoned by intrigues and sorceries."

"My Shah, we'll take you to my house," Hadrith said. "You can't stay in the Sand Palace."

Eshe said, "That would be best. I've a way to nullify the runes, but it could take some time. Until then, best you and your household leave this place."

This was all so sudden, yet the peace deal had already been signed and sealed with my marriage to Kyars. Nothing could be allowed to jeopardize the Shah's safety and the kingdom's peace.

Gholam surrounded the Shah — a golden wall — as Cihan and I

stepped off the dais and gathered with the other Sylgiz. The crowd made way for the Shah to depart, and the guards opened the double doors that led into the antechamber, which itself led to the palace exit.

While watching the clamor, a weakness seeped through my nerves. I leaned against the wall as everything around seemed to… slow. I looked up at the skylight — a drongo sat on the glass dome, gazing upon me. Red eyes of sadness. Red eyes of rage.

I clasped my forehead, dizzy. My limbs numbed, and throbbing nausea crawled through my chest and throat. What an awful time to get sick, to lose yourself. And then my vision cracked, black fog seeping in until it drowned me.

8

ZEDRA

I OPENED MY EYES. THE GREAT HALL SURROUNDED ME: A MESS OF concubines, entertainers, Sylgiz warriors, and viziers, their mouths flapping with confusion and furor. All made way for the Shah, who stood within a wall of golden gholam. My opportunity to act evaporated each second. Though they didn't know who I was, that Disciple had exposed my bloodrunes, and so it was now or never.

"Cyra, you all right?" Cihan caressed my cheek. His Sylgiz costume — a dark blue, fur-accented vest — reminded me so much of our Vograsian outfits.

I pushed his hand off. "Yes, brother. Just a little faint. This is all so sudden." I felt Cyra's fear, which had poisoned the joy of her marriage. Poor girl believed this would be the greatest day of her life. A new chapter. Well, perhaps.

"I don't want you staying here, either. Come with us to camp."

I nodded and smiled. "Of course. Anything you say."

The gholam began marching the Shah out of the hall, in a square formation. Two layers of armored, matchlock- and sword-wielding men surrounded him. How could I, a lanky girl, break through?

I approached a nearby low table and bent down. Looked around, making sure no one's eyes were on me. These sheep were too busy watching Tamaz and the gholam — good. I eyed a cutting knife that had been stabbed into a lamb shank, which itself sat on a mound of rice. I hovered my sleeve over it, then scooped the knife inside.

The gholam and Tamaz marched out the great hall and into the antechamber. I followed with the Sylgiz. In haste, Tamaz and the gholam proceeded beyond the tunnel-like exit and beneath the open sky. I kept up, stepping ahead of viziers, courtiers, and concubines — their brocade brushing against me — so I was just behind. My target passed the ghastly stone simurgh, while the Sylgiz remained back. Good.

Nothing separated Tamaz and me but ten paces and a double layer of trained-to-kill-from-birth warriors. What could pierce that?

"Father!" I screamed, as if I were in pain. "Father!"

Tamaz, peeking through his gholam, looked back at me. But they pushed him forward, even grabbing his shoulders.

"Father, wait!" This time, I had to trap his attention. I slipped the knife out of my sleeve and into my hand, breathed deep, and jammed the blade into my right eye.

Waves of pain washed over my face and brain and bones as I fell to my knees, careful to hide the knife in my sleeve again. "Father! Help!"

Hard to see as blood flowed down my face and onto my lips. Conqueror's blood usually tasted too spicy and metallic — but this time, I savored those notes.

Tamaz glanced back, horror plain in his gaze. He pushed his gholam aside and hobbled to me.

He took my bleeding head in his arms. "Cyra! What happened? Oh, my daughter! My sweet daughter!"

Running steps sounded behind me. Cihan appeared at my side. He put his hands on my shoulder as he and Tamaz bent down and gaped in shock.

"Father, brother, I'm sorry," I said. "I'm so sorry."

"Healer! Get a healer!" Tamaz screamed.

His gholam approached, and now they formed a wall in front of us, with the Sylgiz at our back. Kato pushed through to face us.

"Your Glory." He bent his neck. "We'll find a healer for her. But you must come with us. I know not what dangers lurk."

Now or never. All eyes on me. I slipped the knife into my hand, held it firm, and slammed the blade into Tamaz's heart. "Father." I cut a swathe through his chest. Flesh tearing. Blood flying. Until his mouth foamed red, and he dropped dead.

Cihan gaped, his eyes already watered with horror. He grabbed the knife from my hand as the gholam grabbed Shah Tamaz's corpse.

"She...she stabbed the Shah!" Kato shouted. He unsheathed a sword with one hand and grabbed a matchlock with the other.

Cihan was not armed. All he had was the cutting knife. Still, he jumped in front of me and faced the gholam, ready to defend his sister with his life.

"The sorcerer," he said. "The sorcerer did this!"

"I saw her stab the Shah!" Kato screamed, pointing at me.

As several gholam took the Shah's body and rushed somewhere, the rest formed up and blocked the way out. Kato pushed against Cihan to grab me, but Cihan pushed back.

The raging pain in my bleeding socket numbed, but sour light-headedness threatened to end this cycle. I had to finish Cyra, somehow, but Cihan had seized my knife.

Sylgiz warriors surrounded me. A burly one picked me up and put me on his shoulder. A bright, bone-handle hunting knife was tucked into a sheath at his side. Perfect. As he moved forward with the other Sylgiz, toward the line of gholam, I reached for it. When Sambal had killed the rat, I didn't die, so I was certain I'd survive this — though it would hardly be pleasant.

Gunfire! Shouts and screams filled the air. Sylgiz in front of me fell to gholam matchlocks. Cihan staggered to his knees, clutching a burn in his belly. The Sylgiz still standing pulled out their hunting knives and charged the gholam.

As the warrior holding me ran forward, I put the blade to my neck, pressed it in, and slid it across my skin.

9

CYRA

A FAMILIAR CEILING SPREAD BEFORE ME: THE OPEN SKY. COLD, unfamiliar hands touched me all over. A scythe cut me, bloodying my soul. Then I was thrown. I flowed down a river and up a river. Crashed down a waterfall and got scooped up a waterfall.

I was a drop, and then I was a clot, and then I was flesh. My soul lived in the sheets beneath and the cloth walls around. Blood rain washed over the world and brought with it pain. So much pain — as if swords were hacking me to bits. As if a jinn were being birthed between my ribs.

A familiar face appeared; his name was Eshe. A vulgar poet and former Disciple of Chisti. I turned to look at him and blinked. I could see only half, the other half in darkness.

"I had the strangest dream," I said.

He took my hand and put it to his forehead, then recited something.

A HAMMER POUNDED MY SKULL. A jinn covered in red tulips was nailing my head to the city gate. Each tulip had an eye for a bud, and they kept blinking. The nails split bone and brain. It was as painful as it sounds.

The first nail said: *We can't stay here. The Endless calls. But what to do with her?*

The second nail replied: *Throw her to the Alanyans. Let their dogs pick her to the bone.*

The third: *Gokberk, have you no honor? We must cherish what Cihan would've wanted. Take her with us, to be with her mother.*

Cihan died because of her. As did six others. Let the Alanyans punish her. It's the right thing to do.

She's a Sylgiz. You'd just forsake her?

Look at her. She's no Sylgiz. She was the whisperer in Cihan's ear. She convinced him to forsake the beloved Children, and this is Lat's punishment. Besides, we didn't kill the Shah — she did.

I WAS a camel going *thump-thump-thump* over a dune. I was a man full of sadness, thirsty and baked. And then I was a girl, broken and cold despite the high sun, with barely any blood in her. I was sitting behind the man, roped to him so I wouldn't fall off the camel going *thump-thump-thump* through the desert.

We reached an oasis, and the man sat me against a stone well. I was the well as the man pulled up the pail. I'd been here a thousand years and — with mercy — quenched the thirst of too many to count.

"Are you there?" the man named Eshe said.

I could see my own eyes — open and lifeless.

But I blinked. Again and again. Each time, I was sucked inward, until I was the girl again. Until I bathed in her pain.

"I had such a horrible dream."

THE CRESCENT MOON BROUGHT A BITTER, dry desert wind. It was silent, save for the rustling of palms. My soul slipped into the sand, but it was colder than my body, so I went up again. The man removed the pit from a water-soaked date, then squeezed the flesh and juice into my mouth. Syrupy and happy.

"Where are we?" I stared at the starry sky.

Breathing hurt, each inhale like swallowing nails. My eye hurt, whether open or closed. I wanted to be sand again. Or the well. This body was nothing but pain.

The man was lying in the sand and snoring. When had he fallen asleep? An hour seemed to pass each minute. I touched my neck — thick cloth covered it, wrapped tightly. Was this why it hurt to breathe? I felt my face — more cloth, wrapped around my right eye. Was this why I could only see half the world?

I began…remembering. Remembering a nightmare where I'd cut my eye, stabbed Shah Tamaz, and sliced my throat. I trembled. I didn't want this. I wanted to be sand lifted by breezes to faraway places. Or the breeze itself, blowing to the ends of the earth. Anything. Anything but this.

DAYLIGHT BROUGHT LIFE-GIVING HEAT. Still, I swallowed nails. Eshe was washing his camel while it happily chewed on grass. I was sitting against the well, wearing bandages and a harsh caftan.

"I want to go home," I said.

Eshe dropped his washcloth, then kneeled over me. He put my hand to his forehead and prayed.

"What are you doing?"

"The only thing I know to do."

When I blinked, only one eyelid moved, and what felt like spikes flared in my face and neck.

"What did you do to me?" I asked.

He quenched my thirst from his waterskin, then popped a date into my mouth.

"Why are we in the desert? Where is the Shah? What the hell happened?" Despite trying to shout, I could barely whisper.

Eshe scrunched his eyes and shook his head. "Cyra..."

"You should call me sultana," I said. "I'm a sultana now."

But if that were true, why was I here and not in the palace? Why did the tears streaming down my cheeks taste like blood?

"Where is my brother? Where is Cihan?"

Eshe dumped the remaining water over his head and looked away. "Your brother is dead. The Shah is dead. You're...you're alive."

"What are you saying? Eshe! Look at me!"

But he wouldn't. "I couldn't stop it. Once again, I couldn't stop it."

"Eshe, please don't say these things. You're scaring me."

With a heave that pained everything, I pushed up against the well. The water's reflection showed my face: blood-soaked cotton covered my right eye. A bloody sheet was draped around my neck.

"No, this can't be real," I said with a tremor. "Where is Shah Tamaz? Where is Cihan?"

Neither Eshe nor his camel nor the surrounding palms would answer. So perhaps I ought to crawl back to Qandbajar.

But when I started to, Eshe put his hand on my shoulder.

"We have to get going," he said. "They might be looking for me."

"What? Who?"

"The gholam. They took Hadrith and Ozar captive, and I suspect my name will be on their tongues. The eunuch escaped — I believe he said he was going to Kashan. As for you...I think they believe you're dead. Both your brother and Tamaz died trying to save you, Cyra. You can't let that be in vain."

"But I want to go home."

"You don't have a home! Even your tribe want nothing to do with you."

How could that be? How could this be real? And yet, I'd seen myself. I was floating above my body when it stabbed its own eye, cut into the Shah's chest, and finally...

Was it all true? Had the sorcerer…possessed me?

"If that's true," I said, "then let me die. Bury me here. This place is pleasant enough."

Eshe shook his head. "The other day, when we met at Hadrith's house, you said you loved this country."

"And you said you were just doing this to learn about the bloodrunes. So why are you helping me?"

"Perhaps we both lied, then."

I curled up on the grass. "I didn't lie. I love Alanya. But I can't live like this. I wish I'd died. Stop giving me water, stop giving me food. I won't go wherever you're taking me. I won't! Let it end!"

Instead, he stuck something in my mouth, then forced me to chew. Tasted like poppy seeds.

I woke upon the camel, a rope tying me to Eshe. I'd drooled blood on his back. As we rode, he'd hit the camel's side with a reed. The sun's rays tinted the sky red, a wavy desert in all directions.

"Have mercy," I whispered. "Kill me."

"We'll arrive shortly," he said. "Once we do, you'll be safe, at least."

"You don't owe me anything. Why are you doing this?"

"I am…I was a Disciple of Chisti. We don't ignore injustice, like the rest of you. 'Succor for the weak' — those are our words."

"The best succor is a quick death."

"Ever try praying, lady?"

I had — during that starving winter in the Waste.

"What would I pray for? Which saint can cure my ills? I'm disfigured. I've lost my place in the world. The only two people who love me are dead — because of what my own hands did!"

"It wasn't your fault!"

My tears mixed with my blood on Eshe's thin shirt. I brushed my cheek against the mess I'd made; how rough the skin of his back seemed, as if covered with long, mountainous streaks.

I wriggled my body, hoping to fall off, but the rope stayed taut. Eshe turned his head, looked upon me with pity, and tried to stuff seeds into my mouth. But I wouldn't open up.

"Don't make this hard! We'll both be killed if the gholam find us."

"You're the one making this hard! I don't want to go wherever you're going. Just drop me here. Right here. This patch of sand will do. It's like all the others, but it will do."

"Don't you want justice, lady? Aren't you incensed at the one who did this to you?"

Whoever had was evil, surely. But no amount of anger would help me challenge a sorcerer, bloodwriter, soulshifter — words that sounded like childhood nightmares. I was base, dull, incapable, and now disfigured. All I'd gotten in life had been through luck, and it had turned.

"I just want peace. I can't bear this burden. What will happen to me? Will I have to beg on the streets for the rest of my life? Even the pleasure houses wouldn't take a one-eyed wh—"

The bastard stuffed seeds in my mouth, then squeezed my jaw until I was forced to swallow.

Two MEN GUARDED the mountain pass. They wore green turbans and simple black vests over sand-speckled caftans. Eshe carried me like a baby and approached. He was stronger than he looked, but because I was his height, my head dangled off his shoulder.

"This girl needs urgent help," he said. "Please, let us through to the hospital."

I turned my head to see one of the men, who had small eyes on a round face, whispering to the other. The other nodded; his pointed nose could hook a fish.

"Never heard of this trick," the pointy-nosed one said. "I'm actually impressed. She does look very…wait…that's real blood."

The other one unsheathed his scimitar. "Did you hurt this girl, exile?"

Eshe shook his head. "No. I don't want a fight. Please help us."

The two men picked me off Eshe. The round-faced one held me as if I were a dress he'd pulled from the closet.

"Get out of here," the pointy-nosed one said to Eshe. "I remember the day they whipped you and threw you off the mountain. A clever trick won't get you back in the city."

"Cyra," Eshe called.

I gazed at him with my one eye. How frail he seemed, huffing and sweaty, and how dismal and tired were his eyes.

"Cyra, listen. We have one hope, and one hope only, to defeat a soulshifter. They won't let me in the city, nor will they listen to anything I have to say, so it all rests on you. You must find him, Cyra, and you must convince him to help us."

"Find…who?" I muttered.

"He is a magus. And his name is Kevah."

ZELTHURIYA SEEMED INCREDIBLE, even out of one eye, even while a strange man was carrying me on his chest, my head cradled on his shoulder. The first speck of happiness I'd felt: to be somewhere holy. And, hopefully, to die somewhere holy.

Enormous stone doors had been chiseled out of the mountains, supposedly by a race of jinn called the Efreet — if the stories I'd grown up with were to be believed. The doors had been painted gold and red and green — the brightest hues. Seeing it cheered me up. I'd had a chance to come here a few years ago but turned it down. A pilgrimage of praying and fasting didn't sound interesting to my young mind, unless they sold dresses and shoes in those shrines. Perhaps if I'd gone, my life would've been different. Perhaps I was being punished for all my awful choices.

Crowded streets — men and women wearing white went from

shrine to shrine, in orderly lines, all while chanting to the saints and Lat herself.

"So, what happened to you?" the man carrying me said.

"Soulshifter," I mumbled.

"Oh, I remember hearing about them. The last one died at the time of Seluq, six hundred years ago."

"Rafa," the pointy-nosed man said, "aren't you fasting today?"

"Yah, so?"

"Talking to a girl not of your household breaks your fast, don't you know this?"

"Alir, nearly every part of her body is touching mine. I think my fast is already broken."

Alir said, "That can't be helped. But you don't need to talk to her."

"I haven't talked to a girl in two years. I can fast tomorrow."

"She probably doesn't want to hear anything you have to say, anyway."

"Why not?" The one named Rafa cleared his throat. "So, soul-shifter, eh? What was that like, exactly?"

What was it like? "He made me stab my eye out. Then he made me kill my father-in-law and got my brother killed." My one eye flooded again. It was appropriate to cry, so I let it happen.

"Idiot," Alir said. "Ever even talked to a girl before?"

"That's some story." Rafa tightened his grip on me. "Alir, you think—"

"The soulshifters died out long ago. She's clearly had a bad time, but no, I don't think so."

I swallowed the bitter liquid foaming in my mouth and asked, "Are you two...Disciples?"

Alir laughed. "Do we look like Disciples of Chisti to you?"

Rafa said, "A Disciple? That's the kindest compliment I've ever received!"

"That's the only compliment you've ever received, Rafa." Alir sneered. "Come on, the hospital is just ahead."

The hospital was inside a mountain, too, but windows had been chiseled up the high wall to bring in sunlight. Pallets stretched in all directions, filled with the sick and injured. The two had to walk a few minutes to find an empty pallet. I was just one among the downtrodden, now.

It didn't feel good to find comfort in these rough wool sheets. I'd rather they tossed me in quicksand to drown than on this heap of straw. I wanted to say, *let me die, let me die*, but I knew they wouldn't. Zelthuriyans were known for their charity, if nothing else.

Rafa's smile was sweet. It wasn't soaked in pity, as it ought to have been. Just a simple, kindly smile.

"Do you know—" I coughed. A bit of blood gushed with spittle. I spat it on the stone floor.

Rafa bent down. "You all right?" He turned to his friend. "Get a healer!"

I wiped the blood from my lips, then said, "It's all right. I just wanted to ask...do you know...the magus? What was his name? Keev...Ke—"

"Kevah? Never met him. Everyone knows he's here, somewhere in the city, but I can't say I know where."

What did it matter? Could some magus bring back Tamaz? My brother?

I closed my eyes. Though I'd been asleep most of the past few days, I wanted more. As long as it was dreamless, it was better than being awake. Anything was.

"We're in a saintly order," Rafa said. "I could try and ask my sheikh, if you want."

I shook my head. "Don't bother. It doesn't matter, anyway."

He glanced to his right, down the silent avenue between pallets, then said, "The healer is coming. My friend and I actually have to go. We're on duty. But I'll come visit tomorrow to make sure you're all right."

Charity. I didn't want it. "Don't bother."

The way he pouted reminded me of my little brother, who was also dead. My mother was my only family left, and last I heard, she was near death — a sad end for a line of khagans and khatuns that went back to the time of Temur.

The healer came, washed my face wounds, and changed my bandages. Then some women in white came, scrubbed my entire body with a sponge, and changed me into a baggy caftan, all while a group of stone-faced orderlies formed a wall around me with their backs turned, so that no one except the women washing me could see my nakedness. It was much more than I wanted or deserved, but I didn't have the strength to protest.

I STAYED OVERNIGHT. I didn't get off my pallet in the morning and instead ruminated over the awful events that had happened. Ashamed to say it, but I didn't pray. You'd think a woman in despair would have nothing else, but prayer was for the hopeful. And hope was a bitter thing.

Around me, so many suffered. I saw people die in their beds, carried out in shrouds. I saw a child without legs. A woman without arms. A man who coughed bile until he stilled. Just the everyday suffering of the poor, I assumed, and now I was another among them.

It smelled like death, too, like everything we tried to mask with perfume and incense. As if I was breathing someone's insides. But aside from the occasional cough and heaving, it was oddly silent, as death ought to be.

I didn't want to stay here surrounded by suffering. It only reminded me of Tamaz and my brother. But what about myself? The soulshifter had not only stabbed my eye out, he'd slit my throat. So why was I alive?

The memory blazed through my mind: while my soul was floating overhead like a bird and watching the carnage, I saw myself slit my neck, and then Eshe grabbed my hand and knocked the knife away. He dipped his fingers into my blood and wrote… characters of some sort onto my neck. The blood stopped gushing, as if the wound had closed. Whatever he'd done, it saved me from bleeding out. Was Eshe…a sorcerer, too?

In any case, it was his fault I had to suffer instead of die in peace. Now the best I could do was die somewhere in this holy city, somewhere close to Lat and the saints. Paradise would surely be better…if I were going there. Even eternal nothingness seemed like a salve…if I could be so blessed.

I'd watched my grandmother die of a wretched disease that made her skin fall off. She died helplessly mumbling prayers, in contrast to how she'd lived. A Sylgiz huntress — what a life. How remote I was from anything so noble.

I sat up on my pallet. It didn't hurt so much. My soul wasn't flying into the floor or the air — it seemed solidly in me. Perhaps because the soulshifter had cast my soul from my body, it was struggling to center again. Or perhaps it was the poppy Eshe had been stuffing down my throat.

I got up and walked out of the hospital — just like that. I supposed if you were healthy enough to walk out, you didn't belong there, and so no one stopped me.

The street, which was really a valley between mountains, brimmed with chanting and crowds. The mountains shadowed everything, and a breeze hummed between them. Bright gold, red, and green colored the towering pillars that flanked the doors of the surrounding shrines, the eight-pointed star of Lat blazing above each. The insides all seemed dark and welcoming.

I chose one at random, got into a short queue with eager pilgrims, and went in. I found the woman's section, just behind the sepulcher that housed the saint's body, and sat against the cool stone. Women wearing mostly white came and went — some lit candles at the base of the sepulcher, others sat and recited holy words.

"Kevah," I said, wishing Eshe hadn't told me. Wishing he'd let my hope die so I could rot in peace. But no, he had to give me a name. "Kevah."

I said it again and again, as if I were praying to the man. As if it would summon him. It just sounded so lovely on my tongue. If Kyars and I had a son, perhaps I could've named him that.

What a sad thought. Sitting in this holy cave, among these pious women, I wondered if I could stay forever. Forget. Just pray, night and day. Not have a name, a status, a place. "*A blade of grass, bending in the wind,*" was what Tamaz had said. His final poem.

"Goodbye, Tamaz. Goodbye, Cihan." I heaved and sobbed in silence, clamping my mouth to not attract attention. Were they really gone, or was this a long, cruel delusion? "Goodbye, Cihan. Goodbye, Tamaz. Welcome, Kevah."

Unlike my dead loved ones, this man's name sounded so hopeful on my tongue. Where was he, anyway? I'd not the strength nor desire to search a mountain city for a faint, flickering hope. Let him come to me, if he were so powerful. Let him hear my whispers. "Welcome, Kevah. Goodbye, Cihan. Goodbye, Tamaz."

Tears drenched my face. How sorry I felt for myself. Really, who could compete? Perhaps it started when the Jotrids captured and took me to the palace. Or maybe I shouldn't have tried to marry someone so above my station, someone like Hadrith or Kyars. Couldn't I have been contented with…literally anyone? Just someone to laugh with and have children, like how my mother and father had each other.

And yet, I recalled the cold wave that almost froze off my brother's toes, that killed Sylgiz babies in their cribs. You needed things, if you wanted to survive. Fertile land, foremost, which the Vogras River provided. Gold helped too, so you could buy what you couldn't grow. That was why Qandbajar had spices, silks, metals, books, animals, fruits, nuts, seeds, and precious jewels from the eight corners of the world. And to defend what you've built, you needed soldiers. Specifically, more soldiers than the enemy.

That was why I wanted to climb so high. I was just trying to survive, for Lat's sake. But I'd been outplayed…by someone whom I didn't even know I was playing against. By a damned soulshifter.

"Goodbye, Cihan. Goodbye, Tamaz. Welcome, Kevah." He obviously wasn't coming. I'd have to get off my ass and find him. But where to start in a city this large and mysterious?

I smudged the tears into my skin, crawled toward the woman sitting nearby, and asked, "Uh…do you know where Kevah lives?"

The woman, who was heavyset with light eyes, glared at me and replied in a strange language. Probably a Kashanese dialect. I smiled, then got up and walked outside, embarrassed that I'd even tried.

A yawning, green-turbaned fellow stood in the street. I asked him, "You know Kevah?"

He raised his eyebrows. "Kevah the market inspector? He's my drinking brother!"

"No-no, Kevah the magus. Know where he lives?"

"*Oh*, the magus. No, I don't."

Unhelpful, to say the least. Then I looked up; the Shrine of Saint Chisti stood at the end of the main street, towering over the other mountains. Its door was painted yellow, as if the sun had splashed upon it.

I made my way toward it, until I got stuck in a crowd. No, a line. The longest line I'd ever seen, winding through the streets in rows upon rows. And it was so slow, too; it seemed to move a foot a minute. Were people really waiting this long to pray at Saint Chisti's sepulcher? I supposed if anyone's prayers could help you, it would be those of the holiest man ever.

I'd never waited in a long line before. Now I knew why they were so awful. And worse, I wasn't even sure if Kevah lived in that giant shrine.

So I pushed through, swimming against a sea of people. Hollers and jeers sounded from those I passed, but if they wanted to stop me, they'd have to pull me back. Perhaps my bandaged face and neck scared them — you don't want to touch a monster, after all.

After minutes of pushing against people, covered in the sweat and dust of hundreds, I finally reached the front. But green-turbaned guards blocked the massive, sunshine-colored door. One stuck his hand out to stop me from entering.

"Go back," he said. "This isn't some bazaar, it's the holiest place on earth. Wait your turn, like everyone else."

"Is Kevah here?"

"Kevah?" He raised an eyebrow. "Uh, I think so. He's usually here at this time."

"I need to see him. Please."

Now he chuckled. "The magus doesn't just see anyone. And he doesn't receive intercession."

I had to say something, anything, to get through, lest they send me to the back of that obscene line. "I…I'm…I'm his daughter!" I hoped he had a daughter.

The other guard butted in. "Kevah mentioned he had a daughter. And that he missed her dearly."

"It's me!" I said. "I haven't seen my father in so long. Please, let me through!"

"O-Of course!" they both replied.

They stood aside and told me where he was. Some room behind the sepulcher, down a hallway, down three flights of stairs, then around the corner, and down another hallway, and past the kitchen, then—I'd already forgotten the rest!

If I wasn't huffing and faint from pushing through that line, the shrine would've taken my breath away. A thousand candles stood upon the altar. Paramic calligraphy covered the walls, shimmering in the candlelight. Worshippers filled every space: the men and women weren't even separated. They chanted in unison, low and somewhat somber. How sad that I'd entered this holy place with lies.

I wandered into the hallway behind the sepulcher. Men wearing wool cloaks — like those of Saint Jamshid's Order in Qandbajar — glared with suspicion as I went through doors and down staircases.

Perhaps they were fasting and didn't want to talk with or touch a woman. Was today some saint's birthday that I'd forgotten? There were so many, and I wasn't raised believing in these saints. Each of them had a shrine, a day, a special prayer, and a particular reason for us to pray to them, despite being in Barzakh, where souls go after death. There was even a saint named Death, who always terrified me.

It was far simpler when I lived among the Sylgiz; there were only so many Children to pray to. Twelve Chiefs, in fact, though I couldn't remember their names.

A faded yellow door at the end of the hallway — that's what the guard had told me. And now I stood before that door. Kevah must be in there. Instead of knocking like a mannered person, I opened it, slid inside, and shut the door behind me.

"Melodi?" the man sitting against the bare wall said. "Melodi!"

Before I knew it, my forehead was against his chin, and his arms were wrapped around me.

"Daughter, I knew Lat would bring you back to me," he said in Sirmian. "What happened to your eye?"

I pushed out of his embrace. "No, I'm not. I'm not your daughter."

He glared at me, sorrow-filled, then walked to the corner where his water pitcher sat. He picked it up and splashed the entire thing on his face. Was that some kind of ritual around here?

Now he slid back against the wall and sat. "I'm sorry. I've been fasting for days. I mistook you. Melodi is dead…what was I thinking?"

So his daughter was dead, and I'd used her to get inside. A shameful coincidence that he'd mistaken me for her.

"I've broken my fast," he said, now speaking Paramic with a serious Sirmian lilt, "by talking to you. By touching you. So, in celebration, I'm going to order a feast."

"Is that…really something to celebrate?"

He shook his head. "No." He laughed. Something about how absurd his laughter was made me laugh too.

"So…who are you, strange girl?" He turned his head to the side, then said to the wall, "Oh Lat, don't say such things, bird."

Was this man…crazy? Was a crazy man who talks to walls my only hope?

"My name is Cyra, and I've come from Qandbajar, where a soulshifter used my body to kill the Shah and is probably planning something even more terrible."

He looked at the wall again, which had a cheap sequin-covered tapestry hanging on it, and said, "You're worse than Ahriyya." Then he smiled at me. Such a…beautiful smile on a beautiful man with curly blond hair and a straight jaw. Not that I had time for such thoughts. "Apologies, Cyra. I was talking to a jinn."

"There's a jinn in this room?" I glanced around, unsure if he was serious. There was little else here but a pallet, some books, and a splintered wooden chest.

"He's harmless. But he's been a bit…bored, so…uh…never mind. You said something about a soulshifter using your body to kill the Shah of Alanya. Is that right?"

Whenever I nodded, my neck wound flared. "I was told to find you. That you could help. Because you're a magus."

He sighed like someone with the weight of the world on him. "I've been a magus barely a year. And in this year, my only accomplishment is learning Paramic. I've made almost no progress in achieving *fanaa*."

"I see…" I sighed with almost as much weight as him. "I really need your help."

"Listen, a soulshifter is a serious thing — I don't know much about them, except that they were an ancient order that Seluq destroyed when he conquered this part of the world. They're a curiosity of history, and a terrifying one. Now you're saying a soulshifter…used your body…to kill the Shah of Alanya? And yet, I've heard nothing about Shah Tamaz dying."

"Because it just happened. I'm not lying."

"All right, assuming it's true, I don't know what you want *me* to do."

"Who else could fight a powerful sorcerer but another powerful sorcerer?"

He shook his head. "Seems you've been misled. I'm not powerful, not at all. I haven't gained the allegiance of a single jinn tribe, despite wearing three masks."

"I don't know what that means."

"It means I'm only a magus in name and completely incapable of fighting a soulshifter, of all things."

What could I say to that? Something Zedra once told me popped into my mind. "You don't know your own strength until you try."

He chuckled. "That's a nice saying to encourage children. But we're talking about things beyond the veil. Things birthed from forbidden stars. Things so ancient and evil that…"

He trailed off and began shaking, then grabbed his hand to steady himself. Perhaps a symptom of fasting for so many days?

"If not you, then who?"

He turned once more to the wall and said, "I regret it, all of it." What was he talking about? "That's your job, bird."

Now he strummed his hands against his chest while staring into me. "I'll ask them to give you lodging in the women's dorm. As for your plea, I've heard it. My jinn is going to verify what you've said. Word travels faster in their…circles. But I can't promise you my help. While terrible things may have happened in Qandbajar, I'm supposed to master my training. Lat gave me this task, and I can't just walk away to help you. Besides, from how it sounds, it's beyond me, anyway."

How fanciful to claim that Lat herself gave you a task. Not the answer I wanted, not at all. Still, I held my tears. "Do you want me to go alone? You may be a weak sorcerer, but I've no skills at all. I'll die if I try to fight back…which is fine, I suppose."

He smiled beautifully again. "My jinn says he likes the sound of your voice. He's a useful little creature…he would lament if you died."

I looked around the room again. "If only I could see him."

Kevah pointed to his eyes. "It's not as fun as it sounds, seeing beyond the veil. With the wonders come the horrors. One must be ready to take in both, in mind and soul."

"Were you ready?"

He folded his arms and looked to the ceiling, with all its cracks — perhaps his jinn was floating, now. "Not even a little."

10

ZEDRA

Upon the cliff at the edge of time, Father stared at heaven. The image of a crying woman shown in a cloud; she prayed for her husband's safe return. And then a little boy without an arm appeared, begging for his mother to be saved from the pox. And there was even a king, sitting upon a metal throne, crying for victory against an invading army.

But Father did not grace them with a look. No, he gazed above at the black spot in the ring-lit sky. A spot that seemed to be…growing, as if a disease. What did he see there?

I crawled to his feet. I could not stand, my knees too weak against the heavy air. I clutched his shins and said, "I've done it, Father."

The wails from the supplicants in the cloud intensified. Father Chisti drew out his hand, then swiped it across. The cloud blew away, far into the horizon, taking with it the hopeful and their prayers.

"Such a waste," he said. "They'd be better off praying to stones, like in the days of old."

We'd always been taught that Father Chisti would take our prayers to Lat. How could he dismiss them like chaff? How would Lat hear them, now? Hear any of us?

"What of…all the prayers of your Children?"

"Do you see her throne above? Until we restore the righteous rule of the Children, no prayer will reach Lat."

I was in no position to, and yet I had to press, lest I misunderstand. "How can that be? Are you not Lat's chosen? How, then, can your prayers go unanswered, too?"

His laughter was deep and dismal. He pointed to the black spot in the sky. "Because I've been staring at that for a thousand years. To fight darkness, you must know it, and to know it, you must become it. Don't forget that, Zedra. You've done well, but it's far from over. Go now…and finish what you started."

"I will, of course, I will."

"A word of warning. While you haven't been discovered, you have been noticed."

"Noticed?"

Another cloud billowed. Crying children stretched across its face. Shrieks sounded, and lightning flashed within.

"Save us from temptation," someone said in a strange language that I didn't know but could somehow understand. *"Teach us only what is righteous."*

Father didn't seem to care. He turned toward me, gazing upon my pathetic form. "You've been noticed by the *magus who will wear all masks*. He thinks himself on a path of righteousness, but he is far astray. Steel yourself, daughter. Destroy all remaining obstacles and enemies. And be prepared to do anything — *anything* — to defeat him, lest he take your mask, too."

Father had warned me about him before. His name was Kevah, and he was training in Zelthuriya. More than that, he would not say.

"I will, of course, I will."

· · ·

AFTER WHAT I'D ENDURED, I had to be wheeled around on a chair. The healers said I'd regain my movements with time, but time was an extravagance. I aimed to restore the righteous rule of the Children now while the throne sat empty. Father had told me to destroy all remaining enemies, Kyars being the greatest of them, but I could be wiser: I could have gholam commander Kato destroy them for me.

Vera wheeled me to the great hall. Kato was sitting upon the dais beneath the royal divan, wearing the formal gholam outfit: gold-thread turban, sparkling shoes with pointed-ends, and a plain caftan with a black vest, outlined with golden leaves.

The Majlis stood before him: a collection of viziers, each responsible for one thing or another. The heads of this kingdom now that the Shah was dead. Each wore turbans with the fanciest patterns — I appreciated the marching lions on the rose-colored turban of the governor of Quchan. Each also wore a bewildered, fearful expression. For good reason.

A shah's death is a time for fear and sadness. I'd missed Tamaz's funeral, not that I cared. But the wailers were harder to miss: his wife and concubines, shouting lamentations from their towers. One sounded like demons being beaten to death. Everyone had to pretend to be mournful, at the least, though I'm certain many truly were.

For some, it was a joyous occasion: Tamaz willed his clerks to roam the streets and pass gold, silk, and porcelain to the city folk. Even us concubines got a share. Not that I could do much with gold — it just wasn't my currency.

"My pashas, I'm not a man of buttered words," Kato said, breaking my thoughts, "so let me make plain. Those who planned this had help. Among you." He pointed to everyone in the room. "Until we find the traitors, the Majlis is suspended."

Wise, though expected. By suspending the Majlis, the viziers who despised Kato couldn't act against him in an official capacity.

But it was somewhat like killing a bird with a cannon. I'd not expected Kato to make these sessions public, but I think he wanted to show his loyalty to the Seluqals, so the more who watched, the better.

A clamor arose, of course. "What gives you the right?" someone shouted.

Kato pointed to the seat behind him with his thumb. "An empty chair. And it's going to stay that way until Shah Kyars returns to sit. Now, I don't know who the traitors are. We've caught a few, but assuredly, there must be more. Some of you had to know about the ships beyond the river bend and the thousand khazis waiting within. And if you knew, then you were complicit in the Shah's murder. In Ozar and Hadrith's failed insurrection. Each of you will have to prove your innocence."

Not something the Majlis would easily swallow, but what choice did they have? The gholam around the room were not wearing formal attire but rather their battle armor: golden chainmail, gold-framed matchlocks, and bronze-colored boots.

While I didn't doubt that Kato admired Shah Tamaz, perhaps with some affection, and wanted to behead anyone even tangentially involved in his assassination, I was more certain that Kato would *find* traitors among his own enemies, whatever thin evidence he would use to make it so. He had been railing about the viziers that despised him, that undermined him, and this was his chance to destroy them by whatever loose association they had with Ozar or Hadrith. Good.

"I have a request," a voice boomed amid the nervous clamor. A man stepped forward: Grand Philosopher Litani. Beneath his blue robe, he wore a shirt that clung tightly to his thin frame and ended at his waist, where it was met by a metal clasp that tied his shirt and pants together. I rather liked the style.

Kato said, "Speak, Philosopher."

Litani cleared his throat. "Next moon will be a special time in the heavens. We will have clear view of several stars and wish to study their orbits, upon Mount Qafa, undisturbed. Our instruments are quite sensitive, you see. We request the mountain be prohibited until our study is complete."

Kato stroked his beard, then replied, "Well, all right, fine."

"Ahem," someone said in the crowd, "next moon will be Saint Jorga's festival, which of course must take place upon Mount Qafa."

"Is that so," Kato said. "I just gave the mountain to the Philosopher. Have the festival elsewhere."

"But Saint Jorga received his holy mission upon Mount Qafa."

"Hmm, I'd forgotten that." Kato rubbed his bald head. "Philosopher, find another mountain."

"It's the highest mountain within a hundred miles," Grand Philosopher Litani said. "No others are suitable."

Kato stomped his foot. "This is not pertinent. Our shah was just murdered, and you come to me with such trite matters!"

Litani raised his hands, as if in disbelief. "You just suspended the Majlis. Who else to come to?"

"Don't get sly with me, Philosopher. Sort this nonsense among yourselves."

Seemed like Kato needed help. Good.

WHILE WHEELING me to my room through the carpeted palace hallways, Vera asked, "Did Cyra really kill the Shah, sultana?"

"I wasn't there, dear, but that's what everyone says."

"But Cyra had a good heart, and she loved the Shah. Why would she ever?"

"If only we knew what people hide in their *good* hearts."

In truth, though I'd told Father that I'd steel myself, I needed rest. Too much had happened, too fast, and I didn't know everything I needed to.

Kyars, for sure, would turn around once he got word of his father's demise. And that must've already happened, given how the Alanyans sent messages: archer relays. An Archer of the Eye would shoot a message a thousand feet, and then the next archer would pick up the message and shoot it another thousand feet, and on and on until it reached its intended. When an army departed, they'd leave three Archers of the Eye every thousand feet between Qandbajar and wherever they marched, each working in shifts. The Archers of the Eye also had permanent stations all over Alanya. I planned to use the Archers to send a message of my own, but first: rest, food, and time to think.

Vera helped me settle on my bed. She opened the balcony door so the mid-morning breeze could waft through.

"Go get food and eat with me," I said. "It's best we stay together at a time like this."

"Of course, sultana." Grief tinged her voice — poor little thing. Much had happened that she didn't understand. And yet, by bringing me Cyra's conqueror's blood, she'd made it possible. How horrified would she be to know?

Ten minutes later, Vera returned holding a tray of saffron rice with cumin, a soup of lentils and cauliflower, and lamb chops infused with yogurt and tomatoes. She set the tray on a low table, then helped me settle onto a cushion she'd leaned against the wall.

"Tell me about Ruthenia," I said before stuffing rice and lamb in my mouth. "You remember your homeland, don't you?"

"I was eight when they took me. Rubadi slavers. Ruthenia was very cold. Not just in winter, all the time."

The rice was well-buttered and the tomato fresh. The lamb, though, seemed a tad overcooked. I'd become choosy since living in a palace.

"What was the food like?"

Vera pecked at a lamb chop she'd dunked in yogurt. "A lot of… porridge. Throwing whatever you could in a pot. Sometimes we'd get a meaty boar."

"You ought to eat your fill now, dear. Your ribs stick out. If they don't feed you enough in the canteen, you can come here, and I'll give you whatever you like."

She smiled, twitchy. "They tell a story, in Ruthenia…"

"Oh? What kind of story?"

"About a witch who captures children, then gives them sweets to fatten them up, so she can eat them."

"And do you think I'm like that witch?"

She put down her soup bowl, then looked me in the eye. "Why did you ask me to bring you Cyra's blood?"

"You never questioned me about it before. Why of a sudden?"

"It is not my place to question you, sultana. But everyone knows Cyra and I were close, since I'd been her handmaiden. I fear for myself. I just wish to know if…if I did something wrong."

I took her clammy hand. "You did nothing wrong, dear. You're as sinless as the day you were born." I'd prepared a story for this moment. "I come from the Vogras Mountains, from where descends the river that runs through this city and gives us all sustenance. It's cold there, too. We've a custom, a strange one, but important, none-theless. A little blood in our food, that's all, so we can grow closer to those who are dear to us. I wished for Cyra and me to become good friends — that's all."

Vera nodded, as if she understood. "I see, sultana. It is not so strange. Among certain tribes in Ruthenia, when a chieftain dies, the rest will eat him whole. It is sacrilege, in fact, to leave even a single hair. The bones, too, are chopped into a seasoning. But I fear in Alanya, they would find our customs…savage."

How dreadful. But it was best that I humor her. "That's why they must never know. They look down on us, on our ways, because we're different."

"Yes, sultana. To be true, in Ruthenia, we revere witches. They are our life-givers, our guides through this mortal world. They say my great-grandmother was a witch. Even in the deadest month, she could feed the entire tribe with meat she conjured out of bones. She lived more than a hundred years, they say."

It seemed Vera was probing me. I ought to do the same. "And if I were a witch, would you revere me?"

She slurped up a cauliflower, nodding all the while. "I'd worship your very scent, sultana."

I smiled. But a girl like her, who must've masked so many wounds behind her innocent, strawberry facade, couldn't be counted on with secrets. "Finish your food, dear. These are difficult days — best you be strong."

THE TRUTH: if Kyars entered the city, he would take the throne, and no one could get him off it. But if he didn't return, Kato's power — and ego — would swell, and he'd become the sultan-regent of Alanya. Neither outcome suited my mission. So, to get Kyars and Kato to destroy each other, I'd have to convince Kyars that Kato was trying to seize the throne, and I'd have to convince Kato that Kyars wanted him hanged. Neither was easy, given their long history.

But I could plant the seeds. How fortunate that Kato had many enemies. Wouldn't it be convenient if one would, somehow, escape and make his way to Kyars, bringing whispers of Kato's power-binge?

Another truth: though I'd been careful, writing those blood-runes had risked exposing me. Using Cyra's body to kill the Shah had risked exposing me, and still could. Vera had asked a good question that others were no doubt asking: why would Cyra, who had just been given everything a woman in Alanya could want, do it? And so, I had to stay shadowed while being more careful, clever, and considered so questions wouldn't be asked.

I decided to meet with Kato in the bare room he'd turned into a temporary office. I think it had been used to store linens, but now it sported a low table for Kato and a few cushions for his visitors.

How considerate not to use the Shah's office, or even that of a vizier — perhaps it was to show that his regency was meant to be as temporary as this office. A clever way to avoid making new enemies.

The man was cracking almonds with a dagger when Vera wheeled me inside.

"I'm busy," he said, "make it quick."

"Busy doing what?"

"Looking for traitors. Ozar and Hadrith's lips are as sealed as a good wine, and I can't exactly pry them open, given that one is the Grand Vizier's son, and the other the Crown Prince's — or rather the Shah's — uncle-in-law. So I'm left with less direct methods."

"Do you want my suggestion?"

He popped an almond in his mouth, then put the dagger down. "You're full of ideas, aren't you? Why is it every time you suggest something, it leads to gold?"

Vera wasn't the only one wondering about me, it seemed. "You never questioned me about it before. Why of a sudden?"

"Because you're too clever for a girl whom, when I met her, thought a bullet ball was a big, shiny bead. And given what's just transpired, until Kyars is sitting on the throne, I won't take anything at face."

"I'm perceptive. I notice things others don't. I read a lot — just ask the Philosophers how many books I've checked out from their tower. I'm only as exceptional as I've made myself."

"So many virtues. Must be why Kyars fucked you more than twice. But why lay your blessed fruits at humble Kato's door, hmm? That doesn't sit right."

Just how suspicious of me was he? Before, when I'd made it my purpose to get acquainted with him, he seemed pliable, earnest, and open to my ideas. Perhaps recent events had brought his guard up, which could make planting seeds in him like gardening in the sea.

Although, despite how high he'd risen, the man had no allies in the Majlis. He'd won his loyalties in the field, but he was on a different battlefield now.

"I watched your performance earlier," I said. "You're lost at sea, Kato. If you don't correct course, you'll drown. Alanya, too, will sink if not steered right. It's all on you."

The man wasn't used to being challenged by someone whose jaw he couldn't bash in. He glared at me, as if not knowing how to respond. "Suggest your suggestion and get out, woman. I'm busy." He took up his dagger and resumed cracking almonds.

"The Archers of the Eye have, by now, sent news of the Shah's death to every city in the realm and beyond. The governors will come to give allegiances to Shah Kyars, and Kyars, of course, will come with haste to sit the throne and accept those allegiances. The question is — will Kyars come alone, or with his army? He'll come with his army if he feels there's a threat to his rule. He'll come alone — and far faster, too — if he doesn't. Do you see where I'm going with this?"

Kato raised his hands, palms up. "No, I don't."

"Send a message to Kyars that you've caught all the traitors and announce the same to the Majlis. This way, Kyars will come alone, and the traitors — whoever among them remains — will feel at ease. Perhaps at ease enough to foment a new plan. They're rats, you see — start a fire, they'll run into their holes and you'll never catch them. But put out some bait…"

If Kato did what I was asking, it would only make Kyars suspicious of him. On the one hand, Kato would tell Kyars it's safe. On the other hand, *someone else* whom I had in mind would tell Kyars that Kato was the danger. But would Kato take the bait?

Kato stood, walked over to my chair, and bent down at my side. He whispered, "You want me to use the Shah as bait for rats? You out of your mind, woman?"

He wanted to intimidate me. But I only needed to remind him: "You have much to lose, gholam. Your bald head would look extra shiny hanging from the palace gate. How many would cherish the sight?"

Kato opened the door, grabbed my chair, and wheeled me into the hallway, where Vera was chatting with a eunuch. He returned to his office and shut the door.

THERE WEREN'T ANY TRAITORS — aside from myself — so I needed to create some to make Kato fear for his life. And what's the best place to find rats? Underground, of course.

More specifically, in the dungeons, where I'd put several soulshifting bloodrunes. A soulshifting rune could be written with any blood flavor, but it would only allow me to possess someone nearby, within twenty feet or so of the rune, who carries that flavor. This was among the few scenarios in which my own common flavor could be useful — where any flavor could be useful.

I'd been putting soulshifting runes of each flavor everywhere and taking notes on who in the palace carried which flavor, so I could try to be targeted with whom I possessed. I put a conqueror's blood soulshifting rune in the wine cellar, even, with the intention of having Vera lure Cyra down there, if I wanted to possess her. Obviously, I'd also put one in the great hall because possessing Cyra, while not my first plan, was one of many backups. Though I hid my runes as best I could, that dreaded eunuch Sambal had discovered them, somehow, and so now I wished I'd been more careful.

After Vera carried me into the closet — I told her I felt calm in there — I focused my mind on where I'd planted one of the runes. I *touched* it with my mind, and it glowed.

I found myself brushing a mop back and forth on a grimy floor. Faint candles within hanging metal lamplights lit the hallway. Around me were iron doors with shut portholes. Not ideal to have soulshifted into the dungeon's custodian instead of a guard, but it would have to do.

I opened the nearest porthole. A middle-aged, one-handed man was lying on a pallet. Obviously not Hadrith. I closed it and continued mopping down the hallway, peeking into portholes all the while. A stinking Kashanese man in rags; a singing Abyadi sailor; a man sleeping in his own vomit. But no Hadrith — where the hell was Kato keeping him?

Perhaps the large, red-tinted door at the end of the hallway? I mopped my way to it, then slid the porthole open.

A graying man was sitting on the floor, reciting something. From his straight hair, almond eyes, and patchy beard, I could tell he was a Silklander by blood. And what he was reciting shocked me: the names of the Twelve Chiefs of the Children. I'd seen this man before...in the Tower of Wisdom, behind a stack of books, wearing the tall, felt hat and metal clasp of the Philosophers. But why was a Silklander Philosopher here in the dungeon, the twelve hallowed names on his tongue?

I joined his recitation, so he'd take notice. "Tala," my grandfather, "Sayt," my uncle and father-in-law, "Iban," my husband, "Hafaz," my son, "Zawad," my grandson, "Kazin," my great-grandson, and the final chief, who was only a boy when they strangled him.

"You're one of us," he said, grinning. "Walking the straight path." He put his finger to his lip. "Shh! You must not show them. You must hide it in your heart, lest you end up like me."

"Is that why they put you here?" I asked.

He nodded. "I willingly carry these burdens — someone has to — but you and the others mustn't. Stay safe — lie if you must — but keep their names in your heart, always. So long as truth lives in the hearts of us seekers, it will never perish, no matter what cruelties they devise to destroy it."

How wise. It was men like him I wished to save by restoring the righteous rule of the Children. Why must the good, the truthful, always suffer? Though he was likely ignorant of the true teachings of the Twelve Chiefs, he was trying his best, and that merited something.

"Don't fight," he said, "always forgive. Always. Our reward will be in Paradise — theirs will be here. One day the truth will dawn. Until then, keep it in your heart, always, brother."

"What's your name?"

He put his hand to his heart. "I am Wafiq."

"Wafiq…is there something I can do to ease your burdens?"

He shook his head. "Every day, Khizr Khaz or his Order men ask me 'Who is Chisti?' and when I say 'father' instead of 'saint,' they whip me. My back is not a pretty sight, dear brother. If you do anything to help me, they'll hurt you too. Don't let your faith be known, ever. Just know — there are many of us — thousands, tens of thousands — out there. You are not alone. Though it may be dim, there is always light. Knowing that is succor enough. Remember the saying of our beloved Father — 'Carrying truth is like holding burning coals.' Hold those coals in your heart, dear brother."

That was indeed a true saying of Father Chisti. My husband, especially, loved to repeat it. All books of the Twelve Chiefs had been burned, and I'd learned from my studies that the Sylgiz and other present-day followers of the Path of the Children had attributed fabricated sayings to the Children, so how did Wafiq know a true one? Was it just fortune that a few true sayings had survived in the six hundred years we'd been gone?

Footsteps. Guards approached. I shut the porthole and made mopping motions before the cycle ended and I returned to the closet.

I DIDN'T KNOW what I needed in order to devise the perfect plan to restore the righteous rule of the Children, so I'd have to learn more. I couldn't rest. Too many had suffered, still suffered, for carrying the truth. Just because I lived in a palace and could fill myself with delicacies and lie upon silk sheets didn't give me the right to set down those coals, even for a moment.

But soulshifting had its limits. For one, after soulshifting into a human, you couldn't soulshift again until the sun set or rose. So I went to do something I'd neglected this morning — take a bath.

Celene was there, sitting alone in the hot, corner pool. Other concubines were around, chittering among each other and going in and out of the cold and warm pools, as well as the steam rooms. Vera helped me off my chair, get undressed, and climb into the hot pool. The Crucian girl reminded me too much of myself when I first arrived — aloof — and the harem was difficult to endure alone.

"You all right, dear?" I asked Celene in Sirmian.

That broke her trance. Her cheeks turned from snow to pink as she folded her arms over her breasts. She'd learn soon enough, like I had, there was no preserving one's shame in Kyars' harem.

Wrinkles covered the skin on her hands. How long had she been soaking? "I'm well enough. And are you better?"

"Better every day, aside from this awful tragedy that's befallen us."

"I'm sorry for your loss." Words said so dryly. "I heard he was… a good king."

According to what Sambal and Mirima had told me, Celene was the daughter of the Crucian imperator. She only spoke Sirmian because she'd been the Sirmian shah's hostage. I only did because it was similar enough to one of the three languages spoken in the Vogras when I'd lived there, the others being Vograsian and Paramic.

With her unblemished, baby-soft features, Celene seemed young even for this harem. Sixteen, according to Mirima. How clever could she be at her precious age? Although, some cleverness was surely required to escape from the Shah of Sirm. How careful would I have to be around her?

"It'll get better, dear," I said. "The Alanyans aren't savage like the Sirmians. They've got culture, here." I'd heard so many Alanyans proudly spout that, though I had no idea if it were true. Sirmians weren't loved in this country. I'd read they'd abolished titles like *sultana* and *pasha* after a janissary revolt decades ago, and so slaves were running the place, which seemed the trend here, too.

"Everyone keeps saying that. As if it could ever be good, to be a hostage so far from everyone and everything I love."

A certain other hostage had grown to like it. Poor Cyra. I wasn't sure I'd killed her, and it seemed the other witnesses couldn't say if she were dead or alive. Either way, it had ended badly. She was likely buried in the sand or on her way to the Waste with the Sylgiz. I didn't have the right to feel sorry for her, considering what I'd done, and so tried not to think of her, lest it poison me with guilt.

"Do you pray?" I dropped chamomile petals in the water, submerged my hair, and came back up. "There's a lovely chapel in the city. I'll take you there once I'm walking again. You could even meet the bishop of Alanya."

"I've never stopped praying and never will."

Faithful girl. Though her gods were powerless here, she carried those coals in her own way.

"It would be nice," she said, "to visit the chapel. The Sirmians would not let me. But…I can't really blame them…after what happened."

"After the war with Crucis?"

She shook her head. "Not just the war. The Archangel appeared in the sky, his wings broader than the clouds, his sword taller than a mountain. I saw him too, which is why I can never be unfaithful. I'm like the apostles, now. Faith is no longer a matter of believing, but of seeing. And so many others saw him. They rushed to take our faith, to be saved in the light of the Archangel, which is why Murad outlawed it entirely…with exile, torture, or imprisonment."

Kato had told me the story about the angel appearing in the sky over Kostany, but in his version, Lat had exploded it into a thousand thousand pieces, and the gholam had rejoiced. Either way, it was so fanciful. Perhaps it was sorcery of some sort. Whatever it was, Celene believed it, her voice solid with certainty. We were more similar than I thought. What the Sirmians were doing to the Ethosians, the Alanyans had done to our Path, despite all Latians worshipping the same god and revering the same man.

"They won't forbid you here." I scrubbed my arms with a bar of rose-scented lye, then doused them. "There are even Ethosians in the Majlis. And Kyars doesn't care what faith you keep. The girl wheeling me around — her name is Vera — I couldn't even describe the god she prays to. It looks like…a pillar with faces and arms."

Celene giggled. Her smile truly was precious. "Yormagolgalghar — the Ruthenian dreaming god."

I laughed genuinely for the first time in ages. "I'm not even going to try pronouncing that."

We both laughed — a small relief in a tumultuous time.

"They're a stubborn bunch, Ruthenians," Celene said. "My grandfather sent an army of missionaries up there. They ate half of them."

I don't know why, but that sounded so funny. I couldn't stop laughing, Celene joining me. Other concubines in the chamber stared.

"Hush, dear," I said. "Today is for mourning. If they see us laughing…"

Celene nodded. "Yes, of course." She paused, then took a deep breath, puffing her snowy cheeks. "May I…come see you, later?"

Seemed I'd earned some trust with nothing but a casual and sincere chat. Good-nature and sincerity were rare in this harem, but what is a soulshifter if not an actor?

I smiled as widely as I could. "I would love if you did."

• • •

THE BLACK DRONGO was hatching its eggs when I soulshifted the next day. What a tender warmth, as if your bottom was sitting in a soothing bath. The moment of the soulshift, I also felt her base instincts — a fierce drive to protect those eggs, from any and all, even at pain of death. Drongos were like humans in that way, and I could relate.

I soared into the sky over Qandbajar until I found the training ground: a grassy field — about a thousand feet long and half as wide — littered with straw men. And those straw men were covered in arrows. I dove closer until I could see the Archers of the Eye shooting arrows with their recurve bows in long, almost magnetic arcs.

With their coal-dark skin and white dresses that barely reached below their knees, the Archers were obviously not Alanyan. Next to the training field sat an Ethosian chapel with a white spire at its center — a distinct look to the western-style chapels in the Ethosian Quarter. And as I landed atop the spire and focused my earsight, I noticed them sitting on the floor, like us Latians. Their language seemed to share many words with Paramic, too...so many, in fact, that I shockingly understood everything they chanted.

The Archers of the Eye hailed from Labash, a country to the south of Himyar, and were the most accurate and far-firing archers in the world. So why weren't they off fighting battles? Why did the Seluqal House pay them heaps of gold to send messages? Because, as history had shown, words rang louder than war cries. And the right word, at the perfect time, could win a war — including, hopefully, the one I was fighting.

Amid all these men going in and out of the chapel, in and out of the barrack, and onto and off the training field — all wearing white, knee-length dresses — I noticed someone out of place: a young woman with red hair. She sat in the grass, stringing a bow. I fluttered toward her, careful to avoid the arrows flying about. I absolutely did not want to die...again. I landed on the grass to stay low, then jumped my way toward her until I stood at her front.

She smiled at me. I tilted my head at her, like I'd noticed birds doing to people. Lithe and pretty enough — amid so many men, she seemed like a morsel of halva surrounded by giant ants. Her long, loose, and fur-lined caftan resembled something the Sylgiz would wear — not a popular style in Alanya, for obvious reasons. By her wavy, dark red hair, I could surmise she was a Karmazi from the mountains to the west...but if that were so, why did she just hum a Sirmian song?

Strange. But in any case, I couldn't accomplish much at this training ground as a bird. I'd have to visit in person so I could place runes.

"Agh!" the woman screamed. A droplet of blood flowed off her thumb and onto the grass. She'd cut herself with her knife while fletching an arrow. "Fuck! Am I so out of practice?" She looked at me with a smile warmer than the sun above. "Sorry, did I scare you?"

An animal lover, too. I tilted my head to the other side.

"Ugh, might as well call it a day. Take a bath. So many things I've been neglecting, all for this. No chance I'm going to win, anyway."

She got up and walked off the field. The young woman obviously wasn't an Archer of the Eye, so what was she doing here? What was she trying to win?

Her blood droplet glazed on the blade of grass, as if cream on a cake. I took a peck and stirred it on my tongue. What flavor would it be, I wondered? Seeker, sower, settler, or soldier?

Hot on the tip of the tongue, fiery in the mouth, and burning down the throat.

By Lat. I wanted more. It was nothing I'd ever tasted. It was something else entirely...one of the thirteen rare types. How lucky could I be to chance upon it like this?

But what flavor? Not conqueror's blood, which Cyra had, nor god's blood, possessed by my son Seluq. I couldn't tell because I'd no experience tasting anything else. I didn't even know the names of many of the other eleven flavors.

Stunned, I looked up at the sky, which to a bird was like looking down the street. I so wanted to soar and bathe in a cloud. I'd been alive a long time. Tasted the blood of thousands — nay, tens of thousands — and I'd never tasted a flavor like this.

To figure it out, I needed the book that described and named the rarest flavors. I needed *Flavors of Blood Volume Two*.

11

CYRA

I RETURNED TO THE HOSPITAL FOR A BANDAGE CHANGE. REQUESTED A small mirror so I could look upon my scars before they put fresh bandages over them.

Realizing I was barely the same person stung worse than a red-tailed scorpion. My eyeless socket seemed so dark and endless, as if an abyss. The surrounding swelling would lessen with time, but I'd never be whole. I'd never be beautiful.

And then there was the swollen gash in my neck, accompanied by the bloodrunes Eshe had painted on my skin. A bunch of lines, though one resembled a tree, and another seemed like two triangles, and then, with copious imagination, one even looked like a man waving his arms. From what I remembered, he'd drawn them to stop the bleeding. Perhaps I could imagine they were henna…if blood were a dye color. Worse, no amount of scrubbing washed them off, as if as permanent as my scars.

A relief to have bandages on again. I wouldn't have to see what I'd become and could imagine the same Cyra was behind those wrappings. I also wore a high-collared caftan to hide the wrappings. Too bad I was never good at lying to myself.

News of the Shah's murder arrived in Zelthuriya days ago. Sadly, few lamented. Tamaz had been a great patron here, helping to rebuild shrines, pave fresh roads, and dig new wells. But in his humility, he'd never made a show of it, and so now few here cared for his passing. Supplicants continued to go from shrine to shrine, chanting prayers, though few were for him.

I prayed for him, though. When the sorcerer stabbed my eye, Tamaz rushed to save me. He could've ordered a gholam to do it. He could've secured his own safety. But his instincts took over. Only now did I realize how much he cared for me…how much he loved me…how much he wanted me to be the daughter he never had.

Did he die believing I was hurting him? If there was one salve, it would be that he knew it wasn't me, that I would never harm him, that I only wanted to be the best wife his son could have, the best daughter he could have. I was floating overhead when it happened and did not see his eyes…did not know what they recognized in his final moment.

What would Kyars think? We'd known each other for eight years, and though he never liked me, would he really believe that I killed his father? Was anyone left who'd tell him otherwise? What'd happened to Hadrith, Ozar, and Sambal?

Too many questions. Too few answers.

On my way to see Kevah at Saint Chisti's shrine, I ran into the two green turbans who'd carried me to the hospital. Their names were Rafa and Alir, I recalled.

They were guarding a small shrine in the middle of the street. Rafa eyed me and moved his lips but let out no voice. All the while, Alir glared at him.

"You must be fasting," I said to them. "You don't need to answer. I just wanted to say thank you for helping me."

Rafa moved his lips again. This time, he let out a heavy breath.

Alir grabbed his shoulder. "Don't do it, Rafa. The sheikh will surely cane you for breaking yet another fast."

Rafa's nose twitched as he held in his breath.

"Perhaps when you're not fasting," I said, "we could chat. For now, have a bright morning."

As I turned to leave, Rafa exhaled a gust. "Are you all right? Are you feeling better? You look better. Where are you living? Do you have money? I get off duty in one hour, by the way."

Alir grunted in frustration. "You fool! What have you done? You know I have to tell the sheikh!"

"Tell him!" Rafa pushed his friend away. "I can take a caning from that old bag of sand."

"He might be old, but he's stronger than he looks."

"So…" I said. They both turned toward me. "I'm living at Saint Chisti's. They're taking good care of me. Come visit anytime."

"You're living *there*!" Rafa's jaw dropped. "With the Disciples?"

I'd seen the Disciples around with their black turbans or black headscarves. Each was a sheikh or sheikha, despite several being rather young. But aside from a few polite greetings and smiles, they'd said little to me.

I nodded. "I'm really there to be close to Kevah."

Rafa clenched his jaw and grabbed his chest, as if his heart burned. "Kevah? I saw him with a girl, last year. Karmazi with red hair. What makes him so special that he has girls visiting him all the time?"

I shook my head. "No, I mean, I'm not visiting him. Not like that. Just, he's helping me with…a problem."

"Problem? You mean that Himyarite they threw off the mountain? Is he the one who hurt you?"

"Himyarite…oh, you mean Eshe? No, he saved my life. And… why did they throw him off a mountain?"

Alir pulled Rafa back and said, "Fasting and being in the sun all day has made you insufferable. Go inside before you embarrass yourself further."

But Rafa pushed him away again. "He was guilty of—"

Alir interrupted, "It's unmentionable, what that Himyarite did. Anyway, in Zelthuriya, we don't recount the sins of others."

Rafa bit his lip. "Uh, he's right, actually. Best not repeat such things."

I'd have to ask Eshe myself…if ever I saw him again.

Back at Saint Chisti's, Kevah was standing in front of the sepulcher, which was just a cage within which lay a green shroud. Surreal to think the body of the holiest man ever was wrapped inside. A man so great, he now resided beneath the throne of Lat and would daily take our prayers to her.

After emptying the cavern for twice-daily cleaning, custodians wearing tribal garb broomed the floor and gathered melted candles.

Kevah greeted me with his beautiful smile. "Apologies for my disheveled appearance." What? He looked absolutely radiant, as usual. "Didn't get much sleep. Had quite the nightmare last night."

Well, in that he wasn't alone. "My mother told me that when we dream, it's because a jinn is giving us his memories, which then mix with our own. That's why they're often so strange, terrifying, yet familiar." Mother liked those Sylgiz wisdoms. I said a quick prayer to Saint Chisti under my breath that Lat keep her in this world, though perhaps that was selfish. What if she were in pain, the deaths of her husband and sons too much to bear?

Was she thinking about me when I thought about her?

"The sheikhs do say the jinn bring us our dreams," Kevah said, "but I've never heard the part about them being the jinn's memories."

"Us Sylgiz like to innovate. So…what did you dream?"

He sighed and yawned at the same time. "Well, I was rowing a boat beneath the night sky. I don't know to where, but it was so dark I couldn't see the water, though it was slick and didn't ripple. In the distant horizon, these…*faces*…were watching me. Let's just say they didn't look human." He gulped and scratched his beard. "I suppose it could be the memory of a jinn."

I shuddered. I couldn't remember my own nightmare from last night, but his was terrifying enough.

A cleaner dusted his broom in our direction, then gestured for us to step aside, so we moved closer to the sepulcher. I could scarcely believe Saint Chisti lay in that shroud. I wondered where they'd plant my brother's shrine; there was this one hill he loved climbing, where tall, silver grasses grew in the late summer.

"What're you thinking?" Kevah asked.

"About my family. Were you close with your mother?"

He shook his head. "Janissaries don't have mothers, and our fathers turn us into the Sirmian shah's expert killers…who can also run the kingdom, if needed."

So they were, more or less, like the gholam, then. "You have… had a daughter. Do you have a wife, then?"

"I had a wife." His eyebrows sagged. "I'll tell you all about it, another time. We're not so different, you and I. Everything lost, but still fighting. That's why I want to help you. That's why I spoke with the Disciples. The sheikhs and sheikhas want to hear what you have to say."

Thorn pricks spread across my shoulders. "Have you told them everything I told you?"

"I've told them you have a different version of how the Shah died. One that involves sorcery."

"Do you think they'll believe me?"

He sighed. "The Disciples are a cautious bunch. They've protected this city for a thousand years and prefer not to meddle in outside matters unless there's a threat to the Faith. Bloodwriter, soulshifter — these are dark words that bring to mind the starborn sorceries I witnessed in Sirm. But, unlike me, the Disciples are thorough. Exacting. Prepare to be asked anything and everything. Don't lie, don't hide things — they'll know. All right?"

Honestly, Kevah was even handsomer when serious. A guilty pleasure to stare into his eyes whenever he spoke.

I nodded. He escorted me to a small, carpeted room with a

wooden divider down the middle. The simplicity reminded me of how Tamaz liked to style his living spaces, and like elsewhere in this massive cave, it remained cool and humid despite the dry swelter outside.

Men in black turbans and black caftans entered, sitting to one side of the divider. Women wearing black headscarves and black caftans — though some sported colorful beads — entered and sat on the other side. The elders gathered at the front while the youths took to the back. I sat against the wall with Kevah and faced everyone.

While waiting for the room to fill, these Disciples kept busy with recitals — none used prayer beads, as was the fashion, but rather counted Lat's praises on their fingers. We did the same in the Sylgiz lands — counting sixty praises on our fingers, using the finger creases on our right hand to count the ones, and the whole fingers on our left the tens.

Finally, a man entered and shut the door behind him. But he was not wearing black, nor a turban, just a rough, oak-colored cloak. His white beard seemed to glow. As I stared at him, my breathing quickened, and I almost sprung up and darted away. The last time I'd seen this man was when he'd married me to Kyars.

Grand Mufti Khizr Khaz sat at the front, his eyes on me. He nodded. Though my throat went dry, I managed to nod back.

I whispered to Kevah, "Is…is that man a Disciple?"

Kevah shook his head. "No. That's Khizr Khaz. Some consider him a living saint."

"He's the Grand Mufti of Alanya," I whispered, "and the Grand Sheikh of the Order of Saint Jamshid — in Qandbajar!"

Kevah raised his hands, palms up. "He's so many things, I can scarcely keep track. But he comes here often. The Disciples don't like the Saint Jamshid Order — or any other order, really — but everyone looks up to Khizr Khaz."

I could only think: what if he were here to arrest and take me back? What if he was going to tell everyone that I killed the Shah? And why was he acting so calm in my presence?

"Ahem." I cleared my throat. "Is that everyone?" I couldn't believe I spoke up, but it was entirely from nerves.

Kevah whispered, "Tell them everything. You'll do great, I'm certain."

So I did. From the moment Hadrith apprised me of the conspiracy to when Eshe brought me to Holy Zelthuriya. I emphasized how I saw my body being used by the soulshifter, as if my soul were a bird overhead. I teared up when mentioning how Tamaz ran to help me after the soulshifter stabbed my eye. All the while, the Disciples kept silent and listened amid the somber candlelight.

Once I finished, Kevah whispered, "Well said. The way you told it, none can doubt your sincerity."

Such hopeful words. The Disciples of Chisti were a powerful group, and so was the Order of Saint Jamshid. What did the sorcerer have aside from Kato and his gholam? With the Disciples and the Order backing me, Kyars might believe my story. Perhaps he wouldn't divorce me…despite my hideousness…and cherish the bond his father forged. Tasting hopeful thoughts, for the first time in days, brought me to life.

"Liar." The call came from the back of the women's section — a dagger thrown to shatter my hopes. "Your story has more holes than Yadawiya."

Kevah whispered, "That's where they dig the wells. Clever."

The woman who'd said it veiled not just her hair, but her face, too — the only one in the room who did. How strange. I couldn't see a single feature; the black cloth covered even her eyes. Considering she sat at the back, she must've been young, and the light pitch of her voice affirmed that.

"Ruhi," said an older sheikh, who had a fat lip and red-dyed beard. "I found her testimony rather sincere."

"Perhaps you see a sorry little girl worth coddling," the sheikha named Ruhi said. "Or perhaps her soothing voice has disguised the truth from your ears."

"Disrespectful, Ruhi," the older sheikh said. "If you've an argument, make it without questioning the character of an elder, lest you find yourself beneath the whip. And don't think we won't because of the hardships you've endured."

"I didn't mean to disrespect you, sheikh," she said, "but rather to say that the girl knows how to mine men for sympathy, among other things."

I clenched my fists. I wanted to rip off her veil and bash her eye out so she'd feel what I felt. How dare she?

Kevah grabbed my wrist, whispered, "Don't fall for it. They're testing your character."

I swallowed my rage and pointed to my eye. "Would you like to see it?" I asked the group. "The abyss that stares back when you gaze upon my face? Would you believe me, then? There's nothing *soothing* about it, I assure you."

Ruhi said, "You claim the gholam commander Kato was part of a conspiracy to overthrow the Shah — but then why, in your story, did he try to save the Shah?"

"I don't know. It doesn't all make sense to me, either. But I've told you everything I know."

"No, you're hiding something." Ruhi shook her veiled head. "Perhaps even from yourself. That's what happens with those of base character. They break into pieces, one part hiding things from the other, so they can live with themselves. You're nothing but a shattered vase."

Base character? Such arrogance to assume she knew me! "I might not be perfect, but I loved Shah Tamaz like a father. I care deeply for his son, Kyars, and for their entire family. I've been nothing but loyal to the Seluqals, from the first. I'd never, ever hurt them."

"That's what you want to believe," Ruhi sneered, "but you'd

betray them if it meant your survival. The part of you that you hide, that you're so ashamed of, knows that well enough."

Now my fist shook. Her words went beyond assumptions — they were lies!

Kevah stilled my hand with his touch. "Don't let her get to you. Just remain calm and answer their questions."

I glanced at Khizr Khaz, who was staring at the floor as if lost in thought. What did he think of this?

"Ruhi may be brash, but she is right about one thing," said an elder Disciple, who had dark gray eyebrows. "Your character must be established, because we don't know you. We've never even heard of you. And here you've come, the sole witness of a charge the gravity of which we've not heard in some time."

I shut my eyes and reminded myself that I was speaking true, no matter what they said. Kevah believed me. Surely others would, too. "Ask, then, whatever you wish. I've not a hair to hide."

An elder woman, who wore a colorful bead necklace, cleared her throat. "You're twenty-three years old, and yet you only just married. My daughters all wed before eighteen. Tell me, dear, why were you so unbelievably late?"

"I was the Shah's hostage. He controlled my fate. If it were up to me, I would have married years ago."

Ruhi chuckled. "Twenty-three — impressive to have waited so long. Tell me, when did you bleed for the first time?"

What did that have to do with anything? "I don't remember," I said, hoping to dismiss the topic.

"Liar." More than one Disciple said it: Ruhi and a man at the back. True, it was a lie, but formed from embarrassment rather than malice.

"I think I was thirteen," I said. "That's right — it was the night before my fourteenth birthday. My mother had taken me hunting that morning, and at first, I thought the horse's hard saddle the cause. *True* enough for you?"

"So, ten years ago...a long time," Ruhi said. "And yet, I'm

certain Crown Prince Kyars expects his wife to be pure. Are you pure for him, Cyra?"

I nodded. "I've never lain with a man." I clenched my fist again. "What does that have to do with anything I'm saying?" My voice cracked.

"Everything," Ruhi said. "The way you told your story made plain your desire for the Grand Vizier's son, Hadrith." What? How could she have gleaned that? "Perhaps you wanted to marry him, instead. Perhaps that's why you killed the Shah. Perhaps he's the one desiring power, not some made-up sorcerer or a petty gholam commander."

No. No. No. Such twisted accusations. Such lies. How could she?

Perhaps this was a test, as Kevah had mentioned. Best to answer calmly, then. "Yes, I did have feelings for Hadrith — it's true. But I married Kyars with full hope and every intention to love him. I swear upon Lat."

"You never sinned with Hadrith?" the elder woman wearing beads asked, "or with any other?"

I shook my head.

"Liar!" seven or eight Disciples said. How could they know?

Kevah leaned into my ear. "I told you not to lie, Cyra. They know. I went through this exact thing, and they knew everything. It's written on your face, in a language only they can read. Don't be afraid of the truth, whatever it is. Whatever you've done."

I swallowed a bitter lump. "I thought you didn't recount sins in Zelthuriya?"

The fat-lipped sheikh said, "Normally, we don't. But this is not normal. The fates of the Latian kingdoms may rest on the decisions we make today, based on your words."

"So — what — you want to know every sin I've ever done? Is that how you'll decide if I'm worth helping? Are you all so sinless as to judge me this way?"

"Don't deflect." Ruhi moved closer, mere arm spans away.

"None of us are sinless, but there are degrees. And we must determine—"

"Fine!" I stared at the spot in the black cloth where her eyes must've been. "I get pleasure where and when I can get away with it. I slept with a woman, my handmaiden, more than once. Is that what you wanted to hear?"

Ruhi laughed and shook her head. "That isn't it. This city is rife with such behavior. We've learned to look away." She tilted her covered head toward me. "You're hiding something far worse. And it appears you yourself don't even know what it is."

Kevah's face was in his palm. Had he lost hope in me? Was this whole thing crashing down because I couldn't remember some terrible sin I'd committed?

"Enough," Khizr Khaz said. He stood and turned to address the room. "You need not rely on her character. Everyone here knows mine, and I can tell you what happened."

All chatter ceased. The sheikhs and sheikhas stared up in respect. I didn't know whether this was good or bad, whether to be relieved or afraid, but I felt a bit of both.

"I'll explain what I know," Khizr Khaz said. "But first, Cyra and the magus must leave the room."

Kevah and I shared a bewildered glance. He stood and asked, "Sheikh Khizr...why?"

Khizr Khaz said nothing and gestured to the door.

KEVAH and I returned to his room. I sat in the corner and broke. Was I such a thing to be despised? Hideous, impure, untrustworthy? How foolish to hope the Disciples would help me. That anyone would. I didn't want to cry, but hopelessness forced out the tears.

Kevah put his hand on my shoulder. "If it's any consolation, my jinn wants to steal their shoes and toss them over the mountain peaks."

Even with the tears streaming, I couldn't help but laugh. "Do you think my husband will believe me?"

"Kyars…well…wish I knew him better."

Kevah had mentioned they'd met in Sirm, during their war with Crucis. They were enemies, at first, because Kevah had aligned against the Sirmian grand vizier, whom Kyars supported. But then, during the final battle of the war, Kyars arrived just in time to smash the forces of the Crucian imperator and save their shah — if only he could've done so for his own shah and father.

"Would you believe me?" I asked. "If you were him?"

Kevah hunched his shoulders. "I can't imagine what it's like to be him. A prince…heir to a powerful throne. So many pressures…I really don't know. All I can say is, by your sincerity, I think you're telling the truth." He gazed at the floor. "But…without the allegiance of a jinn tribe, I'm not much."

"That's not true. Everyone looks up to you. They see you as a great hope. Your support means everything."

"Shut up," he whispered to the side, as if speaking to his jinn. "That's just depraved." He looked at me. "If only you knew what it's like…to have Ahriyya whispering in your ear, all the time."

I chuckled. How mischievous was this jinn? Sometimes, it seemed Kevah's patience with it really wore thin. "What did it say?"

He shook his head. "Nothing that ought to be repeated. Anyway, there's something I want to tell you. And to be truthful, it's hard because I'm not the best at…baring my feelings."

"Just tell me."

He cleared his throat. "Hearing you talk about what happened to you…it reminds me of what happened to me. Of the despair I once felt, after I'd lost everything. I never want to feel that way again." His voice quavered. "Truth be told, I came to Zelthuriya to lose my feelings…every feeling…if it meant I'd never have to taste that kind of pain. I came here to…in a way…to die." He sighed somberly. "That's what *fanaa* meant to me. But for some reason…I just can't. No matter how hard I try — with fasting, prayers, meditation — *myself* won't go away. I can't become a pure fire, burning away wick and candle in unity with Lat." He caught his breath. "And so, all this time, I've believed myself to be a failure. But, listening to you, now I don't want to lose myself. Because it's my sympathy that makes me want to help others, and were *myself* to burn away, perhaps I'd become cold like the men and women in that room." He shook his head. "I'm rambling, now. Look, my meaning…if you're going to Qandbajar, I'll go with you."

His eyes shimmered when he spoke. His sincerity, honesty, vulnerability — it pulled me toward him, the way the earth pulls down lightning. Did he feel it, too?

Of course not. I shrugged it off. The Disciples weren't wrong about me — I was sinful. But now, my sinful thoughts were but fantasy. I had not the confidence to try anything, given my ugliness. Kyars honoring our marriage was my only hope of ever having affection.

"Thank you," I said. "It means everything. At least I have you, and…what was his name, again?"

"Kinn."

"Kinn." The book stack in the corner tumbled. On its own.

"Don't do that," Kevah said to the wall. "You'll scare her." He turned to me. "He's just excited you said his name. He's strange like that."

A knock sounded on the door. Kevah yelled, "Enter!" and Sheikh Khizr walked inside, his hood lowered off his head. Kevah and I stood out of respect, then sat back down.

"Cyra," he turned to me, "a terrible thing was done to you. I know you spoke truly, that you're innocent. The Order of Saint Jamshid stands with you."

Those words: a soothing breeze on my ears and more than a flicker of hope in my heart. Many viziers belonged to the Order, as did the heads of several merchant and manufacturing guilds.

Outside the palace gates, only the Philosophers rivaled them for prestige.

"Thank you, sheikh," I said. "That means everything to me."

"That's lovely of the Order," Kevah said, "but what of the Disciples?"

Sheikh Khizr sighed and shook his head. "The Disciples can't be seen getting involved in what could be a succession conflict."

Silence lingered for a moment, as if each of us was surprised. Khizr Khaz, especially, seemed burdened by his words, shaking his head at Kevah's gesture to sit.

"Succession conflict?" I said. "No one is denying Kyars' succession, not that I know of."

"That's where the fog hangs heavy," Sheikh Khizr said. "Few were made aware, but when your brother and the Sylgiz horde surrounded Qandbajar, the palace took measures in case of a prolonged siege. Tamaz sent a letter through the Archers of the Eye to the governor of Merva, his brother Mansur, summoning him to deal with the Sylgiz." He took a deep breath. "By now, Mansur must've heard of his brother's demise. But he also knows how far away Kyars is. An empty throne…I fear it would be too tempting to pass up."

That both surprised and didn't surprise. Of course Tamaz, the wise shah that he was, would've made arrangements in case the negotiations failed. "Are you saying Mansur is going to declare himself Shah, in opposition to Kyars?"

Khizr Khaz sighed as if in mourning. "I'll not hide my part in this any longer — summoning Mansur was my idea. That's why I asked you to leave the room — it's my sin. The man has always been a dear friend and a staunch defender of the Path of the Saints. I feared the Sylgiz, with their fervent cursing of the saints, would level our shrines if ever they entered the city. But now…now I regret this course. Given the timing, Mansur may already be there."

An unwelcome new page had been added to my understanding of this problem. Even so, it didn't fit right. "But Kyars is the designated heir. The proclamation is hanging in the great hall, signed by every governor, Seluqal, and vizier."

"A piece of paper," Kevah said. "What matters is how many gunners you have at your back. Although, Kyars does have tens of thousands of gholam — hard to overcome."

"Hard," Khizr Khaz said, "but hardly impossible. Mansur isn't coming alone. He's bringing Khagan Pashang and twenty thousand Jotrids with him."

Oh Lat. The man who, eight years ago, had torn me from my world and thrown me to the Alanyans, despite once living with my family. The Jotrids were sitting in my blind spot this whole time.

"Pashang is an animal," I said. "What was Tamaz thinking? Why would he summon my tribe's blood enemy to…" I didn't finish asking because the answer was obvious. Of course he'd summon the Jotrids precisely because they hated the Sylgiz and would destroy them if given any chance. Tamaz was as clever as he was wise.

The candle in the corner niche flickered.

"Pashang might be an animal, but he's on a leash," Khizr Khaz said. "And Mansur is holding it. The Disciples want no part of this. They prefer to watch, wait, and see which direction the wind blows."

Were they Disciples of Saint Chisti or cowards?

"This isn't about the succession!" I wished a certain Disciple were sitting here so I could scream in her ear. "Are they going to ignore the soulshifter who began this chaos?"

"A soulshifter in hiding," Khizr Khaz said. "For them, it's only a problem if he acts against the faith or Zelthuriya itself. But for now, the worst thing this soulshifter has done is mutilate a girl and kill a shah."

"That's not bad enough? Cowards! Are they going to wait till the sorcerer is knocking on their door? Till the whole kingdom is in flames? By then, it'll be too late!"

Kevah said, "It's up to us, then. We're not powerless. The three of us are a start." A book in the corner flung open and thudded against the wall. "Four — the four of us!"

Khizr Khaz glanced at the fallen pile of books. "That a nasnas you have haunting you?"

Kevah shook his head. "Worse. A shiqq."

"Exorcised a few of those," Khizr grumbled. "As you were saying — no, we're not powerless, but it might be better if we were. People notice when power takes sides, which is why I won't act directly, not yet. The two of you, however — a girl thought to be dead, a magus in training who no one outside this city knows — could act mostly unseen."

I slammed my fist into my palm. "So you're not going to do anything, either?"

"He's right," Kevah interjected. "If the Order suddenly took up arms against the gholam, with Mansur and the Jotrids and Kyars and his army on the way...even Qandbajar isn't large enough to stew such chaos."

"Maybe that's what we need. Chaos and war to root out Kato, the sorcerer, and the other traitors following them!"

"Or, we expose the sorcerer," Khizr said, "arrest Kato, and assure that Kyars takes the throne. That would be victory, in my eyes." He looked at me. His cheeks loosened, and his lips took a kindly shape — a genuine smile, if there ever was one. "By the way, I was happy to marry you and Kyars. Don't take what the Disciples said about your character to heart. Even in this holy city, great sins stalk us day and night. But in Qandbajar, we eat and breathe sins just to survive. Kyars could do far worse."

That was reassuring, coming from Grand Sheikh Khizr Khaz himself. I nodded, feeling ever-so-slightly restored.

"I'm heading back to Qandbajar, now. Best we travel separately. When you arrive, the Order will have lodging prepared. Kyars is said to be a week's march, and Mansur and Pashang — if my assumptions hold — could arrive any moment. We've a sliver of time to act. And if we fail...Lat help us."

Before he turned to leave, I had to ask, "Sheikh, everyone saw my hand stab the Shah, so why do you believe me?"

Khizr Khaz gazed at the floor as if a memory shown there. Perhaps I should've just accepted his help without asking why. But I needed to know, for the sake of trust, why my allies were my allies.

He smiled and stroked his beard. "They call me *khaz* because I was, once, a warrior. My blade tasted the blood of hundreds — heathens or heretics, all. One of my greatest foes was a certain Sylgiz khagan — Yamar the Young. Your father, Cyra."

I gasped at his mention.

Sheikh Khizr cleared his throat as if preparing a sermon. "About twenty years ago, the first time I faced him. How I looked down on the man. He and his raiders had ransacked a shrine, a hundred miles north of Merva, and were carrying off its valuables when my troop of khazis intercepted them. A bandit — we called your father — nothing more." Khizr Khaz shook his head. "What a blow this so-called bandit dealt us. That was the first and last time I ran from a battle. Truth be told, I have feared you Sylgiz ever since. The ferocity with which you pursue your causes, whether the scant valuables of a shrine or wintering land, inspires a begrudging respect.

"Just as I experienced your father fight that day — thundering at us with nothing but a spear and some frail, leather padding — I saw you fight, in that room, against those Disciples. That's *character*, and if the Disciples can't see it, then they're blind. I'd always prayed to have warriors with hearts like you Sylgiz on our side, because then our side could never lose. You almost made that happen, Cyra. You almost brought them into the light. Just as your father was more than a bandit, you are more than what you think. Far more. And I know that you've the heart to see this through. Bringing to mind how fearlessly your father charged at us and how you didn't cower to those Disciples, I'd rather stand with you than in your way."

• • • •

AFTER SHEIKH KHIZR LEFT, Kevah went to tell the Disciples he was leaving, too. In the meantime, he tasked me with buying a camel for the journey. I wasn't sure what camels cost, but Kevah gave me a pouch of silver and copper coins, so I hoped it would do. I also wasn't certain if he wanted me to buy two camels or one, but I'd probably prefer riding at his back.

While wading through crowds of pilgrims on the way to the camel market, someone grabbed my arm and tugged me off the street into an alley between two mountains. I was about to scream, until I looked upon the hooded man's face: big brown pupils, skin the color of deep soil, and short, ever-curly hair.

"What happened?" Eshe said.

I calmed my breathing, then asked, "How'd you get into the city?"

"I have my ways. And I noticed you have yours. You've been living in the Shrine of Saint Chisti, so I assume you have something good to tell me."

But could I trust Eshe? He'd saved my life, and at great risk. Though I couldn't forget how he kept stuffing seeds into my mouth every time I'd said more than two words.

I summarized what happened. He actually smiled...and didn't stuff seeds into my mouth. I'd heard of such seeds — Hadrith once told me that the Philosophers, through their genius, bred poppy seeds with ten to a hundred times the potency and now produced and sold them as a *palliative*, among other things.

"So good," Eshe said. "Me and a magus, side by side, saving Alanya from a sorcerer. It will surely enliven me more than insulting pimply pashas all day."

Was that why he was doing this? To feel alive? "Can I ask... what did you do to get whipped, thrown off a mountain, and exiled?"

The question seemed to sting as he shut his eyes and slowed his breathing. "I don't think I owe you an explanation."

"I never said you owed me anything. I'm simply curious. People here seem to despise you, but you don't seem like a bad person."

He chuckled. "Have you not realized? Everyone here is bad. The only difference is, I confessed my crimes."

A throng of pilgrims clad in white passed by, chatting in what I guessed was Vograsian, with how soft and smoky it sounded.

I shook my head. "All I know is, you didn't have to save me. Tie my half-dead body to your back and haul me across the desert. I owe you more than I could ever give. So...I don't care what you did to be banished. Whatever it is, it'll never change my opinion of you."

"Sweet words, lady. But sugar dissolves on the tongue. If I told you what I did, you wouldn't look at me like you're doing now. You're probably going to find out anyway, but I'll savor your admiration whilst it lasts."

"If I'm going to find out anyway, better to hear it from you." I clutched his forearm. "What we're attempting is dangerous. If I'm to put my life in your hands again, I need to know everything about you. Right now, Kevah and I have an understanding. But you're not a part of that, and if I wanted, I could shut you out."

He sighed like a slow-blowing sandstorm. "Cup of date wine would help the words flow."

Kevah had mentioned it could take a while for him to sort things out with the Disciples. I supposed we had time.

"Lead the way," I said.

Eshe led me through a maze of alleys between the mountains. We arrived at a sprawling residential area with cave-like houses chiseled throughout the mountainsides. Streams, date palms, and acacias covered the oasis in the central plaza. We sat against a tree, and a vendor from a nearby stall brought us two cups of date wine for two coppers. In Qandbajar, date wine cost ten times as much.

I sipped — sweet and acidic. I recalled Tamaz enjoying date wine while listening to Kashanese poets, who liked to bang on drums as they spouted verse, though few others in the palace seemed to care for it, most preferring grape or cherry wines. It had a simple taste, bouncing between its tangy and sour notes. I wished I could've enjoyed a cup with him, but it was too late. If I could give Tamaz, my brother, and myself justice, it would be small recompense for all the drinks we'd never share.

"Used to love climbing up there." Eshe pointed to a mountain peak in the distance, not too distinct from the others. "To-die-for views. Romantic, even."

"Where are you originally from?" I asked.

"Himyar, by blood and birth. But I grew up far from that land, in Merva. So I am…an Alanyan, I suppose. My father was a merchant. He traded in the usual — spices, silks, ebony, metals — but he'd also trade books. He'd bring wagons of dusty, bulging tomes from Himyar, some the only copies in the world, and sell them to the Philosophers. When the Golden Kingdom fell, vagabonds looted the libraries, as they did all else. My father considered it a duty — a rather profitable one — to recover those books. Spread some light in the world…and make a handy sum thereby."

Perhaps that was Eshe's philosophy, too. Do good and gain. I mean, everyone was trying to gain, but at least it seemed he wanted to do good, as well.

"How'd you become a Disciple?"

He chuckled. "Ah, but what you really want to know is, how did I *unbecome* a Disciple."

I gave him a slow nod.

After a few anxious gulps, he began. "I joined the Disciples with my brother. We'd been part of a saintly order in Merva and were chosen for our upstanding character…as well as a unique familiarity with various obscure methods of sorcery."

"Is that so? Where'd you get such knowledge?"

He tapped his head. "The books my father traded — the rarer ones, we'd copy by hand. It's said that when the Golden Kingdom ruled Himyar, sorcery was rampant — the blood plague was its downfall, after all. My father recovered many sorcerers' tomes, and my brother and I committed several to memory."

"I know you're a bloodwriter. That's how you saved my life."

Eshe nodded. "I am. They say that to gain the power to write with blood, you must be baptized in god's blood. My mother and father told me it rained blood the day I was born."

"Rained…blood?"

He hunched his shoulders. "Don't ask me. The blood plague was a nasty thing, lady."

"Since you can write bloodrunes, can you soulshift as well?"

Eshe shook his head. "No. Even with my knowledge, I don't know how one gains that ability. It's lost to history, I'm afraid."

"Can a soulshifter just possess anyone he wants?"

"Thankfully, no. He can only possess someone whose blood flavor is the same as that of the bloodrune he's using. There's also a range, and each bloodrune can only be used once before needing to be rewritten. So whoever possessed you…it was deliberate."

That, I didn't doubt. For whatever reason, the soulshifter wanted war between the Sylgiz and Alanya, so I was the perfect vessel to stab Tamaz.

The vendor, a kindly old man with spotted skin, walked by and asked if we desired more wine. Eshe and I declined with polite smiles.

"Sorry, you were telling me about how you joined the Disciples."

"What was I saying?" Eshe scratched his thin eyebrow. "Oh, yes. So later, when my brother and I became Disciples, we tracked and investigated reports of sorcery across the three kingdoms, sometimes coming face to face with all manner of terrifying—" He swallowed, hard. "Let me just get the point. Years ago, there was a magus living in Zelthuriya. Her name was Aschere. One day, we overheard her incantations — 'Dreamer,' she kept saying. My brother and I believed she was…that she was calling to something from the void. Something that, itself, called to the Blood Star. That she'd begun worshipping it. Channeling it, to do something truly terrifying."

"Blood Star? I've heard that before, somewhere..."

"There are tribes in the Waste, as well as in the icelands of Yuna, that worship it, though the star itself is no longer visible in the sky, as it was just before the birth of Saint Chisti. But that's a topic for another time. We told the elder Disciples about our suspicions, but they demanded proof. So we followed Aschere around and noticed that she had one friend — an Abyadi girl who sold tea. Sometimes, she'd sit with this girl all day, beneath the sun and the stars. Now Aschere had attained exemplary *fanaa* — she would not eat nor drink nor sleep nor laugh nor smile. What need did she have of this friend? So we followed the tea girl, watched her for weeks. But she was just a normal tea girl — she'd buy leaves at the market, grind tea at her stall, and sell it to the pilgrims. Even used the money to support her sick father."

"And...what happened?"

Eshe took a gulp, shuddered, then tossed his wine on the grass. "I'll just say it. One day while the girl was walking to her stall, we pulled her off the street, stuck seeds in her mouth, and wrapped her in a sack. Took her a few miles from the city, where no one could hear us. I'll never forget her crying, her screaming, her trembling when we woke her. We kept asking her about Aschere, about what they'd talked about, but the girl had nothing to say. So I..."

Already, this story was disturbing enough. "What did you do?"

"I cut her at the wrist, took a cup of her blood, and started writing bloodrunes across her body. Runes that caused...indescribable pain. Runes that would never wash away. I wrote them on her face. Across her thighs. Wherever I could...but no matter what, she wouldn't tell us what Aschere was up to."

Already, I didn't want to hear anymore. Already, my view of this man had plunged when I'd promised nothing could change it. What he described seemed all wrong. The Disciples were supposed to protect the weak and innocent, not torture them. Disgust pooled in my hoarsening throat.

"Why?" I shook my head. "Why did you go so far?"

Eshe couldn't look me in the eye, gazing instead at my wine cup, as if he regretted dumping his. "Because…I didn't want what happened in Himyar to happen here. I felt it my duty to protect the Faith and believed the suffering of one young girl couldn't weigh against that of a kingdom." He sighed, almost in relief. Perhaps it felt good to tell someone his pain. "But…seeing what we did…we took her to the Disciples and admitted our crimes. Accepted punishment. The sheikhs whipped us, then they threw my brother and me off that," he pointed to the mountain peak from earlier, which he'd said had *romantic views*, "a view to die from. As we were falling, my brother pulled me on top of him. He cracked his back and broke my fall. I wrote every healing rune I could across his body, but no bloodrunes I knew could mend broken bones, nor did I possess the flavor to save him." He looked up at me, tears spilling. "So…lady…what do you think of me, now?"

12

ZEDRA

I AM NAUGHT BUT A SERVANT. AND I'M NOT BEING HUMBLE, BUT rather reminding myself of a simple truth: I'm not doing this for myself. I sipped *fanaa* hundreds of years ago, but it has since left me. Once, I was the fire that burned without a wick, without a candle, without even air. And I burned for one thing: Lat and her Children.

Because we were one once and will be in Paradise. But if the Great Terror comes, then we would be remade in fire, and our souls shredded, mixed in a sea, and recycled into other creations, the like of which no mind can comprehend.

Father Chisti warned of this when he walked the earth a thousand years ago. But you won't find it in the Recitals of Chisti because the saint-kings twisted his teachings. To the saint worshippers, the Great Terror is inevitable — simply the cataclysm that precedes the end of the world and the Day of Reckoning. To us, it must be stopped, or else there won't be a reckoning, nor a thousand hells and a thousand paradises in which to dwell. There simply won't be anything we can understand.

I reminded myself of these truths every day so that I acted

167

mindfully. To direct my will toward the ultimate truths, that was my worship, not moving my head and prostrating and singing praises.

"Testimony!" Kato's shout sliced through my thoughts. I focused on the surrounding happenings in the great hall, where Kato was running his public *inquiries.*

"I have given testimony!" the shrill and quavering kohl-faced vizier said. "I've nothing to hide!"

Kato's laugh was iron-steady. "Am I to believe that you *gave* Ozar those ships out of a loving trust? Where are the contracts? If, as you claim, he paid you twenty thousand, there should be a piece of paper!"

The vizier's face reddened like rosebuds. "You ever earned a copper in your life, Himyarite? When men of esteem give their word, it is enough!"

Kato leaned back upon the dais. "Is that all I am to you? A base Himyarite? Darker than a dirty dog's paws? Too bad I am, at this moment, the only one who can save you. And I've heard enough."

I recalled Kato mentioning how much he despised this ship-master vizier. The man had tried to sell Crucian slaves into the gholam, like they did in Sirm's janissary army, to undermine the dominant Himyarite faction who were fiercely loyal to Kato.

Kato gestured to his gholam. The gold-coated warriors grabbed the vizier's arms and dragged him cursing out of the great hall. He'd be sharing the old barrack with dozens of Ozar's friends and Kato's enemies.

That was where Kato put them, rather than the dungeon of the Sand Palace. The old barrack was a rundown compound just outside the palace walls that, decades ago, housed the gholam. It was getting crowded in there. And I had my own designs on it, which I'd have to enact soon — though, unfortunately, I had no bloodrunes in the old barrack.

With a Kashanese steed and a few hundred riders, Kyars could arrive within days. Little time was left to put everything in motion, and yet I needed to know more. More about the man I'd put on strings.

Vera wheeled me to my room and placed me in the closet. Perfect timing: Kato was leaving the palace as I landed atop the simurgh statue. I fluttered overhead and followed him out the gate as he joined the clamor of Qandbajar's thoroughfare. After hailing a carriage, he didn't turn west toward the gholam barrack but east toward the Alleys of Mud.

Drongos have an acute smelling sense — all their senses are heightened, actually — so I almost fell out of flight from the wafting of open gutters. But Kato didn't seem to mind. He walked into a pleasure house, known to be frequented by laborers and tradesmen and sailors. Strange, considering all pleasure houses were closed today for some saint's birthday.

Black drapes covered the windows, so I stood on the roof and listened. Honed my hearing on the happenings in the pleasure house. A jingling — Kato had just handed a bag of coins to someone. The thrumming of fur or something like it, the light scratching of a scalp — he'd rubbed the hair of a child. Then he said, "He's growing strong."

A woman with a tender voice replied, "He'll make a good soldier, one day."

Kato grunted. "Anything but that. Tell the tutor to smack him if he doesn't focus — I won't begrudge it, so long as it doesn't leave a mark. Next time I come, I'll bring *Atash and the Simurgh* — the boy better be able to read it. At least sound out the words. I'll rip out the pictures if I must."

I felt tiny vibrations as the young woman nodded. "Of course, pasha. I'll make certain he does." While the deference in her voice was plain, I didn't sense fear, despite her talking to the most powerful man in the city.

I flew overhead as Pasha Kato traveled to another dwelling, this one in the Glass District. Floral curtains covered the glass walls of the building, which didn't seem like a pleasure house and had a small garden of potted plants atop. I listened as Kato took a crying baby in his arms. With an unexpectedly soothing voice, he hummed a Himyaric lullaby and rocked her gently. A lovely song about animals — the words for tiger, lion, and eagle were the same in Paramic. I wasn't sure why I understood what wasn't the same, but I did. Perhaps I'd picked up Himyaric somewhat by being among so many gholam, though they almost never spoke it around me.

I noted he didn't give this woman any money; considering she lived in the Glass District, I doubt she needed him to.

Kato said, "Lat wouldn't bless Tamaz with a daughter." It almost sounded like he was tearing up. "Yet she blessed me, a mere slave. Next time, I'll bring books. They have a whole shelf for early reading in the Tower. You must start her now, make her eager to learn."

"What will she do with books?" the woman asked, her voice somewhat hoarse. She was clearly older than the girl in the pleasure house.

"She will do whatever she wants," Kato said. "I tell you, Kyars is not like his father. The man is a visionary. And he is strong. He'll break the Fount's hold on the people and crush the corrupt viziers. Alanya will be a land where even a girl with no name can rise, so long as she's knowledgeable."

Was Kato's blade not as double-sided as I thought? He really did admire Kyars. How much harder would it be to set them against each other?

The woman said, "What you're saying makes me hopeful, Kat." Was that his pet name? Adorable.

"In the new Alanya, all will be remade. The strong will become weak, and the weak will become strong. The slaves masters, and the masters slaves. I'll make sure of it."

Kato exuded palpable excitement. Giddiness, even. Did he really believe Kyars, who perfumed his bathwater with a special rose petal that only grew within caves on the snow-capped peak of Mount Azad in Kashan, would upend a system that put him at the very top? My mother once told me, *"Power and wealth do not change a man — they only reveal him."* Kyars was naked to me. He'd never spoken of any grand plans to redesign Alanya, and he'd rarely sought the conflicts needed for that. Perhaps these were Kato's delusions. But they cemented him to his master — a problem.

Most likely, Kyars knew what to tell people to gain their support. He'd likely painted a different vision to Hadrith, and yet another to each vizier and governor whose support he would need to gain and keep power. I knew from the start that I wasn't dealing with fools, but with men whose own cleverness matched or exceeded mine. But even the most cunning had weaknesses to exploit. And as Pasha Kato kissed the cheek of his cooing daughter, I was relieved I'd found his.

I SENT Vera to the Tower of Wisdom to ask if *Flavors of Blood Volume Two* was available. Meanwhile, I tried walking in my room. Mirima was looking after baby Seluq since I couldn't care for him in my state, and so much time apart threatened to break my already strained mind. Despite a few successes, my limbs jittered, and I was cut off from all I'd known and loved...and would always be — though what mattered was whether I acted on these sad, poisonous feelings. Till now, I'd acted to further the cause; the few times I'd let my emotions take over had nearly brought my downfall.

I could walk, but each step seemed to bruise my muscles and buckle my bones, as if I were old again. Was this punishment for getting two soul vessels killed — the rat first and Cyra shortly after? In Vogras, I once soulshifted into an eagle to spy on the movements of Saint-King Nasar's army, and then that eagle had a heart attack while soaring across a cloud, barely surviving. It took months to feel like myself again.

By hobbling from my bed to my balcony, I made some progress. I plopped on the pillow-filled couch and enjoyed the noon breeze.

Closed my mind to every awful thing I'd done and would do. Tried to taste *fanaa* — perfect stillness — though it had been too long.

Vera woke me with a tap on my shoulder. She wasn't carrying the book. "It's past due, they said."

I yawned and stretched. "They'll recover it. Should take a few days — if whoever has it didn't run off. But who would so foolishly risk the Philosophers' whip?"

Vera hunched her shoulders. "Isn't it a healer's tome? May I ask, sultana, what you mean to do with it?"

The girl had gotten curious. Bothersome for me; dangerous for her. "My dear, it merely has some insights on how to help me heal." How quickly the lies flew from my tongue since moving to this palace.

"You told everyone that you fainted. What does that have to do with blood?"

I glared at her.

"Apologies, sultana." She bent her neck as if I were a Seluqal. Good. "I just worry about you. You're always going in that closet."

"As I told you, I used to sleep in a wooden chest as a child. Reminds me of home. I feel good in there."

"I can tell." When I tried to look away, Vera followed my eyes. "It's like you're carrying stones on your back. I wish you'd tell me what's wrong."

"Nothing I can't handle alone, dear."

"But why should you? What else am I here for, sultana, than to ease your burdens? Cyra would tell me her frustrations, and I'd ease them…however I could. I'm a good listener and better at solving problems than I look."

A part of me wanted to share this burden. But my son and I were the last of the Children, and so it was ours alone. Some heathen girl could never understand what it meant to be a part of god. A part that had been severed and left to die.

Trumpets blared in the distance. No, it was a deeper sound: long horns. The wail of long horns disturbed the breeze and reawakened my worries. What could be happening now? Vera helped me off the couch and toward the balcony railing.

Far beyond the city wall, haze covered the fields and dunes at the horizon. I squinted to see. Vera pushed half her body off the railing to get a good look.

That wasn't haze. It was sand. Sand kicked up by horses. Hundreds of them. Thousands, their line stretching a vast distance. They trotted toward the city from the north. Could it be Kyars? But how could he be here so soon? And he would've come from the west, not the north.

The horses were…pulling something. No, not something — many, many things. They resembled…domes…but patterned and formed of cloth. Yurts? As the horses approached the wall, they slowed, and the haze cleared. Riders pulled a city of yurts on massive flat wagons. I considered ordering Vera to leave and shifting into the bird to get a closer look, but a better idea came to mind.

"Vera, take me to Kato. Now."

She helped me into my chair, and we departed. Pasha Kato was in the great hall, sitting upon the dais and talking with other gholam. Vera wheeled me to him, and I asked, "Pasha, what is happening?"

A tender smile stretched across his face. Visiting his children must've warmed his heart. "Nothing you need worry over."

"I am worried," I said. "My beloved is not yet here, and there is another army come to our walls. By Lat, who are they?"

He ordered the gholam to go away. Once they'd walked to the far side, he gestured for me to come closer. Vera wheeled me forward, my knees almost touching his.

"The other day, you said something about rats and bait. Well, looks like the rats have come barreling into the trap."

"Rats? That's a horde!" I reminded myself to stay calm. "Is it the Sylgiz? Have they returned?"

If only I'd noticed it while flying. Riding from the north meant the horde had come through the Zelthuriyan Desert, and the drongo never flew that route, so I'd not had the chance to see anything while soulshifting into it.

"Looks like you don't know everything." Kato seemed to savor my ignorance, his ear-to-ear smile so smug. "That horde is under the command of Mansur."

"Mansur? The governor of Merva? Tamaz's brother?"

"The same. Tamaz asked him to come, with the Jotrids, to deal with the Sylgiz. And yet, the Sylgiz are no longer here. Now, let me ask you — why do you think Mansur still came?"

Tamaz had done *what?* By Lat, this whole time I'd assumed I'd completely outmaneuvered that old man. But it seemed I only got lucky because had things played out the way they seemed to be — and I could still hear the long horns — then Jotrid guns would've driven off the Sylgiz and sundered my plan.

That it all worked out, in the end, was surely a blessing from Lat and not a result of my cleverness.

"Must I repeat my question?" Kato said with a disappointed sigh.

"Mansur is here because…because…" I knew nothing about the man, other than what I'd already stated. He was not part of my considerations at all!

Kato chuckled. "We're not yet close enough to finish each other's sentences, but allow me. Mansur is here to dip his toes. See if he has support to…" He pointed with his thumb at the throne behind him.

What!? For once, I didn't have to pretend to be shocked. "Kato… are you saying that Mansur wants to be Shah?"

"Shh!" Kato put his forefinger between us. "I know it's terrifying to hear, given your son and all, but worry not — Mansur doesn't have the support. Kyars spent the past decade forging bonds with everyone, from the lowliest dungeon sweeper to the grandest of grandiose viziers. He didn't take that paper for grant-ed." Kato pointed to the proclamation hanging above the golden divan, in which Tamaz named Kyars his successor. "So relax. Mansur will come and go, weaker for it."

I let out an anxious breath and shook my head. "But Kyars is not yet here. And you're rather confident for a man with few allies in a city surrounded by enemies. If I were you, I'd stop putting viziers in prison, lest they see their salvation in the hands of another."

"Heh. I have you, don't I?" He raised a playful eyebrow. "An alliance with the cleverest woman in the city must count for something. I'd be more *poetic*, but it may offend the little ears of the girl who wheels you around."

I turned to Vera. She was standing two paces back, her gaze on the ground, pretending not to listen.

The more I thought about it, the worse this problem seemed. Mansur had come with the Jotrids, and that meant he'd brought Khagan Pashang, a man renowned for his disregard of human suffering. Or rather, his delight for it.

"I have the most wondrous idea," Kato said, raising a meaty finger. "You, Zedra, will welcome them yourself. Tamaz's wife never leaves her room, but you and Mirima are worldly women who will convince Mansur that his pretext for being here doesn't exist."

That actually was in my interest. I had to learn what Mansur pretended to want, and what he really wanted. Kato's assumptions rang true, but his overconfidence rattled my bones. Unless he knew something I didn't, he was downplaying the threat and endangering us.

"Honestly, I've been feeling rather useless since my accident. What you've suggested would do wonders for my spirit."

Kato clapped. "You see? I do have an ally in this city." His smile reached his ears again. "And what a wonderful ally she is."

WE TRAVELED by carriage to the Shrine of Saint Jamshid, a yellow-domed, archway-covered compound that could hold a thousand worshippers. It had been cleared out for this Seluqal visit. Within the sepulcher, which was surrounded by a cage, lay the green shroud that encased Shah Tamaz's body, aside other green shrouds — all deplorable men who didn't deserve reverence. One day, if I succeeded, we could burn these bodies and throw them where they'd be forgotten.

Mansur, Tamaz's brother, wore a beige caftan that barely dropped beyond his ankles and leather socks with the typical gold-flecked pointy shoes. He stood and prayed for what felt like an eternity, an entourage of his mirror-armored household guard at his back. Khagan Pashang had decided not to come, it seemed, which unsettled me.

Though not entirely proper since we were in the men's section, I had Vera wheel me forward. The desert air must've dried up Mansur's face; flaky skin surrounded his thin, shaped eyebrows.

"My brother adored the great saint," he said, "first of the saint-kings. Always said he would model himself on the holy man, and now look — they are entombed together."

Jamshid the Usurper, we called him. No, he and Tamaz were not alike. The stories these saint worshippers told conveniently omitted the horrors Jamshid inflicted upon the Children. Tamaz was not so cruel.

"He truly was the spirit of our saint," I said, choking up. "I called him Father."

"That must have pleased my brother. He prayed for a daughter. Ended up having three daughters, but Lat took away what he wanted and gave him what he needed. Two strong boys, last I saw them — now they must be men, hardened by wars against the infidel."

"You're so right, Your Eminence," I said, bending my neck. Mansur was a Seluqal, after all. "Kyars, may Lat bless his reign, is the best of men. Stronger than a lion." I tried to recall some of the flowery wonders from Laughter Square. "Wiser than a saint.

Gentler than a summer breeze. Under him, our kingdom will prosper as it did under his father. I have no doubt."

Mansur nodded and smiled. He'd dyed his hair black, though left his whiskers and beard gray. An odd look, to say the least. "You're a lovely girl. Kyars is fortunate to have you. You know, it's all so…strange…that this tragedy happened while Kyars was on campaign."

"Is it, though? Isn't the best time for assassins to strike while the army is away?"

His belittling chuckle wasn't endearing. "Dear girl, the games people play for power…you wouldn't believe them. They are so layered, so many-faced, so filled with misdirection. Which is why I'm here." An obviously false quavering took over. "When our father tried to have me strangled, it was Tamaz who stopped him. It was Tamaz who convinced him to add me to the line of succession, so I would not have to die. And yet, where was I to stop Tamaz's killers? All I have is a dream of justice." He sniffled, then dried his eyes with a kerchief. "No, I will not allow his killers to go unpunished and will root them out from wherever they lie. I do not trust these viziers and gholam — Lat knows which of them plotted with the killers."

So, *justice* was his pretext. How boring.

Mirima's wail punctured the air. In her airy white mourning gown, she knelt before the sepulcher and pushed her hand through the cage, as if Tamaz would wake up and take it.

I pretended to sob a little. "Of course, Your Eminence. You are so right. I feel so much better now that *family* is here. I've been waiting ceaselessly for my beloved to return — oh, it feels like this torture will never end."

He lowered himself so we could be eye to eye, despite wincing as his knees bent. "My dear, you and the other women shall have no fear now that we have come. Injustice and rebellion will be cast from this city."

"But surely—" I swallowed a sob, "surely Kyars will be here

within days. And he, as Shah, is the fount of justice. Is all this really needed? When I saw the warhorses and heard the blaring of long horns, I almost fainted."

Mansur sighed. "They work for me. Worry not, my dear." Oh, I worried — from what I'd heard, Khagan Pashang liked to use his enemies as seating whilst he supped. "Khagan Pashang has been a loyal retainer to the Seluqals of Alanya. Not so long ago, he helped me crush a rebellion in Merva. Path of the Children have new roots there, it seems — Lat knows how they keep resurfacing. The slaves, especially, seem to love their vile message. Pashang, on the other hand, is a slayer of heretics, infidels, rebels, and traitors, and I know he'll render such service here...if needed."

I smiled and said, "That's reassuring. Those Sylgiz were so deceitful and wretched. I'm sure these Jotrids are nothing like them."

He stood and cast a cool gaze upon me. "Couldn't be more different. Pashang has promised to hunt the Sylgiz for their part in this crime. I'll leave matters outside this city to him. But within, I am the hunter, dear girl." This *hunter* hadn't even bothered to learn my name. "I suspect this plot goes far deeper than anyone realizes. The Grand Vizier's son is a good friend of Kyars — what would he gain from plotting with the Sylgiz to kill the Shah? Ozar, whom I've hosted at my palace countless times, is no revolutionary, either. I'd be interested to hear what they have to say. Another reason why I rushed over — I fear they may be silenced, by the true deviants, before their story can be heard."

A rather astute conclusion, and somewhat worrying. Whom did Mansur suspect, I wondered? Would he cast aspersions on his nephew to seek the throne for himself?

Considering the surprisingly clever moves Cyra made before her demise, I ought not to underestimate anyone. Mansur didn't *seem* too sharp or vicious, and so I didn't find him threatening — especially compared to my image of Pashang — but perhaps he wanted everyone to let down their guards. That was my game, after all, and it'd served me well.

A young sheikh began reciting the Recitals of Chisti, which echoed off the leaf-colored dome above our heads. Curse the saints! I wanted to plug my ears rather than hear that forgery, though his melody was rather pleasant, despite being so mournful.

"Pasha Kato has been interrogating the viziers," I said. "He's made it all open, so everyone can assess their guilt or innocence. He has done wonderfully keeping us safe. The man does not sleep, does not tire, barely eats — he means to safeguard this city until Kyars returns."

"Kato — loyal, yes. I like Kato. But we tend to only see what we're looking for. Kato is a warrior, so he sees a brandished sword. But more subtle weapons may lay in wait for Kyars. No, to safeguard this city, I will need to begin my own investigation. Curious, also, that my good friend Khizr Khaz has run off to Zelthuriya at such a critical moment. Perhaps he fled in fear of the true menace. If Kyars returned today and sat the throne, I'd be worried for his safety. No, it is good I've come first. His nest must be cleansed of vipers."

I let my tears flow. Let Mansur comfort me with his bravado. A brandished sword, I didn't have; tears, frailty, innocence — those were my weapons. Let the battle begin; I'd rip out their hearts when they were done devouring each other.

AFTER MANSUR DEPARTED for the palace, Vera and I traveled by carriage to the Archers of the Eye training ground. With Mansur in the city and Pashang just outside, it was crucial I gained influence and leverage with the Archers, so I could control what messages Kyars received. He still had the largest and most heavily gunned army, and now I feared I might have to use it.

It was on that ride that I began to feel as if I were swimming in a deep sea, trying to reach the light at the surface — a light that kept receding. No matter how much I swam, I remained in darkness, drowning. But surely, it wasn't so hopeless. I needed to redouble my pace, despite not being able to walk.

Unfortunately, I wasn't a bird, so couldn't fly past the guard at the walkway's entrance. He wore the Archer uniform: a white dress that ended just above his dark knees. A few springy ribbons adorned his otherwise plain front — a foreign outfit and inexplicably ugly.

I knew little about Ethosian orders, but the Archers were a large one. An Ethosian order serving a Latian palace in a vital capacity — only one thing could cement such a union: mountains of gold. I suspected other royal families must have vied for their services, but Alanya outbid them.

Vera said to the guard, "This is Sultana Zedra, the beloved of Crown Pri—of His Glory, Shah Kyars. She wishes to tour the grounds and acquaint herself with your order."

The guard looked at us, stupefied. Then he whistled to someone, who jogged up to him. They whispered to each other, and the other man ran inside.

The guard put his hand on his heart. "Please wait a moment."

A minute later, a giant of a man approached. His dense black beard dropped to his waist; it alone was larger than Vera. He wore a white caftan and simple leather sandals — a thoroughly Alanyan outfit. But where did they sew clothes that large?

"Sultana," he said, "the palace did not tell us you were coming."

I smiled up at him. "Just how I prefer it. A surprise. So I can see what this place is really like, not what it's like when the Shah's beloved is visiting."

"Very good, sultana. Allow me to introduce myself. I am Grandmaster Abunaisaros of the Archers of the Eye. If it pleases you, call me Abu."

"Abu it is."

We followed him to a canopied sitting area aside the training field. All the while, Abu explained the history of the order and their role in Alanya. They were called Archers of the Eye by the Alanyans because when Shah Hazam invaded the Labash kingdom, more than a hundred years ago, most of his soldiers returned an eye fewer than when they'd departed. Despite my pressing, Abu would not admit their secret, laughing whenever I asked how they were so superior to a gholam archer, or even the horse archers from the Endless.

"The blood plague ravaged Labash, so now we are here," he said. "Alanya is our home. Some believe we serve only because we are paid to, but the truth is, we love this land. And we would die for it. The Seluqals have ever been good to us."

An enlightening story, but I had to state the obvious. "You were warriors...but now, you're glorified messengers."

He offered me some nuts — puffy and round. Some kind of Labashite refreshment. I declined with a polite smile. Vera popped one in her mouth. Then another.

"We are whatever the Shah needs us to be," he said. "We don't yearn for battle, but we will fight if called upon. And Archangel help the eyes of whoever stands against us."

How confident. I liked that. Even tried a nut, which I wanted to spit but scarfed down to not offend. The syrup within was disturbingly sweet, nauseatingly so.

On the field, the red-haired woman shot arrows at a suit of armor hundreds of feet away. She gazed at the sky, aimed at the declining sun, and loosed. It arced for a lifetime and landed in the grass by the armor.

"Fuck!" she shouted.

I chuckled, then pointed at her. "How peculiar, Abu. All around, I see men. Labashites. Clad in your white dresses. And then, in the midst of it all, one Karmazi girl wearing the garb of a horse tribe." Nearby, a group of young Archers sat, passed around a pipe, and watched her. I gestured to them with my head. "And your men seem to like it. Rather too much, perhaps."

Abu bit his lip, then stroked his unbelievable beard. "We let her practice here."

"Why?"

"She won a bet."

"Oh? Against whom?"

He smiled wide, admitting it was him. "Got lucky. Even an Archer of the Eye can have a bad day. But the girl is good. Very good. Not quite Archer good, obviously, but I've given her permission to practice with us. To learn from us. She wants to enter the archery tourney. I don't allow my men to take part in that, for obvious reasons."

"Well, you'd win every time."

"Precisely. It wouldn't be fair. We'd be resented. As Ethosians, we don't need more of that."

The girl wiped off sweat with a towel and walked by our low table. Abu whistled to her, and she approached.

"This is Sultana Zedra," he said, "beloved of Shah Kyars. She was just admiring your form."

Sweat still dotted her forehead and dripped off her wavy locks. Looked like she'd been practicing for hours. She wrapped the towel over her shoulders. "Pleased to meet you, sultana."

"Please, sit," I said.

"I...I should bathe first. Or at least change clothes."

"No need. I insist." I gestured at the floor cushion beside Vera.

The Karmazi girl sat, then folded her arms.

"What's your name?" I asked.

"Sa...Safia," she said, her gaze on the wooden table.

"You barely know your own name, dear." I chuckled to show it was a jest. "Safia is a lovely one. Your namesake is Saint Chisti's daughter." How lovely to hear it again, after so long. An unheard-of name in today's Alanya, though.

She nodded, not even looking in my eyes. "I see. It was my grandmother's name, too."

Why was she so coy? Something about coyness made me

overeager to draw out the truths from a person. I'd done so with my cousins and nieces and nephews.

"I like your outfit," I said, "reminds me of my homeland. But the Vogras Mountains and the Karmaz Mountains couldn't be more different."

"I wear what suits me." She spoke almost in a whisper. "Nice thing about Alanya, no one cares."

How strange to phrase it like that. "Last I checked, the Karmaz Mountains are in Alanya. Are you not from here, dear?"

Obviously, if she had a rare blood flavor flowing through her, she couldn't be just any Karmazi. Most Karmazi women in this city — the young ones, at least — worked as dancers or serving girls or even in pleasure houses. Ornaments for their exotic features. But this girl spoke Paramic with a lofty accent, and she had bested the Grandmaster of the Archers of the Eye in a bet. What was her story, why did she have a rare flavor of blood, and why was she so careful with her words?

"I'm rather tired, sultana." She tugged on her towel nervously. "Apologies if I've been short with you. I'd like to go home and rest, if that's acceptable."

I forced a smile, but within, frustration reigned. "Of course, dear. I'd like to speak with you again, some other time, when you're refreshed."

She nodded, got up, and walked away.

Before I departed too, I pricked my finger on a needle I'd brought, then wrote a soulshifting rune on the underside of the table. My seeker's blood would be good enough to possess another with seeker's blood. Perhaps even Abu himself, though I couldn't rely on that assumption.

In any case, the events of this morning had thrown everything on its head, and so it was time to return to the palace, lock myself in my room, and think on what to do next.

. . .

I FELL asleep on the carriage ride to the palace. Old age. Once the carriage stopped at the gate, Vera shook me awake. She stepped outside to ask my gholam escort to unpack my chair.

But instead, she screamed.

"Vera?"

No answer. One window faced the thoroughfare and the other the palace wall, so I couldn't see what'd happened. Barely able to stand on my weak knees, I crawled out the door.

Mirima and Mansur stood at the gate with a troop of Mansur's mirror-armored guards. One was tying Vera's hands behind her back.

"What the hell are you doing?" I said, clinging to the carriage door to stay standing.

Mansur huffed. "This girl was handmaid to the assassin herself. Instead of being interrogated, Kato allowed her to enter your care." He shook his head in disgust. "It's a good thing I came. You can't leave justice's pursuit to a Himyarite slave."

"She's done nothing wrong!" I said. "Release her at once!"

Mansur sniggered. "Your heart is too soft, my dear. Surely the assassin's very own handmaid must have some information. Whether culpable or not herself, who knows what she's witnessed? Even the smallest, overlooked detail could unravel the truth masked behind the lies."

I turned to Mirima. "Sultana, Vera was in my service far longer than she was in Cyra's. Kyars is the one who bought her. Should harm come to her—"

"Kyars didn't buy her — I did," Mirima said, her hands clasped at her navel. "I know she's a decent girl. It will only be a questioning, nothing more."

Tears streamed down Vera's cheeks. Her face glowed red and her eyes widened. I, too, wanted to cry but preferred to show strength.

"Don't worry, dear," I said as a gholam finally brought my chair. I dropped onto the seat, my knees strained from standing so long.

"I won't let them harm you." But it wasn't her harm I worried about as much as what she knew. If she told Mansur that I'd asked her to bring me Cyra's blood, and if Hadrith told him about the bloodrunes, that would be enough to expose me.

Curse the saints! Mansur had only just arrived but wasted no time in asserting his authority. I needed time to plan, but he seemed to be rushing for the throne, perhaps out of fear that Kyars could return at any moment. Absent the comfort of time, a breathlessness overtook me, and I strained for air.

"I don't know anything," Vera said between sobs. "Cyra never confided in me!"

Mansur and his guards escorted her inside the gate. I looked on in disquiet and loosened my caftan's collar to breathe better. For now, all I could do was watch and worry and pray this wouldn't be the beginning of the end.

13

CYRA

Turned out a camel costs as much as a decent pair of gold-plated pearl earrings — we'd bargained hard to get what *little* we got. So I had to ride behind Eshe again, though thankfully not tied to him. Kevah's absurdly small camel trailed ours — the seller claimed it to be a full-grown, but it was no larger than a donkey! And thus we began the three-day journey to Qandbajar.

Eshe, who wore a paper-thin caftan and tight headwrap that wasn't quite a turban, turned to me and said, "I heard the magus can fly. It might, you know, shorten the travel time."

I dabbed sweat off my cheeks with a checkered scarf I'd bought for a copper. "I'm not looking forward to this slow roast either, but hundreds of Archer of the Eye stations lie between here and Qandbajar, and I think they'd notice us flying overhead."

Given how cloudless it had been, that was certain. No, we couldn't risk being noticed. If the soulshifter was alerted to us, it could endanger everything. For now, only the three of us, the Disciples, and Khizr Khaz were aware, and given that I mistrusted the Disciples and didn't know what to expect from the Order of Saint Jamshid, worries burdened worse than this scorch.

Because Kevah's camel was so small, ours bore all our belongings. So behind me sat a bundle containing food and clothes. That meant I could lean on it, which gave rest to my back, though I still had to cling onto Eshe's whip-scarred shoulders to stay steady. A camel's gait was rhythmic once you let your body sway with it — not as smooth as a Kashanese horse, but those didn't do well in the desert.

Ironic, because it wasn't long until we came upon horse tracks. Thousands of tracks, as if a horde had crossed these sands. The three of us dismounted to inspect them: the hoofprints were small, typical of Kashanese horses. Aside the tracks, the bones of herd animals were being picked clean by squawking, red-winged vultures.

"Sheikh Khizr had mentioned the Jotrids," I said, "but why cross the desert when they could more easily cross the scrub?"

Kevah bent down to examine the tracks, which remained fresh due to the still wind. "I've sent Kinn to scout ahead. Best we know what we're riding into."

Eshe guzzled from his waterskin. "I can't think of any reason why they'd pass this way. Unless their horses eat sand."

Kevah chuckled. "I heard about a horse that shits gold. How about one that eats sand and shits gold — wouldn't that be perfect?" He and Eshe laughed. I didn't think it was that funny. Probably because I was fixated on something. On one man: Khagan Pashang.

Back in Zelthuriya, when I'd explained to Kevah that Eshe would be joining us and retold the man's exile story, he shrugged it off and said, "I was a janissary. We reaved our way through Yuna. Can't say my hands are bloodless." Also, when I mentioned Aschere, Kevah closed his eyes, looked away, and clenched his jaw, as if overcome by pain. But when I asked if that name meant something, he just shook his head.

I didn't want to pry into someone's pain, so left it at that. Perhaps one day, he'd tell me. We'd all tasted pain and also dished it to others, many deserving, but some undeserving, too. None of us were saints. But Khagan Pashang…the things he was known for…

He'd done the Seluqal's dirty work for years. Tamaz had even imprisoned him, more than once, but just for show, because he often relied on the Jotrids to maintain control over Merva, the restive eastern province of the kingdom.

"Eshe, didn't you say you're from Merva?" I asked. "You ought to know what the Jotrids are capable of."

"Indeed," Eshe said, his grin going flat. "I remember when the Path of the Children were secretly forming a militia, claiming that the return of the Guided was at hand. Governor Mansur didn't want to get his hands dirty, so he called in Khagan Pashang." Eshe shuddered. "Well, he crushed the rebels, all right. First, he got the family books from the palace archive. Anyone who was even suspected of being a rebel, he wouldn't touch. He'd take the family, then go one generation above, and take those families, too. He sent them all to an old mine, left food and water inside, then sealed the entrance." Eshe gulped.

"Oh Lat," I gulped too. I'd heard this story once, and didn't want to hear it again, but listened to remind myself of the man who'd kidnapped me — and the boy who'd sat with my family for meals and raced horses with my brother and me.

Eshe continued, "Pashang brought the men accused of joining this militia to the mine entrance, just to hear the screams of their families trapped inside. Once the food and water ran out…well, you can imagine. The screams turned…inhuman. Every day, he'd make the rebel men hear the shrieks of their families as they ate and ripped each other apart. Until, one day, it went dead silent." Eshe shut his eyes — hard. This next part always froze my blood. "And then, if the stories are to be believed, something broke that silence — laughter. Utterly maniacal and insane laughter. The laughter of Ahriyya himself. Khagan Pashang let the rebel militiamen go, but none had the heart to fight. Not anymore."

"You tell it as if you were there," I said, putting my hand on Eshe's shoulder.

Eshe shook his sweaty head. "It's not that — one of the families sealed in the mine used to work for my mother. Good people… though, yes, they were heretics. It broke my mother to learn what happened to them. How is it that in this kingdom, we let Ethosians and all manner of infidel worship what they wish, but fellow worshippers of Lat on a different path are so cruelly crushed?"

Even Kevah seemed rocked by that story, discomfort obvious in his gaze. "Because aside from coastal raiding, the Ethosians aren't a threat to the Seluqals here, like they are to the Seluqals where I'm from. The Alanyan kingdom was built on that of the saint-kings, who built their kingdom upon the graves of Chisti's descendants, the Children. They'll always haunt this place." Kevah sighed, long and weary. "Now, as a practical consideration, I suggest conserving water. A horde has been through here, so the oases' wells are likely dry."

"He wasn't always like that," I said, trying to wrap my head around how Pashang had become so depraved. "I think it started after his father took him on a ranging into the deepest part of the Waste — a place we call the Red for the color of its sky. Lat knows what he saw there, but he left a boy and returned a monster, his father's flesh inside him." That was what Cihan had told me, anyway.

Kevah said, "I think we know enough to conclude — let's avoid Pashang and get to Qandbajar."

We rode on, but Kevah's camel lagged, so we often slowed so it could catch up. You'd think the Disciples would've given him more support, but according to Kevah, they were disappointed he was leaving without the allegiance of a single jinn tribe, which meant that he was a magus in name, not ability. Still, they couldn't stop him because he'd *made the covenant with Lat herself* and so only she could punish him.

I wished I were riding with him. I mean, that camel had an oversized head on a small body with a tiny hump, but that only meant our bodies would be closer. Such thoughts were obviously wrong since I still pinned my hopes on Kyars accepting me, but I couldn't help it.

All day, we rode. Eshe and I chatted about everything: his life growing up in Merva and mine growing up in the Waste and Qandbajar. At one point, his father owned fifty slaves, he claimed, and they served him in a house larger than Governor Mansur's palace. But when the slaves in Merva revolted when Eshe was still a boy, they burned his house and almost killed his family, and so his father and mother decided to live more modestly. They joined a saintly order and devoted half their wealth to it, which also encouraged the city folk, who regarded them as foreign Himyarites, to be more accepting.

After a while, we stopped to make the sunset prayer. Kevah and Eshe argued about who ought to lead it.

"I'm a depraved hashish addict," Kevah said, "no way I can lead."

Eshe sniggered. "You know what bought my camel and these clothes?" He tugged on his shirt. "Money earned by disparaging half the asses, breasts, and cocks in Qandbajar. You want the same tongue sending your prayers to Lat?"

"You're a former Disciple and a scholar of high knowledge."

"You're a magus who claims to have been chosen by Lat herself."

"What about her?" Kevah gestured his head toward me.

"Her it is." They both lined up and glared in my direction.

I spat out a date pit and shook my head. "I once…killed a frog."

They looked at each other, bewildered.

I grunted in frustration. "I once said…very disgusting things… about another woman in the harem…behind her back!"

"We're wasting time," Kevah said. "Please start." He stared up at the reddening sky. "Where the hell is Kinn? He should have been here by now."

I practiced the prayer words in my mind so I wouldn't mess them up. My head needed to sway left, then right, then right again, then left, then up. It had been so long since I'd paid attention to any of this.

But just as I was about to raise my hands and begin, something landed on my head. A white flower petal? But why was it cold? And then on my nose. And then it was falling all around.

Snow.

We stared up: a rosy sunset. And yet, it was snowing. What in Lat's name?

"How is this possible?" Eshe said, hugging his body.

I shivered too as the air chilled. As if the warmth from seconds ago had been sucked out.

Kevah pushed his head back until he was looking directly above. "Oh Lat. If only you two could see this."

"See what?" I asked.

"I was expecting to meet her," Kevah said, "but not here. Not like this."

"Expecting who?" Eshe rubbed his arms.

"Marada." Kevah pointed at the setting sun, which now seemed to be turning blue. "Sultana of the Marid, one of the great tribes of jinn. Her wings are the span of clouds. Did the Disciples really expect me to gain her allegiance?"

The snow fell in clumps, now. The sand beneath chilled my feet as it froze. A howling wind screeched my ears, whipping up cold sand that mixed with snow, and the sky fogged.

"The Marid tribe live in the Waste," Eshe said, "the hell are they doing here?"

"She's looking right at me," Kevah said. "Why? What does she want?"

In seconds, the landscape turned white. A blizzard raged. I couldn't even see our camels.

"It's...upset with me." Kevah dropped to his knees. "You two, go, get out of here. As far as you can."

Eshe grabbed my arm. "Come on!"

I resisted. "We can't just leave him!" But I did want to run. The cold burrowed into my bones. Just like those frozen days in the Waste, when I'd starved and vomited nothing but my spit, which I'd swallowed so much of, just to taste something.

"He's a magus," Eshe said. "His power comes from submitting the jinn tribes to him. Perhaps this is the consequence of leaving Zelthuriya without doing that."

"Consequence or not, he's our friend!"

"Don't worry," Kevah said, hair covered in snow. "Marada's not going to harm me. I'm wearing her mask, after all. But you two… you're not but ants to her. So go! Get clear of the storm!"

I let Eshe pull me away. We shielded our faces from the blizzard and trudged through the snow. Everything froze, even the water in my eyes.

The wind shrieked like the dying. I could barely see Eshe in front of me but clung to his hand as icicles formed in my veins. My legs buckled as if my joints had frozen, and I fell upon a couch of snow.

Eshe pulled me up. Then he screamed. Something was pulling him, too. The air was too white to see. I clutched his hand, but the force sent him flying.

"Eshe!" I shouted. None answered but the wind's shrill cry. Nothing but white every way I turned. I couldn't even shout: the air was ice and so were my throat and lungs.

"Payment for your sins," someone whispered hot in my ear.

No, my sins didn't deserve this pain. The thousandth hell is a place of absolute cold, the Recitals say. I was falling into it, ten cold hells passing me each second.

"Remember what you did," the whisper said. "Remember, so you can beg forgiveness."

I didn't do anything. I'm good. That's why they wanted me to lead the prayer.

"Liar," every disciple in the room said, their eyes black-in-black. "Liar!"

"Follow the straight path," Khizr Khaz said, his eyes only whites. "Worship no other god aside Lat."

"I am on the straight path," I cried. "I've made mistakes, but I'll be better."

"You're hiding something," Ruhi said, her black veil covered in snow. "And you don't even know it."

I crashed into ice water and became ice. So brittle that a whisper could shatter me.

"Cyra," Cihan whispered in my ear as we huddled beneath a torn blanket. "Wake up."

Slap! It scathed my cheek like fire. I did wake up, with Eshe cradling my head.

"What happened?" I asked.

"Can you stand?" he said. "I've not the strength to carry you." As he spoke, snow fell gently upon his headcloth. It seemed the blizzard had become a pattering of snowflakes, though my toes and fingers still numbed.

I sat up and stuck my hands in my shirt, near my core, for warmth.

"We need to keep going," he said. "Get up."

Eshe pulled me up by the arms. I fell again, onto my knees, and then toppled to my side. My caftan was soaked and my knees numb.

Eshe unsheathed a dagger, clutched my numb hand, and pricked my finger. My blood flowed onto the blade's flat, though I didn't feel it.

I glared at him in horror. "What're you doing?"

He drew a pattern on the flat, then mumbled some words. The pattern glowed, and the blade enflamed.

Life-giving heat emanated from the flame. Eshe pulled off his headcloth and wrapped it around the burning blade; the cloth caught fire, providing more heat.

"You have useful blood," he said, brandishing the flame. "Fire and ice, both, run through your veins. A conversation for another time. Warm up and let's go."

After a few minutes of huddling near it, the heat helped me feel again. Helped me stand. Eshe and I held hands and trudged through the textureless surrounding. White the sky, white the ground, white the air. Where were we going? Any direction was better than staying still, I supposed. And was Kevah all right?

As we went, the ground hardened. Sand intruded on the snow, grain by grain, as if we entered another world. The desert world from before this madness began. And then, as the storm died to a whisper, dunes appeared in the distance. The cold eased with every step as the red, setting sun crept out of the haze that had been choking it.

A hooded man stood just ahead, his back turned to us.

"Kevah?" I shouted. I broke out of Eshe's handhold and ran forward.

"Wait!" Eshe huffed as he followed.

But as I approached the man, I noticed he towered compared to Kevah. Freakish. Almost double my height. And then I stared at his feet: they faced backward.

"Turn back," he said in a whisper that boomed. Had it come from the man or the sky?

I stood still. Eshe caught up and grabbed my hand. Beyond the man was the sand and sun we craved. Behind us, the snow and cold. He was the line between two wastelands.

"You are about to enter the Palace of Bones," the tall man whispered across the sky. "A fate worse than death."

I looked behind me. Nothing but snow. Please, no more cold. Cold was starvation. Cold was death.

"This place has swallowed armies whole," the tall man said. "What are two strays?"

"This isn't good," Eshe said. "The Palace of Bones is a cursed place. It's said to travel between the deserts of the world, snatching up the lost, sending them to the realm of the Dreamer. Scholars say it even caused the blood plague that destroyed my homeland. We should turn back."

"A palace that…travels? But if we turn back, we'll freeze."

Eshe said with a tremor, "Lat help us, but I think I'd rather freeze."

"Lat has no power here," the tall man said. "Turn back."

No. I wouldn't go into the cold. Never again. Not after all that had happened.

But when I stepped forward, Eshe yanked my arm. "You crazy?"

Snap. The hooded man's arm bent at an odd angle and…grew. *Snap-snap.* His whole body grew, like a tree sprouting, with each bony snap of his neck and limbs.

"You're right," I said to Eshe, whose eyes were bulging grapes as the thing continued to *snap-snap-snap.* "I'm not thinking clearly. L-Let's go back."

We turned from the creature and hurried into the snow, trudging into the cold that I hated, ice making a home inside me. The heat of Eshe's flaming dagger kept us going. Until, once again, we saw sand, dunes, and sun in the distance. Eshe and I hurried onward, hope thudding in my heart.

But as we neared the sand, there it was again: the bizarre, bent-limbed creature, its many arms and legs sprawled in the air and across the sand. What resembled octopus tentacles bored into the ground off its stone-like torso. Its head towered several feet into the sky, mouth open and hundreds of eyes bubbling on its face.

I bit my trembling lip, then said to Eshe, "But we turned back."

"Whatever it is, it's having fun with us," Eshe said with a quaver. "We're ants, remember?"

Its laugh sounded like a broken flute being blown into by a man gasping before death. "Did you really think there was a choice?" it said from everywhere. "Perhaps there was, long ago, before you did what you did. But now…there's no way back."

The thing swiped a tentacle in our direction, flinging sand waves in the air. The burning grains scathed my eye. I yanked out of Eshe's handhold and pressed against my tear duct. Eshe screamed, his voice getting fainter, as if he were flying away.

"Eshe!" I cried, feeling around me as my sand-filled eyelid refused to lift. I rubbed until it flickered open but couldn't spot him. All I saw were tentacles snaking forward as a sandstorm whirled around me.

I AWOKE in a mound of sand. So hot — the red sun burned it and my skin with an angry gaze. That sun had been setting for a long time; why hadn't it fallen below the horizon yet? Despite the heat on my skin, my insides shivered, as if ice filled my core. How torturous to feel uncomfortably hot and unbearably cold at the same time.

I blinked and blinked to confirm what my eyes told me: in the distance stood a building that dwarfed the Sand Palace, the Tower of Wisdom, and the Grand Bazaar pyramid combined. I pushed to my feet, rubbed sand from my hair and nostrils, and approached the structure. White and shining and built of bone and skull — was this what that awful creature had called the Palace of Bones? It looked as if the populace of twenty Qandbajars had built that thing…from their own skeletons. Would I be another among them?

Why was I walking toward it? Because it was whispering my name and more things that I couldn't understand. It was at once familiar and also filled me with noxious dread.

Before I could think, I was staring up at it. The top of the pyramid pierced the sky like a spear tip. And then…a low rumble sounded. I expected a pathway to appear and a door to open, leading me within, but as I stared at the bones and skulls, the sweet and deathly stench of flesh and guts filled the air. Every bone in the pyramid rattled, and then the *thud-thud* of the rattling became a *thump-thump* as flesh was painted upon the bones. Meat filled the skulls, and the sockets even had eyes now, all staring at me. Skin appeared on the flesh, as if sewn on, and then features like hair and moles and lips and lashes. Finally, the skulls and bones screamed. Each alive, each tortured, each begging for the end with their bulging eyes and flailing tongues.

This was not a Palace of Bones. It was a Palace of the Living, of the trapped, of suffering I hoped to never understand.

But I couldn't move. I could only stare at the faces, at the shaking arms and legs and torsos. As the mouths closed after screaming, they bit down on the flesh, and now blood poured down the pyramid. That was when a giant, eyeball-covered hand pushed out of the pile of flesh and heads, grabbed me, and pulled me inside.

I FLOATED IN A BLACK SEA. Stars burned around me. Each one tried to pull me toward it, as if they had hooks, but I stayed in place. I flipped onto my belly and realized I was falling, not floating. A distant light blazed, growing as I fell, though no air pushed against my face. As I screamed, no sound came; a silent terror streamed from my throat.

I was falling into fire. Into a sea of surging, whirling, flaming waves and tornados. Into the sun itself. But it was red and bulging and oblong. And strangely...beautiful, like the swollen belly of a laden mare, seconds from birthing.

I flipped around and saw twelve stars. They danced on a black tarp, swapping positions every second. Slowly, they all dimmed until only two still blazed. The two stars continued to dance, closing in as they coiled. Closer, closer, until they borrowed each other's light. Spirals of rainbow wisped off one and onto the other.

Somehow, I felt their love. Their utter devotion. And then the last two stars in the sky, with a blinding flash, became one. For a moment, their union painted the black tarp with every color imaginable and unimaginable, known and unknown, pulsing from the center. Their dance had resulted in a rebirth, utterly magnificent. Two had become one and were better for it.

But then, the combined star shrunk until it was the size of Qandbajar. It pulled inward, compacting its fire, turning cold and blue. No longer loved, nor loving — all alone, seething. It would watch everything die.

It sucked me in, pulled me around itself, and then launched me into the black sea. I passed through a sky of giant rocks, each icy and whirling like dervishes. I swam into a sparkling red cloud that somehow smelled of rose wine. And then another star — green and calm — sucked me in, hymning as I neared. After it, too, spat me out, I watched rocks pull together, becoming a flaming cauldron and then turning into a smooth, blue marble, which was destroyed by a spreading wall of flame.

And through all this, I couldn't think because I couldn't breathe. I was a witnesser without a will, doomed to spend eternity slinging across stars at the mercy of their anger and sadness and hatred and love.

Until, a thousand thousand years later, a hand tore through the darkness, grabbed me, and pulled me out.

14

ZEDRA

With Vera taken, I asked Mirima if Celene could attend me. Life in the harem was dull, even during tumult, and the girl hadn't been doing much aside from learning proper Alanyan etiquette and Paramic. Mirima felt my lofty manner would be a good influence and so agreed.

Alone in my room, as I sat on a floor cushion and pecked a sugared jelly, I said to Celene, "Tell me, dear, did they question you?"

She stood by the door and nodded. "They asked about the girl who bought me."

"What did you say?"

"Nothing. I haven't talked to her since the day she brought me here."

"And they accepted your answer?"

She hunched her shoulders. "Mirima confirmed it, so I suppose."

Celene didn't seem as fearful about Mansur's inquisition as me. I supposed she already felt like a prisoner, so getting locked somewhere dank was a mere degree worse.

"I'm going to ask you something," I said, "and I need you to be truthful. Given what's happening, I require honesty from those who serve me. Tell me, do you hate the Alanyans?"

She twirled her hair and stared at the floor. "I don't hate any—"

"The truth," I interrupted. "Don't think I can't see past your meekness. Inside, you're raging, aren't you?"

She believed me to be one of them, of course, but my rage burned hotter than hers. A rage she endured in silence as she continued to twirl her hair.

"I was taken by them, too," I said, "but I know that to survive, I have to be whatever they find agreeable. What I mean to say is, as different as you may think we are, we're the same."

She sighed, tense. "You've done more than survive. You're the mother of a prince. Where I come from, that would make you a queen. I'll never be anything like that unless I go home."

"Home — it's always on your mind, isn't it? What if I told you I can send you home?"

Now her eyes glistened with hope. "H-How? I'm told there are no ships heading for Crucis."

"Serve me — faithfully, with absolute trust — and I'll see you to your home, no matter what."

"A promise," she said. "But based on what ought I to believe your promises?"

A good question; the right answer could gain her loyalty. And with Vera imprisoned, I needed someone to help me. But Celene was no servant at heart, though it seemed she could play the role. And a Crucian princess could be useful in ways I hadn't yet conceived.

I asked, "What is something you want, aside from to go home?"

She twirled her hair again — an anxious quirk. One of my granddaughters did the same. "There's nothing else I want."

"Surely, there must be something. Some comfort that would ease all this. Because that I will give you, whatever it is."

She shook her head. "The only comfort are my prayers, and that you can't give or take."

"Then let's go to the cathedral, meet the bishop, all of that. They won't let you leave the palace on your own, but I can always take you." I popped a sugared jelly into my mouth. The brass plate lay empty, now, save for crumbs and bits of sugar powder. I hoped her next words would be as sweet.

Celene sniggered — the first hint of impoliteness cracking through her facade. "Why? What is it you want from me? What does my *trust* mean to you? Because I'd think the trust of some heathen girl trapped far from home entirely meaningless. Unless..." She held up a finger. "It's my desperation that you're trying to play. Maybe you think I'll do anything, and that's why—"

"I'm not so depraved." Though I was...in a sense. It seemed Celene's trust could only be gained with trust. "I wasn't just ripped from my home, Celene. Everyone I love was killed, by them. By the Seluqals. But I'm not here for revenge. I'm the mother of the future shah, and I..." What wonderful lie could I come up with? "...intend his rule to be a better one. A just one, for all his subjects. Even for Ethosians like you. But to do that, I need help. Allies. People I can trust, because enemies will surround me."

"What makes you think I care?" she said with venom. "You people are so despicable, you don't just enslave us, you enslave each other. You're worse than even the Sirmians. I'd rather Alanya burn than prosper. And if Ethosians burn too, the Archangel knows his own." Her cheeks twitched as she shook her head. "I'm not going to help you. I'm not going to be your pawn in the games played here. If I did become useful to you, then there'd be less reason to send me home, so there's nothing in it for me."

Curse the saints! I needed more than words. Without leverage over Celene, she couldn't replace Vera in my service, which meant I was alone. While Celene could wheel me here and there, carry me into the closet, and guard my door, I couldn't trust her with more vital tasks. And each day, it seemed my mission grew more difficult. Too difficult for one frail woman. I could search high and low in the harem but wouldn't find someone like her: without any attachment to this land or a nearby tribe, who wasn't already in the service of Mirima, Kyars, or some vizier, and who, like me, hated these people enough to burn her own with them.

"The cathedral is beautiful. I'm certain a visit will brighten your spirits." I patted the pillow next to me so she would sit. Once she did, I took her hand: so unblemished and smooth, not unlike my own.

I said, "If you had truly lost hope, you wouldn't still be praying. You believe you'll one day see your home again, and I believe that too. I don't pray anymore because my home doesn't exist, except in my memory. Time has erased it, worse than any war ever could."

Celene stared just below my eyes, as if it hurt to face the truth. "Your home…doesn't exist?"

I ignored her comment and continued, "The truth is, you're stuck here for now. And I'm the only one who will understand you. I'm your best bet, and you know it. If you can't trust me entirely, then trust me enough to give me a chance. Is that fair?"

She nodded.

I smiled as if I were staring at my daughter. "Good. Let's go, then."

I COULD ONLY PRAY Vera hadn't said much about me, though given how Mansur dealt with the Path of the Children rebellion in his province last year, I doubted she'd last. And what if Kato told Mansur it was my suggestion that led him to the fingerless scribe? Certainly, Kato knew I wore an innocent face over my cleverness, but I was hardly the only concubine to do so. He wouldn't so easily swallow that I was a sorcerer, though. As for Mansur, if he sought the throne, then painting me as a sorcerer would be perfect: if the mother of Kyars' son killed the Shah, then Kyars himself could be a guilty party. I'd have to silence these worrying thoughts with proper action.

But to do that, I needed an ally and a plan. By carriage, Celene and I traveled to Basil's Cathedral. I did my best thinking on these carriage rides, as I stared out the window at the oblivious city folk. The death of Tamaz, the arrival of Mansur and the Jotrids — it hardly changed the rhythm of the street, which was an assured yet ordered chaos. Did the people of Qandbajar believe their high, double-layered walls kept them safe? Perhaps from the khagans. But not from me.

Stone doesn't stand against a determined host. I'd been alive for the deaths of three saint-kings. The last of the saint-kings, Nasar the *Honorable*, had once considered Seluq his vassal. The Children once counted Seluq as a friend, too. But then he had that dream of a thousand black birds devouring the sun, and a thousand stone walls couldn't contain him.

One rather trite vision changed history's course. Now, I had to change mine. Instead of dividing them, I had to align with Kato and ensure Kyars took the throne. Weakening either would empower Mansur and endanger my son. Nothing frustrated me more than how I'd put so many plans in motion, but now had to form a new one to deal with an enemy I'd been oblivious to. I'm sure it had been the same for Nasar the Fool, last of the saint-kings, when some brute from the Waste overran his glorious kingdom. I had to do better. Had to coddle as close to Kato as I could, hide in his golden armor until Kyars returned and ended Mansur's threat, hopefully forever.

"You always so lost in thought?" Celene asked.

My mother once asked me something similar. I had one of those faces that exposed its musings. "I'm worried about Kyars." How strange to say that so sincerely. If anything happened to him, Mansur would have no obstacle save for my son — a rather tiny obstacle.

"Kyars." She chuckled with bitterness. "I was there the day he became a *hero*. My grandfather would have prevailed and freed me, if not for him."

"Your grandfather…who came back from death." If only I knew such sorcery, I'd bring back all the Children. But ought I to darken my soul with powers that controlled death itself? Though Father Chisti had said, *"to fight darkness, you must become it."*

"The Archangel brought him back," Celene said, "only to die days later. Wish I knew why, but we mortals must be content in our ignorance."

What an odd thing to say. Why content yourself with not knowing? And yet, Father Chisti had mentioned his *sip* of truth and how it awakened him to the Great Terror. Perhaps it was better to be content in ignorance.

"I knew a man," I said, "a great man, like your grandfather. God had promised him so much. Verdant land, gushing rivers, vineyards filled with every fruit. And yet…" Once more, I chewed this bitter memory. "They knew it was forbidden to spill the blood of a descendent of Chisti, so they strangled him. There's no blood when you're strangled. Nor when you drown. So they strangled or drowned us all."

Silence lingered as I sipped my sadness. The hum and bustle of the streets outside our thin carriage doors wouldn't permit a moment of peace.

"Descendent of Chisti?" Celene whispered. Seemed I'd let that slip, but what did she know about us? About our history? About the true heirs of this land, of the Latian faith?

"Sounds like you're a descendent of your faith's founder," she said. "Do the others know?"

I shook my head. "If they did, they'd strangle me too."

"I don't understand." She hunched her left shoulder. "Why do they want to kill the children of a man they revere?"

"I've been asking that question for longer than you've been alive."

Her eyebrows reached the top of her forehead. "How old were you when you started asking questions?"

That was the wrong question, but I wasn't about to reveal my secret. In any case, Celene wouldn't believe it.

Our carriage halted at the outskirts of the Ethosian Quarter, just next to the Glass District. Celene climbed out first, asked the gholam to unload my chair, and then helped me onto it.

I'd always found this cathedral impressive: three floors in a triangle shape composed of gray brick and covered in stained glass. I'd read that artisans from Dycondi had fashioned it in their style. A sprawl of spires crowned the top, along with a pointed red dome. It stuck out, to say the least.

Word had gone ahead that we were coming, so I wasn't surprised to see the bishop at the entrance. He resembled a middle-aged peasant I once bought kababs from outside the Grand Bazaar — thin frame, somewhat unkempt black hair, potbelly, and a face that needed a few extra scrubs. He wore a lovely white robe accented with vivid star patterns and greeted us with his hand on his heart. "Archangel keep you," he said in Crucian to Celene. She smiled, her straight teeth showing, probably relieved to hear her language again.

Whereas I shuddered: how strange that I understood what he'd said. No way I'd learned Crucian in the past. They continued chatting, and I continued understanding, hearing them talk about angels and apostles and trials and truths. My comprehension of their language was a curiosity, to say the least. One that raised the hairs on my neck.

While our gholam escort waited outside, we entered the chapel. On the altar beyond the pews, a statue of the Archangel stared with lifelike eyes. Its eleven arms and eleven wings were spread, as if to claim as much air as possible. On the other side, a choir of girls and boys hymned in Paramic.

And the angel said,
We are only a trial, so do not disbelieve.

How terrible the price for which you sold your soul.

Beneath the light of Aurora — the dead star of morning.

I shuddered at the ominous verses. *Dead star of morning?* By Lat, what did that mean?

I was about to ask the Bishop, but seeing the sweet smile stuck on Celene's face, I decided it better to let the two chatter. Instead, I approached the angel on the altar. *"They'd be better off praying to stones, like in the days of old,"* Father had said. But this angel statue was metal, not that metal was more intelligent than stone. Had the people of Kostany really witnessed this creature in the sky? I shuddered once more at the thought.

I'd been doing much shuddering in this bizarre place. Just then, I noticed someone in the pew to my right. It took a few seconds to recognize him, though he wore the familiar felt long-hat and metal clasp at his waist: Grand Philosopher Litani. He put his hand on his heart when he saw me.

"You're one of these people?" I said. "I had no idea."

He smiled politely, then stood. "I am, in fact, the highest-ranking Ethosian in the Majlis."

"Impressive. Tell me, did you get the mountain for your stargazing?"

He sighed, heavy and annoyed. "We lost that battle, for now. But I have hope when Shah Kyars returns that he'll see it our way."

Everyone seemed to be pinning their hopes on my *beloved*. Even opposing factions saw Kyars as their proponent. I'd only known him a year but never noticed this immense character that might as well stand in place of that angel statue. The Kyars I knew was vain and base — I'll never forgive the vile things he made me do with himself and other women in the harem — though he did possess a certain cunning. Thank Lat that since birthing him a son, I was safe from his immorality. It seemed he was as many-faced as the cleverest in Qandbajar — disappointing I hadn't realized it sooner.

These Philosophers, though — I was glad they kept so many useful books, but their severe lack of practicality bewildered. "Considering the death of his father and the coming of one horde and the going of another, I somehow doubt my beloved Kyars will care either way."

"On the contrary, we all ought to care about the heavens. Doesn't your faith teach that stars birthed us all?"

Something the saint worshippers and the Children agreed on.

I nodded. "And what do the Philosophers teach about the stars?"

He tilted his head forward, as if out of surprise for my question. "We have a different way of knowing than this faith or that, and we don't claim to know anything we can't observe or deduce."

"Nothing of import, then."

He chuckled in a mocking tone. "Not to small minds, no. But yours isn't. You've quite the reading habit, I hear. A woman who likes books. The dream of many a Philosopher."

"Is that so? Does your wife read?"

Again, that mocking chuckle. It did not endear. "I didn't say it was my dream. Rather, I believe everything has its place. Religion belongs in the chapel. Stars in the sky. And a concubine, certainly not behind the pages of obscure medical texts."

So he'd seen my record at the Tower of Wisdom. Why did he care? His condescension chaffed on my already frayed nerves.

"I'm not just any concubine, Litani. Only a second-rate Philosopher would fail to deduce that I've the ear of the man you're placing your hopes in. You'd do well to remember that."

"You have his ear — and other parts, clearly. I understand. But we Philosophers don't fear power — we are power. When they needed to reverse engineer those fast-firing Crucian guns, who did the palace turn to?" He double-tapped his collar, which had a metal pin on it that resembled a throne. "Knowledge isn't a game, Zedra. It isn't a dress or tiara to make you gleam. It is the fount of victory. You'd do well to remember that next time you borrow a book."

After that speech, I somewhat admired the fellow. He knew well who I was — or rather, who I was pretending to be — and yet, like

Kato, didn't try to suck on my toes. Rather, he stepped all over them because he possessed something weightier than the throne — his knowledge. My great grandfather once said, *"A hopeless person sees difficulties in every chance, but a hopeful person sees chances in every difficulty."* I wouldn't let Litani's obstinance hinder me.

I smiled as warmly as I could. "If you'd rather I didn't read obscure medical texts, then grant me access to the highest two floors of the Tower. I just might find something more appropriate to my station."

Litani winced as if he'd eaten a sour date. "So you can embellish yourself further? Have you been listening? Only three have access to the top floors, and one of them is in jail for being a Path of the Children sympathizer." Wait...did he mean Wafiq? The Philosopher I'd found in the dungeon, repeating the names of the Twelve Chiefs of the Children? I had no idea he was regarded so highly, no idea who he was in the first place. "I've already said too much." Litani came to my ear, whispered, "Point is, I'd rather burn the whole thing down than see you prancing around my office."

So he *really* didn't like me. Didn't fear me. Didn't think I'd make a good ally. Whereas Kato didn't fear me but liked me enough to consider an alliance, which then bloomed. How was I to endear myself to this Philosopher?

I tapped the armrest of my chair. "I won't be prancing, if that's any consolation. Consider it an official request. I want to read what you're keeping on the top two floors." More out of curiosity — just what could they be hiding there?

Litani folded his arms. "Then consider this an official denial." He raised a finger. "No."

MY ONLY CONSOLATION was seeing the brightness on Celene's face as we rode to the palace. Not merely because it endeared me to her, but also because it made me happy to see her happy. Praying in the house of her god had warmed her. Familiarity is comforting. Which is why it stunned me when she said, "The bishop is a heretic."

"Come again?"

She bit her lip. "They don't obey the Patriarch in Hyperion."

Well, obviously not. The Seluqals would never permit a clergy that took orders from a power outside Alanya.

"They worship your Archangel though, right? Isn't that enough?"

"They do, but they place Marot above Cessiel as the closest angel to the Archangel himself. Blasphemy. That's what happens when you're severed from the source of faith."

Marot? Cessiel? Such strange names — who cares what angel was above the other? I did understand what she meant by *severed from the source of faith* — that was what happened to mankind when they murdered the last of the Children. It had put us on the path toward the Great Terror. The reminder that I bore this whole thing almost paralyzed me.

Celene smiled, her chin turning pink. "No matter, the chapel was holy enough. Thank you for bringing me."

"My pleasure, dear. Seeing you bright like this makes me joyous, too." That wasn't a complete lie. Celene, Vera, even Cyra — whenever they'd smile, it reminded me of my daughters and granddaughters and great-granddaughters. And if anything could pierce my shell, it was remembering that time, that place when we were together, joyful, and free.

Upon arriving at the palace, Celene wheeled me to my room. A eunuch was standing on my bed, wearing a red sash, his back turned. Sambal? How dare he soil my bed! But he'd run off to Kashan. And this one...he was far too lofty...

He turned around: his dark hair fell on his face, almost covering his eyes. I'd been staring at his feet and back since we first met; I barely recognized those emaciated cheekbones and sharp chin. But worst of all were the lifeless pupils that seemed to stare at nothing, even as they gazed into me.

I turned to Celene. "Dear, best you go now."

She nodded and left us, glaring at the man all the while.

"What are you doing here?" I asked.

Father Chisti stared down at me, also something I wasn't used to. He'd barely ever looked at me.

"You're having a lovely time, aren't you?" he said. "Enjoying a life you didn't earn. Making friends in every quarter of the city. Devouring delights that hadn't even been conceived when I was alive. Is this the sum of your purpose?"

"What are you saying? I'm doing everything for our cause!" I banged on my armrest, my coolness dissolving before the father of our faith. "You warned me about Kevah but said nothing about Mansur and Khagan Pashang! Do you realize how much that's set us back?" I hugged myself to ease the trembling.

"Shh, dear daughter," Father said. "You don't want to startle your minders. Khagan Pashang is under a cloud that even I cannot pierce."

"What does that mean?"

"It means that, like you, his intentions and actions are not of this world."

I shook my head. "Can you not be so cryptic, for once?"

His thin smile, too, barely seemed of this world. "I deal in cryptic, lovely daughter. That's what makes me such a good saint for the masses. But for you, I'll be clear — Pashang is now your primary problem. Get rid of him."

"I don't need you to tell me that. But it's not so easily done. The man won't enter the city, and he's surrounded by tens of thousands of riders."

"Easy or not, you'd best defeat him soon because Magus Kevah is coming for you. As we speak, he's confronting Marada, sultana of the Marid. Or rather, she's confronting him. Surely, you've not forgotten her?"

I rubbed my suddenly frigid arms. The image of a cloud filled with snakes out of which shot three dragon heads, each with eyeballs of fire, flashed through my mind. Oh Lat…not Marada… how many horrifying enemies, worldly and otherworldly, would I have to face?

Father reached behind his back and plucked something, as if out of the air: a book. He held it forward so the spine faced me. *Flavors of Blood Volume Two by Aligar of Zunduq* was sewn onto the spine in gold thread.

"The time for subtle methods is over," he said.

My jaw dropped. "You had that all this time? Why?"

"I was solving the puzzle for you."

"Puzzle? What puzzle?"

He opened the book; blue ink covered the pages, some letters circled, others crossed out. "It's not merely a medical tome. Aligar was a bloodwriter, and he filled this volume with coded rune recipes. I've deciphered it for you. Use the recipes, destroy Pashang, and get our plan going again."

A wonderful reveal, and yet, it all seemed so strange given who it was coming from. "Are you alive, Father? Have you been living in Qandbajar? How can you be here? How are you checking out books from the Tower of Wisdom and deciphering codes?"

He stepped off the bed and approached, then took my hand. "Occultation is as lonely as it sounds. A trip here, once in a while, doesn't hurt." He clasped our hands together. "But if I do anything more, *they'll* know." He gestured at the sky outside the open balcony door. "I have to be careful. You, though, never mattered. There was a time when I never mattered, too. That's the only time when you can change the world…because *they* won't be looking."

"Who are *they*?"

He bent down and whispered, steamy in my ear, "I pray you never, ever find out." Then he slid his hand up my thigh.

"What are you doing?" I asked, trembling.

Then across to the other thigh. "What is a saint without miracles?" He kissed my cheek.

I shut my eyes, resigned to let him do whatever he wanted. I tried to take a deep breath, but the trembles wouldn't let me.

Instead, Father Chisti got up, opened the door, and walked out of the room.

"Father?"

I was stuck in the chair with no one to help me off. I pushed out, ready to fall and crawl, but somehow I stayed on my feet. My knees didn't buckle, either. I walked forward a step — no pain. I walked backward, then forward again. I rushed into the hallway, but Father was gone.

Miracles, indeed.

Flavors of Blood Volume Two — finally, I held it in my hands. I smelled the cover — old and leathery. It was bound in the traditional fashion, with a flap on the back that wrapped around to the front. The vellum pages bulged unevenly, typical of older books, though I found it rather charming.

With this heft, it would take two days to read if I did naught else. But I had much to do. Father had stuck notes into the back with the bloodrunes he'd deciphered, so I pulled out those papers.

Looking at the scrawls he'd made in red ink, I shuddered. He'd noted the specific widths and lengths each character had to be. And these characters…I'd never seen them before. They were more like paintings — of animals and stars and trees. And given how large each character was…these weren't bloodrunes. These were…

I gasped, then put the papers back in the book. I closed my eyes — I saw the patterns blazing across my inner eyelids with the red light of the Morning Star. I wanted to forget them, but they'd been seared onto my mind.

Perhaps I should read the actual book first. This volume contained descriptions of the eleven rare flavors I didn't know about, and I particularly wanted to know what flavor the red-haired woman possessed. I ought to close the blinds, order a pot of cardamom tea, light a lantern, and get to reading. To be truthful, while I could learn much to further the cause, I also enjoyed Aligar's lavish, metaphor-reliant prose.

I began from the beginning, which was a rehash of the first volume. So I skimmed until I reached the descriptions of the rare flavors. Conqueror's blood came first, but I knew that well enough. After was god's blood, which my son possessed. And then…

My door burst open. Curse the saints! I'd forgotten to lock it. Mansur marched in, two of his mirror-armored household guard at his side, clutching the silver daggers in their sashes.

"What if I was changing?" I slammed the book shut. "How dare you enter without permission?"

"It wouldn't be the first time another man has enjoyed your nakedness, would it?" Mansur's tone was a dagger, too.

What the hell was going on? Just what was he insinuating? "H-How dare you? What will the Shah do when I tell him his uncle said something so untoward about the mother of his son?"

With a sickening grin, Mansur's whiskers reached his ears. "And what will my nephew do when I tell him that your son is not his." He tilted his head toward me. "Hmm?"

Unexpected…yet typical.

"So…this is the game you've chosen. It won't work, Mansur. You're declaring war on your nephew, who is even more loved than his father. You think casting doubt on my son as heir will win you the support to become Shah of Alanya?"

Mansur shook his head. "Like I said, I'm here to find the vipers, dear. I don't covet my nephew's throne. The Ruthenian handmaid, Vera, has told us everything. All the high viziers have heard her confession. How you would go into the city and visit strange men, all to satisfy your licentiousness. This is what Kyars earned by being so permitting with his women."

I never expected Mansur to stoop this low…but I didn't know him. Had he tortured Vera until she agreed to spout such lies? Did this gray fool really believe calling me a whore would make him Shah?

"I'm disappointed," I said. "You've bent over and plucked such low-hanging fruit, it must've been buried in the ground."

"You and I both know that my nephew has bedded hundreds, with not a son or daughter to show. And then you come along, and of a sudden, a miracle pops out."

Of course. He wouldn't accuse me of being a sorcerer; no one would believe that without hard evidence. But a whore — completely understandable, given that I looked like a beautiful, young girl. A believable lie was always better than an unbelievable truth. Even though, ironically, my son wasn't Kyars' — though Mansur didn't know that.

"You're disgusting and wretched, Mansur. Your lies don't merit a response. Kyars will have much to say, I'm sure, though he'll let his steel do the talking." I gave him an assured smirk and held out my hands so he could chain them. "Well? Have you a cell prepared?"

He shook his head. "'Course not. I'm confining you to this chamber until Kyars returns. No more dallying about the city. Such freedom is the ruin of modesty, of innocence."

He and his guards turned to leave. I was meant to destroy him and Khagan Pashang, and now I couldn't leave my room. Though I could soulshift from my closet, I couldn't rely solely on sorcery to achieve my goal. The truth is, I was never good at reacting to surprises; careful planning had always been my strength. But the plots I'd set in motion, from when I'd arrived here a year ago, had been smashed with a hammer. I'd lacked foresight. Curse my lack of insight, too; I'd not read Mansur as well as I should've. My hopes now rested on one man: Kato.

"Did Kato approve this?" I asked, "or are you going over his head, too?"

Mansur paused at the threshold. "Over the head of a coal-skinned slave?" He sniggered. "Seluq is my ancestor, my blood, that means I was born with my feet on the heads of everyone, the least of which is some Himyarite. All serve us."

"Spoken like a true Seluqal." I chuckled with venom. "But Tamaz was not so haughty, and neither is Kyars. If you think all before you so base, then you won't notice when they come for you. Hadrith, Ozar, Cihan, Cyra — four of Tamaz's *subjects*, and yet they killed him."

"Only them?" Mansur shook his head. "I'll fill the old barrack with *all* the conspirators, not just convenient scapegoats."

So, he would continue Kato's policy of using the old barrack to imprison his enemies. Good to know.

He walked out and shut the door, leaving me with acrid thoughts. I couldn't let them trap me. If Mansur controlled the palace, how long would it be until Pashang's horde entered the city? The gholam still controlled the city walls, and Kato was no fool to allow it. But what had happened to him? Was he also being kept in the old barrack?

Kato had underestimated Mansur. But I couldn't blame him. To refuse Tamaz's brother entry would have been a dangerous gamble for a slave. Kyars, it seemed, would have to save us from his own blood.

No. We couldn't wait for him; I'd have to do it. I stood on my bed — how wonderful to have working legs. I hoped to never take them for granted. Now that I could walk, I had to get my son back from Mirima. And then I had to get out of here.

15

CYRA

Desert. Snow. Bones. Stars. And…slap!

I coughed water that had snuck into my nostrils and slid down my windpipe. Then I rubbed my left eye and the bandage covering my right socket. Ground my knuckles into my tear ducts.

For a moment, I thought I was eight years old again. A yurt ceiling stared down, colored with paintings of vines and flowers and lions. In the center, an ice-filled stove cooled the air. Casting their shadows upon me were a group of men; they wore sky blue caftans with bear-fur shoulder pads and hard caps plumed with dark, spot-filled argus feathers. How I hated those outfits.

I recognized two men: Tekish, wiry as ever, arms folded and consternation stuck on his thin face. And his brother, Khagan Pashang, his calloused hand on my raw cheek.

"Oh, you felt that?" he said. "Apologies, Cyra, but naught else would wake you."

"Where am I?" I whispered.

He matched my low tone. "Somewhere with more even lighting."

My head throbbed. Dry aches chaffed my throat. "Water would be nice."

Tekish, whom I recalled was younger than Pashang, handed me a furry waterskin. I sat up and smelled it — just water, thank Lat. I sipped until the dryness eased.

"I heard you were coming," I said, glaring at Pashang. "Waking up to your face, just a continuance of my terrible fortunes of late."

He smirked. "I wouldn't want to wake to my face, either. Thankfully, I'm the only one who never has to."

"Shut up," I said. "Nothing you have to say could ever — ever erase what you did to me."

Pashang removed his plumed hard cap, then scrubbed the sweat from his straight, brown hair. Not an imposing man — rather soft-faced and pleasant, especially those light brown eyes — but within, there wasn't a darker soul this side of the earth. Slightly frail in build, though tall — some would say *lanky*, others *lean*, to put a more positive spin. In his neat, formal Jotrid outfit, he seemed rather proper. It was disarming, and being disarmed around Khagan Pashang ought to terrify you.

"Sour over old times, are we?" he said with a sigh. "I did as ordered. Tamaz wanted a Sylgiz hostage to keep your tribe from expanding onto his territory. I asked him whether he wanted a son or the daughter, he said the daughter would do. Just to be fair, I asked your father what he preferred to part with, and he also chose you. An amicable deal, brokered by none other."

What lies! Tamaz had said he didn't know the Jotrids kidnapped me, and ordered me brought to his palace for my safety, as well as the kingdom's peace.

"Did Tamaz tell you different?" Pashang said, obviously noticing the trouble in my downcast gaze. "Of course, he did. Blaming us Jotrids was one of his many clever tricks, but everything we did was by his or his brother's design. I was but the towel he used to soak up blood, so his floor could sparkle."

"Just because someone else gave the order doesn't absolve you!"

I grunted. In any case, Tamaz was dead and Pashang not, so it was a fruitless argument.

"My two traveling companions," I said. "Are they here?"

"The Himyarite man and the Abyad woman. They, too, are our guests."

So Eshe was here. Kevah, probably not. But what woman was he referring to? The Abyads were a collection of desert tribes from the south, near the Yam Sup Sea and the border with Himyar. I had no companions from there.

"Are we your guests, Pashang, or your prisoners?"

His smirk was insufferable. "I'm sure you've heard tales of how Khagan Pashang treats his prisoners." He gestured at the surrounding comforts. "This isn't it."

"So you'll just let me leave…despite what everyone is saying about me?"

"I couldn't care less. Actually, that's not true. It's refreshing to find someone as reviled as me in this kingdom. After hearing about what you did, my shoulders feel a slight lighter."

Nauseous, I rested my head on the pillow and turned to my side. "You're a client of the Seluqals. Won't they order you to turn me over, like before?"

From this angle, I stared into his brown beard. Unlike most men his age, it seemed Pashang kept it trimmed close to his face. Some would call it *womanly*. But thinking back on the days when he lived with us, his beard was always rather patchy. Perhaps he couldn't grow it full, which wasn't that uncommon in the Waste.

He looked at Tekish and gestured at the flap.

"Feel better, Cyra," Tekish said as he walked out of the yurt. The other men followed him.

"You obviously don't trust me." Pashang sat at my bedside, too close for comfort. "Which is sensible — trust requires trust. The gulf between us is wider than the Endless. But I've no design against you, and neither does Mansur. Go wherever you like — I won't be your problem, so long as you won't be mine."

"Pashang, I—"

"When we were children, you used to call me something else. Remember?"

I winced at that thorn prick of remembrance. "You've grown out of that name, surely."

"Say it. Say it one more time, for the sake of our memory." His hungry smile showed a yearning for the past. Too many seemed to live there, building homes with their last happy memories. I despised the thought of living in what had gone — always better to look ahead.

"Forget it," I said. "I'm not the same person, and neither are you. What kind of monstrous woman would kill the Shah of Alanya…haven't you asked yourself?"

"Say it, Cyra. Just hearing it would be a salve."

"I won't." That came out hoarser than I wanted. "You're a sad creature, Khagan Pashang, and always have been. 'Our memory,' you say. I don't have a single fond memory of you. Even when we were children, I found you cloying. Just as insufferable as you are now."

"You used to scold me in the same way." He inhaled as if nostalgia scented my words. "I'll have to make do with that."

I turned onto my back and stared at the ceiling. For a moment, I saw stars shimmering in the daylight. I blinked and blinked and saw only the yurt ceiling, with all its magnificent patterns. From the shock of meeting Pashang, I'd neglected the more pertinent questions.

"Where did you find me?"

"We brought a storm with us from the Endless. The Zelthuriyan Desert hasn't seen a summer snow in decades. We rescued hundreds — dug them out of mounds, gave them rest, medicine, food. You were, thankfully, among them…"

That didn't sound right. The Palace of the Living flashed through my mind: tormented souls, stuck within a pyramid of flesh, each mouth singing its pain. And I'd been in heaven, floating with stars, watching their births and deaths.

Dreams, perhaps? Yet they carried the scent of memories.

"You're such a saintly man," I scoffed. "I want to see my companions. Now."

Pashang raised his hands, palms up. "Go see them, then."

I threw my blanket off and pushed to my feet. A heavy layer of sweat stuck to my body.

Pashang folded his arms and said, "You've turned red." He sniffed — was he smelling me!? "Sweating sickness, seems like. Cold never agreed with you."

"Where is my Himyarite friend? I want to see him. I want to know he's healthy."

"You've one mind, eh, Cyra? Always admired that. I recall when your cousin sewed a lovely fur cap, which your father wore on his rangings. Your face was red with jealousy. You wanted to make a prettier one and spent days just—"

"Shut up! I'd sooner gouge my remaining eye than reminisce with you!"

He tightened his shoulders and winced — was that all it took to silence the fearsome Pashang?

Upon walking out of the yurt, the sight of Qandbajar's gleaming saffron wall stunned me. Beyond, the Tower of Wisdom tasted the clouds, and the Sand Palace shimmered like crystal on its hill. The Grand Bazaar pyramid pointed to the sun like a brandished dagger. Last I remembered, we were two days from Qandbajar. Seemed they'd brought me a long way.

"You know, you're adorable when you're confused," Pashang, who'd followed me through the flap, said.

I wanted to retch at the thought of him finding me adorable.

"We brought you here by cart. You were asleep the whole time. Your friends, though, fared better and have been doing well."

Fitting that I'd departed Qandbajar in sleep and had returned in sleep.

Pashang gestured his head at the seven-row prayer line facing northwest, toward Zelthuriya. In the midst, there he was: Eshe, swaying his head with each repetition of Lat's name.

I rushed over, pulled him out, and hugged him. Unthinking. It was good to see an ally, amid so many enemies. He stumbled into my arms, bewildered at first, then exclaimed, "Cyra! You finally woke!"

"Where's Kevah?" I asked.

He shook his head and sighed. "No idea what happened to him. I got covered in snow after that whirlwind separated us."

"Whirlwind?"

"I'd rather not remember. Are you feeling all right? Your face is…redder than a monkey's ass at sunset."

Quite a comparison. "I don't want to stay here a moment longer. Khizr Khaz mentioned he had a place for us at the shrine. Let's go."

Eshe and I turned toward Pashang, who watched us with his hands neatly folded below his chest.

We approached him together. "Pashang, we're going into the city," I said. "As much as I begrudge it, you have my thanks for saving and looking after us."

"And your other companion?" Pashang said. "You don't want to see her?"

"You're mistaken." I shook my head. "Our other companion was a young man. His name is Kevah, a Ruthenian by birth and Sirmian by raising. If he comes here, tell him we went where we were supposed to."

"Kevah's certainly not a young man," a woman behind me said.

I turned to see another I never wanted to see: the black-clad Ruhi. Lacking in height, she seemed like a child wrapped in a tablecloth, which I so wanted to rip off.

"What in Lat's name are you doing here?" My hand formed a fist without me even knowing.

"Followed you. That was my mission. Until the sky fell. Then I tried to save you but ended up needing saving myself."

My jaw hung in shock and disgust. "So…the Disciples sent you to spy on us. You certainly don't stand out." I chuckled, then turned to Eshe, hoping he would appreciate the jape. But he gazed at the ground, eyes closed, his body wincing as if from shame.

"You think I stand out like this? Wait till you see what's underneath." In one motion, Ruhi pulled off her veil, then threw it to the ground.

Patterned blood covered her face. On her nose was a character that resembled a cup with a dot in it, and across her forehead, one that looked like the sea. On her cheeks shown what I could only describe as a snake eating itself. All manner of lines went down her neck and onward beneath her caftan. Bloodrunes covered this girl.

Eshe wouldn't look. Now I realized why. Because he and his dead brother had painted those bloodrunes when they tortured her.

We went to the yurt I'd woken up in to talk, out of earshot of Pashang and his riders. Bone-crafted pitchers of water and kumis sat on a low table, which the three of us shuffled around.

"Still won't look at me, Himyarite?" Ruhi said.

Ignoring the bloodrunes, she had a pleasing face. Gentle, wheat-colored hair, slightly up-slanted nose, and pupils like coffee beans.

Eshe finally looked at her, but not with remorse. "My father had a saying, a Himyarite wisdom. 'When webs of a spider coalesce, they can trap a lion.' What web did you spin for the Disciples, I wonder?"

Ruhi huffed. "All this time, I thought you'd repented. But looks like you're still on the path that got you and your brother thrown off a cliff. Want to know how I became a Disciple? It's thanks to you."

"What?" Eshe said.

Ruhi pointed at the bloodrune on her forehead, which looked like sea waves. "*Thousandth Hell* — that's what this one is called, right? The pain it caused has never ceased. Even now, my skin is boiling, and every time it cooks, new skin replaces it. It's only by perfect *fanaa* that I'm able to endure living, which is the trait the Disciples value most."

Eshe stared at her with watering eyes. He looked like a man who was sorry, and yet he said nothing.

"I always wanted to ask you," Ruhi said, showing no emotion, "why did you go so far? Did you...enjoy it?"

Eshe shook his head. "No. I went so far because...because to save the people from whatever Aschere had planned, was worth the suffering — even death — of one girl."

"What you gave me was worse than death. But I see truth on your face. In the moment, you believed you were serving the good. And yet...even now, you're not sorry."

"I'm not sorry because I still don't believe you. Hearing your cries that day, my mercy overcame my wrath. But when I heard about what your friend Aschere did — how her wicked actions led to the deaths of tens of thousands of innocent Latians — if there's still a chance you know an inkling about the evil she served — I'd do worse to you, right now, where we sit."

"E-Eshe..." I clutched his shoulder. How could he say such a thing?

Ruhi sighed. "All I know is this — even an evil woman needed a friend. Aschere would tell me about the life she left behind. A loving husband, a baby son, an adopted daughter, a father. She was lonely, and so was I, to be true." Ruhi shook her head. "You know what? I don't think she believed herself to be evil. Like you, I'm sure she thought the suffering she brought worth it."

"You'd compare me to her?" Eshe glared with fire. "I was trying to prevent calamity! I would have even confronted Aschere herself, but a bloodwriter is no match for a magus."

"So you tortured a little girl?" Ruhi sneered. "If you still can't see how wrong that is, you are truly lost, Eshe."

Is this how it had been when Eshe and his brother tortured her? If so, we weren't going to solve this now.

Eshe took a chug straight from the kumis pitcher. "Someone has to do what others won't, to protect the land. If the Disciples don't understand that, then I'll be their shadow and let Lat be the judge."

While I felt for Ruhi and understood Eshe's position as well, none of this mattered.

"Stop! Right now!" I turned to Ruhi. "I don't know what you want, but best we go our separate ways. And if I see you following us, I won't be so kind next time." Now I turned to Eshe. "I thought you regretted what you did to her, but I guess not. In any case, it was never my business. Lest you forget, we're here to find a sorcerer, and your problem with her has nothing to do with that."

"What makes you so sure?" Eshe said. "What if Aschere and the sorcerer in the palace serve the same evil?"

"Fanciful," Ruhi scoffed. "But you've no evidence. You're clutching, like you did with me."

I got up and tried to pull Eshe up too. I didn't want to stay in this camp another moment. But Eshe yanked out of my hold.

"I'm glad you're here," he said to Ruhi, "out in the open, again. Watch yourself, because I'm not done with you."

"And I'm not done with you," Ruhi replied, her slight lips plump with disgust. "I've my own mission, on behalf of the Disciples. Best not get in my way, because I'm no longer a little tea girl for you to abuse."

"Spy," Eshe said, pushing to his feet at last. "I know a liar when I see one!"

I dragged him out of the yurt. A string of horses passed by, tied to each other. All around, horses, men, and women went about. The sweet tang of fruits filled the air; a young Jotrid woman sorted muskmelons, pomegranates, and dates into baskets. They grew in the cultivation beds along the Vogras River, though I wondered if they'd paid for or taken from the sowers who tended that land.

"Listen." I grabbed Eshe's shoulders. "Forget about her. Let's go find Khizr Khaz and finally do what we're supposed to — unveil the soulshifter. Kyars is going to arrive any day now, and if we don't have a truth to tell him..."

"Do you think I'm doing this for you?" Eshe said, his voice laden and sad. "Or for some pompous fucking prince?"

"Why are you, then?"

"I track and hunt sorcerers. Aschere was the worst of them — she brought an infidel army into a Latian city and nearly caused the ruin of a kingdom. I won't let it happen again, no matter what I need do to stop it."

I nodded as quickly as I could. "I'm with you, brother. I might be a victim of the sorcerer, but doubtless he has worse planned. But if I were you, I'd forget about Ruhi. Her and all this," I spread my arms, gesturing at the Jotrid camp, "it's a distraction. I want to expose the sorcerer that took my life, took my face, took every shred of happiness. Maybe then I can get something back. We might have different reasons, but our goals are one."

"One goal, then," he said. "Nothing should separate us, and no mercy for the wicked. I'll hold you to that."

We shook hands, reaffirming our shared purpose. Though whether our methods and values aligned was an open question.

"Did your camel survive?" I asked.

Eshe winced and shook his head. "Fluffy wasn't made for snow."

She was rather fluffy for a camel. Poor girl. "I could try asking Pashang for two horses. Although…I'd rather not speak with him, again. The gate's not that far — we could just walk."

"You mean the man who had every healer in his camp attend you, who would watch you sleep for hours to ensure you weren't dying? Pashang worships you, and there are five horses for every rider here. Go ask him."

Well, I supposed I had to.

Pashang was sitting at a fire pit, alone, roasting what smelled like yak on a spit. I recalled it being his favorite, and I rather missed its juiciness and delicate flavor. But did the *great* khagan of the Jotrids have nothing better to do or anyone to sit with? How quaint.

"Do me another kindness," I said, straining to be as tempered as

I could with him. "Lend me and my companion horses. They need not be mares, or Kashanese. Whatever you can spare."

He looked up with concern. "Sweating sickness is like this, you know? Lively enough to move mountains in the day, but come the moon, you'll be clutching your sheets."

"So long as they're not your sheets, I'll endure."

He sighed, almost out of resignation. "Doesn't being here, with us, remind you of home?"

I pointed to the Sand Palace, which looked fuzzy at this distance. "That's my home, Pashang. That's where I'm ending up. Either there, or in the grave."

"So ambitious. Like your brother. I lost to him twice, you know. Was looking forward to a third try at some of that Sylgiz grazing land, but now…" He raised his hands in defeat. "Guess I'll have a go at Gokberk."

"A Sylgiz has ten times the spirit of a Jotrid." My father's words spewed out of my mouth.

Pashang chuckled. "And a Jotrid has ten times the strength of an Alanyan. So that would make you a hundred times better than any man in those walls. Why, then, are you finding it so difficult?"

"And why are you here?" I didn't want to ask, but his mere presence chaffed. "Why bring the horde? The Disciples say you're here to make trouble for Kyars. They, like everyone else, are so scared of you." I stepped closer, so that he sat in my shade. "Call me foolish, but I'm not. After what I've seen, what I've experienced, I know you're a just a small man casting a large shadow."

He stood, reminding me how much taller he was. About Cihan's height. "Do you remember, Cyra?" He came to my ear, whispered, "Do you remember what happened whilst you floated with all those brightly burning stars?"

I stepped back, my eyebrows raised in shock as the memory of falling into a star burned through my mind. "What did you say?"

An almost otherworldly smile stretched across his face. "You were falling. Floating. Flying. I took you by the hand, and we swam across a thousand worlds."

I shut my eyes as the memories burned with every word. Stars birthing, dying, exploding, crying. I'd experienced too much for one mind, for one lifetime, that was why—

Pashang grabbed my hand, like he'd done in the memory. "*She* felt your suffering, as if it were her own. And so, in her compassion, she gave you something."

I pulled away, overwhelmed by celestial images and sensations. I looked up at the sky; the stars burned like emeralds, each hymning its own distinct song.

"Two horses," I said, barely able to stand. "Give us two horses."

"You can have anything you want." Pashang spread out his arms. "My camp is yours. My Jotrids are yours." He tugged his collar. "I am yours."

ONCE THROUGH THE CITY GATE, we stopped at Eshe's house in the Glass District. His third story loft featured a stunning view of the glass sculpture of Saint Nora. On the saint's birthday, once a year, men and women gathered to stone the statue, to show that it was unbreakable. It was the saint's final miracle before she ascended to Barzakh and was so astonishing they built an entire district around it.

Eshe's loft was not only spacious but filled with tapestries and carpets with a simple, geometric style I didn't recognize. Himyaric, I assumed. He'd devoted an entire room for books, with niches on every wall.

Now he was tossing all the books on the floor.

"It's not here," he said. "Could they have…recovered it?"

"You're really that worried about a book?"

"It's one of the only copies of *Flavors of Blood Volume Two* in the world. And it contained a hidden code that I'd been deciphering, after learning the truth about its author from a drunk Philosopher.

Perhaps the Philosophers broke in and took it back…but the door was locked and latched when we arrived…so how?"

"I'm more surprised the gholam didn't break in. They must've gotten your name from Hadrith, Ozar, or Sambal and so know you were involved."

He picked up a stack of books and dropped them one by one into a niche. "You've no faith in your friends?"

"None were my friends. And I know that to save themselves, they'd give up Saint Chisti himself. So best we not linger, lest someone sight us."

"Do you really think we can trust the Order, though?"

"We've no other choice. And Sheikh Khizr was as sincere as I've ever seen anyone be. As the Grand Mufti of the Fount, he has tremendous access to the palace, to everywhere in the city, really. With his help, we'll expose the sorcerer, surely."

As Eshe continued to ransack his house for the book, I sat on his balcony and watched people dally about the district. Being among the richest areas in the city, too many buildings sported a dome — either green or gold — and around those domes hung vines. Glass panels, some colored with flowery patterns, replaced whole walls. Unlit streetlamps perched on the sides of the clean, cobbled streets.

It was then I began to feel faint. Sweating sickness — I'd had it twice or thrice before. Always best to stay in bed and sweat it out, but we hadn't time for weakness. I rested my head on a silk pillow, hoping fresh air would relieve the scorch spreading from my core.

A dry hand clasped my forehead. I looked up to see Eshe crouching over me. "You're heating up," he said. "Perhaps it's best we stay for a night. Trust me, my lodgings are a lot comfier than the Order's."

Too weak to argue, I nodded and moved to his bedroom. Silk sheets and a wool blanket, just like I had in the palace. While I got comfortable, Eshe pressed leaves into a bowl, mashed them with a stick, then headed to the kitchen to boil water. He returned with two steaming tea mugs. I sniffed; sugarcane and cinnamon streamed into my nose, calming me.

"I've memorized most basic medical tomes," he said with a huffed chest. "Short of an actual healer, you won't find a better man to look after you."

As I stared at his unfamiliar ceiling, I saw the faint edges of stars burning through sky and stone. I closed my eye, but that only vivified them, so I turned to my side and faced Eshe, who was sitting on a cushion and watching me.

"All that knowledge," I said, "and yet you insult people for a living."

"Knowledge is one thing, perception another, and insight a third. I honed all three weapons so I could serve. But they cut both ways."

Watching him savor his tea, only then did I realize how alone Eshe was. As alone as me, expelled from where he belonged and grasping at faint, flickering hopes.

"I wasted my life," I said, "I should have been sharpening my weapons, too. Because now I'm forced to fight with nothing but a dull blade."

He smiled and shook his head. "You're too hard on yourself. Yours isn't a dull blade, not at all. You're clever in ways that I'm not. And you rode that horse like a true khatun."

"You flatter me, Eshe. But while you were memorizing rare books and hunting sorcerers, I was sipping coffee, watching dances, and gossiping with other vain, tortured women."

"So you know their game, then. The game they play in the palace, where a poisoned word must be hidden beneath a pound of flour. I'd say that'll come in handy."

I chuckled, catching the bitterness on my tongue. "I wish I were more than that. I wish I were something. That's why I wanted to be..." I hesitated to speak my shame.

"Married to Kyars? Or that little shit, Hadrith? It's perfectly understandable. What other chance would you get to be something? We're all hemmed in by our births. Being a Himyarite — dark as coal, as they say — people would think me a slave, if I didn't wear silk, live in the Glass District, and speak with a lofty lilt."

He really did have a lofty accent. But mine was just as lofty, so I hadn't noticed. "You're the farthest thing from a slave. In fact, you might be the most complicated person I've ever met."

Eshe laughed, almost choking on his tea. "Now that's a compliment I could never come up with."

"I'm not sure it's a compliment."

"I know."

We both laughed. How nice to feel camaraderie after so long.

I said, "When I was a child, we had nothing, but we were free. And then as a grown up, I had everything, but I wasn't free." I chuckled at the sadness of it all. "And now, I have nothing, nor am I free. But you, Eshe…you have everything, and you're free. Why not find a nice wife and live out your days, savoring it all?"

"I'm not made for that." He spread his arms, palms up. "This house, the gold — it's wasted on me. I was happiest as a Disciple, sleeping on the sand, because I had purpose as fuel. Now…I'm starting to feel that again."

"So my problems bring you happiness?" I chuckled.

"Something like that."

I DRIFTED to sleep amid our conversation. Dreamless, thank Lat. In the deadest part of the night, I awoke gasping for breath. My nose had congested in my sleep, and perhaps I wasn't breathing well on my side. A layer of sweat swamped my skin, and heat radiated from my chest and forehead.

Eshe snored serenely, on his stomach. Best to let him rest.

I thirsted, so I got up and, despite my heaviness, headed for the kitchen. On the way, I passed a mirror. Amid the moonlight streaming through the open windows, I saw me, a soggy bandage wrapped over my right eye. But now, I didn't feel sorry for myself, and a hopeful glimmer lifted my spirits. I wasn't the only one in this struggle. I wasn't alone.

Something buzzed at my ear. I swatted it, missed. It landed on the mirror: a firefly, twinkling green. How luminous.

It flew toward the ceiling. As I followed its path, stars burned on my eyelids. An endlessness of them, orbiting each other without pattern — twinkling in and out of existence — exploding — growing — shrinking — wailing — singing.

Pashang's words played in my mind: *"She felt your suffering, as if it were her own."*

I couldn't hide it from myself. Not anymore.

I pulled the bandage off and stared into the mirror. Stared into my right eye, which was black and without a pupil. When I shut my right eye, I saw only the world, but when I shut my left eye, I saw only stars.

"And so, in her compassion, she gave you something."

And what a thing it was.

16

ZEDRA

By pretending I couldn't walk, they'd let Celene continue to attend me. In the morning, we got permission to use the bath — naturally. And so Celene wheeled me there.

"There are new ships in the harbor!" Celene said as we passed through the sunlit hallway, the cool after-dawn air flowing through the open windows. "I noticed them from the balcony. They've the emblem of Principus on their sails — that means they're Sargosan ships! Sargosa is a client of Crucis. Perhaps...perhaps they can take me home."

I'd noticed them, too. Ghastly emblem that resembled a jellyfish with a single, bulging eye.

"Don't get your hopes up, dear. They sailed from the east, from the Sargosan outposts on the islands south of Kashan. That's even farther from your home than here." I knew this from following Ozar as the drongo. He bought spices from the Sargosans and oft used their ships.

Celene heaved with disappointment. "Well...ugh...I knew it was too good to be true, like all my hopes."

Once at the bath, I asked her to join me in the hot pool. The eunuchs had lit sticks of nutmeg in the incense burners: spicy, sweet, and penetrating. The water, though, seemed a tad frothy. With the fountain gushing, I whispered my intention.

"We're leaving. Right now. If you want to go home, you'll do everything I tell you, all right?"

She gaped, jowls pink. "What? What do you mean leaving? Where will we go?"

A steam cloud bubbling from the coal burner separated us. I waded to her front, so she'd see me clearly and not mistake my seriousness. "I promise, if you do what I say, I'll see you home. Do you accept, Celene?" I held out my dripping hand.

Her agonized glare said it all. "I told you, how can I be sure?"

"How are you sure there's an angel in the sky, hearing your desperate prayers?"

"I saw him."

"Before you saw him, you had faith, didn't you?"

She snickered and shook her head. "Are you comparing yourself to my god? That I ought to believe your words, the way I believe Angelsong?"

How to convince her that I deserved her faith? That I, too, possessed miracles?

"Come with me." I pushed out of the pool.

Celene gasped as I walked on my two strong legs. "How long've you been deceiving everyone?"

"Longer than you've been breathing." I took her hand and helped her out of the pool. "I want to show you something."

She followed me into the steam room. I breathed deep, then pushed on the coal burner; getting it to budge burned my meager chest muscles. But with it aside, the bloodrune, and my handprint beside it, lay revealed.

I knelt and traced the rune with my fingers: three eyes around a star. How agonized I'd been when I made it, only a day after being brought here. To a new place, a new people, a new time.

"What is that?" Celene asked.

"Where I came from…and when I came from…there was nothing like this bath chamber. I was at once struck with wonder, full of agony, and suddenly alone. Not knowing how to even balance in a place like this, I slipped and hit my head. Thought I was going to bleed to death. So I made this bloodrune…for one final, joyous memory."

"Blood…rune?" Celene gasped. "Are you some kind of…"

Trust requires trust, so I hoped to earn some with my truth. "Yes…I am. Deep in the Waste, in a place called the Red for the tinge of its sky, lies the God Sea. I was baptized there when I was six years old. I still remember how the water tasted…as if my mouth were full of coins. My ancestors learned about it, and how to make these runes, from a jinn tribe, and they claimed to have learned it from a god."

"Not a god. An angel. The angel Marot." Celene gulped. "Marot came to test mankind. All who learned magic from him would be cast into the fire, their lineages cursed for eternity, which is why it's forbidden in my faith. Which is why I can't be a part of this!"

I took her hand again, but she pulled away and turned her back.

"Will you at least listen to my story?" I asked.

She wasn't covering her ears, nor had she left the steam chamber.

I said, "When I made this rune, I was just like you — yearning to be somewhere else. I hoped it would ease my longing. It does something remarkable, despite being written with my own, simple blood."

"There's nothing simple about you," Celene whispered, her back still turned.

"I'm going to make it glow, and then I'm going to hold your hand, and you're going to touch it."

I whispered the incantation to the Morning Star; the rune glowed briefly.

Celene turned to look. She stared into it, almost entranced. "This

is sin. You and your ancestors failed Marot's trial. You're cursed —
I'll not join you!"

I took her hand. "You want to go home, don't you?"

She nodded. "Of course. It's all I want. But I can't touch that!"

"The moment we entered this palace, our rules didn't matter.
What we wanted didn't matter. Kyars made me realize that rather
quickly. Now, I'll do the same for you."

I took her other hand. She tried to pull away. I caught her terrified eyes with my assured gaze, as I'd done countless times with
my daughters.

Her hands fell limp, as if she'd resigned her strength. "Marot
forgive me. Twelve forgive me. Archangel forgive me."

She'd feel less guilt if I forced her. So I hung my arm around her
neck, then pushed her trembling hand onto the bloodrune.

I AWOKE IN ANOTHER BATH, but it was nothing like the one I'd come
from. A water clock hung on the stone wall, numerals written on
the glass for each hour of the day. *Drip-drip-drip.*

An organ sat on the far side, its pipes stretching to the ceiling.
No one played it, and yet it bellowed. The keys…pressed down by
themselves! Could it be a jinn intent on mischief? I moved closer
and studied it; this was no magic: as water from the glass pipe on
the wall passed through, some clever mechanism pushed the keys.
The Philosophers had similar contraptions in the Tower, I recalled.
And the music this organ made: so thunderous, as if some world-
ending battle were to begin. Around me, water gushed from the
walls like they did from the waterfalls where I grew up. But I
wasn't anywhere near there — no, I was farther than I'd ever been.

I stepped into a fall and let the water douse my long, tawny hair
and fair body. Whoever I was inhabiting, they were more carefree
than I'd ever been; I even twirled and hopped, landing on my
tiptoes — what country's dance was this?

"Adonia, my flower, are you ready?" Foreign words — as if you took Paramic and stretched it, then sunk it under the sea — yet, somehow, I knew what they meant.

I turned to see Celene, wearing the daintiest outfit, whilst I was damp and naked. A necklace with layers of diamonds and sapphires in a chaotic mix hung around her neck. A bright purple cape covered her shoulders and wrapped around her front; marching lions in rose gold adorned the base. But more stunning was the tiara that sunk onto her head, a size too large: pearls dangled from it, intermixing with her bright hair. I could scarcely huff out a word with how awestruck I, or rather Adonia, was.

"You like it so much?" Celene said, giggling. She twirled. Then she closed in, as if to hug my dripping, naked form with her royal garb. But instead of putting her arms around me, she pushed her lips up to mine.

I stepped back. Whereas I was stunned, the mind I'd inhabited fluttered, enraptured by the kiss.

"No one's watching," she said. "Stop being so coy."

My cheeks got hot and red. "Sorry, my lady. I'm just overcome by…how beautiful you look." Speaking a language I didn't know, yet somehow understood, was like plucking flowers out of air.

"Don't 'my lady' me. We're in my home now, my castle. There're no priests here to fear."

I wondered where we'd been before. I could smell the memory, though it wasn't mine. Some place…holy. Long, drafty dark-stone corridors. Thin air, views of the lowlands, as if we were perched on a peak. Crucian hymns, thick dusty robes, old tomes, and tiresome chores.

"You'll do wonderfully today." Celene put her hand on my bare waist. It was warmer than the steam around us. "Remember, if you get nervous, it's only the imperial family." She snorted mischievously.

Laughter came from high in my throat. "That's supposed to make me *less* nervous?"

"You can imagine us naked." Celene pressed her head against

my breast, wetting her gown. "Though you've left naught to my imagination." Another chuckle.

I eased her off. "I'd best get ready, then." I could only guess what for.

Celene grinned and nodded. "You will do great, I mean it." She blew me a kiss while twirling out the bath, bereft of a princess's grace.

I returned to the water falling from the wall. I put my hand in my armpit, then brought it to my nose — the salty smell of someone else. I pooled spit in my mouth and swallowed. Tasted like someone else, too — though she possessed seeker's blood, like mine.

Adonia was her name. I washed, letting the waterfall feel every inch of me. The water tasted different, too: sediment-filled and sweet. I'd come to a new world.

Afterward, I dressed and walked through a tapestried stone corridor toward my room. Golden angels were emblazoned on the bright, hanging carpets on the wall: Adonia knew their names. Malak with a spider eye and legs taller than towers; the jellyfish Principus and his lightning tentacles, each large enough to hold a galleon; Cessiel with her wispy, feathered form and kind eyes arrayed in a diamond; Micah, his ten vertical eyes open or closed in no clear pattern.

I stopped at the angel Marot. Marot was just a man — faceless and indistinct. He held four cards in his right hand, each symbolizing a variety of sorcery: demonbinding, bloodwriting, sungorging, and — most terrifying — starwriting. He hid his left hand behind his back, not ready to show his other cards to mankind.

How pious Adonia was to know this story in detail. In fact, she'd memorized the hymns — they bounced around my head, melodious and deep. Somber, because they were about man's failure to resist temptation, to choose faith over forbidden power.

In Adonia's room — a guest room in the castle — a high and wide bed covered one wall. To climb it seemed a chore; while

Adonia didn't mind, I wondered why it was so far from the floor. The couch of blue and gold thread against the other wall seemed more inviting. Everything here was soft and pillowed and carpeted, like in the Sand Palace.

A half-woven tapestry, featuring winged men and women flying around a cloud, sat on the couch — Adonia's hobby, perhaps?

But not her *favorite* hobby. When I opened the wooden dress closet, it was like opening a window to the sun. I pulled out the outfit of gold thread, with a headdress that resembled a spire. Sequins were sewn onto everything — the Alanyans liked to do the same but with pillows, not clothes. Although, the Abyads liked to sew sequins on their caftans — I wonder who came up with the idea first.

Adonia dressed, then twirled in front of the mirror pane. The leggings clung tight, though the sequin and gold dress covered them. Her twirling dizzied me, but only excited her. This was no hobby; it was her purpose.

I'd enjoyed hundreds of dances since coming to the Sand Palace: Kashanese, Sirmian, Abyad, Abistran, Silklander, Dycondian, and more from places I never knew existed. Some flowed, others made generous use of pauses; some were supple like streams, and others roared like tides. But I'd never seen a Crucian dance, and as Adonia left the room and strutted toward the great hall, I realized in horror that I'd be performing one.

There I stood; the sunshine through stained glass painted me red and gold. Upon the highest dais I'd ever seen sat the Imperator, his face shadowed by a canopy. Then I realized there was no dais; his throne…floated. Celene had told me magic was forbidden in her faith, but could that be anything else?

Around me in the massive, hollow hall, the court sat in groups of two or three on separate balconies. Purple was never out of fashion in Crucis, though some men and women sported teal robes, and yet others draped themselves in gaudy gold. How Alanyan. Adonia glanced at the balconies above, searching for Celene. She craved the smile of the one she adored — a sweetness to soothe her nerves.

I found her. Celene stared down from the third story. She leaned on the railing and smiled a honey-filled smile. I smiled back. Then the Imperator clapped twice, and I began to twirl.

Beneath the Imperator's floating throne, a choir appeared, as if by magic. Perhaps they'd been on a platform that moved upward. All wore white and sang with deep, somber voices that sprang from their bellies and souls. I twirled and stepped, my toes holding my weight, as a wind blew from my heart and through my arms. A holy song, a holy dance — and I was one and holy — in the east, we would call it *fanaa*, but it was union with god, nonetheless.

How could a toe hold my weight as I twirled? I lifted my other leg backward and leaned forward; as I spun, I dragged the world with me. Time ceased, and the air itself disappeared, as if I would forever spin.

To finish the dance, as the chorists' tempo quickened with alternating high-and-low pitched hymns, I pranced forward, chest out, and spread my arms as if wearing wings, then stopped, turned, and slid onto my knees, arms above my head and back flat. *Angelfall*, the move was called, and I performed it as an angel would.

Clapping echoed across the four walls; it seemed millions cheered me. An entire empire. I'd never been under such attention nor felt my heart *thud-thud* with both elation and relief. A dance I'd practiced for months had been born — and now, I bathed in love.

The Imperator's throne descended with a steamy hiss. The chorists parted, and he walked toward me, his metal-sole boots clanging on the marble. He held out his hand for me to kiss. On bended knee, I glimpsed the face of Celene's father: youthful, hazel-haired, and handsome.

"Lord Imperator." I put my hand on my heart and kissed his ring finger.

He said, "The priests say Cessiel performed this dance after the

Fall. I fear we have all been witness to a miracle, this day. I fear faith is no longer enough for our hearts to enter heaven."

Praise...cloaked in faithful words that Adonia understood, though I struggled to make straight. Nevertheless, I lowered my gaze and smiled at his boots.

"My daughter told me you were magnificent, but that is a shade of what you are. Ask for anything, and you shall have it." But the one thing I wanted, he would never give. All Adonia wanted was Celene, and in Crucis like in Alanya, such a thing — even if attained — ought not to be spoken.

After leaving the great hall, I rushed to Celene's room, where I knew she'd be waiting. It was, fittingly, in a tower, and I trudged up too many stairs in shoes meant for dancing. But I didn't fall until I found her arms at the doorway.

She pushed me onto the bed. I wanted to resist, but perhaps it was best to let Adonia have her happiness. More importantly, to let Celene taste the reason she conjured this *fantasy*. In my mind, I pictured the drained water clock — *drip-drip-drip* — the cycle would end any moment.

Celene had just pulled off my clothes when cracks erupted on my vision, as if a bird had crashed into a window. When she stuck and wriggled her tongue in my mouth, Adonia melted with joy while I tried to stay apart from the ecstasy. I tasted Celene's spit: milky with salty notes, almost like ayran, though unlike any flavor of blood I'd tasted. Could it be...yet another rare flavor?

The cracks shattered my vision, exploding it to pieces, severing Adonia's ecstasy.

I AWOKE in the Sand Palace's steam room, laid out as if asleep in bed, my towel a damp blanket. Celene shivered on the floor, her towel wrapped over her face.

I pulled the towel away to see red, tear-filled cheeks.

"Ad-Adon-Adonia," she mouthed. "How...how..."

"I told you I'd send you home."

She grabbed my hand. Squeezed. "Please, send me back. I want to go back. Please."

I shook my head. "Dear, that would be all wrong. Where I come from, there were sorcerers who spent each day *going back*, who couldn't endure their actual lives because what the bloodrune created was so much better."

"You don't understand," Celene cried. "You don't understand how good it felt...to be home again..."

"You didn't go home, dear. It was a mirage. That's the power of the bloodrune. It conjured what you wanted most. And I *do* understand. I was there, too. I felt...everything."

She glared at me in disbelief. "You were watching?"

"No...I was there. I was..."

It seemed my eyes told her; she backed away in shock, redness filling her cheeks. "You...no..."

"It just so happens Adonia and I have the same common flavor of blood. You've nothing to be ashamed of." I paused to breathe; that journey had taken much out of me. "I understand you now, dear. I understand all you left behind, all you long for. I can't even say I understood my own daughters as much."

She said, hoarsely, "But I don't understand you. I don't know who you are at all. I don't know what you want from me, or why. You...you *revealed* me, and yet you hide everything!"

"Because I have everything to hide. I'm the farthest thing from an open book. If you saw into my fantasies like I've seen into yours, you wouldn't find some giddy girl prancing around a castle. You'd see a river of blood, snaking through time itself and stinking from the corpses of entire generations, entire dynasties of my enemies."

Celene stood and wrapped her towel around herself. "I can sew the holes. You're a sorceress. You're much older than you look. You're a descendent of Chisti, and it appears you're on a mission equally as weighty. Perhaps you caused the chaos in this kingdom, or perhaps you're trying to stop it. But either way, it has nothing to do with me. And if I choose a side — whether your side or the other — then it'll just be more reason for someone to lock me up."

I, too, stood and wrapped myself. "Everyone will have to choose a side, Celene. I promise you. This is your chance to be on the winning side — your one and only chance. Because I'm going to leave this bath on my two feet, and then I'm going to fan the flames of a war — one that will engulf not just Qandbajar, not just Alanya, but the whole east."

"Is that what you are? A bringer of war and ruin? I've had enough of that!"

"You'd rather just waste away in this harem, the plaything of some prince? Come with me, and I'll make sure you go home. To your real home, not some mirage. And if this Adonia girl is still alive, you can make love to her every day for the rest of your lives." I held out my hand. "You know what I am. You know what they are, out there. You're either with me or with them. Choose."

She stared at my hand. Stared at it for so long, it hurt to keep holding it out. I was about to retract when she said, "Last I heard, Adonia was alive. And so was my father. And I'd like nothing more than to be with them again. You've told me your secrets, and that means you trusted me, so…I'm going to trust you."

We shook hands. And then I explained to her what I was about to do.

I STILL HAD some conqueror's blood remaining from when Vera had collected it from Cyra's lip gash, and I'd brought the tiny bottle with me to the bath. Once clothed, we began enacting my hastily crafted plan. First, I wheeled my chair to the doorway, then stood on the seat. With Celene holding the chair steady, I dipped my finger in the bottle of diluted blood and wrote a rune on a part of the doorframe that protruded an inch from the wall and faced the ceiling, so none would notice. The pattern resembled three eyes with a line cutting through. I invoked the star, and it glimmered.

"Close your eyes when you go through," I said.

Celene did so, mumbling "Marot forgive me" as she walked out the bath and into the hallway.

"Someone help!" she cried in her awfully accented Paramic. She'd learned something, at least. "The sultana is hurt!"

A maroon-robed eunuch rushed into the chamber.

"Sultana," he said, "are you all right? What has happened?" Then he clutched his head. "Oh my...suddenly I'm...very...sleep—"

His eyes glazed over; he fell in a heap on the damp, marble floor. I pulled him into the steam chamber, straining my muscles and bones, so the others wouldn't notice him.

As Celene ran through the halls screaming for help, more eunuchs dashed in and met the same fate. Their snoring resembled a cave of sleeping bears I'd once encountered in the Endless, long ago. After five minutes, we had most of the harem eunuchs on duty asleep in the steam rooms.

I closed my eyes and walked through the door. In the emerald-lamp lit hallway, dozens of concubines had gathered to see what the fuss was. Among them stood Mirima; I stepped to her.

"Where is my son?" I asked.

"You're walking again, Zedra dear?" She raised her eyebrows, obviously bewildered. "I heard you'd been hurt in there."

"I'm fine, just had a little fall. Where is Seluq?"

Mirima's eyebrows lowered into a limp expression. "My brother took him. You know what he's been saying. I'm afraid I..." She cleared her throat. "I don't know what he intends for your child."

Hearing that was like swallowing a sword covered in flames: my worst fear realized, and not for the first time. I clasped my throbbing forehead and steeled my tightening limbs. While I could send a bunch of eunuchs into slumber, to get my child from Mansur, I'd have to pierce through his armed and armored household guard. And bloodrunes, whilst powerful, were no substitute for armies.

"Do you believe him?" I asked Mirima. "That I'm the worst kind of whore?"

She shook her head. "Of course I don't believe such vile drivel. I've known you to be an honorable woman. I remember how you bled the first night Kyars laid with you, and the precise day and hour the healer deemed you were with child. My sight had not left you in that interval, and you didn't so much as glance at another man."

I took her ring-studded hand, which was rougher than I'd expected. "Thank you, sultana. Your faith means so much to me. But I cannot simply endure this while we wait for Kyars to return. I must do all I can to safeguard my son."

With the eunuchs snoring in the steam chambers, the way out of the harem lay open. But the gate guards outside were Mansur's, and they wouldn't let us pass. For that, I had a simpler bloodrune in mind, and it was time to go.

As I walked toward the exit, where I'd told Celene to wait, Mirima called, "Where are you going, dear?"

I turned and said, "I cannot save my son while a prisoner here." Though I wasn't sure where I would go.

Mirima picked up her dress and hurried to me. "Don't be so hasty. You won't get far alone. I'll request a carriage, and we'll ride to the one man who has any chance of saving you and your son."

"But Kyars is not here," I said, shaking my head.

"Not Kyars. I speak of the Grand Mufti of the Fount, Khizr Khaz."

Mirima cleverly dressed Celene and me in teal caftans and veils so we'd resemble her handmaids. Her affection for my son had always resembled my own, and so I didn't doubt her earnestness. By carriage, we rode to the Shrine of Saint Jamshid, home to both the order of the first saint-king and the Fount of Holy Scholars. Law set down by Tamaz's father stated only the Fount could order the death of a Seluqal. And as the entire country considered my son to be one, it made Khizr Khaz a powerful ally in this struggle.

The flickering thought of my son crying in the clutches of that devil Mansur filled me with bitter despair. How many of my children had I already watched die? I would not let it happen again, no matter what. Not again, not again, not again. Let the world bleed, the Great Terror remake us all, but my son would not suffer.

And yet, I had a higher purpose than being a mother. My son was the Children. The Padishah of the Final Hour. I had to ensure his future, for everyone's sake.

The carriage *clop-clopped* to a stop amid the traffic of Qandbajar's thoroughfare. A wagon full of metal ingots had spilled onto the lane, so the riders guarding our front had to dismount and help clear it by hand.

"The steam…put them all…to sleep," Mirima said, shaking her head. "I can scarcely believe it, and yet I saw it with my own eyes. What is this world coming to when servants think themselves entitled to our luxuries?"

After the eunuchs had woken, they'd been embarrassed to find themselves sleeping in the steam chambers. Any excuse they could make, they did. Sorcery, thank Lat, wasn't one. Not one of my most thought-through plans, surely, but we were out.

Celene stared out the window, seemingly drenched in her thoughts. Perhaps Adonia was dancing upon her mind. We sat across from Mirima, who clasped her hands and complained about the poor service in the Sand Palace.

"What are the servants like where you come from?" she asked in Sirmian, meaning she was talking to Celene.

But Celene continued staring out the window. I nudged her.

"Oh…my apologies, sultana," she said. "Where I come from, we don't have slaves. It is forbidden in our faith for one soul to own another."

"Surely you must have eunuchs, though," Mirima said. "Who keeps watch over the women?"

Celene nodded. "Yes, we do have eunuchs, but they are free men, too."

"And what does *free* mean, exactly? Can they just abscond from their service, any time they wish?"

Celene twisted her lips, as if perplexed. "Well, no, but they are paid, in the very least."

"So is every slave in Alanya. What's the difference?"

"A free man has his pride," Celene said, her tone lacking confidence.

Mirima sighed bitterly. "A servant with pride — that's the last thing anyone wants. Pride and service cannot share the same heart. To serve, you must admit you are beneath."

"I've been serving," Celene said, "and yet, I'm still proud of who I am. Of where I come from."

Mirima, her back straight and regal, glared into Celene's downcast eyes. "That's the problem with you, dear."

Wisely, Celene let it be. An uncomfortable silence reigned over the remaining ride.

I sipped hope when our carriage halted in front of the large shrine. Mirima still had a gholam escort, which surprised me, and they entered ahead of us. Minutes later, they beckoned us to leave the carriage, then guided us through a myriad of arches. Air seemed to pass so fast here, like there was more than a breeze. We came to a flat-roofed building behind the domed shrine. We stepped through its sunlit hallway, which the gholam had cleared ahead for our arrival, and into a room with a creaky door.

On the floor behind a low desk stacked with books and scrolls sat Khizr Khaz, his back against the wall. He stood to greet us. The man wasn't wearing his typical carded wool cloak but rather a rough-looking caftan that ended just above his bare ankles.

He gestured for the three of us to sit, though there weren't any pillows. Just cool, uncarpeted stone. Celene and I did so; Mirima took an age to lower herself and find a comfortable position: her usual high back and clasped hands. Stark contrast to Celene, who rested her chin on a fist.

"Apologies, but you gave me no warning," Khizr Khaz said in a matter-of-fact tone. "I would have come to the palace, where you'd be more dignified, had you summoned me with some notice."

"It's not dignity we're lacking," Mirima said. "Surely you're aware what's happened in the palace. What your old *friend* is doing."

"My friend and your brother." Khizr sighed.

Mirima turned to me. "Go on, dear. Best he hear it from you."

I put my hand to my chest. "Mansur has accused me of infidelity and taken my son, claiming he is not of Kyars' seed. He will murder my son, I have no doubt, as part of his scheme."

"His scheme to claim the throne," Khizr said, noting, with a faint smile, our surprise at his frankness. "The man has never stopped believing it was his right, despite Tamaz removing him from the line of succession that their father decided for this kingdom. There's a reason the Sirmian shahs still kill their brothers."

"Sheikh," I said, my voice fearful and heavy, "we can't wait for my beloved to return. Every day that he doesn't, Mansur grows more brazen. That's why we've come here. You're the only one who can stop him."

"Not the only one." Khizr Khaz knocked on his desk.

The door swung open, bringing sunshine from the hallway. Amid that light stood a man clad in golden chainmail, gleaming in the glow. He looked upon us and bent his neck.

"Sultanas," Pasha Kato said, "how lovely to see you healthy."

"Kato." Mirima looked up in surprise. "I was wondering what happened to you. Mansur was rather tight-lipped when I asked him why the palace had been emptied of gholam. I could barely convince him to let me retain my escort."

Kato put his hands on his hips. "He ordered us to return to our barrack, so he could take the palace and seize the heir, unimpeded.

But with the men of the Order, we've the numbers to overwhelm his household guard."

Just what I wanted. While Mansur was busy fighting off the gholam and the Order, I could ensure my son's safety, my own way.

"No!" I exclaimed, shuffling to my knees. "You'd make a battle of this? If Mansur finds his back to the wall, he'll dangle my son's life to save himself!"

"There's yet another problem," Sheikh Khizr said. "The Jotrids. They've shown no desire to enter the city, though I doubt they'll sit by if we attack Mansur."

"The gholam still control the walls," Kato said. "But…we'd have to divide our force to both retake the palace and hold the walls."

"Precisely." Khizr gestured for Kato to sit next to him. "Even with the Order augmenting your force, can we stop so many with so few?"

Kato sat cross-legged, across from me. "We need only keep Pashang from entering until Kyars returns. But Mansur's arrest can't wait. The longer he remains in the Sand Palace, the more people will believe he's in control. We must secure the heir and the Sand Palace without delay."

I squeezed my chest. "Did you not hear me? Mansur has all the leverage. He could kill my son. I came here believing the Fount and the Order would pressure Mansur into giving up this foolish power grab. I didn't come for blood." I came for nothing but blood. An ocean of it.

"Pressure?" Kato scoffed and shook his head. "Sultana, we are well beyond negotiating. The moment Mansur accused you, the mother of the shah-to-be, of infidelity, he turned traitor. I'm going to take his head off, embalm it, and perch it at the tip of the Grand Bazaar. Then I'm going to march to Merva and do like to his wife, two sons, and daughter, so none may ever challenge Kyars and your son."

Good. My faith in Kato seemed repaid this day.

I sighed, as if in resignation. Noting my trembles, Mirima

hugged me. "It's been hard on her," she said, "as it would be for any loving mother. And I share her concerns. But…though I hate the stench of blood, even I cannot think of another way. My brother must die."

I gave them a few sobs. "Please, get my son back. He's all I have in this world. Him and my beloved, who is so far away." And now, a gush of tears.

As Mirima held me close, I met Celene's gaze. She'd been quiet the whole time, sitting in the corner, and couldn't understand much Paramic anyway. But, as she stared into my eyes, she showed the briefest smile, as if she understood me. And, by every indication, she was the only one who did.

17

CYRA

"Your bandage is soaked in sweat," Eshe said as he set my breakfast tray at my bedside. "I'll run down and buy some gauze, help you change it."

I sat up in bed and stared at the clear broth as my stomach knotted without appetite. I absolutely could not let him help me change it, given what was underneath.

Eshe mixed the bowl with a spoon — whatever paste he'd added spread and thickened the broth. Still, I winced as he brought the spoon to my mouth.

"Eat," he said. "Your body has a fight of its own, needs what nourishment it can get."

"Ugh, all right." I slurped and swallowed. Not entirely tasteless — the chickpea paste had an earthiness to it.

"Cooking isn't one of your many talents, clearly," I said with my wryest smile.

Eshe chuckled. "I made breakfast for a sick woman. Return when you're healthy, and you'll see just how talented I can be."

Surprising confidence. "Really? I've been eating palace food for the past eight years. You'll need more than confidence to impress me."

He brushed my bandage. I turned away, fearful he'd notice. Notice my featureless black eye. But it stayed covered, and he only seemed concerned with how much I'd sweat during the night.

"I'll go get the gauze." At that, he left.

What the hell was I going to tell him? *Oh! I hadn't even noticed I grew a new eye! Haha!* The man hunted sorcerers and things arcane — well, I'd become something worth hunting. The eye showed me stars, and yet I'd no idea why, nor who gave it to me. All I knew was Khagan Pashang — of all fucking people — knew something about it.

Whatever it was, I couldn't let it distract from my purpose. We'd come to Qandbajar for a reason: to find and expose the sorcerer who killed Tamaz. To make certain Kyars, my husband by law, would take the throne knowing the truth. Many stood in our way: the sorcerer, Kato, and Lat only knew who else. The time for wavering and weakness had long passed.

I couldn't hide this from Eshe, though. He hadn't hidden his secrets from me, and we were partners in this ordeal. I had to tell him, I just…didn't know how. So I went over it in my head:

Eshe, my dear friend, I grew a weird eye that makes me see stars, even in the daytime. Oh, and it's entirely black…you know, like the wicked jinn from all those children's tales.

Wording confessions was obviously not my strength. But, like pouring alcohol on a wound, better to get it over with. I ought to just show him the eye and let him think what he will. He had to know, and he had to know now.

Ten minutes later, he *thump-thumped* up the stairs, entered my room, and tossed a bundle of gauze at me.

"Come on, take it off." He paused mid-step. "Your bandage, I mean."

"Bet I'm not the first girl you've said that to in this bed." I took a deep breath and reached for my bandage, ready to reveal my secret.

Knock-knock sounded on the door.

"Who could that be?"

As he went to answer the door, I got up and watched from the threshold of my room. Eshe opened the door, peeked through the crack, then backed away as the person on the other side pushed it wide.

Persons. Three men wearing flowing, ocean-blue robes with bronze scimitars on their belts entered the room and surrounded Eshe. I recognized the tall felt hats they wore, so exaggerated they nearly brushed the ceiling, as well as the metal clasps. Philosophers.

"This must be about the book," Eshe said. "I was just meaning to return it."

A man who wore a foreign shirt that featured an even larger metal clasp at the waist stepped forward. "You think the Grand Philosopher would barge into your lodging to retrieve a book?"

"You're…Litani?" Eshe asked as I backed against the wall, content to listen and not see or be seen. The Philosophers often seemed rude, dismissive, and blunt, even the ones who tutored me. I hoped Eshe wasn't in trouble.

"Pleasure to meet you, Eshe," Grand Philosopher Litani said. "How is Hakaim, by the way?"

"My father? He was well, last we corresponded."

"Happy to hear it. Your father did a great service for mankind. He only salvaged a fraction of the Ten Thousand Tomes of Tinbuq, but enough to be a torch in the night." He sighed like a disappointed father. "And then there's you…losing a book, darkening the world. I know you don't have it. But in that mind of yours, there are so many more books, aren't there, former Disciple Eshe?"

"If you want something, you need only ask. No need to barge into my home. I am a free man, with rights."

"*Rights.*" Litani scoffed. "You forfeited your rights the moment you didn't return *Flavors of Blood Volume Two.*"

"Is this or isn't this about the book?" Eshe asked, his tone perplexed. Obviously, Litani was using the lost book as a pretext for something else. "Like I said, I'll find and return it. Fine me, if you must, for the delay."

"*Fine* you," Litani said. "A fine you could obviously pay, given your lodging. That just won't do. We'll talk more at the Tower. Bring him!"

Eshe gasped and struggled and shouted as they grabbed him. A *thwap* sounded; Eshe wailed. I peeked to see him spitting blood on the wall — oh Lat, he was hurt! I backed away and heard rope tighten on his wrists as he huffed and pleaded. I wanted to jump out and save him…but what could I do?

Litani, though, continued to walk through the apartment. He stepped toward my room as I covered my mouth to douse my hurried breaths. He was a hair from entering when he said, "We can ransack this place later." He whistled. "Let's go. Master is waiting."

Master? But Litani was the Grand Philosopher — no one was higher than him at the Tower. Just who was he working for?

From my window, I watched them push Eshe into a black-roofed carriage. Before his head sunk inside, I caught sight of his bloody lips and fear-drenched eyes. By Lat, the Philosophers were a powerful group. What had he gotten himself into?

With daytime fueling me, I resolved to help my friend. Coming to Eshe's loft had been a mistake. We should've gone straight to where I now trotted: the Shrine of Saint Jamshid. Straight to Khizr Khaz, the most powerful man we could count on.

Heavy crowds made passing through the streets slower than wading through pudding, even on my spotted steed. A stinking sweat stench wafted in the breeze. The impatience was palpable: shouting and cursing alternated through the air. Awful to get stuck in this mire.

By the time I arrived at Saint Jamshid's, heaviness bore on my chest. Climbing off my steed, tying it at the nearest stable, and tossing a coin to the stable boy — just these rudimentary actions made me want to collapse on silk sheets. Or any sheets.

Out-of-rhythm chanting replaced the shouts and cursing of the streets as worshippers streamed in and out of the shrine. After walking through the colorful stone arches and main doorway, supplicants would reach through the cage that separated them from Saint Jamshid's sepulcher, as if they begged him to take their hands along with their prayers.

I plodded past the shrine toward the flat-roofed building where the Order lodged. Before I could reach the door, it swung open. I dashed behind an arch as several gholam, gilded scimitars on their belts, walked out. Upon sighting the bald, steel-faced Pasha Kato, I gasped. He was talking to a woman at his back; she was wearing dove-like brocade with silver accents, fit for a queen. What was Mirima doing here?

More shocking: behind them, Zedra walked out, wearing the breezy teal caftan of a handmaid. A relief to see my friend on her feet, but why was she dressed that way? Behind her was a familiar young and pale girl, similarly garbed. Was that...Celene? The Crucian princess I'd bought for Kyars?

I held my breath and listened as they passed. Difficult to make out what was said. Zedra and Celene spoke in Sirmian, though, and they mentioned the name Seluq. Her child?

Once they'd disappeared beyond the arches toward the back of the shrine, I let my breath out. What a strange grouping — why were they with Kato? And what were they doing in the Order's lodging?

I opened the door and entered the hallway. Bereft and emptied of people. The doors were shut, except for one, and within was the only man I cared to see: Khizr Khaz, sitting behind a low desk, writing a letter with a feather pen and blue ink.

He raised his eyebrow. "You can't be seen here, girl. Come in and close the door!"

I did as told. A candle burning in a corner niche provided dim light.

"Sheikh Khizr, I desperately need your help." I got on my knees, eye to eye with him. "Just now, one of my allies…my friend Eshe, was kidnapped by the Philosophers."

He crossed his arms. "Philosophers? What do they have to do with anything?"

"It's all so complicated." I pieced it together as I spoke with tense breaths. "He didn't return a book or something, and so they took him. I know we have a thousand other things to discuss, but this is urgent. It can't wait. If they hurt him, I…I…"

"It's all right, Cyra. I tell my own daughter, one bite at a time. Here you are, trying to gulp the whole apple." He pretended to chomp an apple.

He was right. "Eshe saved my life." I described how he'd written the runes that stopped me from bleeding out.

Sheikh Khizr nodded. "Ah, the exiled Disciple. So…the Philosophers have him." He sighed as if worn by the thought. "I'm going to be frank with you. Though several in the Order are Philosophers too, I don't have influence in the Tower of Wisdom — its leaders don't like me. And right now, what influence I do have, I'm putting toward saving this kingdom. One man, though a dear friend of yours, can't weigh against that."

"I understand, Sheikh Khizr. I ask so much of you. Yet, I've nowhere else to turn." I shut my eyes, but the tears flowed anyway. This burden weighed too much, and I needed someone to help me bear it. Without Eshe, it was all on me.

"Forgive me for changing the subject, but what happened to Kevah?"

I shook my head. "I don't know. He said something about a jinn tribe and jinn sultana when the desert snows started. After that…I don't know."

"We could have used him…in what's coming."

"Did something happen?"

Khizr Khaz cleared his throat. "Just as the Disciples feared, this succession has turned more than messy. I believe the sorcerer, whoever he may be, is not backing Kato — like you assumed — but Mansur and that dreaded khagan at our gates." He explained how Mansur had seized Zedra's child and expelled the gholam from the palace, which shed light on her visit here.

It truly was messier than I'd imagined. So many factions, so many vying men, yet all I wanted was to find the sorcerer who destroyed my life and to help Kyars keep his throne, perchance he may still consider me his wife.

"What should I do?" I asked, though I knew what I wanted to do. Even before my earnest hopes, the one thing I couldn't stomach was Eshe hurt. He'd saved me, and so I owed him everything.

"Nothing." Khizr Khaz shook his head. "You can't do a thing." Did he have to state the obvious so mercilessly? "Only warriors can defeat Mansur and his household guard, who are all hardened khazis from Kashan and beyond. You are no warrior. We'll need your gifts after the blood has dried, when it's time to uncover the sorcerer."

"I've no gifts." I lowered my head in self-pity. "Just rage, bitterness, and heaps of despair."

"You're more motivated than anyone, then. And you know what motivates me? Enforcing." He knocked on his desk — a woody bang. "Enforcing laws, good conduct, and godliness. Enforcing marriage contracts, like the one I presided between Kyars and yourself. In mine eyes, you are the Sultana of Sultanas and naught less."

By Lat, to hear such from the Grand Mufti enlivened my spirits. I managed a hoarse "thank you."

"Regarding the Philosophers, if you're going to try something in the interim, be careful. They are not what they seem. I suspect, as I've always suspected, that their loyalties are to a foreign power."

I'd never heard such a thing, and the thought of yet another enemy tightened my chest. "What foreign power?"

Khizr Khaz leaned across his desk. "The mightiest country in the world — the Empire of Silk."

I knew from geography lessons that the Silk Empire was on the far side of the earth, across the Waste, and beyond two seas. Theirs was a country built on metal and secret knowledge. Could they be related to the *master* Litani had mentioned? Perhaps they wanted Eshe for all the books he'd memorized. Perhaps they'd send him to the Silklands, and then I'd never get him back.

"I really don't know what to do, sheikh," I said. "I can't just walk into the Tower and demand they return my friend."

"No, you can't. You need an ally with influence. But Kyars, your best bet, is not here. Hadrith, your next best option, is in prison. Ozar, a likely number three, is in there with him. There are other viziers who could help you, but why would they? Everyone believes you murdered Shah Tamaz." He grunted, reached behind, then dropped a bare scimitar on the table. "This is my answer to Mansur. I suggest you find your answer to the Philosophers."

I stared at the scimitar's deathly sharp curve. Perhaps I, too, needed something to cut with.

It took two hours of nauseating, thigh-bruising riding to get to Pashang's camp. Where else was I to go? Khizr Khaz, though supporting, wasn't willing to spend his influence to help me. And expelling Mansur consumed his time and thought. But these Jotrids…they seemed oddly bored.

So bored that I found Pashang cutting the hair of his little brother, Tekish, with a heated blade outside an enormous, palatial yurt. I watched them from afar; he seemed enamored with the task, slicing hairs as if sculpting a statue. He would even pause and rub his beard, as if pondering his cuts.

The Pashang I saw seemed at odds with what I imagined and remembered. A rough boy, who punched first, with thick hands that broke what they touched. He'd become khagan of the Jotrids by killing seven claimants, each sadistically, if the stories were to be believed.

And yet, now he held that heated blade with slender hands. His cuts seemed considered. As I trotted near, he looked up and gave me an acknowledging nod, then resumed making deft cuts to Tekish's mop-like head.

A line of warriors sat on a log, waiting their turn. Some munched on seeds, others rolled bones, a crude version of dice. Was Pashang going to sculpt them all such considered styles?

"You could use a haircut," he said with a familiar wryness, "though, the women here are often stunned — in awe or anger — when I'm through with them."

"Want to do something useful, Pashang?"

"Not really. I'm enjoying this sojourn. Though I know it won't last."

I jumped off my horse and let it go where it may. This was its home, after all.

"Can I talk to you in confidence?" I asked as he made cuts.

He gestured his head toward the palatial yurt. Alanyan-style dancing lions patterned its entire width. "Wait in there."

I pushed through the flap. Inside was an auditorium of sorts. A dais sat at the center, bereft of any chair, and around it, cushioned floor seats laid out in concentric circles. On the far side, a dozen men holding quills clustered behind low tables. Upon my entrance, they hushed their buzzing conversation. This Jotrid gathering yurt didn't resemble that of the Sylgiz; most things here were of an Alanyan style. They used less bone and more wood. Their carpets were silky with flowing patterns, whereas ours were rougher and geometric. No wonder my brother had defeated the Jotrids thrice: they'd grown soft, they'd grown Alanyan. It was easy to prey upon helpless rebels, but I doubted they could overcome Kyars' richly provisioned, heavily armored gholam.

I settled on a cushion near the dais. Five minutes later, I was lying down from a crushing heaviness and staring at the open spot in the yurt's center. Daytime stars flickered on my vision like phantoms. My sluggish, sweaty limbs cried for rest and sleep, and so I gave in, despite the discomfort of being surrounded by strangers in a Jotrid yurt and Eshe's cry as a Philosopher hit him bloody ringing through my mind.

When I awoke, I wiped the slobber from my chin and sat straight. Khagan Pashang was next to me, scribbling on a parchment with a golden quill.

"You look healthier," he said. "Not quite radiant, but getting there."

"I don't feel any better."

"Oh? I hope your Himyarite companion is taking good care of you. Where is he, anyway?"

"That's why I'm here. The Philosophers took him." I breathed deep and could barely believe what I was about to say. "Pashang, I need your help to save him."

He set down his quill and parchment, giving me full attention. "Philosophers?"

I nodded. "They took him to the Tower, and when the Philosophers take someone, it doesn't end well. What hope do I have of getting him back, all alone? I need your help."

"You want me to storm the Tower?" He hunched his shoulders. "The gholam won't let us within a thousand feet of Qandbajar's wall. How am I supposed to help?"

As I stared at his manicured, sand-brown beard, I wondered what the hell Pashang's plan was. Khizr Khaz had made plain that the Order was about to move on Mansur, and yet Mansur's most powerful ally remained so distant and detached. Just what was going on?

"You said something to me," I inched closer to him, "last we spoke. Something about stars and a gift." I wasn't about to tell him I was seeing stars, nor that I grew a fresh eye, but had to extract what he knew. "What did you mean?"

Pashang folded his arms. "That's the question, isn't it?" He reached for my bandage.

I grabbed his wrist. "What are you doing?"

"Let me see it."

"See what?"

His smile poisoned me. "I know what's hiding there, Cyra. I saved you from the snowstorm, remember? And not just that. It wasn't my first time in the Palace of Bones. I guided you through the stars and saw the gift you left with."

I shuddered as memories stormed my mind: Pashang dragging me through a tide of whirling rocks and flaming comets toward a white tear amid endless black. "What is the Palace of Bones?"

"A fate worse than death," Pashang said, his expression plain. "And a new beginning, for us both."

"I don't understand," I shook my head. "I..."

He closed the distance, his dry breaths on my face. "I've never told this to anyone, but I'm going to tell you. I was lost in the deepest part of the Endless — the Red — for more than a year. Day and night, the sky never changes — puffed with bruised and bloody clouds. I found the Palace of Bones there. I went inside. And I, too, left with a gift."

"What gift?"

I winced when he took my hand, but still, I let him.

"The gift of a new path." His smile stretched. "One I walked alone. Until you. And visions...three visions, to be precise. We are in the midst of the second one — it began when I dragged you from the Palace of Bones, and it ends tonight. But my gift is nothing compared to yours. You, Cyra, are a starwriter."

I shook my head, perplexed. "The hell is a starwriter...and why is it worse than dying?"

"A starwriter, with a flick of her fingers, can bring a city to heel." His laugh was so guttural, the one familiar thing from his boyhood. "As for why it's worse than death...I suppose you'll find out."

Too much to understand and too little time.

"I just want to get my friend back, Pashang. If you can't help me, I'm leaving. And may we *never* see each other again."

"You can leave. You seem to think I'm here to hinder you, but for me…" He clasped his hands. "Only one thing matters."

I stopped myself from standing up. "One thing?"

"Getting my horde into the city. If only you could help me, somehow."

Oh Lat, that I couldn't do. If I counted Khizr Khaz as my ally, how could I help his enemy?

"Why? So you can back up Mansur? I won't aid in his power grab. He's trying to steal my husband's throne!"

Pashang chuckled. "Do you really think Kyars will honor a marriage with the girl who murdered his father? And, you know, they say Ahriyya has eyes of all black." He sighed, sharp and deep. "Insensitive of me, but I ought to state what is plain."

"I didn't kill Tamaz. I'm going to bring the truth to light. Kyars is a fair man. He'll see it."

"You didn't kill Tamaz?" Pashang glared at me, eyebrows zagged in obvious confusion. "Then…who did?"

Seemed he didn't know everything. "A sorcerer! A soulshifter who used my body!" I hushed, wary of the others on the far side of the yurt. "Has no one told you?"

"Soulshifter?" His jaw dropped, revealing worn, chalky teeth. "She's here, in Qandbajar, now?"

"*She?* You know something?"

Pashang looked up, as if into his own mind. "I saw her in my third vision. But she was…at least a hundred years old…her face as dry and cracked as tree bark." He shook his head as if shaking away the vision. "She's on our path, Cyra. A broken branch blocking the road to Paradise."

"Paradise? Must I repeat what you said? 'A fate worse than death.'" I suppressed a shudder. "Regardless, I'm going to save Eshe. And then I'm going to expose her, and then Kyars will know the truth."

"Yes-yes." Pashang grunted with annoyance. "It's like a litany for you. I wish I could see my purpose so clearly. If we could get into the city, I'd help you with all of it. Not next week, not tomorrow — this moment."

To my weary soul and body, such words were the sweet, uplifting beat of a tambourine. White-garbed men walked by toward the low desks on the far side, humming in conversation. After they'd passed, I said, "But how can we possibly get you into the city?"

"So you agree that we help each other?" he asked, eyes pleading.

If he could save Eshe and aid in exposing the soulshifter, then perhaps it was worth it. But could I trust the man who'd kidnapped and sold me? Who pulled me from my mother's arms?

"What if you're lying? What if you get inside, and then you run to Mansur?"

No, how could I?

I stood, content to leave and abandon all thought of getting help from such an awful creature.

Pashang got to his feet and grabbed my hand. A shock passed between us — lightning in our veins. In a breath, I felt hot and cold, numb and awakened, frozen and on fire. The stars flashed in every direction, and as they orbited through my vision, they hymned like a breeze on my ears. With my other hand, I reached out and touched one; the star began to spin, and so I drew a line from it to another star. The line pulled them together, as if through a taut string, and then they danced around each other.

A scathing ache raged through my skull; I plunged, knees first, onto a cushion, clasping my forehead. Pashang held me, then laid my head on a pillow.

"What the fuck — what was that?" I said.

"I saw…a star. Did you see it, too?"

"I saw more than *a* star. Ugh, it hurts." As if horses with iron hooves trampled my head.

"What if…this is the key?"

"Key?" I blinked until the stars disappeared, though the headache only intensified.

Pashang pulled my bandage off. I was in so much pain, I let him. He didn't seem bothered by the freakishness of my black-on-black eye. With the cloth off, the stars spun around me once more, and only shutting my eye would put out their twinkling.

"The key to the city," he said. "I've been praying for a way in, because one thing is certain — we're attacking the wall tonight." He spread out his arms. "The lack of readiness, of appetite you see among us — it's a ruse. Meant to put the gholam at ease."

"What? Why?"

"You were right about me, Cyra. I do intend to help Mansur. But I can't let them know it until the moment we strike. So…tonight… you're going to watch us attack the walls, you're going to watch us try to get over them, and — unless you can align those stars in our favor — you're going to watch us die."

LIKE THE SYLGIZ or any respectable Waste tribe, the Jotrids were able to form up fast. Within hours, Khagan Pashang had thousands of riders hurrying to join the battle lines stretched across the landscape. I peeked out the yurt's flap to see them fletching arrows, packing their steeds, testing matchlocks, and sharpening steel. Weary, I lied down and listened as they barked orders, dictated their last wills and letters to their loved ones, and sang throaty songs that inspired men to kill and die.

I got no rest hearing all that. Sunset came, and I sweat all over my pallet and sheets, so much that I hated my smell. When I sniffed my shoulder, the stench of a damp horse assaulted my nose. And it was everywhere.

Horse girl the concubines would call me when I arrived in the harem eight years ago. Although many hailed from the Waste, their tribes had been pacified, unlike the Sylgiz. So I truly was an odd thing.

While I could cover that up with glossy brocade, a fashionable hairstyle, and Alanyan manners, my accent was harder to shed. *"You speak Paramic as if a horse is neighing,"* someone once told me. I kept trying to speak like the others, like a proper Alanyan woman, but that only made it worse. A sad attempt is worse than no attempt, and trying so hard, everything out of my mouth sounded so falsely stretched. *"Now you speak like a cow is yawning,"* they would jest. So, for months, I barely spoke.

Tamaz noticed my silence, though. Once he'd pried the reason out of me, he assigned me a teacher, and for half a year, four hours a day, I practiced speaking a language I already knew with an accent that seemed impossible. The teacher had these special methods; she would make me sing, recite these tongue-tiring poems, and even instruct where I ought to settle my tongue for each word.

And it worked. All I needed was someone to tell me the right things to do, and I could follow. Sometimes all we lack is a little knowledge, some light to illuminate the path. The way I look and sound now, no one would guess that I lived my first fifteen years in the Waste with a tribe of horse warriors. I'm as Alanyan as it gets — for better or worse.

Pashang entered while I was on my side, itching my sweaty scalp.

"It's time." The man wore mirror armor inscribed with saintly verses and knotted with metals in six different colors. The Philosopher who tutored me once remarked that the mirrors on such armor were as useless as the inscribed verses — a ward for superstitions, particularly the *evil eye*. But if words written with blood could have power, and if I could touch stars with my fingers, then why not armor made of mirrors?

As Pashang held out his hand, I saw my sorry self in its reflection.

"I look like a yak took a shit."

"A little excitement's all you need." Pashang chuckled. How was he so jovial?

With a heave on my throbbing muscles, I sat up. "You're really going to throw yourselves at that high, gholam-filled, double-layered wall...for Mansur?"

Pashang shook his head. "For what Mansur promised — heaps of treasure and river-fed land."

"I'd say you already have enough, but a wiser fellow once told me that riches and power make a man more ambitious, not less."

"It's not about what I want. The Jotrids, as you know, are more of a...confederation of tribes. Our lands once spanned from Merva to the Vogras." He sighed. "Then your brother took half. If not for Mansur's golden embrace, I'd be a bloated corpse at the bottom of the river. And if I don't continue to provide for those above and below me, I may yet be."

I almost retched upon imagining a bloated corpse. "You know what I think? You're too at ease to be guided by fear."

"Because I've seen this day — I know how it ends."

"Tell me, then. Because I'm...afraid."

He looked away, as if hiding something. "You need to be."

His expression reminded me of when he and Cihan shaved a crude Sylgiz word onto a camel's side and then pretended it wasn't them. But far gone was that innocent time. I knew, in my soul, that we were invoking something we shouldn't. Everything about the Palace of Bones, about that giant, snake-limbed creature who guarded it, and even swimming with the stars — these were not things on the path of a faithful Latian. *The straight path.* And yet, when had the straight path worked for me? What had it gotten me, except maimed and left for dead, my hopes drowned in a deluge?

I grabbed Pashang's hand; he pulled me up into his chest. His armor emanated a coolness, and I let it relieve the boiling between my bones. For a moment...until I felt disgusted at his touch and pushed away before it got too awkward.

I followed him outside to a breezeless evening sky. The crescent moon hung high and cast everything in a milky tone. A thorny disgust pooled in my throat upon seeing these Jotrids lined up on their steeds, backs straight, bone bows hugging their shoulders. The Jotrid sea filled the grass plain by the Vogras River and extended into the bushy scrub and even the desert with its dunes. They were the enemy of the Sylgiz — my enemy — and yet, I let Pashang escort me into a carriage. To my surprise, he sat with me.

"Shouldn't you be in the vanguard?" I asked as I settled on a pillow and covered myself in the horsehide blanket I'd brought.

Pashang sat across from me, facing away from the direction of travel. "Tekish is leading."

"I neglected to bathe today," I said. "And now...I'm sweating like a glass blower."

He leaned over and sniffed me, then sat back, his face plain.

"Don't do that," I said. "It's not endearing." I huffed. "Might as well tell me — do I smell like a damp horse?"

He shook his head. "You smell...but they don't call it sweating sickness for naught, so what's the matter? You weren't so self-shamed as a child."

"You don't know what it's like...being so uncomfortable in your own skin. Stuck between two worlds, neither this nor that."

"Do the sultanas in the harem sweat musk and ambergris?" he said with a restrained bitterness. "Fuck the Seluqals. I saw Kyars, once. If that shit wasn't born a prince, he'd be an underthings sniffer."

I chuckled with less restraint. "And you lived your adult life serving such people. What does that tell you about the way of things? You've got your horde, but long gone are the days when Seluq conquered the east with arrows. You'll be up against gholam guns — and I've heard they fire very fast, now. They'll throw bombs and launch rockets from the wall, and your horses will scatter in fear. That's why we live free in the Waste or die in Alanya as servants of these...*underthings sniffers*."

The carriage started rolling. The smooth, canal-fed grassland made it a bearable ride, even in my abject and pained state.

Pashang must have felt the sting of my words; he sat in silence, staring out the grated window.

"You're not wrong," he said. "Sometimes I want to turn it all on its head. But…it's like you said — gone are the days when some khagan from the Waste could subdue the world. Unless…"

"Unless?"

He smiled with a fire's warmth. "I once listened to two Philosophers argue about fate. The first said there was no such thing — that we, each, choose our paths. The second said we were like ants crawling on a fine Abistran carpet, deciding our way but ignorant of the wondrous pattern already laid out. If only we could see it from a bird's eye, then we would know…but if we could see from a bird's eye, we wouldn't be ants anymore, would we?"

I shook my confused head. "By Lat, why are you so bad at explaining things?"

"Something is happening, Cyra. I've been shown the pattern on the carpet. And that pattern…it's you. All three of my visions…are about you."

"You tease me with talk of visions, and yet you won't tell me what happens." I turned away and covered my head with the blanket.

"Consider it…a mercy," Pashang said.

I slept the rest of the ride. I dreamt I was a simurgh, flying through a thousand heavens. Then Pashang nudged me awake. He helped me out of the carriage, and we stood on the thorny scrub beneath the cloud-covered crescent. The torches of his riders throbbed in the windless night, as did those of the gholam standing atop the high walls of Qandbajar. The gold-plated warriors filled both the higher inner and lower outer layer, their chainmail glowing in the firelight.

We walked a few paces to Tekish, who sat high upon his silver-spotted Kashanese mare.

Pashang said, "May I?" He gestured at my bandage.

I let him remove it. I blinked my star-seeing eye — though saw nothing through it. Just a starless black.

Khagan Pashang closed his eyes and said words under his breath. Was he going to blast through two layers of wall and thousands of gholam with his mumbled prayers?

After a minute, he looked at me, serenity in his gaze, and held out his hand.

I stared at it — taking someone's hand had never felt so fraught. I didn't know what would happen — if anything would happen — but it was as if Alanya itself sat on my shoulders.

Why did I agree to this? To helping the man I despised most? What the hell was I doing? Had he bewitched me? Seduced me with talk of visions and fate? This was the farthest thing from the straight path. Why was I here, with thousands of Jotrid riders, standing against the walls of the city I called home?

I thought of how I watched the soulshifter jab out my eye and then stab Tamaz to death. I thought of the Disciples, who accosted me and refused to help. Of Eshe as the Philosophers beat him, bound him, and pushed him into that black-roofed carriage as I watched from the window. How I begged Khizr Khaz for help, and how even he turned me away.

Watching — that was all I'd done. Powerless — I was nothing but. I'd been dragged, helpless, from both my homes and now belonged nowhere. Was this a chance to change that?

Perhaps all I needed was some light on what had been a dismal path. And there was no grander luminance than starlight.

I reached out and took Pashang's hand. His was dry and rough. Mine was soaked in sweat, so it wasn't the most comfortable handhold.

Seconds passed. Nothing happened.

"I saw you praying," he said. "So pray, Cyra."

"Pray…for what…to who?"

"Three visions, I was given. One already passed, one is passing now, and one will pass. You know, as I know, to whom you prayed, that first time, all those years ago."

I mouthed a name buried deep in my heart, but no sound emitted, as if I were too ashamed to say it.

"You were hungry and freezing that day, remember?" Pashang said. "Your father and mother had been on a hunt for weeks and left you and your brothers with nothing. A snowstorm howled against the cloth walls, and you and Cihan huddled for warmth beneath a motheaten blanket, his bony knee jutting into your empty belly. No other yurt for miles had food either, so bereft was that winter. So, with naught else to do, you prayed."

I didn't want to remember — my most shameful secret. The sin I'd hidden, even from myself.

"You prayed to Lat, as a good girl ought to. But when Lat didn't answer, in your desperation, you prayed to other things. First, you prayed to the stones on the ground, then to the mud, then the grass, then the sun and moon — but none heard. Then you looked up and saw the very stars burning through the ceiling, and so you called to each. But they, too, did not hear. So you prayed to the space between the stars — the darkness where the dead stars dwell — and *it* heard. It saved you, saved your family — remember?"

Of course I remembered. The hour after my prayer, Father and Mother's hunting party returned with hundreds of horses and bison, and we feasted for months.

Now I looked up at the space between the stars — the void — and with only my mind, called out for help. Called out, ironically, for light.

In the periphery of my vision, a star blazed. I touched it; it hymned somberly, then vibrated. I drew a line from it to another star that burned just above my head, and from there to tens of more stars that suddenly shone around me, careful to follow the order of their appearance. The lines now resembled a shape with many sides, and as the stars orbited each other, this shape changed forms. Every second, the stars would rearrange into a new, many-sided shape, but it was getting faster: five new shapes a second, then ten. Faster and faster, until I could no longer count, until it seemed like chaos. And with each new form, the hymns changed too — but they were always somber and sunk deep into my soul.

The many-sided, constantly shifting shape vanished, and with it the stars. I'd done something, but what?

Wind blew against my ears toward the city. And sand came with it, nestling in my hair. A sandstorm? I turned around; other riders did as well, and so did Pashang. Not only wind and sand — something else was coming.

A fat and jittery thing flew by my head. An awful bug we oft saw in the Waste and Alanya. A locust.

And a locust, of course, doesn't come alone. More chittered by my head, zooming toward the walls, as if our vanguard. But Qandbajar was not unaccustomed to locust plagues…so what was it for?

Rumbling. The very air stirred and whirled. An endless buzzing sounded in the distance, and it loudened each second. The locust mass looked as if a wall were surging toward us. And as it neared, it took a shape…or rather, a face…a face with a hateful, open smile. I shut my eyes and ducked; thousands of riders did the same. I pressed my fingers into my ears and curled into a ball, yet still felt the bugs flutter through me like thousands of prickling fingers. The chirps deafened the whinnying of the horses and the shouting of the men.

The moment it ended, Pashang pulled me up. The locust mass was so encompassing, I could scarcely see the walls of Qandbajar as they swarmed it.

Pashang escorted me toward my carriage. Once I was inside, he shut the door and shouted, "Now!" I watched from my window as riders charged the wall. Would the locusts really be enough cover for them to break through?

Given that it was the answer to my prayer, I didn't doubt.

18

ZEDRA

Earlier that day...

Honestly, it shocked me how easily Mirima settled into the Order's lodgment. Our shared room had three crude, feather-stuffed mattresses with coarse linens and three wooden bowls for the broth they were stirring downstairs. The earthy air of lentils and peas wafted through the window; outside, hooded women went about the garden, tending to herbs jutting from the grainy topsoil.

Mirima seemed content to sit on her pallet and *click-clack* her prayer beads, which were so shiny they could be pearls or well-polished teeth. Not a peep out of her about this austere, though tidy room. Perhaps she'd endured a few hard days that I wasn't aware of.

Celene, also a princess, wasn't fussing either. She lay on her side and stared at the wall. In the middle between the two, I sat against the window and listened to the breezy, idle chatter from the garden below.

Much had to be done; waiting, mostly. The Order and the

gholam had to gather, arm themselves, and devise a plan to retake the Sand Palace — one that didn't need the input of three princesses who'd never fought a battle. Of guns and swords, at least. Our task was to wait, though I, of course, had other plans.

The entire city seemed to be waiting. Waiting for Kyars. Who was in no rush, apparently. And if the Archers weren't reporting his whereabouts, it was likely because he didn't want them to. Ultimately, only he could save us, and so we waited.

But I couldn't wait to hold my son. I had to find somewhere quiet, dark, and cool so I could soulshift and disrupt Mansur's plans. Though I'd been plotting to pit Kyars and Kato against each other, for now they were my unquestioned allies, and I had to help them bring down Mansur.

I cleared my throat. "I would go and pray in the shrine. Perhaps Saint Jamshid will grant us his ear."

Only the Children could intercede with Lat, but regardless, I had to find an appropriate place to keep my body whilst I soulshifted.

"Celene, dear, would you accompany me?"

She turned on her back and gave me a tepid nod. Mirima ignored us and continued *clack-clacking* her prayer beads as we left the room.

We didn't go far — downstairs in a small room by the foyer sat a massive chest laden with rough-spun robes. Celene watched, a wince stuck on her face, as I climbed inside and sank into the pile. Thankfully, they didn't smell of sweat and other body odors, so they must've been fresh.

I poked my head out. "Celene, dear, don't let anyone disturb me."

"Are you doing…witchcrafty things?"

I nodded. "Only because I have to. No one is to come near, all right?"

"Well…" She folded her arms. "What if someone, you know, wants a robe?"

I threw a few on the floor. "There you go."

She picked one up. "How long will you be gone?"

"A soulshifting cycle is only thirty minutes. I think you can manage to guard me for that long. Much depends on this."

She nodded, jittery. "Marot forgive me," she said in Crucian.

I pretended I didn't understand. "Is that a prayer?"

She twirled a lock of hair. "Oh, it's just…I'm aiding in sorcery, and the angel Marot is the teacher of all sorcery, though only as a temptation, a test. So I asked him to forgive me…or rather, to beg the Archangel for forgiveness on my behalf. I mean, I'm not the one doing the sorcery, so perhaps it's not a sin, but just in case…"

I supposed that made sense. Sin or not, we needed the prayers of those closer to god.

I sank into the robes. Barely any light poured through the rough wool pile. They were cool and dry on my skin and even muffled the outside noise.

I closed my eyes, focused on the bloodrune I'd written in the Sand Palace guards' lodging, and pricked it with an imagined fingernail.

The man whom I'd possessed was tossing dice in a noisy, incense-filled room. I choked on the seed in his throat; I banged on my chest — once, twice, thrice — to get it out, but looked down to see a distorted reflection in the mirror plate. Futile to bang on that. A fellow guard ran up, held me hunched over, and smacked my nape. The seed flew out.

"What'd you roll for that luck?" the other guard, who also wore mirror armor, said with a hissing laugh. He spoke a Kashanese tongue that I didn't know, but like Himyaric and Crucian, could somehow understand. "You rolled the evil eye, didn't you?" His mustache seemed to be growing out of his nose.

I had no idea what was on the faces of those dice. I coughed to relieve the squeeze on my throat.

The real trouble was that I didn't know who I was, what rank I merited, or much else. The mirror armor meant I was a khazi under

Mansur's employ. I didn't have time to digest the ebbing memories, emotions, and thoughts that flowed from this man into me like a river leaking into an ocean.

In the room were pallets, low tables, bowls of sesame seeds, trinkets, and, on the far side, a weapons rack: guns, scimitars, and spears. A dagger hung off my belt, its hilt well-worn steel with a falcon imprint. Falcon…the sigil of the Seluqal House of Kashan, which bordered Merva, the province that Mansur governed. Perhaps the man had picked it up as a spoil, fighting off a Kashanese raid. But the memories dropping on my mind suggested the dagger was a requisition — was this man in the employ of the Seluqal House of Kashan? I probed my mind, only to find stressful memories of a dark place, as constricted as a strangled throat.

I could at least glean I was battle-hardened, loyal to Mansur — when paid — and had a wife and four children back in Merva. The hard lines on my face suggested some age. And with age, hopefully, came respect. Strange that my eyebrows seemed lacking, with faint, hardened hairs sprouting where a thicker forest ought to be.

I left the room to a Sand Palace hallway, with its emerald lamps and mosaic-covered walls. On my right, open windows with golden, star-patterned grates let in a breeze, which soared into the ceiling beams, spreading coolness.

Mansur's guardsmen stood straight at every door. Some nodded at me, and I nodded back. Ideal that it seemed I wasn't too highly ranked, nor too low; after the soulshift ended, this vessel wouldn't remember anything, but he'd obviously be blamed for what I was about to do, and perhaps they'd think him a spy, which would suit my purpose.

As I passed by the ornate double door that led into the great hall, I spied a rather wide man walking within, wearing gold- and leaf-colored brocade, a similarly dressed woman at his arm. No question: the pink face of spice master Ozar, and his wife, who happened to be Mansur and Mirima's younger sister.

So, he was free; what deal had he made with Mansur, I

wondered?

Either way, I hadn't the time to find out and so continued through the antechamber that led toward the exit.

Finally, I arrived at the archway that preceded the simurgh statue. I quickened my pace through the palace grounds — the gardens and sandstone-lined walkways — until I'd left the gate. It was a ten-minute walk through empty, palm-lined streets to the old barrack, where Kato, and now Mansur, kept the so-called conspirators of Tamaz's killing.

Staring at the pasty, gated compound, I wondered what I ought to do. Kato had stored his enemies here, and Mansur was doing the same. The enemies of your enemies make good allies, but some enemies of your enemies are your enemies, too. So behind that gate were enemies of my enemies, enemies of my allies, but no allies of my enemies, surely, and quite a few allies of my allies. It was getting confusing; I couldn't waste precious time sorting it out and had to strike like a hammer.

I unsheathed my dagger, admired the falcon on its hilt, and sliced a line through my palm. Sipped the seeker's blood, which tasted much like my own. I wrote a bloodrune on the dagger's blade: two eyes, interlocked, within the sun. I whispered, "O' Morning Star, take from me and give from yourself." The rune brightened.

I approached the two mirror-armored sentries guarding the gate and gave them a nod. "Mansur wants to see the Grand Vizier's son. I'm to escort him to the palace."

They looked at each other with raised eyebrows. One said, "Why'd he send the damned sapper?"

So…I was a sapper, which is why I barely had eyebrows. No wonder memories of scalding rooms and strangling tunnels floated about my head. My job was to detonate bombs and bring high things to the ground.

"I asked for…more responsibility," I said in a shaky voice.

Judging by their deadpan stares, my tact wasn't working.

"By the way, have I ever showed you my dagger?" I unsheathed it, displaying the hilt and bloodrune. "That falcon...such lovely craftsmanship, don't you think?"

"You've got some...blood on there," one said as he gazed into the eyes of the rune. "Beautiful...blood..."

They straightened their backs and stared forward with bulging eyes. I snapped my fingers in their faces: no blinking. Perfectly tranced.

I patted them down until I found the gate key dangling from a belt buckle — a rusted, hefty piece of metal. Took a bit of fidgeting with the keyhole to get the gate to unlock, but now the creaky thing swung open.

The old barrack was a wide square with rooms on every side. Sand covered everything, even the dried-up well in the center. The rooms weren't even locked, only barricaded with a wooden plank and latched. I lifted the plank off the nearest door, then unfastened the latch and pulled the door open. The room stunk of unwashed skin and urine. A flat-nosed man sat on the floor, itching his scalp. I'd seen him before, knocking on doors in the Glass District. Wasn't he a tax collector? I wondered whether he'd offended Kato, Mansur, or both. I left the door open and proceeded to the next room.

One by one, I removed the barricades on each door, speeding up as I went, not bothering to see whom I was freeing. Slowly, the square filled with viziers, clerks, notable pashas, and all manner of folk who'd been imprisoned, each stinking and dusty. Some joined me in freeing the others, and soon more than a hundred doors in the old barrack stood open.

Hadrith, his beard now beyond his chest, emerged from an open door, looking as if he smelled something odd. Prison should have done his haughty character some good. The son of the Grand Vizier possessed influence that Khizr Khaz and Kato lacked, and a shrewdness that matched or exceeded mine. Better he be for us than Mansur.

I studied the rabble overtaking the square, particularly the wives shouting for their husbands. Too noisy — I eyed with worry the overlooking guard tower. Though considering the sultry afternoon sun and the lack of interference, the sentry must've been napping.

I paced around the square. Vera wasn't here. Just where was Mansur keeping her?

A clamor arose as the prisoners approached the gate and argued whether it was wise to run. The sentry sitting in the wooden guard tower overlooking the area finally woke up, grabbed his matchlock, and rushed down. That lit the spark: the prisoners stampeded through the gate, screaming "run!" and "go!" and "to freedom!" Soon, the square was empty and still, save for the increasingly distant rumble of people running for their lives.

My part in this was at an end. I sat on the sandy ground as my vision cracked like a glass pane. It shattered, and I was back in the massive chest, buried beneath a pile of robes.

Not an hour later, a rabble arrived at the Shrine of Saint Jamshid. Some men nursed burns and worse on their backs, likely the targets of gunfire as they ran for freedom. At least a hundred congregated amid the stone arches in the shrine's square, loud and pleading with Khizr Khaz for help. How delightful to see Hadrith standing at the head.

Khizr Khaz, Kato, Hadrith, and a dozen other viziers went inside the Order's lodging and into an empty room with a grass-colored carpet. I followed.

"Why is she here?" asked a thin-faced vizier, a man I remembered as responsible for shipping grain from one of the western provinces. If only he knew I'd just freed him.

"You're going to be discussing how to free the heir. He's my son."

Hadrith leaned against the far wall, a wooden mug in his hands. We eyed each other — his mellow gaze didn't see me as a threat.

When I'd worried earlier that he was on to me, I was being rather presumptuous — he clearly had no inkling of my involvement in the intrigues he blamed on Kato.

Kato stood on the opposite side with folded arms. "Are we going to free the heir with the ingrates responsible for the death of his beloved grandfather?"

Hadrith chugged the mug and shook his head. "I was trying to save the Shah! If only you'd listened, Himyarite!"

"You accused me!" Kato wagged his finger. "Accused me of consorting with a sorcerer to kill the Shah! And then you plotted my downfall!"

"Then we were both played!" Hadrith approached Kato, head forward. "Don't you see? The sorcerer blinded us to the real threat — Mansur and his henchman Pashang!"

"I think your own avarice a better blinder!" Kato raised an open palm in Hadrith's direction. "So who's to say you're not among them? And what *real* evidence have you that a sorcerer was involved?" He chuckled — how absurd it must've seemed to him. "Let's not forget the testimony of Cyra's own gholam minders. You met with her, in secret, more than once before she assassinated the Shah. When I asked you earlier what matters you discussed, your lips were sealed." He gestured at all the viziers and Order men in the room. "Now that they're flapping again, we await your *truth*."

"The truth is Cyra would never kill the Shah. She was as harmless as a feather fluttering in the wind. The sorcerer used her body!"

The viziers seemed to heckle in unison. Of course, Hadrith's story didn't make sense to them. Good.

While the viziers bickered among themselves, Khizr Khaz stood in silence near the window, gaze low as if in reflection. Whereas I'd once worried about what Hadrith knew, now everything pointed to Mansur and Pashang — they were traitors, after all. Nothing whatsoever pointed at me. I was interested to see how they would piece their different stories together, as if trying to repair two broken vases with each other's pieces.

"The Sylgiz had every reason to murder Tamaz." Kato's hard voice silenced the room. "Cyra could've been coaxed by her brother. Mansur is acting to seize an opportunity that *you* helped create!" Kato understood half the truth.

"How convenient." Hadrith crossed his arms and shook his head in utter disgust. "Is your vision too narrow to see the pattern on the carpet, Kato? We — each of us in this room — have been used like playthings by a much shrewder entity that is aiding Mansur's power grab." Hadrith understood the other half. But combining these half-truths somehow made a whole lie, one that served my purpose.

"Entity!" Kato scoffed. "You'd have us believe Ahriyya himself schemes against us!"

The two were about to butt heads when I pushed forward and stomped my foot. "If you're with Kyars, then you're on the same side. When he's here, he'll decide who to punish for which crimes. And if my son is hurt, that crime will be on everyone's head!"

Khizr Khaz stepped forward. "She's right. We can bicker later about what has passed. Getting her son back and retaking the Sand Palace is all that matters." He turned to Hadrith. "How many men can you muster?"

Hadrith replied, "Hundreds of pashas owe me favors. They'll answer my call, and so will their men-at-arms."

"You've gone from the banging of a pot to the strumming of a sitar," Kato said, his gaze on Hadrith. "We need more men. I can't spare too many gholam. That wall is vast, and if we leave even the sparsest gap, you can bet your jewels that Pashang will be crawling up it."

Pashang had enough riders to overwhelm the gholam, the Order, and whatever men-at-arms Hadrith could muster. If he entered the city, our hopes would turn to ash.

An idea struck. "What if..." I hesitated — perhaps it was a foolish idea. "What if we ask the Archers of the Eye to man the wall?"

Stares from the men in the room. Silence. Then came the shaking of heads and disdainful grunts.

Kato chuckled. "In Himyar, they say 'never trust a Labashite. He'll shoot an arrow in your ass the moment you show him your back.' I'm dutybound to that wall. I won't give it to an order of heathens."

"The Seluqals trust them enough to relay their most vital messages," I said. "They fulfill that role faithfully."

"Do they?" Kato scoffed. "The Archers have said nothing about Shah Kyars — no sightings or messages, despite that I was sending him messages daily, apprising him of every happening."

Perhaps Kyars didn't want anyone knowing his whereabouts or day of arrival.

"Did you send riders?" the thin-faced vizier whom I'd freed asked. "In addition?"

Kato nodded. "Of course. But none have returned. Sometimes I fear we are being caged in this city…with a red-striped tiger."

Was Kyars preventing the riders from returning, too?

Silence lingered as everyone digested their thoughts.

Kato broke it again. "I determined a few possibilities regarding his arrival, based on his speed. Shah Kyars could have been here yesterday if traveling with a light escort atop Kashanese horses. But if bringing the army, he would arrive six days from now. And with the artillery he left with…two weeks."

Khizr Khaz sighed. "Six days may as well be six years with Mansur in control. Everything depends on us. If Kyars returns to a city fortified by the Jotrids, we'll all be in the grave, and he'll have to siege the city to retake it."

"Every reason not to fail," I said. "Every reason to stay united, stay the course, and save my son." Everyone looked to me. Hadrith's hopeful smile, Kato's assured gaze, and Khizr Khaz's slight nod. Though I had the three most powerful men in the city as allies, it still felt as if it were all on me. "So, shall we plan, then?"

· · ·

KATO WOULD HIT the Sand Palace tonight with enough men to surround every gate, scale the walls, and eliminate Mansur's household guard. As for Mansur, they'd take him prisoner, and Kyars would decide his fate. What would I do? Wait, of course. Wait within the chest of robes, where I could ensure my son's safety.

The Jotrids prickled my mind, though. Father had said Pashang was *"acting under a cloud"* that even he couldn't *"pierce"* and that his actions were *"not of this world."* Though everyone feared Pashang, I feared they didn't fear him enough. We needed more men guarding the city wall while the gholam and Order retook the palace. So I sent an Order man to summon Abunaisaros, Grandmaster of the Archers of the Eye.

He arrived just before sunset with three other archers and that red-haired girl whom I'd noticed earlier. Amid the madness, I'd forgotten about her and her unknown flavor of blood. Perhaps, if I played this right, I could hatch two eggs in one sitting.

Alongside Kato, we sat at a wooden low table in the Order's canteen, which had a stone floor and unadorned walls. Footsteps, water pouring, and clanging pots sounded from the nearby kitchen, which always seemed busy. It all smelled pleasantly of lentils and mint.

Abu wore a beard that kissed his navel when he walked; he was so tall he towered even when sitting. He made Hadrith look tame.

The Order's kitchen didn't have rosewater, nor sherbet, nor any intoxicating beverages, so they served water. Safia, the red-haired girl, sipped her mug, then brought it down with a frown.

"She's squiring for me," Abu said. "In exchange, I'm teaching her skills only known to the grandmasters of the Archers of the Eye."

I wondered how she'd secured that deal. Clearly, she wasn't the shy, elusive girl she appeared to be. I'd have to learn more after this meeting.

Kato kept his back straight, hands folded, and gaze on Abu. I wondered how acquainted they were; regardless, Kato's prejudices would likely weigh heaviest.

"I've only five minutes to spare," Kato said after huffing a breath. "Convince me these Labashites are worth trusting with more than just paper."

Abu said, "The blood plague destroyed our land just as it did yours, brother. We both serve Alanya, now."

Kato snickered. "Right. How much are they paying you?"

Abu snickered too. "How much are they paying *you*?"

Both grumbled.

"Listen," I said, "my beloved Kyars expressed tremendous faith in the Archers." He'd never mentioned them, but invoking the one man everyone treasured seemed a good idea. "He counted them among Alanya's most loyal servants, just as his father did, and his father before him. Abu, will you help defend our walls from the Jotrids?"

Water moistened his beard as he took a swig from his mug. "I've no hesitation. As you're the mother of the heir to the throne, we'll do whatever you ask. Besides, we cherish every opportunity to gain the people's trust."

Kato grunted in disgust. "She could be the mother of Saint Chisti himself, but here in Alanya, mothers don't give orders — not yet, at least. You'll need my approval, and I'm yet to be convinced."

"Are slaves giving orders, now?" When Abu shrugged, his shoulders almost reached his ears.

"Slaves have ruled many Seluqal lands," Kato said. "They say the janissary Grand Vizier of Sirm commands more loyalty than their shah."

Abu replied, "Oh? And I heard their shah's wife has him on strings. A fierce, fiery-haired woman who helped crush the Crucians."

"Concubine." The almost-whisper came from the red-haired girl. "Not wife."

I'd not heard of her, but no matter. "A slave, a concubine," I said. "Rather like me. But I've got no one on strings, and I'm not giving orders. It's a proposal, one I believe would benefit all." I turned to Kato. "Khagan Pashang outnumbers us ten to one. If you leave even a sliver of that wall undefended, he'll take it from you. If you decide, here and now, to refuse the Archer's help, then it's on you if something happens. And I'll make certain Kyars knows it."

Kato sighed. "And if these Ethosians," he gestured at Abu, "betray us? Will I bear that on my back, too?"

I shook my head. "I promise — if they do — I'll tell Kyars it's my fault, not yours."

"Fawning lovers don't find faults," Kato scoffed. "It'll still be on my head, and you know it. Sometimes I wish I'd never sold myself to this palace." He glanced at me. "You Seluqals are more trouble than you're worth."

That was the first time I'd been called a Seluqal. I forced myself to take it in stride. "You sold yourself? Why would anyone choose to be a slave?" I'd chosen the same for the sake of my mission.

Kato never talked about himself, so hesitated as he scratched his beard. "I was, for a time, a warrior in service to the Sultan of Himyar…the paltry scrub that remained for him to rule, after the blood plague poisoned most of the land. With so little cultivation and so many mouths to feed, the Sultan daily sent us to round up, enslave, and sell off entire tribes — men, women, and children." He grinned at Abu. "All the while, we fended off attacks by *your people* over what little remained. Killed more Labashites than I have teeth." So that was why he still had a Himyarite accent. He wasn't enslaved at a tender age, like most gholam. "I…got tired of it all. Turned out, the blood plague wasn't the true horror. What we did to each other in its aftermath was far worse. I wanted more than to be part of an endless cycle of blood and enslavement. So, one day, sick of it all, I joined a caravan of those I'd enslaved." He put his hands behind his head and leaned back. "And would you believe it — now here I sit, most powerful man in the greatest city in the world."

"We're not so different," Abu said, nodding as if impressed. "The Archers, too, wanted more. Alanya was our sworn enemy once, but who can deny its promises? Tell me, do you ever miss Himyar?"

Kato shook his head and chuckled. "Not at all. I don't look back. A waste of good faculties to hunger for what's gone."

Abu smiled. "You must miss some things. The tangy, sweet syrup of the sappa nut. The sultry air of the Yam Sup Sea. Coffee beans roasted fresh from the still-hot stool of yellow-horned mountain goats."

That last one…a tad sickening. But Kato closed his eyes and breathed deep, as if sniffing that coffee. Then he smiled and shook his head. "Ah-ah-ah. Now you're pulling at my strings." Kato raised his finger at Abu. "I told you, I don't look back. So let's look forward — if the Jotrids enter the city, we're all dead."

Abu cracked his knuckles. "Then the Archers of the Eye will make sure they don't. We are the greatest defenders of walls the world has ever witnessed. Both our arrows and words are true and find their marks faster than any bullet."

"Your arrows better be better than your words." Kato chuckled, then gulped his water. "By Lat, they better be a lot better."

"Is that an agreement?" I asked Kato.

He banged his cup onto the table. "Time is tightening its noose. I've been forced to trust Hadrith, now I'm forced to trust a Labashite. But that rope — I feel it closing in, taut on my skin. I'm a dead man in a thousand scenarios and alive in only one. Let this be the one, then." He held out his hand.

Abu shook it and sealed the deal with a jovial grin. "You won't regret it, my Himyarite friend."

AFTER THE MEETING, I followed Safia into the shrine, which had been emptied and closed to the common folk. She didn't raise her hands in prayer and just stared at the sepulcher, as if lost in thought.

I stood nearby, my presence snatching her from her trance. She managed a weak, almost intimidated smile, then averted her gaze.

I tried to recall one of the few Karmazi phrases I knew, then realized I knew Karmazi. Why did I know Karmazi? Or Crucian? Or Himyaric? "How are you?" I hoped I'd gotten the accent right.

The girl answered "fine" in Karmazi, though with a nervous lilt, and she'd used the casual form, which wasn't appropriate when addressing someone from a royal household. Why did I know so much about this obscure language?

"Sorry," I said, speaking Paramic, "I don't know much more of your language." Or rather, I shouldn't know. Just another mystery for the pile.

"Why would you? We all speak Paramic."

I tried to recall if Karmazis were known to possess a rare blood flavor, but *Flavors of Blood Volume One* didn't mention such a thing. Perhaps if I'd had time to read *Volume Two*, I could've learned about such a flavor and its possibilities. I'd left it hidden in my room and hoped to return to it soon.

"Will you be defending the wall, as well?" I asked.

"If Abu wants." She always kept her answers so short.

It made me more eager to dig. "What do you want? Do you care about any of this? A war between an uncle and nephew?"

She moved her lips, then hesitated. After a moment of thought, she said, "Kyars...he's a good man."

Her, too? Why did everyone believe that? Couldn't they see through his obvious chicanery? Though such beliefs bolstered my cause, it bothered me how easily people were deceived in this day and age.

"Yes, he is," I said. "He's touched every Alanyan, in some way." He liked to touch the women especially, whether they were his or not. "In what way has he bettered your life, dear?"

"He saved my father," she whispered.

Now that could have many meanings, metaphorical to physical. "Oh? How so?"

She finally gave me her gaze. Those sun-colored irises…sharp, yet somber. "My father fought for the Sirmians at the Battle at Syr Darya. The Crucians would've slaughtered him had Kyars not rode in, just in time, to rescue him."

Unexpected and perplexing. "Is your father…a janissary?"

She shook her head. "Janissaries didn't fight in that battle. My father is…a khazi…in the service of Hayrad the Redbeard."

"I'm sorry," I said, embarrassed. "I don't know much about the battle, aside from my beloved's heroics."

"I owe Kyars," she said. "I'll defend his wall."

The feeling that something wasn't adding up wormed through my gut. But I couldn't quite finger the false string in her story. Meanwhile, a sweeper entered the room — a gray-haired woman clad in one of those robes. She said a quick prayer with raised hands and broomed the already tidy space, keeping her distance.

I thought of another tact, despite being annoyed by it. "You know, for the poets in Laughter Square, *beauty* and *Karmazi girl* might as well be synonyms. And even among the Karmazi girls I've seen, you're stunning." It was a bit of a stretch. While she was pleasant looking, I'd seen better among the dancers who frequented the harem. "Why, dear, hasn't some wealthy vizier's son snatched you up?"

"I'm of low blood," she said. "The daughter of a khazi. Why would anyone—"

"You're not of low blood. Your Paramic is loftier than Sultana Mirima's, at least when you're pressed to speak more than two words. And your accent…I can't quite place it, but it's not Karmazi, that's for certain. You barely speak that language, and you stumbled on your own name. No, you're something else."

Her weak shrug and slanted frown showed a lack of bother. "So what if I'm something else? What's it to you? And could this be a case of a sour tongue accusing a sweet grape? Perhaps you're not what *you* seem. You speak Paramic as if you authored the Recitals of Chisti, and your accent reminds me of an old play set in the time of the saint-kings. But I don't care enough to pry."

How perceptive. I would back off, but that wasn't my style. "Daughters of khazis watch a lot of plays, do they?"

Her snicker stung a little. "'Slave' — that's what you said about yourself. Describes my mother, too, but she was so much more. We all have to be *more*, don't we? To break through the cages we're birthed in?"

How true. But that water clock was draining, and much had to be done. "Well said. I'm afraid I don't have more time. I hope I haven't...put you off. I'd so like to chat again."

"Takes more to put me off."

At that, I left the shrine. On the way to my lodging, Celene ran up to me, her breaths quick and raspy. "Zedra, I must tell you something — you may not believe it — but I must tell you."

I touched her cheek, which was pink with worry. "What is it, dear?"

"That girl in the shrine...do you know who she is?"

"You were eavesdropping?"

She shook her head. "No, I came to find you, but when I saw her — by the Archangel, by the Twelve — I'm certain it's her."

"Calm down. You've all the time in the world." I clasped both her cheeks, which used to relax my eldest daughter. "Now, tell me what you want to say."

That didn't seem to calm her; she choked on her words. "I...I was..."

"Just say it."

"I was at her funeral! I saw them bury her in the Sublime Seat's garden! *Plant* her shrine — however you people say it. Like my grandfather, that girl should be dead!"

Not a word of it made sense, but Celene seemed sincere. "Who should be dead, dear?"

"Her name is Sadie. She saved my life. But she's also the daughter of the Shah of Sirm!"

Those words were like a thread, weaving disparate parts together. Of course — that was why she'd corrected Abu during the meeting; she was talking about her own mother, whom she'd proudly mentioned during our conversation in the shrine. And indeed, Kyars had saved her father, the Shah of Sirm. "And you say...she died?"

"My grandfather killed her with a stone! Everyone in Sirm believes her to be dead! But that's her! I swear by the Twelve, by the shining apostles, by—"

"All right. I understand. Relax. Thank you for telling me." It was the second time, according to Celene, someone had come out of the grave. The story of the Crucian imperator was well known, but now this girl, too? Could it be related to her unknown flavor of blood?

The sun laid in the earth, now, leaving us with a windless evening. I looked toward the hanging crescent. Kato had described time like a noose, and it began to choke me. Our hastily assembled coalition had to act before Mansur and Pashang could bolster their positions, and I had to secure my son, who wasn't just my son; he was the Children. The shield against the Great Terror. The Padishah of the Final Hour. That ought to be my focus, not some princess who'd supposedly risen.

Something chittered by my ear: a grasshopper. It landed on the nearest arch, its horns twitching. Four more joined it, each colorless and fat. Locusts. Their cries reminded me of broken bells.

A swarm of them descended on the shrine. Celene winced and hugged herself. Did they not have locust plagues in Crucis? They would no doubt devastate the crops, but the common folk, not us, would bear that suffering.

"It's no danger, dear." I touched her shoulder. "Come, let's go inside. There's much to be done."

And yet, as I gazed at the sky, the swarm obscured the crescent, and even the stars dimmed.

19

CYRA

THE LOCUSTS CLINGING TO THE TOWER OF WISDOM FILLED THE CITY
with a shrill, spine-numbing cry. They twitched upon the limestone,
as if the Tower itself fluxed in the night. It reminded me of the
Palace of the Living, which was formed from screaming eyes and
mouths. Given what I'd done, I wondered if I'd one day join that
tangled mess of human parts.

Pashang, I, and hundreds of riders galloped through the streets
toward the Tower. I rode behind Pashang's brother, Tekish, since I
was too weak to ride on my own, digging my fingers into the chainmail around his waist to keep steady. No Alanyans in the streets —
what else could they be doing but huddling together and praying?

I'd not watched the battle but, from the elated chatter of the
Jotrids, surmised that it had been quick and brutal. They'd rushed
toward a part of the wall where the locusts hovered so thickly that
the gholam couldn't see, scaled it with ladders, and overwhelmed
the surprised gholam atop. Once the Jotrids opened the gate, the
surviving gholam retreated to the second wall, where minutes later,
the same course of events repeated. Apparently, Pashang killed
three men with arrows. Everyone was boasting about how many

they'd killed. In a way, I'd killed as many as all of them put together, though this wasn't the time or place to digest the thought.

But as we rode, I started to feel brighter, knowing that I was the reason we'd broken through two layers of wall and cut through hundreds of gholam. Because they were Kato's gholam, and it was good to strike back at the men who killed my brother. Though Khizr Khaz believed the sorcerer was aiding Mansur and Pashang, if that were true, then why didn't the sorcerer help Pashang get into the city? No — in my mind, it still pointed to Kato because if Mansur hadn't come, he'd still be in charge. And Pashang was his enemy, so the enemy of my enemy was my ally — at least, for now.

Wasn't that how everyone in this city behaved? One day an enemy, the next day an ally, and the next an enemy again, all for self-gain? Pashang had believed that I killed Tamaz, and yet he didn't mind, as if I'd slew a bug rather than the Shah of Alanya. It seemed he was the best ally I could have, but only until I'd exposed the sorcerer and cleared my name.

Philosophers crowded the plaza outside the Tower, locusts sitting on their tall, felt hats. Some held glass jars and collected the jittering things, as if to eat them. But being Philosophers, they probably wanted to study the creatures I'd conjured out of the air.

As we circled them on our steeds, they huddled together; a few clutched the matchlocks at their sides. One pulled his matchlock out; Pashang unleashed an arrow, and it zipped through the air and pierced his neck. The man fell with bulging eyes as the other Philosophers raised their hands.

Litani pushed through to the head and faced Pashang. "You just struck down the foremost catopter expert in the country."

Pashang tucked his bow behind his back and shrugged. "Catopter? Isn't that a fish?"

"You're making a dangerous enemy, Khagan Pashang." Litani smiled — too at ease for my liking. "Or perhaps you took a wrong turn on your way to the Sand Palace?"

"No, I'm precisely where I want to be." Pashang jumped off his horse. The moon reflected in his mirror armor, between fresh flecks of blood. He gazed down at Litani. "I'm here for Eshe. Release him and we'll go. Refuse…" He gestured with his head at the dead Philosopher.

"What do you want with the former Disciple?"

Pashang put a hand on the Grand Philosopher's shoulder. "Litani, remember last we met?"

"At Mansur's granddaughter's wedding. What of it?"

"You were with your wife and three sons. Blessedly beautiful family, though I recall one of your sons being a bit overfed. I think he'd make a nice chair for my victory meal tonight. My brother is a bit frailer, so your wife would do. Oh, you live in the Glass District, don't you?"

Litani shook his head. "How many times have you practiced those lines?" He chuckled with indifference. "Let me make something clear — we Philosophers are beyond some pitiful Seluqal succession. We are like the clouds in the sky, entirely undisturbed by the battles below."

Pashang grabbed an arrow from his quiver. Without taking his eyes off Litani, he tossed it up. It flipped a few times in the air and clattered on the cobblestone, tip facing a young Philosopher with a rather long neck.

Two riders grabbed the man. He howled and writhed in their grips as they bent him over and faced him down. Other Philosophers protested and screamed the man's name. Litani, though, remained cool and expressionless.

Pashang put his boot on the young Philosopher's neck.

Tekish turned to me and said, "This will be…crueler than the usual. Look away."

I shook my head. "I've learned that if people don't fear you, then they're likely to hurt you. I know I'll have to do like to succeed."

Tekish chuckled. "Wisest thing to ever come out a Sylgiz mouth."

Pashang took his boot off the screaming man's neck. "You know what, I've changed my mind. Let's be merciful, for once."

Two Jotrids brought the young Philosopher to his feet. Then one clutched his right arm, and the other the left. They each pulled, as if his arms were rope. The man's wails heightened in pitch. Dear Lat. Bones snapped. The Philosophers gazed, mouths agape, while the Jotrids smiled. *Snap-snap.* The sound churned my stomach. The neck tore off the shoulder at the left side, and now the man's neck dangled to the right — it seemed the Jotrid warrior on the right was stronger, and he shouted with joy, as if he'd won.

I forced my horrified eyes to look as Pashang unsheathed his scimitar and sliced the tortured, now silent Philosopher down the middle. As the two Jotrids pulled him apart, his blood and innards spilled onto the cobblestone, smelling of copper and cold, rotted meat.

I shut my eyes, yet those innards glowed on my eyelids. Is that what we were made of? Could my own flesh be pulled apart like that? Now I regretted not looking away, regretted even coming here. But I had to steel myself for what was to come.

"For a cloud, he bled quite a lot." Pashang smiled at Litani. "But perhaps you don't care so much for blood. Now, the next word out of your mouth better be more pleasing than a maid's teary moans, else I'll fill the river with ink and bones."

Litani glanced toward the Tower's entrance and said, "Ask him if he's willing to part with the former Disciple." Then he turned to Pashang. "You've made a grave mistake. There's a reason the Sand Palace never interferes with our affairs. You're going to regret this."

"I'll add it to a long list, at the top of which is eating my father bloody and raw. Wish I'd seasoned him first."

I stayed behind Tekish, careful not to be seen. Pashang's talent for cruelty had won. And the Philosophers, for all their enlightenment, were still blood and innards. Their Tower was stone and paper, and if determined, Pashang could end them this night, as he was known to end things.

"Not willing to suffer for all your ink, eh?" Pashang said to Litani as we waited. "That's why I'm not afraid of you."

"Oh, we're all willing to die. But it's not up to us."

"I never said 'die.' Dying is peace. It's the very opposite of suffering. How many hells would you burn in for a book, hmm?"

With locusts still swarming through the air, Eshe stepped out of the Tower's double doors. I almost jumped off the horse and ran to hug him, but Tekish raised his hand to stop me.

A man wearing a flower-patterned cloak escorted Eshe to Pashang. His hood shadowed his face; I couldn't make out much detail, except for some kind of covering over his eyes.

Eshe, though, wouldn't raise his gaze. He wore a white caftan meant for a man twice his size. His body didn't seem injured — though from his trembling, his spirit certainly did.

"You all right?" Pashang asked him.

But Eshe said nothing and continued staring at the ground. I could barely stay on my horse with the worry coursing through me. Why wasn't he saying anything?

"He's not," the man in the flower-patterned cloak said, a voice from somewhere dark in his throat. "Let's just say he drank too much."

Pashang stared into the shadowed face of the cloaked man, then said, "You…I know you…you were there…"

Did they really know each other? Just who was he?

The man in the flowery cloak turned and walked toward the Tower. Before he could go through the double doors, Pashang grabbed his bone bow, nocked a wooden arrow, aimed with a squint, and loosed.

The arrow cried through the air, enflamed, and turned to cinders before it could pierce the man in the flower-patterned cloak.

"If you want to try again," he said, "I'll be at the top."

By Lat, what sorcery was that?

Litani smirked, then followed his master through the doors of the Tower, locusts singing the while.

. . .

Without resistance, we rode through the streets to the Sand Palace. Mansur's guards let us through the palace gates. I was eager to check on Eshe, but Pashang wouldn't allow it until we were safe. When I glanced at my back, I couldn't see my newly freed friend, which ate at me. He was riding behind someone in the rear, hundreds of horsemen between us.

Returning to the Sand Palace, like this, filled me with a prickly dread. Had I just led the enemy into my home? How would Kyars take the throne now that Mansur had rebuffed his hold with thousands of Jotrids? And yet...

So long as I could live here, in my home, did I really care whether Kyars or Mansur sat the throne? So long as I was at the top, as far from the grave as possible, did I care whose shoulders I stood on?

As we rode through the archways and locust-infested gardens, with crystal fountains shimmering in the moonlight, I realized I barely knew myself. Barely knew what I was capable of, what I was willing to do, just to feel better. Did I not have loftier, more honorable motives than helping myself and my friends? How was I different from a corrupt vizier, Ozar, or Mansur? Hadrith, self-serving as he was, still showed loyalty and friendship to Kyars, who was without question the designated and rightful heir.

But why show loyalty to a man who'd never cared for me? Though Kyars was my husband by law, could Sheikh Khizr enforce our marriage, especially when the country believed I'd killed Tamaz? So many things were up in the air, and I was relying on others to settle them. When had relying on others ever gotten me anywhere, aside from one-eyed and left for dead?

"Cyra." Tekish broke my thoughts. I was still clinging to him as we trotted through the palace garden, my hands sweaty on his bloodied chainmail. "You can't be seen here. If some vizier recognizes you, there'll be trouble." He handed me an orange turban and an eyepatch. "Put these on. You'll be my beardless boy for the night."

"You like the one-eyed boys, Tekish?" I said, surprised at my brazenness.

His boisterous chuckle clashed with the grating, endless chirping of locusts. "Don't make me say something I'd regret saying to a *sultana*."

"Why not? I may enjoy it."

"Jotrid humor is rather merciless. Do you enjoy that kind of thing, Cyra?"

I didn't think so, but I barely knew myself. "No," I whispered, hoping it to be true.

Someone shouted something at Tekish. A woman rider to our left, with zealous eyes and hair that didn't reach her ears. Blood covered the spear on her back. I'd noticed her in the vanguard as the Jotrids charged the city gate.

"My wife isn't happy you're holding me so tight," Tekish said with a chuckle. "Maybe she'll feel better if you looked like a boy."

"Why? She lets you fuck boys?"

He took a chug from a waterskin, then handed it to me. "It's true, she's less jealous when it's a boy licking my cock."

I cringed, not wanting to know about Tekish's perversions. My own bothered me enough. His satisfied smirk didn't reveal whether he was jesting.

His wife's glare revealed much, though, and filled me with a nauseous caution. I didn't need more enemies, so loosened my grip on Tekish's armor and sat at the saddle's edge.

"I'll be your boy, then." I had no idea how to wrap a turban, but after much tugging and scooping and tying, managed to bundle my shoulder-length locks into it. The eyepatch snapped on easily enough. Now I was truly unrecognizable — mind, body, and soul — to myself, most of all.

An unexpected man stood at the palace entrance, along with

tens of Mansur's household guard, who were all garbed in mirror armor inscribed with holy verses.

That man was Ozar. Was he on Mansur's side? I hid behind Tekish, fearful the spice master would recognize me, despite my disguise. I peeked over Tekish's shoulder to see just what was happening.

Ozar and Pashang conversed, though in a whisper. Pashang seemed…surprised…agitated by whatever Ozar was saying. The two talked for minutes until Pashang ordered us to dismount.

Mansur's guard opened the palace door and welcomed us to enter. We passed by the massive stone simurgh, which seemed to eyeball us, and entered the Sand Palace.

I waited at the entrance as tens of Jotrids walked by. Waited for Eshe. As I fidgeted, a sweet breeze seemed to kiss my shoulders: that familiar, Sand Palace air, propelled so lightly by the ceiling rafters. I was home. And yet, who knew what enemies remained? If a spy spotted me and reported to Kato, I could be captured. Killed, even. No — until my home was safe, until I'd defeated my enemies, I couldn't let myself enjoy relief.

Finally, Eshe walked in, his eyes downcast.

I hugged him. His trembles flowed into me, and he didn't hug back. I looked upon his haggard, weak appearance as he gazed at me with short but heavy breaths.

"Eshe," I said, gripping his shoulders. "What did they do to you?"

"Cyra…" He managed a soft, kind smile. "You look like a beardless boy."

"You'll have to do better than that, or the line to your throne will empty."

He chuckled; raising his spirits filled me with a fluttering relief.

"Thank Lat you're here, Cyra. Was it you who asked them to save me?"

I nodded. "You saved me, didn't you? Do you think I'm the

kind of person to forsake a friend?" I hoped I'd never be. "Tell me you're all right, Eshe. You're all right, right?"

But if he was, why were his lips still trembling? "I..." He shut his eyes, hard.

"It's all right." I hugged him again. "You should rest. I'll find a room for you."

"Don't leave me alone," he said. "When I'm alone, I see it."

"See what?"

He looked to the ceiling with its shiny blue lattices and golden, bird-patterned mosaics. "I see the egg."

I LED Eshe to a room a few hallways from the great hall, where the Shah would house visiting dignitaries. I lit the lanterns in the niches, fluffed the pillows, and wiped the silk sheets, though there wasn't a speck of dust. Amid the throbbing candles, the gold-plated etchings on the low table, wardrobe, and desk seemed to glow, filling the room with golden light. On the wall hung a painting of a simurgh carrying a man across the sea, a rendition from *Atash and the Simurgh*, a childish story I never cared for.

I poured water into a crystal cup as Eshe settled on the bed and sat against the pillows.

"Drink." I handed him the cup. "I should get you food, too."

He sipped. "I'm not hungry."

"The food here is *really* good. Fit for shahs, quite literally."

"Just my luck, then, that I've no appetite."

He seemed...morose...to say the least. Though I wanted to know what happened to him, more than that, I wanted to see his full smile.

"I want you to rest. Whatever happened, we can talk about it tomorrow."

"I've no appetite for sleep, either."

I sat on my knees at the base of the bed. "Eshe, I was terrified when they took you. I'm sorry I didn't try to stop them."

He shook his head. "You jest. What could you have possibly done against three armed men?"

"I don't know…thrown my soup in their faces? Anything…just not cowered, the way I did."

"Cyra, you saved me. I don't know how you did it. I don't know what devil's deal you made with Pashang…but thank you. Really, thank you."

"Devil's deal…you don't know the half of it." I crawled over and sat next to him. "The truth is…it's been a long night…and I'm very tired." I let myself slide against the pillow until I was reclining.

"I recall you sweating gobs the other night. Couldn't have been easy to do all you did in that state."

"I feel better. Much better. Must've sweated it out."

"You can take off that turban, too."

"Oh, Lat no — it was impossible getting my hair in here, and I'll have to go out there," I pointed to the door, "soon enough."

"The viziers will line up to fondle you," he said with a wry, half-smile. It seemed I was cheering him up, and that made me hopeful.

"Well…they'll be quite disappointed, I imagine."

As we laughed, I remembered my star-seeing eye. Surely, this wasn't the time to tell Eshe. Better for him to digest the day's events before adding another awful layer.

We both laid in silence and stared at the ceiling for a slender, happy moment. A thought interrupted that peace: *what was I?* Pashang had called me a *starwriter*, but what did it mean? What could I do with this new power, and how? Was it a gift or a payment? How much did Pashang know, and who else knew something about it? Should I be happy or terrified?

"I have something to tell you," I said, looking him in the eye, "but it's hard to sound the words."

He shifted to his side and faced me. "I don't mind if you keep secrets. But if something burdens you, you know I'll help you carry it."

Sweet words...but Eshe had once said *sugar dissolves on the tongue.* "I aided the Jotrids. I helped them get into the city. A tribe I despise — enemies of Kyars, the man I bound my soul to. And I didn't just do it to help you. I think I did it because...because..."

"Cyra, no one likes the Jotrids. Least of all myself. But I saw the way Pashang lingered at your bedside as you slept. And I saw the remains of that Philosopher he cut in two. Now that he's in the city, he's the kingmaker. You've put yourself in quite a position."

I shook my head. "Whatever happened to loyalty? Whatever happened to the straight path?"

"All I know is the straight path doesn't lead to a palace like this. And I'm not one to give guidance...I gave up trying to be good, long ago. We're always going to hurt others. Sometimes it's about choosing the right people to hurt. Sometimes a few people have to die so that many people can live."

"Eshe...I should be cheering you up...but..." I jammed my tear duct with my finger to stop the tears, to no avail, as usual. "It's all been so hard."

"Well..." He took my hand and squeezed it. "I'm right here, suffering with you."

"Eshe..." I bit my lip, then forced out the words. "If I'm being honest, you might be the only one left I don't want to see hurt, ever."

"That's reassuring, I suppose." He smiled.

Whatever passed between our eyes, it struck like lightning, straight into my heart. I leaned away and did the most foolish thing: I smelled my sweat-soaked caftan.

"You know, I really need to take a bath," I said with a nervous chuckle.

Eshe smelled his caftan, too. "You know, you might be on to something. A bath would cure my ills, surely."

"I can show you where the bath is. Oh, and it's quite nice."

"Did the Shah himself bathe there?" He raised his eyebrows in excitement.

I nodded as I got to my feet, though he likely never did. Nothing wrong with a little white lie if it made him happy. "Come on, then."

I peeked out the hallway door; a serving girl was walking away from our room, her back turned. Something about her gait...so familiar...entrancing, even. Short. Lithe. Straight hair the color of a peeled almond, down to her nape. No question.

"Vera?" I whispered to myself.

She turned the corner. I tip-toed after her. But by the time I'd reached the corner, she was gone.

Was she...eavesdropping on our conversation? Had she recognized me?

I turned to see Eshe at the doorway. "Something the matter?" he asked.

"Thought I saw someone I knew...I hope she didn't notice me. I better stay clear of the harem."

The bath was away from where she'd walked, in the western arm of the palace. Strange to see the place so empty, but I assumed it was because Mansur had replaced Tamaz's guards and servants with his own, and they seemed busy with whatever was going on in the great hall.

For now, I wouldn't involve myself in the intrigues between Pashang and Mansur and Kato and Khizr Khaz. I simply wanted to go home — and I'd done it. All I really needed was to expose the sorceress and clear my name, but other than Pashang's vision of a hundred-year-old woman, I had no leads. There was no one that old whom I knew of, but tomorrow I could begin investigating. Perhaps get birth and death records from the registrar — there couldn't be too many women in the city over the age of a hundred.

That ought to be my focus. I had no part to play in the bloodshed between the gholam and the Jotrids and the Order and whoever else was relishing a chance at more power. For now, I'd rather just soak.

But the bath's layout doused my plans. I'd never been inside since it was for men, but to my surprise, there was only one pool that extended across the far wall. The water, also, flowed faster than what I was accustomed to in the harem. Massage tables dotted the room, which our bath lacked. Aside from that, the tile was bright blue and similarly star-patterned, but the mosaic here depicted a battle between a mounted army and a staunch wall filled with mustachioed men.

Without a hint of shame, Eshe pulled off his too-big caftan and stood topless. The whip-marks on his back reminded me of crude etchings children in the Waste would chisel onto bones.

"I was hoping there'd be two pools," I said, "but you go first. I'll wait outside until you're done."

He grabbed my arm as I turned. "Don't leave me alone. Please. When I'm alone, I see it."

Right, he'd mentioned something earlier. "The...egg?"

He nodded. "We're the egg, Cyra. This whole world. All it needs is a little fire, and it'll hatch. He showed me what would happen." Even his eyelids trembled. What torture had the Philosophers devised? And why Eshe? "I don't want to talk about it right now. Just...stay with me."

"Of course, I will." I turned away as he undid the lace on his pants and stepped into the pool.

"By Lat, the water's soothing," he said.

I kept my back turned. "I've actually...never seen a man naked." Ugh, by Lat, why did I let that bit of honesty slip?

"Even your brother or your father?"

"I mean, they don't count."

Eshe splashed water on himself. "You really are a good girl. Lucky Kyars. Another maid to deflower."

I chuckled bitterly.

"I'm sorry," he said. "That was...a senseless thing to say."

"Why? You think I pine for him? I've known him for eight years. I know I won't be his nighttime fancy. I mean, there's Zedra, who is heaps more alluring. She could never pass for a beardless boy."

"Sounds like a lovely marriage. But you knew what you were agreeing to, I imagine."

I made a fist. "I agreed to be Sultana of Sultanas. Kyars can fuck and love whomever he wants. I want my position back. I want what that sorceress took away."

"*Sorceress?* A woman?"

I didn't want to tell Eshe about Pashang's visions. That we'd entered the Palace of Bones. I feared he'd look upon us like the evils he hunted. "Sorcerer, sorceress, whoever. He or she took away the only thing I wanted."

I could hear the water shift as Eshe floated on his back. I almost wanted to peek.

"Cyra, I don't know what it's like being you. We're nothing alike. But at the end of the day, everyone wants the same thing. To be happy."

I snickered. "*Happy?* That's the least wise thing you've said to me. While I lived in the Sand Palace, all day, every day, I witnessed viziers and concubines and even the eunuchs compete, not for happiness, but for *more*."

"Because they think *more* will make them happy. But you know what? I know that's false…because I was happiest when I was a Disciple, living in a cave on a bed of sand and stone."

"So you were happy when you had purpose. We're not so different, then. I don't want to waste any more of my life idle in the harem or freezing in the Waste. As Sultana of Sultanas, I could do things that mattered to this country. Shape its destiny, even."

A splash of water dampened my back. I screamed and, without thinking, turned toward Eshe, who was standing in the pool and laughing. He wound his arm and splashed another gale onto me, soaking the front of my caftan.

I shivered as I stared at his nakedness. I couldn't deny that I liked what I saw.

He sank back into the pool, obscuring what I was staring at.

"Sorry, I just had to. My mother always said I had a bit of Ahriyya in me."

I was shivering, and I hated shivering. Cold reminded me of those frozen and starving days in the Waste, which I'd prayed to the void to escape. A prayer that had eventually led me here, to this bath, with this man.

Without a second thought, I stepped into the pool and submerged in the rippling, warm water. It eased the shivers.

"Are you really going to bathe with your clothes on?" Eshe asked.

I glared at him, though I wasn't as furious as I pretended. "So… was this your way of getting me naked? Well, sorry to disappoint."

He grinned. Just how shameless was he? "I swear, I don't have any ill-intentions."

"Earlier, you said you gave up trying to be good…well, I haven't yet…completely…"

"That's admirable. To be fair, while I gave up trying to be good, I didn't give up trying to do the right thing…if that makes sense."

In a way, it did. What you were on the inside and your actions could be entirely different. "Was getting me in the pool the right thing?"

"You're the one who got in the pool. I only splashed you." He scratched his beard. "Splashing you was not the right thing, no, but now that you're in here, I don't regret it."

I smiled. Was I blushing? "I don't regret it, either."

A knock sounded on the door.

Whoever it was entered before I could get out of the water. And it just had to be him: Khagan Pashang, still in his bloodied chain-mail, wearing a shameless smile above his bright brown beard.

He was obviously delighted to catch us in this sordid situation. And his smile only stretched as he stopped at the pool's edge.

"Cyra, Eshe, I honestly never knew," he said. "Now, I'm not one to interrupt pleasure, but a serious matter has presented itself."

I wanted to say that nothing happened between us but swallowed my shame instead. Besides, it seemed Pashang wasn't the jealous type. "What matter?"

"Two matters, actually." Pashang held up two gloved fingers. "First, someone claims to know who the soulshifter is. And second…oh, that you'll barely believe."

20

ZEDRA

INTO THE CHEST, I went, Celene on guard. With the Jotrids —
somehow — in the city, it was time to use my most treasured bloodrune, lest it all unravel. I'd saved it for a crisis like this when subtler
methods had failed, and a direct, though far riskier approach was
needed. I touched the bloodrune with my mind, hoping it would
do what I needed it to.

I stood at the head of a prayer line, hands raised and head going
left to right, left to right. These saint worshippers prayed all wrong,
too: the head should start on the right, not the left, and you should
never raise your hands.

I dropped my hands, folded them, and said in a gruff voice,
"I'm not feeling well. Everyone out."

The viziers in the rows behind me looked at each other, bewildered, so I shouted, "Out!"

At that, they streamed out the room. I studied the rings on my
fingers: an emerald partly encased in gold, a topaz within which

was some sort of twinkling water, and a flat, golden disc with the sigil of the simurgh, its wings high and august.

I didn't need more confirmation. The bloodrune I'd scrawled under Tamaz's table the night I'd supped with him had now worked. I'd used some of Kyars' sower's blood — which I'd cleaned up when I'd *so clumsily* left a needle in his bed — instead of my own seeker's blood to make the rune, suspecting his father possessed the same flavor. Well, his father didn't, but his uncle did. I was now a Seluqal. I was Mansur.

I tried to remember where baby Seluq was. Mansur had given him to…a serving girl…somewhere…not far. I couldn't tell precisely who or where, so I'd have to search. I'd only get one chance: was half an hour enough time?

In the hallway, a gray-mustached man who wore chainmail over brocade bowed his head at me. "Your Highness. Khagan Pashang was last sighted at the Tower of Wisdom."

Tower of Wisdom? What was he doing there? "Why?"

"We don't know. Some of his force has already arrived at the palace gates. We're well secured from the Order's treachery. Khizr Khaz will pay for this betrayal."

Betrayal? Was Khizr Khaz originally on their side?

"Where is Kyars' son?" I asked.

The man's mustache twitched. "Where he's always been. With the Ruthenian handmaid."

With Vera? But Mansur imprisoned her, even forced a false testimony from her.

"I'm off to the harem, then," I said.

"Harem? But the girl and the child aren't there."

"Then where are they?"

He scratched his head — I ought not to let my ignorance show too much, from now on, lest they grow suspicious. "Where they've always been. In your bed chamber."

So…Vera had more cunning than I'd realized. She always was good at getting baby Seluq to stop fussing or crying. She'd sing, rock his crib, and put him to sleep. Seemed her skill with children extended to old men, too. Good for her.

After a short walk, I entered the Shah's bed chamber. There Vera stood, polishing the golden trellis that surrounded the bed. Kyars had the same in his room — when we'd *make love*, I'd feel like a caged animal.

Vera straightened her rose scarf and bent her neck. "My Shah." Was she already calling him that? How profane.

In the crib slept baby Seluq. Seeing him…tears misted on my eyelids, one trailing down my cheek and into my beard. I scooped him up, kissed his forehead, and hugged him close. Tucked him between my shoulder and neck.

I turned to see an astonished Vera, dimples aside her soft, strawberry lips.

"You've taken to him," she said. "That's a relief. He's always been a good boy."

"And have you been a good girl, Vera?"

I'm sure Mansur loved that mischievous smile. She said, "I hope so, my Shah. I've not denied you any request, have I?"

I caressed her powdered cheek. Nauseatingly sweet, this girl, like an underripe date dipped in molasses. "You'll do something for me, now."

She got on her tiptoes and kissed my cheek, finishing with her tongue. "Anything, my Shah."

I handed her baby Seluq. She cradled him over her shoulder.

"Follow me."

Mirror-armored soldiers guarded every room in the hall, bending their necks as I passed. Servants also went about, though I recognized few — seemed Mansur had brought his own. After several minutes — I was acutely aware of the draining water clock — we arrived at the archway to the exit.

Just my damned luck that a bubbly and over-perfumed Ozar stood there, as if lying in wait. He bent his neck.

"I've no time for you," I said. "Find me later."

"Your Highness," he called as I passed, "I've received word from *you-know-who* at the shrine."

Curse the saints. They had a spy in the shrine? For everyone's sake, I had to find out who.

I turned back to Ozar and said, "What did he say?"

Ozar eyed Vera. "We should speak in your room, never know who's listening in a vast hall like this."

No, I hadn't the time. "Tell me here. Now. I'm in a hurry."

He shook his head. "That would endanger *you-know-who*. And I won't put an ally in harm's way."

Was it Hadrith? It had to be; the two were known allies after having been enemies for so long. "Find me later, then." The water dripped out the clock every second that passed. I had to get baby Seluq to safety within twenty minutes, and there was a long way to go.

Vera followed me through the archway, past the simurgh statue, across the gardens, and to the palace gate, which was open. Jotrid riders flowed through — an endless sea of them, filling the palace grounds with horse stink. They weren't the only pestilence; locusts flew overhead, their fluttering wings like Ahriyya's whispers. Already, they were devouring flowers and trees, and the pleasure garden began to resemble a bullet-riddled battlescape.

"I hate-hate-hate these things," Vera said as she waved her hand in front of Seluq to shield him from the bugs. "Where are we going, anyway?"

I put my finger on her lip to silence the question. "Give him to me."

She handed over my baby. I held him to my chest, his tiny breaths against my beating heart.

"Please don't hurt him." Vera's eyes wetted. "I know someone who'll take him. Raise him on a farm. He'll never know who he really is." Trembles overtook her breaths. "Just...don't..." She sobbed. "Don't hurt the child."

If she truly cared about my son, then she wouldn't have called his mother a whore. Nothing had endangered him more than her aspersions. I turned away, letting her chew on a painful uncertainty.

"Don't hurt him!" Her cry echoed in the night as I walked through the gate against the tide of Jotrid riders.

A gate guard, also clad in mirror armor like the rest of Mansur's ilk, was standing by and watching the Jotrids pass. I said to him, "I need a carriage. Right now."

He bent his neck. "Your Highness, yes, of course. I'll have one here in five minutes."

"Did you not hear me? I said *right now!*"

His neck stayed bent. "But…this afternoon…you ordered us to fortify the palace and not allow anyone in or out. The carriages were moved from the remise to the stable grounds."

I turned to the Jotrids. "Whoever gives me their ride right now, I'll give you a thousand gold pieces come morning!"

Four men and two women dismounted. I handed Seluq to the gate guard, then grabbed the nearest mare — golden-haired and fair-maned — and climbed on. My bones and muscles groaned with each stretch and pull, a reminder that Mansur was old. After the gate guard handed Seluq back, I clutched the reins with one hand and my baby with the other, somewhat worried about how much Mansur's groin ached on the hard, tanned saddle. Could this frail fool even survive a ride?

No time to consider it: I spurred the mare, and we were off, galloping in the opposite direction to the Jotrid wave engulfing the streets.

As the wind whipped against us, Seluq began crying. No time to stop and comfort him, so we rode on. The fastest way to the Shrine of Saint Jamshid was through the Glass District, which was thankfully devoid of Jotrids. The buildings here always seemed so odd and mismatched, with their glass walls and bright domes. Now locusts covered them, their song like the wails of demons. We passed by the unbreakable statue of that saint — I could never remember her name — and down the winding lane that led to the bridge of Saint Jorga, past which sat the Shrine.

Except…men armed with long-barreled matchlocks guarded the bridge. Through the locust-infested air, I could only discern that they wore the rough, hooded cloaks of the Order.

With minutes remaining, I trotted toward them until they took notice and approached.

"The bridge is closed," one said. "Turn around, old man."

I climbed off the horse as two aimed their matchlocks at me.

"Turn around!"

"I've a message for your sheikh," I said, holding my baby tight. "For Khizr Khaz and him alone."

They lowered their guns once they noticed the baby. "Who are you?"

"Just a vizier." A crack appeared in my vision. "I must speak with your sheikh. Now. Right now. There's not a moment to lose. I've just come from the palace and have much to tell him."

Another man, who was standing near the river, approached. Fair-haired, like my horse, with light skin and eyes. He spat a chewed-up jelly delight from his mouth, then studied me up and down. "I know you."

I walked toward the bridge, but the men continued to block my path.

Another crack erupted across my vision. I trembled. Only a few more steps to reach the shrine, and yet…

"Please, I must speak with the sheikh. Let me pass!"

The jelly-chewing man grabbed my hand, fingered the flat ring with the simurgh seal, and looked at my face with flaring pupils. "No question. Saw you when you visited the shrine, the other day. You're Mansur!"

More cracks nearly blinded me. I handed my baby over to the jelly-chewing man. He held Seluq out in front, as if ignorant about how to carry a child.

"Khizr Khaz, now!" was all I could say before everything shattered and I awoke in the pile of robes.

I pushed out of the chest and onto my feet. Barely glanced at Celene as I ran out the building, through the arches, and toward the shrine itself. I took a shortcut through the area around the sepulcher, then ran down the steps toward the street, where gun-toting hooded Order men waited and chatted. They took notice; one shouted, "No one's allowed on the street! Jotrids are everywhere!" as I ran by toward Saint Jorga's Bridge. They gave chase. I sprinted harder than I ever had, locusts streaming through my hair.

Ahead, another cohort of Order men blocked the bridge. Too many. They formed a wall; I tried to run aside, but one of them grabbed my arm and pulled me into him.

"How dare you touch me!" I screamed. "Kyars will cut off your hand!"

"You can't be here!" the bear-like man said. "Return to the shrine!"

I pounded his grip. Smashed it with all my strength. That did nothing, and he only tightened his hold. I writhed and screamed and cursed. I needed blood. Any blood.

I pulled his dagger from his belt. He grabbed my wrist before I could cut myself, then squeezed so tight I couldn't grip the dagger. It clattered onto the ground.

"Let me go!"

"It's dangerous! There are Jotrids all over! Return to the shrine!"

"No! Let me go!"

I tried to peer across the bridge but couldn't see the other side amid the locust swarm. Where was Mansur? Where was my son? Surely, just beyond the bridge!

"Let me just go over the bridge! Please!"

But the men wouldn't heed. The bear-like one put me over his shoulder and carried me toward the shrine. He didn't flinch as I pulled his hair and punched his back. I could only resist so much before I huffed, breathless, my strength consumed by rage and longing.

They dropped me on the floor of my lodging, then barred the door. Celene ran up to me, still holding one of those robes, her cheeks tight with worry.

I SPENT the remaining hours screaming at the guards. Begging them to ask Khizr Khaz if they'd brought my son to him. Trying to get out through the windows, but they guarded them, too. All for my *safety*. If anything happened to my son, not a one would be safe from me.

If only I could have soulshifted again, but the sun needed to rise. I lamented the limitations of my powers, both worldly and otherworldly.

At dawn, they relented and escorted me to Khizr Khaz's office. The old warrior was conversing with some stoop-backed vizier.

"Out!" I screamed at the vizier. He winced and crawled out of the room.

Khizr Khaz folded his hands and glared at me. "Sultana, I heard about your…behavior. I apologize for not addressing you sooner, but last night kept me occupied. Now tell me, what's the matter?"

"Last night, I had a dream. I saw my son. I saw him being brought to this shrine. Where is he?"

Khizr bade me to sit. I didn't.

"A dream?" he said. "Sultana, I don't know what you're talking about."

"Father Chisti himself brought my son to me in the dream. Where is he?" I wiped the slobber which had burst onto my chin.

Khizr shut his eyes and sighed. "You look like you haven't slept. No one has, after what happened. We're all going mad. But I assure you, I don't know where your son is. Last I heard, he was at the palace, with Mansur."

I wanted to throw his desk in his face. How could he not know?

I'd delivered my baby with Mansur's hands to one of his Order men. How could he not be here? Was he lying? Was he a traitor?

My arms shook as I glared down at Khizr Khaz. He stood.

"Listen to me," he said. "Go back to your lodging and rest, sultana. Your son is my foremost priority. Are you even aware that, last night, the Jotrids broke through the wall? They've reinforced Mansur's hold on the Sand Palace. The awful truth is — we've been dealt a hard blow that—"

I turned away and marched outside to the fresh morning air. Tugged on my hair. Paced back and forth, retreading it in my mind. I'd handed Seluq to that cloaked, fair-haired, jelly-chewing man. He had my baby. He was an Order man, and so he had to be here. I'd turn over this whole shrine if I had to!

Either Khizr Khaz was lying, or his men were not loyal. But then where else would those Order men take Mansur and my child? Surely not back to the palace.

I turned to see Khizr Khaz, hood down and white hair blowing with the breeze.

"You called him *Father*," he said.

"What?"

"Saint Chisti. You called him *Father*. Slip of the tongue, I assume?"

Had I? How foolish of me. "So what? He is the father of our faith, so to speak."

Khizr Khaz shook his head. "He is, but no one refers to him that way, save for those far astray, on a path descending to hellfire."

I wanted to smash his head against the stone arch. "My son is in danger, and you chastise me for a stray word?"

"Stray words oft reveal the truth. Does Kyars know you're Path of the Children?"

"Freeze in hell." I spat at his feet.

As I turned and walked away, he said, "What else are you hiding, I wonder?"

· · ·

I WENT to the women's section of the shrine for some privacy. Sat in the carpeted area nearest the sepulcher, which was covered by a wire cage. I shut my eyes and allowed the cool air blowing down from the leaf-colored dome to soothe me. But it didn't. Nothing could stop my heart from pounding with rage.

Nothing could stop the tears, either. I covered my face, but they flowed onto my lips, tasting bitter and dark. I'd gotten my son back. I'd held him, kissed him, felt his beating heart. How could this happen? He was there, just outside, across the bridge, across the cursed saint's bridge!

No matter my power, I could never stop it. I'd watched Seluq's horde drown my daughters, granddaughters, and great-granddaughters. My son, his son, and his son's son had been strangled. Three of the Twelve Chiefs of the Children — I could do naught for them.

Why did I survive? Because I was a bird watching from a treetop. After the cycle ended, Father Chisti brought me to this time, this place to rebirth our lineage. It was all on me, all on me, but I was never enough, never enough.

Footsteps pattered on the carpet. I turned to see that girl — Safia, or rather, Sadie, rubbing the crust out of her eye. She seemed as bleary as me as she sat in the middle of the room and stared at the sepulcher, her lips still and prayerless.

Khizr Khaz had asked what I was hiding. Well, nice to know I wasn't the only one. I scooted over to her; she welcomed my presence with a gulp that rolled down her throat as if she'd swallowed a leather ball.

"What were you doing last night?" I asked.

She covered her mouth as she yawned. "Guarding one of the bridges. Not much else we could do."

How had Shah Murad's daughter become so masterful with arrows? The Seluqal women in Alanya were not trained to fight. The Alanyans liked to cast the Sirmians as warlike — if even the princesses were warriors, it must be true. Whereas the Seluqals in

Alanya embraced the ways and words of the saint-kings they conquered, it seemed the Seluqals in Sirm clung somewhat more to the ways of the Waste.

"Did you…" I sniffled. "Did you see an old man carrying a baby?"

She raised an eyebrow, then shook her head.

Why was she here? Why wasn't she with her family? Did she not understand how precious a moment with your blood is? With your mother and father and brothers and sisters and daughters and sons? All that matters is blood. Only blood.

I sobbed as I stared into her kind pupils — the color of late afternoon sunshine. I seemed to spread my sadness to her; her eyes watered.

"What happened?" she asked.

I covered my sobbing face and shook my head. "Don't trouble — yourself with — my sorrows, dear."

"I heard Mansur has your son captive. I wish I could help."

"Why? Why help me?"

She let out a heavy breath. "I've seen so much death. Seen death itself. I thought by helping your son's father that I could help spare Alanya…whatever it was that happened…up in Sirm, where my father fought."

She wanted to relate her wisdom yet couldn't expose herself. A fine seam she threaded, but I'd let her.

I said, "I would've been proud to have a…sister like you." I really meant daughter. "The Jotrids have their women holding bows, but the Jotrids…there's nothing good about them." They reminded me of Seluq and his horde. "They're cruel and uncultured. You, on the other hand, seem to hold every virtue." If I could wield a bow like her, perhaps I could've killed Seluq and stopped this awful history from unfolding.

"That's not true," she said. "I'm a coward. I always do the easy thing. I run away." Had she run from her family? Was that why she was so far from home? "I'd rather fight someone else's battles, because my own scare me so much."

I rubbed away my tears. "Do you know the story of Safia, your namesake, daughter of Fa...Saint Chisti?" My great-great-great-great-grandmother.

Sadie shook her head. "I had no idea it was his daughter's name."

Of course she didn't. The saint worshippers pretended like his children never were — their shame for killing us all. I began, "When Safia was twelve years old, she was taken by..." I pointed to the sepulcher.

"By Saint Jamshid?" Sadie raised her eyebrows.

I nodded. "Jamshid wanted to resolve the rift between himself and the family of his teacher, Chisti. As his best student, he considered himself the heir, and I think he really believed it because Chisti had no sons, only daughters. So he took his teacher's favorite daughter, without asking, to be his wife. That way, his children would have Chisti's blood, and there'd be no conflict."

Sadie shrugged. "Sounds reasonable...sort of...but he kidnapped her...so maybe not..."

"Safia had already been promised to her cousin, and he swore he would save her."

"Cousins? Well, I know the feeling..."

I rather enjoyed how engaged she was, but I'd barely begun the story. "Armies were raised, and a battle was to be fought over a twelve-year-old girl, one that would decide the future of the Faith."

"Right," she said. "I think I remember something about that battle. Though the way I learned it, Jamshid was fighting to keep the Faith together. Fighting heretics who had manipulated Saint Chisti's family and sought to divide the Faith of Lat."

Of course they'd tell such lies. In truth, it was Jamshid who split the Faith with his avarice.

"Well, either way, we all know Jamshid won. And it wasn't even close. But he didn't get what he wanted. Safia, through sheer cleverness, escaped and traveled to the Vogras Mountains, where she married and founded a great tribe. They became known as the Children."

Sadie put a finger to her chin. "Hmm, the Children. A few zabadar tribes in Sirm still follow their path."

"Is that so? The Seluqals there permit it?"

She nodded. "In Kostany, they have their own sheikhs and shrines. But they don't call them shrines — they call them *gates*, I think. But...I don't want to overstate things...their followers are very few."

Those who called themselves Path of the Children today were like a shadow cast by a long-dead flame. They barely knew what to believe. They called their shrines *gates* because they imagined, by entering them, they were walking through a gate into the presence of the Twelfth Chief, my great-grandson, whom they believed would return to save the earth from the Great Terror.

Nonsense. He was strangled to death. I was the only one who survived that bloodbath. I, and my son Seluq, would save them by uniting the east under one padishah with the blood of Father Chisti, as it was always meant to be.

But I couldn't blame them for inventing falsehoods to give themselves hope. At least they were trying to follow the true path, unlike these saint worshippers.

"Are you...one of them?" Sadie asked.

"If I were, they'd lock me in a dungeon until I recanted. Do I look like I'd do well in a dungeon?" I smiled. "My mother, though, believed. That's why I know the story."

"Saints. Children. Angels. Lat. I never understood why everyone hates everyone else for the sake of things we've never seen. Although..."

Well, she was looking at the Children, so that wasn't true. But could I be like the best of us, like my grandmother, Safia? Could I survive this and rebirth our tribe? Rekindle the flame of truth?

Dwelling on her story — how she persevered despite all

seeming lost — calmed my heart. There was hope. I needed to find my son and wipe out Mansur and his Jotrids. I'd use every blood-rune I'd ever learned if it came to it.

Later, I returned to the Order's gathering room, where a meeting was taking place to determine our next steps. Sitting scattered across the grass-colored carpets were the obvious men: Khizr Khaz, Kato, Hadrith, and various viziers. As soon as I entered, Khizr Khaz rose and stepped to me.

"You need rest, sultana."

"I'll rest with Mansur buried and my son in my arms."

He shook his head. "I'm afraid, for your own well-being, I must order you back to your lodging."

"Go ahead and order it," I said. "But keep in mind, I'll never forget. I'll tell Kyars, the next time he's undressing me, that I'm not in the mood because I can't forget the day Khizr Khaz ordered me to go away. I'll tell my son, too, when he's grown enough. We'll see how long you remain Grand Mufti or grand anything."

Kato, who was sitting within earshot, glanced at me, his ring-laden hand barely covering his grin. Let him hear. Let them all hear.

Khizr said, "We're all upset by what happened last night. As a mother, it's broken you. Running into the street, screaming…because of a dream…the Jotrids could have captured you, killed you. For your own well-being, you'll be escorted to your lodging, where you'll remain for the next few days. Besides, this meeting is rather sensitive — we could have defections if we don't play it right — and I'll not have you disrupting it with your outbursts."

Outbursts? He had no idea what I was capable of. I could draw a rune that would send his mind to a place of utter torment. But no…he was right…it had broken me.

"You're right." I swallowed every bitter feeling, as I'd been doing. "I will take to my bed, then."

But as soon as I returned to the women's lodging, I pulled Celene out of sleep and dragged her to the robe's chest.

"Again?" she said, picking up the robes I'd thrown on the floor. "Shouldn't you rest?"

"My son is out there, and I'm going to find him. No matter what."

"All right." She yawned. "Marot forgive me."

THE DRONGO WAS SWALLOWING A LOCUST, whole, atop Qandbajar's wall when my soul entered it. The bug chittered as my throat forced it down, crying with flapping wings. I pushed it through, and it died from the bath in my stomach. Then I jumped into the air and soared toward the shrine.

I landed on the windowsill of the room where the meeting was taking place. Dark drapes covered it, so I aimed my ear and listened.

"My contact assures me that it's true," Hadrith said. "They've been looking for Mansur and the child through the night."

So Hadrith had a contact in the palace. Who else could it be but Ozar? The two played both sides; if Mansur won, Ozar could vouch that Hadrith had spied for him. If Kyars won, then Hadrith could vouch that Ozar had spied for him. Both would be spared, no matter what happened. Clever.

Kato cleared his throat. "Why, though? Could it be that Mansur feared the Jotrids?"

"No-no," Hadrith said. "Mansur was overjoyed. He even led a prayer in thanks after the Jotrids entered the city. Then he suddenly stopped in the middle of the prayer, took the baby, and walked out of the palace."

"The old man's mind snapped like a rusted sword." Kato snickered. "That's why I always bet on fresher steel."

So Mansur and my son hadn't been returned to the palace; a relief. They were somewhere in the city, then. Maybe even in this shrine — what if Khizr Khaz was hiding them? But why would he?

The old sheikh spoke up. "Strange that you mention this. The boy's mother told me she had a dream that Saint Chisti was walking down the street, bringing her baby to her. Turns out it was actually Mansur." From his tone, he seemed genuinely confused.

Those Order men I handed baby Seluq to must've been corrupt, must've brought Mansur and my son to whoever would pay them the highest sum. But Ozar didn't have them, as Hadrith made clear. Who, then?

Kato said, "We find Mansur and the heir, we win. It's that simple. We could scour the city, but the Jotrids will be doing like, and they've ten for our one."

Hadrith let out a weary sigh. "I have a theory. Most of you doubted me, doubted that a soulshifter killed Tamaz. I believe that the soulshifter possessed Mansur's body, seized the heir, and brought them to him."

Grumbles and shifting. Somehow Hadrith had become the bearer of truth. And because of my failure, it was starting to unravel me.

"I, for one, believe it to be possible," Khizr Khaz said. "Why else would Mansur just disappear on the night of his apparent victory? But if it's true, it introduces a troubling possibility. That the soulshifter isn't fighting for Mansur and the Jotrids, nor for anyone here, but for another faction."

The grumbling heightened. The viziers didn't like these complications. Nor did I. I was supposed to be in that room, leading them toward my truth, not the actual truth!

"Another faction?" Kato released a long, stinging sigh. "By Lat, aren't there enough?"

Khizr Khaz said, "Who benefits most from a prolonged conflict in Alanya? Who benefited, in the first place, by Shah Tamaz dying?"

"You sound like a sitar with snapped strings," Kato said. "I've no inkling where you're leading with this." Nor did I.

"Think about it," Khizr said. "Who is an enemy to us, to Mansur, to everyone? Path of the Children."

The scoffs and grumbles vibrated beneath my talons. They were putting the pieces together, but could they see my image on the cracks?

Hadrith grumbled loudest. "The Path of the Children have no face. No leader. Their followers are scattered, hiding. I very much doubt this."

What had led Khizr Khaz to such a perceptive conclusion? I hoped it wasn't our earlier conversation. Did he know it was me? Was that why he wouldn't let me attend the meeting?

"I have another theory." The light and airy voice of a girl. Twisty Abyadi accent. But when I'd been there earlier, I didn't see any girl.

"Yes, Ruhi," Khizr said. "I, for one, am relieved the Disciples are taking an interest in this affair. Tell us what you think."

She was a Disciple of Chisti? I assumed they'd stay away from a succession conflict.

"Most of you don't know me," she said, "but I'm well-acquainted with sorcerers of various varieties." The sound of cloth being pulled off. Gasps filled the room. What had just happened?

"A bloodwriter covered me in these runes," she said. "There isn't a part of my body left unscarred by them. These runes…if you sipped the agony they daily put me through, you'd beg for ten deaths. This one right here, on my forehead, they call it *Thousandth Hell*." Thousandth Hell was a bloodrune meant for torture and punishment. It made manifest one's deepest fears — though I'd never written nor experienced it. "Let's just say, it's as bad as it sounds. If not for *fanaa*, I'd be writhing in agony, even now." The room was silent aside from her voice. She had them enraptured. "Other than the bloodwriter who tortured me, I was once friends with another variety of sorcerer. Her name was Aschere, and she was a starwriter."

More gasps.

"The magus who brought calamity to Sirm?" some vizier said.

"Yes, her," Ruhi continued. "But before that, she used to visit my tea stall. She seemed…decent, though melancholic. Anyway, one day, I saw her standing atop a hill. I saw her…drawing shapes in the air…with her hands. At the time, I thought nothing of it. Only later did I realize she was writing on the stars. And by doing so, invoking one star, in particular — the Blood Star."

All sorceries were conjured from one of two stars: the Morning Star — which birthed all life — and the Blood Star — from which all life would be rebirthed in the Great Terror. Of course Aschere had invoked it for her evil.

"I tell you this," Ruhi gulped, "I tell you this because last night, I was hiding in the scrub, and I saw someone make those shapes in the air. And afterward, I saw the very air turn into a swarm of locusts, and I saw those locusts fly toward the wall, clustered so thick that the gholam standing guard couldn't see the Jotrid's rush."

"Told you it was the locusts," Kato said. "My gholam are no cowards. Go on, girl, tell us who it was. It was that bastard Pashang, wasn't it?"

"No, not Pashang. He was holding her hand, but it wasn't him. It was the one you all know as Shah Tamaz's killer. It was Cyra."

21

CYRA

OZAR AND VERA WERE SITTING ON CUSHIONS AROUND A WOODEN TEA table in the dimly lit meeting room. At first, neither recognized me in my eyepatch and orange turban amid the weak candlelight. But once Eshe and I plopped down on sequin-covered pillows across from them, Vera grabbed her chest and said, "Cyra!"

Pashang, who sat to my left, *shhd* her with a raised finger. Ozar stuck his elbows on the table and leaned close.

"Sultana," he whispered. "It really is you. Thank Lat!"

Looking at them was like peeking into the past, into a life I'd lived long ago. And yet, it'd only been days since I'd seen them. Some days can be longer than years, I suppose.

I undid my orange turban, letting my curled locks fall on my shoulders. What could I say to them? Was I happy to see Ozar and Vera? Not truly — as much as I'd appreciated Ozar's respect and Vera's affection, they weren't the ones I missed. If it were my brother and Tamaz sitting at this table, perhaps I wouldn't have to force a smile.

I said, "It sweetens the soul to see you both healthy."

Ozar gestured to Eshe, who was at my right and still smelled of lye and bathwater. "Himyarite, I so wanted to hear more of your *poetry*. What a relief that there's still time."

"Is there?" Eshe folded his arms. "Given what's happening?"

"Oh, of course," Ozar said. "The warrior-poets would conjure verse whilst bolting up fortress walls, wading through rivers with warhorses snarling at their backs, even amid a melee, sword gripped in one hand and pen in the other. *'Quavering hearts birth beauties.'* Verse by Taqi himself."

Pashang chuckled. "I must be the midwife of beauty, then." He gestured his chin at Vera. "Tell us, girl. Tell everyone what you told me."

Vera's cheeks pinkened as she shriveled from the attention on her. Insufferably adorable. "I don't know where to begin. I suppose I'll start with Mansur. You see, Mansur — I'd seen him hold the baby a few times. Baby Seluq. He would always hold him out in front, as if he were a big stone — not even flesh. But then, a few hours ago, he took the baby. But this time — the way he held him — I'll never forget it…"

Pashang explained on the way that Mansur had left the palace with the baby and was now missing. But by Lat, what did exposing the sorceress have to do with how he held him?

Vera continued, "Before he disappeared into the night, Mansur kissed the baby's head then tucked him between his shoulder and neck. Very motherly, don't you think? And you know who used to hold baby Seluq in that way?" She sucked in a long, tense breath. "Zedra, his mother!"

I laughed. Ridiculous! "Is that all the evidence you have? Mansur has children. I'm sure he knows how to comfort a baby. And Zedra…she spent her time watching dances and swooning over verse in Laughter Square." As soon as the words left my tongue, I realized: wouldn't apparent vanity be a great cover for a sorceress?

Vera said, "You two were such good friends. I know it's hard to hear. But Ozar told me how you all suspected there was…someone possessing other people's bodies. Well, in Ruthenia, my mother told me stories about such possessors. A god named Nyarlot descended and taught men how to do that, and other magic too. Once, there were entire tribes of men and women who could steal bodies, but only for minutes at a time."

I grumbled. Ozar was nodding. Pashang stroked his trim, brown beard, gaze on the ceiling as if deep in thought. Eshe stroked his beard too, eyes squinted.

Vera gulped hard. "Cyra…I'm so sorry…please forgive me." She looked away and sniffled.

"Forgive you for what?"

"Zedra asked me to bring her your blood. So, whenever you'd… have an accident…I'd wipe it up and bring it to her. She said it would cause your friendship to bloom. But now I realize…she was doing magic with it."

Eshe slammed his fist on the table. "That's proof enough. The bloodrunes I saw were made with conqueror's blood! You have that blood, Cyra."

So…not only did Zedra betray me, but Vera did, too. The two whom I was closest to in the harem. My throat tightened with sadness. How alone I'd always been; even when I thought others were being affectionate, it was all a sick jape.

Vera sobbed as tears flowed. I took her hand and caressed it. "Vera…you couldn't have known…no one did. Thank you for telling us." I withdrew my hands and clenched my trembling fists beneath the table. Rage simmered in my core, but I didn't want to show it.

If what Vera said was true — and she didn't seem to be lying — then it was almost certain proof that Zedra was the soulshifter. But *almost* wasn't enough.

Ozar cleared his throat. "I've a man in Jamshid's shrine, where Zedra is staying along with Kato and others. I can ask him to confirm this, if more proof is needed. Khagan, what say you?"

Everyone looked to Pashang, who still seemed lost in reflection, his gaze on his own lap. "Hmm," he said as he scratched his cheek. "Has your man said anything about where Mansur took the baby?"

"I've already sent word — we'll get his answer shortly, I hope."

I thought about Zedra. Her friendship...it always seemed so genuine. We'd fought once or twice but always due to my pettiness. She seemed so mature, and that drew me in. Whereas I was like a raging sea, she was an island, placid and unmoved. I wanted to be like her, but my childishness never let me.

"You said she was an old woman," I whispered to Pashang. "But Zedra is years younger than me."

"You're right," Pashang replied, loud enough for all to hear. "But magi are known to appear young, despite being old. Could be the same magic changed her appearance." He sighed — heavy. "The worst of it all — if we don't get Mansur back, this was all for naught. Without a Seluqal on our side, we have no side. Every vizier worth a copper will turn against us."

Kyars was obsessed with Zedra. He groveled at her feet. If she were against me, no way he'd ever accept our marriage. Perhaps I'd done right by opening the city to the Jotrids. Perhaps Mansur's side was the only one where I had a future.

Ozar nodded. "Mansur and the baby must be at the shrine with Zedra. Where else would she bring them? Once we have confirmation, we'll have to get them back."

"It's not foolproof," Eshe said, "soulshifting. There's a chance her soul was forced out of Mansur's body somewhere in the city, before they reached the shrine."

"Until we know for certain," Pashang said, "it's all worth considering. For now, everyone go rest. It's been a night for the ages."

Rest? Not with what stirred within: a storm of rage, confusion, sadness, and frustration. Why did Zedra use me to kill Tamaz? Had she planned it from the first? Or was it in response to my marriage to Kyars? I'd been slapped in the face with a hammer, by my best friend, and the bruise would never heal. What evil was she serving? And most importantly, how could I get justice?

After the meeting, I asked Vera to show me where the so-called soulshifting of Mansur took place. She guided me to Tamaz's chamber, though he only slept here when his wife or a concubine was staying the night. Half the room was a bed, surrounded by a golden trellis. A chest of overflowing jewels sat in the corner, next to an empty crib. Vera relit the candles.

"It was here he kissed the baby, just like Zedra would." She rocked the crib, longing in her eyes. "Oh — how rude of me — may I get you something, sultana?"

"Wine would do."

Vera reached atop a shelf for a ruby-encrusted cup and a flagon of wine.

"For yourself, as well." I gestured to the second cup she'd left on the shelf.

"I better not…it doesn't agree with me."

"I don't care. Pour yourself a cup."

She did as ordered, then stood across the room, as if I were a tiger about to pounce.

"Sultana, please understand — I only did what she ordered me to."

I opened the gate of the trellis and pointed to the bed. Once Vera and I were inside, I shut it. We sat on our knees, across from each other. Vera covered her mouth with her emerald-studded cup.

"You're not telling me everything," I said. "You're no fool. You knew she was up to no good. She sent you into my service for a reason, and you merrily played the part."

"I-I didn't know why." She slurped the wine. "I swear!"

"That's why you…did those things to me. It was all in service to her." I was as sad as I was angry. "Did you know I'd lived here eight years and couldn't count anyone as a friend until she came along, only a year ago? My only friend…someone I could just be with, laugh with, without thinking about why...but turns out she was the worst kind of enemy...and so were you."

She sniffled. "I'll do anything. Please — please forgive me."

I gulped the wine. The intoxicant overwhelmed the rose flavor, and it burned down my throat with a peach aftertaste. "How many others would you do *anything* for? Kyars? Zedra? Mansur? Whoever else holds your leash for a day? You're worse than a worm-rotted date. How can I trust you?"

What if she told Zedra I was here in the palace? And what if Zedra came for me? She had bloodrunes everywhere, which put us all in danger, though I recalled Eshe telling Shah Tamaz he had a solution for that. Still, the last thing we needed was Zedra's spy worming among us.

"I...I could have kept it all to myself," Vera said as tears flowed. "But I chose to tell you."

"So you chose to betray Zedra, your sultana. How does that make you trustworthy?"

"No. I...I...when you walked into the palace, I saw you. Wearing a turban, but not even that eyepatch could obscure your lovely face. I overheard your conversation with your Himyarite friend. I could have fled and told Zedra everything, but I chose to stay. For you."

I snickered. "Right — *for me*." I picked up a silk pillow. "I could smother you this moment, and naught a one would care. No, that's not true — Pashang and his Jotrids would likely cheer it. Perhaps I should. It would soothe my worries. Balm my wounds."

She dropped her wine cup on the bed, reddening the sheets. Then she clutched her hair and covered her face, all while trembling and crying.

"You were part of it." I fluffed the pillow. "I attained all I ever wanted. I became Sultana of Sultanas, and you helped her ruin everything."

"I-I-I didn't know!" Her sobs resembled a bleating goat.

"Didn't know? Since when is ignorance an excuse? I don't have a good choice here. It's dangerous to keep you — it's dangerous to let you go. Killing you is the only way. Why am I the only one who sees that? Are the others so delighted by your sweetness that they can't taste the poison? Is it on me to make this awful choice?"

"I don't want to die. Please, sultana."

"I don't want to kill you." I inched closer, then put the pillow aside. I took her crying form in my arms, which both warmed and revolted me. Such an insidious little thing, whom I wanted to kiss and crush with a rock.

"I want you to do something for me." I stroked her hair. "It's going to make everything better."

"Anything," she managed amid sobs. Her hair smelled sweet and damp.

"You fooled me, you fooled Zedra, you fooled Mansur. But can you fool Khagan Pashang?"

She shuddered. "No. He's not kind like the rest of you. There's a frost in his eyes. He terrifies me."

I whispered in her trembling ear, "I should terrify you."

She shuddered even harder. "What do you want me to do?"

"Find out what his intentions are. At the meeting, he lamented Mansur's absence, but I suspect he may not mind it so much. After all, now there's an empty throne...for him to sit." Which only bothered me insofar as Pashang would lie about it. Why hide his intentions from me, whom he claimed to be truthful with?

"How am I supposed to manage that?" Vera asked as she nestled her head against my neck.

I kissed her forehead. I took her hand, placed it on my thigh, and moved it up to the warmest part. "Just how you managed me."

I AWOKE AFTER TWO HOURS, a pounding ache in my belly. I'd barely eaten anything yesterday, and so my insides seemed to tighten on air. I retched in a precious tulip-patterned vase that was sitting atop its own small carpet.

Afterward, I sat against the wall and watched an unclothed Vera snore on her side with small, rhythmic breaths.

Was I really, honestly, truly going to kill her? Earlier, when I'd held that pillow, I wasn't jesting. And it shocked me — how coldly I considered her fate. Was this what was necessary, now?

In the Waste, I'd watched men kill for the pettiest reasons: an insult directed at one's horse, a sideways glare, and I even saw a man bludgeon another for wearing yellow. Here in Alanya, men killed each other for weightier considerations: justice and moral order. Even so, the killing never ceased.

When I'd written on the stars and summoned those locusts…it led to deaths. Scores of gholam and Jotrids died fighting atop the walls. All because of something I did. I'd returned to this city to clear my name, but in doing so, I'd drenched it in blood. And worse, I'd become something as arcane as the sorceress I was fighting. What was it for, then?

Could I turn back, could I find the straight path, as Khizr Khaz admonished? But the path to anything worthwhile could never be straight. It would twist and turn through mountains and forests and jungles, and as you walked, sorcerers and jinn and Ahriyya himself would beset you. From here on, any path worth walking would be paved with bones and painted with bile.

So why didn't I suffocate her, then?

I got more much-needed sleep and woke after dawn. Vera wasn't next to me — perhaps she'd gone to ingratiate herself with Pashang. It was a tenuous reason, at best, to let her live, but it gave me room to breathe and decide what I ought to become.

I went to Eshe's room; he wasn't there. After searching for a while, I found him in the guards' lodging, asleep on a pallet, a book cradled on his chest. He awoke with a snort as I sat beside him.

"Are you ready, now?" I asked.

He rubbed his eyes and looked around, as bewildered as a just awoken man ought to be. "Can we have breakfast before I find out what I should be ready for?"

He settled the book on the floor — the spine read *Garden of Embers.*

"What's that?" I pointed at it.

"It's about a man who," he stretched and yawned, "discovered an underground kingdom of jinn while searching for his dead wife. Frightening tale...not sure how the author dreamed up such horrors."

"I want to know what they did to you, Eshe. You said you saw an egg. What did you mean?"

In the Waste, I used to love devouring the eggs of this fat, tall-necked bird called a *bustard.* The eggs were bronze-colored and barely fit in my hand — that was the only egg I wanted to see.

Eshe pulled on his utterly curly hair. "The man in the floral cloak — he wanted to know about a book my father salvaged from the Golden Kingdom after the blood plague ravaged it. A book I'd committed to memory." He itched his scalp. "The strangest thing is...the book is about flowers." Eshe began reciting:

Red tulips, one of the seven hundred species of tulip. They are endemic to the areas north and south of the Syr Darya, west to the Yunan Sea, and east toward Merva. Local legends claim that the petals turned red from the bloodshed of when Seluq's sons warred for the title of Padishah of the East, but this is entirely fiction. However, it is quite a coincidence that the red color appeared during that war, which lasted a century, and to this day is the worst calamity ever to befall the Seluqal kingdoms.

I tried to hide how impressed I was that he could pluck whole tomes from memory, as if verses of a much-loved poem. "Tulips? Perhaps it has a hidden meaning, like the other book you mentioned."

"My hunch, as well. I told him that I knew nothing about it, but he knew I was lying, and so...that man in the floral cloak...he..." Eshe swallowed hard. "He pulled out a book. When he flipped through it, I saw that a different bloodrune was painted on each page. And then, he took my hand and forced me to touch one." Eshe winced and shook his head. "I can't describe what I saw.

There was an egg, and screaming mouths, and the bitterest song from the coldest hell." The Palace of the Living had mouths that sung of pain, too. "'Why are there creatures on my womb?' — that's what the mouths were screaming. It was a memory…"

A shudder seized me. Nightmares beyond our understanding. I put my hand on Eshe's shoulder. "Did you do what he asked, then?"

"He wanted a particular chapter — the one about red tulips. I'd just finished it when you all came."

I rubbed my turban. "I just remembered something — Zedra loved those red tulips. She'd ask the servants to bring her fresh ones from the garden each day." Now I made a fist. "Just who do Litani and that flower fellow think they are, torturing you for such nonsense?"

A few of Mansur's guards nearby eyed us and walked toward a weapon-covered wall, chattering in some rhapsodic Kashanese tongue. Some grabbed swords, others guns. On the far side, several guards snored in sleep — how could they rest with their paymaster missing?

"The Philosophers *know* who they are, Cyra. Theirs isn't a false confidence. I'd rather fight a sorceress than them."

"Why? Their tower is just stone and paper. A well-placed bomb could end it all."

"Do you know who taught us how to make bombs? Men were fighting with bronze before the Philosophers appeared. It's said they have knowledge hidden in the top two floors of the Tower that could destroy a city faster than a hummingbird flaps. They keep it from us out of compassion."

Pashang had claimed that a starwriter could bring a city to heel. It seemed the Philosophers were sorcerers in their own right.

Another group of guards passed by, munching on seeds and laughing.

I said, "Khizr Khaz told me that the Philosophers are loyal to the Empire of Silk."

Eshe shook his head. "I've heard that, too, but people cast similar aspersions on us Himyarites." He took my hand. "Listen, let's ignore the Philosophers, for now. We have to find Zedra and stop whatever she's planning. One doesn't kill a shah for fun."

I rubbed the eye beneath my patch — my star-seeing eye — careful not to let Eshe see. Although, it was long past time to tell him.

"Eshe, there's something I need to tell—"

"My failure to stop Aschere led to tens of thousands of deaths in Sirm." He cracked his knuckles. "I won't let it happen here. I won't let darkness win."

Darkness…if only Eshe knew how it called to me, how I prayed to it, perhaps he'd strike me dead this moment.

"Sorry, I cut you short," he said. "You were saying?"

I swallowed my secrets and nodded. "Nothing. You're right. We must stop her."

But my intentions weren't so noble. I didn't share Eshe's horror over what happened in Sirm. I just wanted revenge, to restore my place in the world, and ensure I kept it this time by destroying my enemies before they destroyed me. A stew of rage and longing drowned me. I hoped, after I'd defeated Zedra and secured my place, I could seek nobler ends.

"You're wrong. You are a good man, Eshe. Or at least, you're still trying to be."

He shrugged his shoulders as if unsure of himself. I knew well that feeling.

WHILE ESHE WENT to find breakfast, I sought out Khagan Pashang. He was in the great hall with Ozar and a few viziers. I waited by the entrance, then caught the two as they were leaving.

Ozar was garbed in a maroon and bronze vest with emeralds for buttons. He greeted me with a nod and smile. Pashang wore a fresh white caftan with an almost glossy blue turban.

"Bright morning," Pashang said. "Eshe was right — Mansur and the child never made it to the shrine."

"My man confirmed it," Ozar said, "and more. Last night, Zedra was stopped from running into the streets, claiming she'd dreamt Chisti himself was delivering her son to her."

It was now beyond doubt. Zedra was the soulshifter. She'd stabbed my eye out, killed Tamaz, and slit my throat — for reasons unknown. Reminded of her evil acts, I felt better about my own.

"So," I said, "why don't we march on the shrine and demand her arrest?"

"We won't have to," Ozar said. "My man has already informed Khizr Khaz. The sheikh has confined Zedra to her lodging, with a thorough guard, and is weighing when to tell the others in his coalition. The ruse is up — everyone will awaken to it soon. My good name, and your most exalted name, will no longer be curses uttered in the dark."

It truly was a bright morning. Brighter with every word. Khizr Khaz was no fool. He'd seen through her veil, and soon I'd have everyone on my side.

Pashang sighed. "We still haven't a shadow of where Mansur and the child are. Without them, what are we doing here? What authority have we?"

"Authority?" I scoffed. "When did Mansur have any authority, to begin with?"

Ozar said, "Mansur was the heir before Kyars was born. Shah Haran, Tamaz and Mansur's father, made them stand atop the peak of Zelthuriya and swear an oath that Tamaz would rule first, and then Mansur after him. But Tamaz betrayed the oath — and those of us old enough to remember, remember."

"You chose his side because of an oath?" I said. "That's not like you, pasha."

"Why are we arguing this?" Ozar shook his head. "I thought we all agreed that Mansur should rule. That's why we're here and not with Khizr Khaz and his ilk."

I said, "I'm here because an injustice was done to me, to my brother, to my father-in-law. I'll stand with whoever rights that wrong. But I won't pretend it's because some words said on a mountain before most of us were born."

Ozar smiled, almost out of pity. "I don't envy you, sultana. Your hand will always be what struck down Tamaz. But deeper truths oft lie beyond the veil — and time is the thickest of veils. Regardless — you're right. I am not a truth seeker. And so, I ask myself — does it really matter *who* killed Tamaz? *Who* should be shah? Rather, what matters is we're on one side, and those who want to kill us are on the other. And if I were you, I'd bring to mind that Mansur, unlike Kyars, isn't beholden to Zedra, whom we all know was bedding other men."

I rolled my eyes. "What she's done is bad enough. We don't need to heap lies on top of it. We'd start to sound ridiculous if we did."

Pashang cleared his throat. "I'll tell you what I think. Forgetting your enemies are your enemies — there's nothing worse in war. Make no mistake, Cyra — this is a war with Kyars, and we'll be heads on walls if we lose."

"Kyars is my husband by law. Khizr Khaz will enforce the contract. Just because I'm your ally, for now, doesn't make him my enemy."

"By law." Pashang sniggered. "And in the same law, do you know how easily a man can end a marriage he hasn't consummated? Not more than three words, and your marriage is undone," he snapped his fingers, "just like that."

"No, Khizr Khaz won't let him."

I turned my head toward the wall as a few viziers I recognized walked by, chatting the while, sweet myrrh wafting from their brocades. I couldn't let myself be known — a reminder that I was still in danger, in my own home, from all sides.

Ozar put a stiff hand on my shoulder. "Sultana—" I backed away.

"If you don't believe I'm the wife of the Shah, why call me that?"

"You know I always called you that," Ozar said, "not because of whom you're married to, but because you have a sultana's grace. But I fear you're putting your hopes in the wrong men. Khizr Khaz — powerful as he may be — won't save you. Kyars never liked the white-haired devil. He'll want a more *permitting* Grand Mufti, one that matches his own vision. Which is why Khizr Khaz supported Mansur, too, before stabbing him in the back."

Was Khizr Khaz, the one honest man who seemed to believe in me, just another double-dealer? Did I have to abandon the hope Kyars would honor our marriage? And what would I be to Mansur? Just a trinket to display? I didn't want that; I wanted to be someone who could make a difference. I wanted to be the Sultana of Sultanas!

"Kyars is a good man," I said, though it sounded so false. "Everyone is going to tell him about Zedra's treachery. Then he'll know I was innocent, and he'll honor our marriage!"

Pashang grumbled. "Then go, Cyra. Go to Khizr Khaz. But once you choose their side, ours will be shut to you, forever."

Did I really have to choose? Why did there have to be a war, anyway? Was I foolish to have revealed my feelings? So many thoughts stirred, and I couldn't grasp what to do.

One thing, though, was obvious: Mansur and the heir were missing. Whoever found them would decide the fate of the country. Perhaps the stars would help me be the one.

I FOUND Eshe in the hallway outside the great hall, staring into a mirror and combing his hair. He kept it so short, I couldn't conceive why he needed to style it.

"Did you eat something?" I asked.

He nodded. "Not the shah's food you promised. Curry and a bit of lamb — what the guards were eating."

Watching him comb his beard, I realized I hated everyone... except him. Everyone in this place was so twisted, so devious, so double-sided...me included. But Eshe, he was the kind of person I wanted to be: purposed. I wanted a purpose above myself, too. And yet, I remained so mired in my anger and appetites.

"Eshe...I don't think we should be here."

He settled the comb beneath the mirror. "I could have told you that. The history tome won't praise the Jotrid side — well, unless they write it."

"I heard Khizr Khaz has placed Zedra in confinement. He's aware that she's the soulshifter. We should go there and join him, like we were supposed to. Besides, I want to talk to her. Find out why she did what she did."

"Cyra...is that wise? While the Jotrid side isn't the good side, it may well be the safer one, for now. The numbers tell it — there's naught between that shrine and tens of thousands of loot-mad Jotrids."

True...but rather shortsighted. "And when Kyars gets here with enough gholam to even the odds, won't he catch us on the losing side, then?"

Eshe sighed. "I don't know. But until Kyars returns, the last place I want to be is that shrine. I don't think Kyars would begrudge his wife for playing it safe and remaining here, in her home."

"What should we do, then?"

"Wait and see, lest we get caught in the mire." He beamed, teeth wide and white. "In the meantime — I've never been in the harem before. What's the Shah's bed chamber like, I wonder?"

I chuckled. "There's a golden cage around the bed."

He widened his eyes in surprise. "Oh? You've been there? Not as innocent as I thought, perhaps."

"I slept there, in fact...last night."

"Last night...when you were supposed to be sleeping with me. Forced me to go with the guards so I wouldn't be all alone."

"I wasn't alone, either." I grinned.

His jaw dropped. "What? Don't tell me…P-Pashang?"

I nodded, eyebrows high, and then laughed.

Eshe breathed a sigh of relief. "Oh, thank Lat."

"You were jealous for that moment, though."

"Not even a little. I've got a trove of lustful nymphs waiting at my brass throne."

We both laughed. He seemed to be in a better mood than last night — his old self — and that made me happier than I expected.

I touched my chin. "I think I know a room you'd like."

"Before that, we need to do something I should've done the moment we got here." He pointed at the ceiling. "Take me to the highest place in the palace."

That would be the eastern guard tower. It was a short walk, during which I explained the history of the Sand Palace to Eshe. It was built by Saint-King Zabur, but then Seluq's son Rukan leveled it when he seized the city from his own brother. I think Eshe already knew this, or he was uninterested, judging by how tepidly he nodded and *hmmd*.

Climbing the winding steps of the guard tower terrified me somewhat, and Eshe more so — there was no railing — but reaching the top was worth it. A sand-colored city spread in all directions, hazy in the dusty air. It seemed so still and peaceful.

"Romantic views," I said to Eshe.

"If only that was why I brought you." He frowned and unsheathed his dagger. "Cyra, I need your blood."

"My blood?"

"With conqueror's blood, I can write a bloodrune that will protect us from Zedra's soulshifting. I'll have to write it at four corners of the palace, as well, so I'll need quite a bit. It's like spreading a net, you see."

Of course. I hadn't really thought about it, but it seemed my blood was special. "Am I the only one with this blood?"

He shook his head. "No, but it's rare. I'd never written a rune with conqueror's blood until the day I saved your life. It's the basis of many potent bloodrunes." Eshe took my hand. "Just a prick on your finger, all right?" From his caftan pocket, he took out a tiny, emptied perfume bottle.

I winced at the thought of being cut. I closed my eyes; the dagger prick lasted a blink, but the sensation of my blood being squeezed from my finger hurt worse. Seconds later, it was done, and Eshe wrapped my finger with a bandage.

Eshe dipped his finger into the perfume bottle and painted a bloodrune on the wall: an eye within the blazing sun. Then he mumbled something, and the rune glowed for a moment.

"It's done." He breathed with relief. "We'll need to go to the other extremities, now."

"Why do I have such rare blood, Eshe?" I fingered the high collar of my caftan, which hid the bloodrunes that Eshe had written on my neck, with my blood, to save my life and protect me from being soulshifted again.

He raised his hands, palms up. "Aside from your ancestry, I don't know."

"Is it a blessing…or a curse?"

"Maybe neither. Maybe both."

What about the star-seeing eye, hiding behind my eyepatch? I so wanted to show him, but how could I? Then he'd know I was the very thing he hunted. Beholden to the void, to a star so dark it ate light.

"Eshe…what if I was evil? What would you do?"

He crossed his eyes in confusion. "There's a difference between not being good and being evil."

"You think you're so insightful, but you can't see what's standing in front of you."

"I see someone struggling, like everyone else, for a place in this world. Firing a bit high, sure, but as the Archers of the Eye say, 'aim at the sun and you'll hit the moon.'"

I shook my head. He really didn't get it. But I needed him to know. I couldn't go on, hiding from the one person I didn't hate.

I fingered the back of my eyepatch, ready to pull it off and show him what I'd become.

In the corner of my eye, a light blazed. Shimmering red stars exploded beneath the sun. I hadn't even pulled the eyepatch off, and already I was seeing stars.

"Fireworks?" Eshe said. "Where are they coming from?"

The bursts sounded over Qandbajar. Fireworks indeed…but stranger than that, they were coming from the shrine. And everyone knew red fireworks meant one thing: war.

22

ZEDRA

It was bad enough being trapped. But when Khizr Khaz ordered his men to stand guard *inside* my room, it became intolerable. Mirima had gone to stay elsewhere — in fact, so had everyone aside from me and Celene, who was asleep on the pallet next to me.

Of course, I protested. Demanded to see the sheikh. Reminded them that I was the Crown Prince's beloved. But these Order men didn't care.

So I threatened them with beatings, whipping, hanging, burning. Who were they to trap me? Some dirt-faced beggars whose only skill was fasting from sunrise to sunset? Is that all faith was to them, depriving yourself?

Their utter indifference to my pleading enraged me. But I couldn't let that rage dictate what I would do. I had to take the time to think, so my actions would help, not harm.

I'd been a fool; somewhere, somehow, I'd exposed myself. Someone clever had put the pieces together and told others. And so it became quite clear: the old sheikh knew. And if he knew, so did others. The alliance I'd forged to stand against Pashang were now my captors.

Worse, I had an enemy I never expected: Cyra. She always was full of surprises…but a starwriter? How could that be? And if true, which star spoke to her?

So there I sat, on my pallet, surrounded by three Order men watching my every move. In the end, I could sit here and think and think and think, but it wouldn't save me.

"Father, do you hear me?" I whispered under my breath. "I need you, Father." I'd been repeating that for hours, to no avail. Our son was somewhere in the city, and his father wasn't here, helping me save him. It was my burden. Always my burden.

"I need to go relieve myself," I said to one of the guards.

He tossed a bucket at me.

"Surely, you jest. Can followers of Saint Jamshid be so indecent?"

He said nothing and stared at me, a disgusting smile stuck on his lips. So I grabbed the bucket. Rotated it until I found a splinter sticking out the side. I pricked myself on it and wrote the perfect bloodrune for this.

I rolled the bucket to the man's feet. He stared at it, entranced. The other two looked as well, and then they stood and stared straight, hands at their sides, eyes wide and unblinking.

I crawled over to sleeping Celene. How foolish of them to keep her with me — likely, they didn't know the extent of my power, nor the power in her blood. I dabbed my finger in the slobber on her chin and licked it; beneath the obvious disgust of someone else's spit was a salted milk aftertaste. I didn't know this rare flavor, which meant it was powerful, and there was a decent chance it shared some bloodrunes with conqueror's blood. If I had to guess, I'd say it was angel's blood because long ago, that flavor was found among a tribe that lived in the icelands to the west, though they'd gone extinct before I was born. Not the soundest reasoning, but a wild guess was better than nothing, I supposed.

I shook her awake. "I'm going to cut your finger." I reached over and pulled a dagger from a tranced guard's belt. "Your blood is going to get us out of here."

Celene yawned and rubbed her eyes. "My blood?"

"You have a rare flavor beating through your heart. And rare flavors can do…well, if I'm right, you may yet see."

She looked up at the tranced guards; I snapped my fingers in front of their unblinking eyes.

"By now, I ought not to be surprised by anything you do." Celene gulped. "You've been fighting so hard…it seems no one can get in your way. To be honest, you scare me…and yet, I kind of admire what you're capable of. I hope, one day, I can fight as hard as you for the things I believe in."

I let out a *hah*. I wasn't trying to be an exemplar. "Celene, I hope you never have to do a shadow of the things I've done. I hope you grow old with those you love and die happy. I almost had that…but it all ended so badly, and then I was cursed with this second life."

"Is it such a curse? If you can be with your son, would it be so bad? Is it not another chance at happiness, as well?"

She was right. How unexpected: wisdom from someone who hadn't a wrinkle on her jowls. "Thank you." I rubbed the wetness from my eyes. "Knowing that you care is actually…well, it makes this a bit easier."

"I'll help you be with your son. Whatever I can do. Just…don't forget your promise to me." She held out her hand. "And may Marot forgive me."

"I won't forget, dear. I will get you home." I hesitated, not wishing to see blood on her skin. "Thank you again…for believing in me."

I pushed the point of the blade into her fingertip. Blood oozed, and she sucked in a breath; I squeezed the flow into a small perfume bottle. Once I'd gotten enough, I doused her wound with water and wrapped it with a bit of cloth.

Before leaving the room, I grabbed a scimitar from a guard. On the way down the stairs, I wrote a bloodrune on the flat of the curved blade, one I'd never tried: a six-sided star, a seven-sided star, and an arrow shooting through them. Whether it would work depended on if this bloodrune could be written with whatever blood flavor Celene possessed.

I whispered the invocation. To my astonishment, it glowed.

I didn't even know how to wield a sword, but that wouldn't matter. As it was rather hefty, I simply held it forward with both hands. Celene stayed behind me.

"You know how to use that?" she asked.

I nodded, hoping to comfort her.

Three Order men stood outside, their hoods on. They laughed at the sight of me wielding a sword. So I slashed it in their direction.

The air caught fire, and the fire roared, catching all three on their cloaks. I stared, horrified, at the three burning men — each flailing and crying and running. I gaped in shock at what I was able to do. Celene, too, screamed and covered her mouth. I should've used the ice rune — the frozen can't move or make a sound.

Nevertheless, we had to go. I took Celene's hand, and we ran into the bushes at the back of the shrine, thorns grabbing at our clothes. We pushed through the growth, the shrieks of the burning men resounding, until we reached the alley behind the shrine. We darted toward the street as the screaming became fainter, until there was silence.

But the street wasn't empty, like I'd hoped: gholam blocked the road toward the river. They noticed us, then formed up, guns forward.

As they neared, I held out my sword. I was about to enflame the air when someone stepped through the line and came forward: Kato, helmeted and shining like a freshly minted coin.

"Zedra, my-my-my." He sighed. "I thought you better at keeping secrets."

"Kato, there's no time. Let us go."

He whistled; the wall of gholam parted, leaving a way for us.

"A girl who brandishes a sword — *mmm* — lights a fire inside."

He leaned his matchlock on the ground. "I have nothing against your kind, you know."

"My kind?"

"Path of the Children. I couldn't care less. Khizr Khaz overreacted. Fool is the man who makes enemies of dogs while wolves roam."

Wait, what? Was that why he'd imprisoned me? But why did he have guards *in* my room, watching my every move?

Or, perhaps, that was only what he'd told the others. I'd exposed myself by running onto the street and shouting for my son. Surely Khizr Khaz knew. Perhaps he even had my son and Mansur — somewhere — and Mansur had confirmed to him that he'd been soulshifted. Khizr Khaz merely put the pieces together and figured out it was me. And yet, it seemed the sheikh didn't trust his own allies with the truth.

Or perhaps Kato was playing me for a fool? Laying a trap? By Lat, I was supposed to be a fearsome sorceress yet had no idea what was happening!

"Zedra," Kato said as we walked past, "you do realize the streets ahead are no-man's-land. You're going to be captured by the Jotrids, and they won't be as polite as me. I know a place where you'll be safe." He came close and whispered. "A house in the Glass District. Tell them Kato sent you, and they'll never betray your trust." He described the location: the same house where his daughter lived. He wasn't lying; I'd watched him go there myself after he visited his son in the Alley of Mud when I followed him as the drongo.

"I'd send an escort with you," Kato said, "but that would attract attention. And your clothes…you'd be better off in rags or robes, you realize?"

I nodded. We should've grabbed robes on the way out. "Your help…you've no idea how much I appreciate it." It seemed I'd been wrong about Kato from the first. He was as well-intentioned and true as anyone in this city could be.

He raised an eyebrow. "We're friends, aren't we? Always have been. The next time Kyars is pulling off your clothes, you'll whisper 'Kato saved me' in his ear." He stepped back with a smirk.

The Glass District lay just beyond Saint Jorga's Bridge, but Order men guarded it. Celene and I could take Saint Rizva's Bridge into the Metal District, then cut across. We hurried past the gholam and continued down the street, my sword hanging awkwardly from my pant lace.

A layer of sand seemed to cover everything, the result of the streets not being cleaned for a single day. Children watched us from their windows, as if our nervous scurrying was entertainment. We stayed away from the doorways and alleys, wary about being pulled inside, which was a danger for unguarded women even in the best of times. The afternoon sun brought a breeze, but still Celene and I heaved, neither of us accustomed to such a pace.

Finally, we arrived at Saint Rizva's Bridge. From my conversation with Safia, or rather Sadie, earlier, I knew it was being guarded by Archers of the Eye. And there they were — tens of them, formed up on the far side, Sadie among.

They noticed us as we crossed. Sadie put her bow on her back and approached. Celene cowered at my back, like a scared puppy.

"Zedra," she tugged at my caftan, "what if she sends me back to Sirm?"

"She won't, dear. She ran away, just like you."

Judging by the sweat on Sadie's forehead and shirt, she'd been standing there for a while. "What're you doing here?" she asked, trying to peek at Celene, who had pushed her face against my back. "And who's that?"

I dragged Celene in front of me. She covered her face with her hands, so I pulled them off.

Sadie gasped. "C-Celene?"

Celene finally looked at her. "Been a while, Sadie."

"Sadie," I repeated. "There are enemies behind us and worse beyond this bridge." I held out my hand. "Will you help us?"

She gasped again. "How long have you known who I am?"

"We'll talk about it later. Please help — Khizr Khaz will torture me, for naught but my faith. If I must, I'll die like my ancestors — fighting — but neither can I swing a sword nor shoot an arrow."

Tremors. Behind us. Order men were marching up the street toward the bridge.

Sadie took my hand. "All right. I'll ask the Archers to delay them. Lead the way."

We ran across the bridge into the Metal District — my least favorite part of the city. But today, the air didn't choke with black smoke because no one was working. I took the lead, with Sadie behind me and Celene behind her. We crossed the thoroughfares and even took shortcuts through alleys. No Jotrids to be seen. We were about to cross the archway into the Glass District when a rumbling sounded.

The three of us darted behind a low wall and lay on our bellies. Horses galloped by, hundreds of them, kicking up dust that obscured the air. They brought the smell of the Waste: damp horsehide, shit, grass, and rider sweat. After a few minutes, they'd all passed, heading in the direction of the bridge. Were the Jotrids attacking the shrine?

We stood. Arm spans away, a dismounted Jotrid was pissing in the road, painting a pattern with his stream. His eyes flared upon sighting us; he didn't even put his cock in and reached for the bow hanging off his horse.

And then an arrow burst through his neck, spraying blood, and he fell into his piss puddle, eyes wide.

Sadie was not only accurate, she was fast. I hadn't even noticed her draw, but there she stood, huffing, bow clenched tight.

We stayed low and entered the Glass District. The unbreakable glass statue of that saint greeted us, her hands outstretched as if to hug all who came here. I could never remember her name, but what did it matter?

The house where Kato's mistress and daughter lived was just

ahead, the domes of the neighboring buildings dim beneath the clouded sun. One more street to cross to safety. Once there, I could soulshift into the drongo and search for my son, without any fear of Khizr Khaz or Pashang.

We ran toward the door. Dark drapes covered the glass walls, like all dwellings in the district. I banged the knocker on the wooden door, then folded my arms and waited while staring at Sadie and Celene.

We hadn't said a word to each other since the bridge, but their fearful eyes told me everything. Sadie was tough, but by appearances, we were just three women running around a city engulfed by war. And though Celene had been through much, she was barely more than a child and couldn't be expected to be fearless. As for myself…my heart wouldn't stop thudding into my throat.

I knocked on the door again. What if they weren't here? I tried to turn the knob, but it wouldn't budge.

A shadow loomed. Down the lane, a man emerged wearing a cloak. An Order cloak.

"Sadie!" I called, pointing to the man. While I gripped the hilt of my flame-flinging sword, she pulled out an arrow and nocked it in the man's direction.

The man pulled down his hood and walked toward us, chewing the while. By Lat, it was him! The light-haired, fair-skinned, jelly-chewing man! As he approached, Sadie pulled her arrow taut.

"Don't, Sadie! He knows where my son is!"

"You…" she said to the man, ignoring me. "What the hell are *you* doing here?"

Footsteps behind me. I turned to see another Order man; he lunged at me, grabbed my neck, and put me in a hold. I pushed against him but couldn't break free. More men appeared, grabbing Celene and Sadie, who could scarcely resist. I flailed and pushed and cried but couldn't weigh against the man's strength. He stuffed something in my mouth: seeds. They dissolved on my tongue, and it all went limp and dark.

. . .

I AWOKE in a room that smelled of mold and seaweed. It rocked, as if built on pudding, making me want to retch. I almost did, but only managed to spit on the floor. Throbbing candles sitting on a desk — a rather high one — lit the room.

I turned to see a man dressed in the soft, maroon robe of a eunuch, staring out a porthole. I was on a ship, obviously. The man turned to me, his hair a mess over his eyes, which seemed so devoid.

"Father? Where am I?"

"You've been discovered, Zedra." He turned away and looked back out the porthole. "Hadrith found out and told Khizr Khaz, but the old man is keeping it to himself, for now."

"Where is our son?" I asked, trembling. "Without him, what is it all for?"

He snickered. "I heard your prayers. Remember what I told you? You might as well pray to stones, for all I can do for you."

"Our son!" I threw off my blanket and sat up. "Where is he?"

"The time is at hand. You cannot lose this battle. You were right, by the way — the Crucian imperator's daughter does have angel's blood." He raised a hand to his mustache, casting a shadow over his smile. "Did you read my notes from *Volume Two*? There's a wonderful bloodrune you can write with angel's blood, but you'll need much of it. The Crucian girl likely has just enough."

Was I going to sacrifice Celene the way I'd sacrificed Cyra? Was that what was required to save mankind?

The thought sickened me. Those runes I'd learned from his notes...they ought not to be called runes. They were more like paintings, and they required buckets of blood.

"And the Sirmian shah's daughter, would you like to know what blood she has? Just enough of it, too, for precisely the same rune. Which of the two you use is up to you."

"Are you really going to patronize me like this? Just tell me what her flavor is."

His chuckle came from a dark place. "The girl was rebirthed from a star, you see. She has star's blood, and she's the only one walking the earth with it."

I shuddered. Star's blood...along with angel's blood, it could also be used to make that *painting*.

I shook the thoughts off. "No, they're good girls. They don't deserve to be—"

"THEY ARE NOT YOUR DAUGHTERS!" Father banged against the porthole, cracking the glass as I huddled against the bedframe. "Just like Cyra wasn't your friend." He climbed onto the bed, pinning me between himself and the wooden wall. "And now she's a starwriter, in the service of the Dreamer, come to destroy our best-laid plans. If you aren't as ruthless as her, then we'll lose. The Children will truly end, and the Great Terror will remake us all in fire. Do you want *that* on your head, dear daughter?"

"And you are not my father," I said, tasting the tears pouring down my cheeks. "My real father...I was precious to him. He would never ask me to—"

Chisti jabbed my shoulder, sending a painful pang through me. "Do you think I wasn't watching? The end of my bloodline? If I could've saved one of my sons, I would have! But I only managed to save you! A foolish old woman, kept alive by magic!"

I rubbed the bruise he made and sobbed. "Why me? Why is it all on me?"

"You think I didn't ask the same thing, a thousand years ago, when I was forced to save mankind?" He climbed off the bed and moved to the door. "One more thing. Beware. Magus Kevah is no longer alone. Marada, sultana of the Marid, has submitted to him. He will come for you."

I shuddered as the image of that cloud-sized monster flashed in my mind: a floating black mass of snakes, glowing red from the sun's outline, with three heads and six blazing eyes. "How can I fight that nightmare?"

"Like I've been telling you this whole time, use the bloodrune I gave you. Cyra and Kevah are no match for what it'll conjure. Now…clean yourself up, my dear. You have a visitor."

Father opened the door, then bowed to the man standing at the threshold. "My Shah, she is awake."

Father Chisti left the room, and Kyars entered, holding baby Seluq in his arms. I dashed off the bed and grabbed my cooing son, crying while I kissed his forehead. So warm to have your own blood in your hands. Meanwhile, Kyars put his arms around us, and I finally felt soothed after what seemed like a lifetime of agony.

I cradled my son between my shoulder and neck, then looked up at Kyars. Was this really real? Or was I dreaming?

He kissed my cheek. "Oh thank Lat you're here."

"Where is here?"

"You're with me. What else matters?"

I stayed in his embrace as my heart calmed. His heavy breathing and muffled sobs made plain how much he missed me. I, too, in an unexpected way, missed him.

After taking in much warmth, I asked again, "But really, my love, where are we?"

"Come…I'll show you."

He took me by hand down a wooden hall and up creaky stairs to the deck. A flag fluttered above, the image of a jellyfish with a thousand lightning tentacles on its face. The emblem of Sargosa. What were we doing on their ship?

"I must apologize for the method of bringing you here," Kyars said.

"So those were your men, wearing Order cloaks and stuffing seeds in our mouths?"

Kyars nodded. "I wasn't sure if your companions could be trusted, and couldn't take the chance that you'd refuse to come."

That made sense, I supposed. Though I would've followed

anyone anywhere to find my son, Kyars didn't necessarily know that.

"Mansur is here, too, then?" I asked.

"He is. Won't open his mouth, though. Not that he'll have one for long."

Good to hear that. Mansur wouldn't know who soulshifted him, but better for me he not tell Kyars anything about his out-of-body experience.

We floated in Qandbajar's harbor, surrounded by more Sargosan ships and yet more ships bearing other flags: Redbeard's scimitar beneath the sun, the winged elephant of Koa, and the Kashanese falcon.

"All ships I captured," Kyars said. "We hoisted the flags as a deception."

I nodded, impressed.

The air here stunk of oily, dried fish. On the adjacent land sat rows and columns of empty wooden cages: the Stable, where slaves were herded and sold. The Sand Palace stood on its hill, some distance away, glowing in the almost noon.

Kyars, his black hair blowing in the breeze, looked more muscular than when he'd left. He'd filled into that gholam armor, the bronze and gold seeming like the shell of some animal. Even his sailboat-shaped nose looked broader.

"You missed the fireworks," he said. "The Jotrids are just about to attack the shrine."

Oh yes, I'd watched what was likely an advanced group gallop through the street. "And...what's going to happen? What will you do?"

"That depends on you, Zedra. You were in that shrine."

"Meaning?"

Kyars beamed as I kissed Seluq's barely budding hair. "When I was a boy, I once asked Khizr Khaz 'if Lat is real, why isn't she here? Why doesn't she show herself?'" An obvious question. "And he said that Lat was always watching, but that she was testing us, testing our faith and deeds." He folded his arms. "And so I've been watching. And more importantly, you've been watching." He pressed his lips onto mine, and then his tongue onto mine, kissing me with more passion than my husband ever had. When he backed away, he said, "So tell me, my beloved — are those in the shrine worth saving?"

"Worth saving? They're your allies, my love. What do you mean?"

"Are they? Khizr Khaz convinced my father to summon Mansur and the Jotrids to deal with the Sylgiz, bringing this whole calamity upon us. Is he worth saving?"

No...Ozar had confirmed that Khizr Khaz was duplicitous. I shook my head.

"And Hadrith?" Kyars said. "Is he truly my friend?"

I shook my head again. "No, my love. Hadrith and Ozar are playing both sides." Only one man had stayed true to Kyars, stayed true to me. "Kato is loyal. He helped me, so many times. He is your staunch ally, my love. I know it to be true."

"Kato is but one dove in a den of vipers. Should I risk my position to save one true man?"

No, not just one man. "The Archers, my love. The Archers of the Eye are loyal — they fight for you."

"Ethosians. Am I to risk believers to save heathens?"

I nuzzled my nose on Seluq's scalp to ease his cooing. "What, then? Will you let the Jotrids overrun the entire city?"

"Precisely that. Let them think they've won, and then I'll strike. The Jotrids are aching to plunder this city of gold. That's why they came. They'll be drunk, looting and raping — completely out of order — and then I'll cut them down."

Though Kyars' plan was clever, forsaking Kato and the Archers seemed wasteful. Perhaps I could soulshift and find a way to save them. But...why? Saving Kato wouldn't further my mission. Getting rid of him was part of it. So why was I bursting with worry for him?

I said, "Kato still commands many gholam, and the Archers are numerous, too. You can never have too many loyal men fighting for you, isn't that right?"

Kyars nodded. "My father always praised Kato. 'Kichak and Kato are more loyal than my own sons,' he'd say. He was right. I'll send a man to bring Kato into our fold."

I kissed my son's cheek. "It's the best course, my love."

"As for the Archers, I'll send word to Abu asking them to withdraw to their training ground. Let the Order alone perish. I'm sick of their hold on this city, in any case."

That seemed right. And yet, manipulative for Kyars, letting his enemy destroy a group he didn't like. It sounded more like something I would do.

"My Shah," I said. "Are you aware of the starwriter?"

Kyars shook his head. If he wasn't aware of the starwriter, then he wasn't aware that Hadrith and Khizr Khaz had discovered my secret. All the better, then, that they perish in the shrine.

"My love," I said, "Cyra killed your father. And afterward, she didn't die or go away like we thought. She's back…with the same power that Aschere wielded in Sirm."

His face grew cold and sad. "They say it was Aschere who summoned the Archangel, who brought a dead imperator to life, who summoned a fireball that melted men alive, who led Micah the Metal through Labyrinthos. And you're telling me…that Cyra now wields that power?"

I nodded as forcefully as I could. "She's a sorceress. She fooled everyone. She fooled me."

"I'd heard whispers of a sorceress. Now you've confirmed it. If only…if only we had a magus in our service." He shook his head. "Cyra, though? When I'd heard she killed my father, I couldn't believe it. And yet…" He huffed as if blowing smoke from a hookah.

He had better than a magus: a soulshifter. "I share that shock, my love. She seemed my honest friend…and yet, are not friendship and love the brightest blinders?"

"If Cyra is as powerful as Aschere, then we need Kevah. He would help us…if only we knew where he was."

Kevah, the magus Father had warned me about. I hoped not to see him; I didn't need yet another adversary.

Kyars hugged me. One good thing I could say about him: he always smelled fresh. "Now…" He looked down at me with wide eyes. "There's the matter of your two companions. Do you realize who they are, Zedra?"

Kyars, the hero of the Battle at Syr Darya, certainly knew them both. But he didn't know that I knew them. Perhaps some honesty wouldn't hurt.

"Sadie and Celene — are they here?"

Kyars' nose ruffled as his eyebrows zagged in disbelief. "In what…utterly impossible-to-believe story are you found wandering the streets with the captive daughter of the Imperator of Crucis and the dead daughter of the Shah of Sirm?"

"This one, apparently."

He grasped my shoulders. "I was there the day they buried that girl. My greatest shame was arriving minutes too late to save her from an imperator who had also come back from death. And Celene…do you realize that when the Shah of Sirm asked what I wanted as a reward, I chose her?" No, I didn't know, and — I could scarcely believe it — I felt a jealous ache. "He refused. But it turns out I always get what I want, in the end."

"Can I see them?"

"Of course." Kyars nodded. "My love…I will consider everything you've told me before making my next move. Your suffering won't be in vain, I swear upon Lat."

Kyars led me down the stairs and into their room, then left to put baby Seluq in his crib.

Sadie was sitting on a raised bed, a glass bottle in her hands.

Celene was on a wooden chair near the porthole, gazing at the blurry river.

"Thank Lat you're both all right," I said.

Celene stood. "Kyars said he opened the way."

"Opened the way?"

"He defeated the Ethosian pirates, and the way to Crucis is now open. I can go home. Please…ask him to send me home."

He really was a man of unexpected ability. How had he rooted them out so fast? Was that why he was in one of their ships?

"Of course, dear. He will."

Sadie gulped whatever was in her bottle: something red, but it was too dark to be rose water.

"You all right?" I asked.

She chuckled. "Everyone's seen me now. Soon, word will get to Sirm, and my mother and father will hear rumors of their dead daughter's return. How cruel would I be, then, to deny them? How cruel have I been, all this time?"

I didn't understand her reasonings, her past, her life, any of it. But I couldn't say I didn't feel guilty for bringing this pain upon her.

"I'm sorry," I said. "It's my fault all this happened."

"What are you fighting for, Zedra?" Sadie asked. "Because if you're fighting for something good, then maybe it was worth it. But if you're just like the others…"

If only I could tell them. Tell them how I was fighting to restore the Children, who could then be a shield against the Great Terror. But in truth, neither of them were believers.

But was any of this…good? Was Father…good? Were the Children…good? For the first time, I didn't know.

I sat next to Sadie. "What's that?" I gestured at the bottle.

She shook her head. "No idea…some Sargosan something, I suppose."

"Ginja," Celene said. "It's made from sour cherries…and alcohol."

Sadie gulped another mouthful.

"Dear," I put my hand on her shoulder, "is it wise to drink so much, so fast?"

She wiped her chin. "What are you, my mother?"

I wished I was. All I wanted was to be a mother, but Seluq had destroyed that when he drowned my children. I was a mother again, to baby Seluq, but my mission called me to be something greater. The mother of a new tribe of the Children, the mother of a unified east, under my son, the Padishah. I had to cling to that, otherwise, what had it all been for?

Sadie said, "You know, history will write Kyars as the hero who saved Sirm, but they're wrong."

Celene came over and sat next to us. "Can I try it? My grandfather loved ginja."

Sadie winced. "Ugh, you just ruined it for me." She handed Celene the bottle. "The real hero…" Her face reddened as she smiled somberly. "The real hero was Kevah. He sacrificed everything…even what he loved…"

Father had called him *the magus who will wear all masks.* The first time he mentioned Kevah, he also called him his *"replacement."* What did it mean? Replacement…as Lat's chosen? Why was Father severed from Lat in the first place? Weren't Lat and the Children one and the same blood?

Suddenly, I couldn't make sense of anything. It was as if an earthquake had brought down all my neat, stacked-up beliefs. Nothing made sense, and yet…I could only swallow the bitterness, the rage at what the saint worshippers had done to my tribe, to my family, to my children. It was too late to turn back…but what did I have to look forward to?

Sadie continued her drunk talking. "Kevah loved me. And I still love him…that's why I stayed here, close by…that's why I didn't go home."

What? Her and the magus were lovers?

Celene sipped the ginja, then swallowed bitterly. She settled the bottle on the floor. "I remember Kevah…he treated me well. Far better than Micah did." Her sigh was laden and impatient. "I just want to go home."

"Me too." Sadie stretched and yawned — poor girl had been guarding that bridge all night and day.

I picked up the ginja bottle and took more than a sip. A sour and bitter sea seeped down my throat, stinging everything it passed. But it wasn't bad.

"Me too," I said.

23

CYRA

AND LIKE THAT, IT BEGAN. WITHOUT TELLING ME OR OZAR OR ANYONE aside from those involved, Pashang had ordered Tekish to attack the Shrine of Saint Jamshid, prompting them to launch a desperate, red firework — a cry for help, which it seemed none heeded.

And like that, it ended. By morning, Tekish and his riders returned, ululating and cheering their victory. The shrine defenders had either died, surrendered, or scattered.

Tekish marched the notable prisoners into the great hall. At the head was Khizr Khaz, wearing a blood-stained cloak.

"Where is Mansur?" he asked. "I'd like to see my old friend."

Pashang, who was sitting on the dais below the golden divan, snickered. "Wherever he is, I'm certain he's in bed, recovering from the stab wound you left in his back."

Khizr Khaz glanced around the room, which was filled with Jotrids, Mansur's household guard, and the smattering of viziers who'd chosen Mansur's side — though their number was far less than yesterday. I wore my orange turban and eyepatch, yet still kept behind Eshe, careful not to let Khizr Khaz notice me.

"When I strike, it's never in the back," the white-haired sheikh

359

said. "How about it, Pashang? Just you and me and a pair of swords. You'll learn why they call me *khaz*."

Pashang rested his head on clasped hands. "It's no fun making gray men scream. The screams of your daughter and son, though, would be sweeter than plums."

"I know Mansur isn't here to hold your leash. Let me caution you, then — don't even think of looting and raping. When Kyars returns, he'll chase you across the Endless Waste for stealing a single stone of this blessed city."

"Where is Kyars?" Pashang stood and approached Khizr Khaz. "Where is Mansur? Where are our overlords?" He breathed deep as he clasped Sheikh Khizr's shoulder. "You're right. A dog without its master turns wild — rabid, even. Best help me find my master, then, before it's too late."

Sheikh Khizr shook his head. "I don't know where Mansur is."

Pashang returned to the dais. "That's too bad — for everyone."

ONCE THE GREAT HALL EMPTIED, I rushed to speak with Pashang.

"Did you capture Zedra?"

He shook his head. "'Course not. That would've been too easy." He sighed, long and sharp. "Cyra, in council with my tribe, I've made a decision, one you won't like. We're going to claim our booty and go."

"You mean...plunder this city? But this is my home!"

"Your home is the Endless. Without Mansur, I can't hold this place once Kyars returns. And my scouts have now sighted his army, only three days away — two if they march at night." He tugged at his beard. "Fear is not enough — I need a Seluqal, and I lost mine. I'm sure you noticed our support has dwindled, and with news of Kyars' return, these halls will shortly be empty."

Right, that might be true. But conquerors, I'd learned, made their own truths. If Kyars arrived in two days, without Zedra's capture and confession, how could I prove my innocence?

"How disappointing." I wanted to spit at Pashang's feet, but my mother always said that was bad manners. "Are you so meek? Craven? Indolent?" I stretched my vocabulary to find a word for how bitter he was making me. "Tell me you're jesting. After all we've done, to just—"

"There's no one Alanya hates more than me, aside from maybe you. Mansur is likely dead, and Kyars will see we join him. We don't have any of those fast-firing guns the Philosophers made for the gholam — they say Kyars departed with over five thousand, meaning one in four in his army carries something we simply can't counter in open battle. I always knew that if I found myself on the losing side, I could betray Mansur and throw his head at Kyars' feet — that would be enough to save us. But I no longer hold that card, and I won't lead my tribe into extinction."

I sniggered. "Then plunder what you will and go. I'll sit on that chair," I gestured to the golden divan, "and await my husband."

He chuckled somberly. "I remember...I remember how you waited for your father to return from a hunt. You'd sit on his bed, keeping it warm. Smell his clothes. Even drink that awful, salt tea he used to make — though you hated it as much as me."

I so wanted to backhand him. "Is that all you have left? Reminiscence? Home isn't a place you build in your memories, it's where you keep your hopes. And for me, that's the Sand Palace, not some frozen plain hundreds of miles away."

"You know what the Jotrids hoped for? Why we followed Mansur here? Why we obeyed the Seluqals, in the first place?" He opened his empty hands. "We like shiny things, and we like slaves. This city has it all. Without Mansur here to give us our due, we're going to take it. If I don't allow a full day for claiming booty, then the Jotrids will find a khagan who will."

"There are greater rewards on offer, surely you realize? Stay and help me capture Zedra, and maybe we can claim them. You talked to me about your visions — well, what do you envision about yourself?" I took his hand. "I didn't walk out on you. I chose your side."

I rubbed his fingers, chaffing on his silver and gold rings. "I can't find and defeat a sorceress on my own."

He snickered and shook his head. "Even after everything I did for you, you never chose my side, Cyra. You allied with me while it was convenient, but I realize now you'd sell me to Kyars in a breath if it meant he'd keep you as his *sultana*. To be honest…I thought you'd be the same caring girl I knew in childhood, but I suppose it's my fault for seeing you as I wanted to see you…not as the changed person you are. As for my visions…I saw three, and only one has yet to happen. And perhaps…" he shuddered, "perhaps it's best if that one doesn't."

He was right that I'd changed and that I hadn't chosen a side. Even now, I hedged. If Pashang had captured Zedra, I wouldn't mind if he ran. It was all I needed him for, and perhaps I'd made that too obvious. I'd neglected to cover my bitter truths with sweet deceits, and that could cost me — a lesson to remember.

Pashang said, "You know how a warrior knows his commander is committed to the fight? He scorches all behind him — every field, village, burg, and bridge, so there's naught for his enemy nor his own to find comfort in. Want me to stay and fight with you, Cyra? Then burn your comforts down."

"My comforts?"

"The old sheikh, Khizr Khaz. Ask him to stand here, in front of everyone in this great hall, and terminate your marriage to Kyars."

I could never! Khizr Khaz believed in me. He could make Kyars see the truth. And yet, without Zedra captive, without her willing to confess her crimes, what proof was there?

"Pashang, if I did that, what place would I have here, in my own home?" I'd be doubtless joining the losing side. Pashang was right — the Jotrids could smash a few thousand defenders with their numbers, pillage the city, be kings for a day…but they couldn't defeat Kyars' fully provisioned, fast-firing, and heavily armored gholam army. Only now, considering my own stakes, did I understand what the Jotrids had to lose.

Pashang pouted like the boy who'd lost a foot race to my brother, except now a brown beard hid his sour chin. "See? You don't believe we can win. You'd be giddy for Kyars to destroy us, so long as you get what you want — a place at his side, and your soulshifter enemy in chains. You couldn't care less if I were planted beneath the sand, nary a red tulip to adorn my shrine."

"That's not true, I—" I choked on how right he was. Perhaps it was inevitable that Pashang and I parted ways, here and now, as our paths no longer joined. And yet, I didn't want that. He'd shown me a new world — a power from the stars — when he'd taken my hand the day we smashed through Qandbajar's wall.

"You and me, Cyra." What was he insinuating? "Want me to fight the soulshifter, fight Kyars, give me something to hope for." He let out a jittery breath. "Give me a home."

"I need time to think," I said, turning away.

"You have the day." Pashang began to walk away. "In the meantime, I'll be out there, making sure my men don't overstep. Even pillaging has rules."

WHO ELSE COULD I talk to about this but Eshe? My only confidant...and yet, he didn't know about my star-seeing eye. How could he, then, understand my dilemma?

I ran into Vera in the hallway. She'd just bathed, her hair wet and fragrant.

"Have you been doing what I asked?"

She gazed at the flower-patterned tile. "Sultana, I was with Pashang earlier. He invited me into his room...for coffee...actually."

I pressed my hands together, excited. "That was fast. You're so good."

She shook her head. "No, sultana. The thing is, all he did was ask about you. He knew I'd been your handmaiden and so wanted to know all your likes, your dislikes, your habits. He wasn't the least bit interested in me."

I sighed, disappointed. "You'll have to try harder, Vera. Your task is to learn about *his* desires, not tell him *mine!*" I came to her ear. "He'll be drunk on victory tonight. Make sure you're in his room, or you'll be punished in mine."

She nodded, keeping her gaze low. "Of course, whatever you ask. But…do you want my advice?"

"What's the advice of some Ruthenian strumpet worth, these days?" I grumbled at myself. Of course, I was trying to be mean — this girl had bled me on behalf of a witch, after all — but I didn't want to be Mirima, for Lat's sake. "Just say what you will."

"You should talk to Pashang. You should go to his room, not me. He'll tell you whatever you ask."

I snickered. "I'm not a base little whore who spreads her legs for whoever holds her leash that day." But truly, I needed to leash my tongue, lest she resent me.

"I don't mean anything so vile. Just talk to him. He would tell you things he'd never tell me. Believe me, I know when I have a way in and when I don't — and I don't with Pashang."

"But I do?"

Finally, she looked me in the eye — with some force, too, like a kitten with its back to the wall. "You do, and you know it."

At that, she walked away. I supposed she was right, though I was only trying to make her useful to me, so I could justify keeping her around. Otherwise…I shuddered at the thought of what she deserved. What all traitors deserved, whether in Alanya, in the Waste, or anywhere else.

I let my task distract me from the thought. I checked for Eshe in his room, then remembered he refused to be alone. He was probably with the guards, again. But on the way to the guard lodging, I ran into Ozar, dabbing his sweaty head with a silk kerchief.

"Sultana." He gazed at me with dismal eyes.

"What's wrong?"

"My wife has tasked me with locating Mirima. But Tekish informed me she wasn't at the shrine. Where could she be?"

I hunched my shoulders. "Doesn't your *man* know? Or has his beard grown over his eyes, too?"

Shaking his head, Ozar resembled a nervous pig. "Hadrith wasn't fool enough to get caught there. With Kyars army sighted only three days away, he must've ridden to them."

"Well, maybe Mirima went with him?"

"Mirima's not like you, she can't ride. Kato and his gholam weren't there, either, nor were the Archers. Strange, don't you think? Where everyone went, just moments before we struck?"

It wasn't all that strange. Better to run than die. With Kyars now known to be days away, only the Order must've cared to defend their shrine from the Jotrids.

I put a warming hand on Ozar's shoulder. "I'm sure Mirima is fine. Everyone respects her. Who could ever hurt her?"

"Things happen midst the fog of war. Horrible things. Curse Zedra for killing Tamaz — he coddled us with his peace, and now here we are, at each other's throats. For what?"

A spice trader, it seemed, had much to lose and little to gain in war. Perhaps that was why he hedged his bets — he didn't care who won, so long as someone won. Was I so different?

I was, wasn't I? As Kyars' wife, I wanted him to win. But if Kyars wouldn't uphold our marriage, then I wanted him to lose. But — and I couldn't believe I was thinking this — if Kyars lost, was Pashang willing to sit the throne...with me as his wife? Two *massive* uncertainties.

Everything was uncertain, and yet, I had to decide. If I made the wrong choice — no question — I'd end up a head on the wall of the palace I called home. It truly was win it all or perish.

But not for Ozar. He wasn't trying to win — just survive.

"She'll turn up," I said. "Have faith."

He nodded. "Your strength is a brightness in the fog, sultana."

• • •

I FINALLY FOUND ESHE, outside, sitting below the simurgh statue that was likely larger than an actual simurgh, if they'd ever existed. It was also where I'd bled…where he'd saved me. Come to think of it, the simurgh's head loomed precisely where I'd watched Zedra use my body to commit horrors, as if my soul were inside it. Quite a coincidence.

A layer of sand now covered the stone ground, and Eshe was drawing patterns in the sand. They looked like runes, with all the stars and lines that resembled things in nature.

"What're you doing?" I asked.

He bade me to sit, but I didn't want to get sandy.

"I heard they're going to loot the city," he said. "You know what my first thought was?"

I shook my head.

"*Did I lock my house?*" He chuckled. "Isn't that sad? I was a Disciple in what feels like another life. Our whole reason for being is to help others, and all I care about is my house."

Eshe hadn't even had the chance to lock his house. "I forgot to lock it," I said with a nervous smile.

"Good. I hope the Jotrids take all I own. Maybe then…maybe then I'll remember how I'm supposed to feel."

Perhaps it was my fault. I'd put him on this path, given him the hope that he could help. But what we'd done had only hurt…what I'd done…

"Perhaps I was too obsessed with the arcane," he said, "I forgot the evil in front of my eyes. We should stop them…before the sky fills with screams."

"How can we stop them? We're two against a horde. Even Khizr Khaz failed — now he's their prisoner."

He seemed to soak in that thought.

"You said it yourself," I said, "we're not *good* people. But we're not evil, either. Isn't that so?"

"What is evil, Cyra? Is it not evil to do naught while others are hurt?"

I shook my head. "I don't know. If I had power, I wouldn't let anyone get hurt. I wouldn't have let that bitch hurt Tamaz." I wanted to tell Eshe. Tell him how I'd used my star-seeing eye to save him. "I wouldn't have let you be hurt, Eshe. Pashang listened to me then, but now…"

I wasn't being honest, as usual. Pashang had said if I burned my bridges, that he wouldn't loot the city. I just wasn't willing to pay that price.

"It doesn't take a sorcerer to inflict suffering," Eshe said. "When men join to take what they believe is theirs but isn't, that's calamitous enough."

So true. Ultimately, the Jotrid horde was a worse catastrophe than myself or Zedra, and if I couldn't spare my home that, what good was I?

"Eshe…Pashang told me he'd spare the people if I asked Khizr Khaz to dissolve my marriage with Kyars. And I didn't do it. It's not you who's evil, it's me."

He looked up at me with soft, trembling eyes. "I can't tell you what to do. It's your life. A hard heart is easy to live with, but a soft heart never stops bleeding. Which one have you?"

I nodded, fully understanding. Eshe saw the whole, like a bird perched on a tower, while I was always stuck in the muck. I needed his perspective, lest I escape that muck only to find myself in a fire of my own making.

Perhaps if I hurried, I could catch Pashang. I ran through the garden, toward the palace gate, heaving the while. Once there, I asked the guard, "Where's Pashang?"

He took me outside the gate and pointed to a cluster of walled villas aside the thoroughfare in which great viziers lived. Most were made of limestone, whereas the rest of the city was mudbrick and sandstone, and so gleamed like pearls in the dirt.

I ran over and found an open gate, Jotrids going in and out. One carried a porcelain vase with strange, colorful fish painted on it in the style of the Silklands. Sapphire-encrusted diamonds and emerald diadems were dangling out the overstuffed sack of another Jotrid, who was also chugging a waterskin with the sour stench of kumis.

I stepped between them and into the open gate, then through the villa door, which was surrounded by limestone columns and a fragrant rose garden.

Inside the high-roofed villa, a Jotrid man and woman guarded what looked like a family: a middle-aged man in a relaxing, silk caftan, his wife in a big, silk sleeping shirt, two teenage daughters, tears trailing kohl down their faces, and a handsome boy of no more than twelve years. They stood together in the middle of the room, hands clasped, as evermore Jotrids went about tossing their possessions into big, horsehide sacks.

Pashang was upstairs, in a pearl-themed bedroom, sitting on the bed's silk sheets. He was holding a puffy pillow and…sniffing it?

"I'll do it!" I told him, breathless. "I'll ask Khizr Khaz to break my marriage. Just don't…don't hurt anyone. This city is my home!"

He tossed the pillow away, what little of his cheeks shown aside his beard turning red. He resembled a boy caught touching himself. "Earlier," he cleared his throat, "you seemed rather disinclined. Why the sudden change?"

"What will you do to that family downstairs?"

He smiled. "Is that why? You're aching for *these* people? Do you know where the limestone comes from to build a villa like this? All the way from the Karmaz Mountains. Slaves cut out the rocks and carry them down, breaking their backs the while. These people don't deserve your tears, Cyra."

"What will you do?"

"The girls are ripe. The boy is hairless. We have a system — my riders will throw bones, just how you toss dice. The winners will get firsts, the next highest seconds, and so on. It'll be orderly — no one will be hurt, who doesn't resist."

No wonder Khizr Khaz didn't like these Jotrids. "They are

Latians, Pashang. Have you no regard whatsoever for our faith? You can't rape believing men and women!"

"Oh, don't worry. We'll gift plenty of Jotrid babies to the Ethosian Quarter, too."

I wanted to suffocate him with that pillow he'd been sniffing. "That's not what I meant! Stop this at once! Everyone in this city, whether worth a thousand diamonds or a single stone, are my people! How dare you touch them? Call off the looting, now!"

He stood and loomed over me, his breaths dry on my forehead. "Or what? Do you know whom you're speaking to? Have you even a flickering image of the things I've done? Looting your beloved city is a mercy. I could fill the river with blood and decorate your streets with skulls, if I so desired."

I stared up at his vengeful eyes in fear. I backed away until I hit the wall. "I told you...I'll do what you ask. I'll tell Khizr Khaz to end my marriage. Follow through on your end and spare my city. You're a man to be feared, for true, but aren't you more? Show me who you are, Khagan Pashang."

His gaze softened. "Tell me...who do you think I am?"

I wanted to say *evil*. If anyone was evil, it was him. The things he'd done...

"I don't know."

"No, you don't. You don't know a thing. You think claiming spoils, so my riders get their due, is so wrong? Do you know how many I've made scream because Tamaz or Mansur needed blood to be shed, so they could rule in peace? So their hands could stay clean? If I'm wicked, so are they! So is every Seluqal! So is Kyars!" His cheeks turned fiery. "I'll tell you what — they made me into their mad dog, and now I enjoy it. I savor each scream, every shrill 'no!' Truth is, I've been looking forward to this day."

"Does your affection for me weigh so little against the gold and slaves you'll claim? Was this all just a false choice?" I made a fist. "Well, *Khagan Pashang*, here's a real one. If you claim even a single stone more, we're done. I'll never, ever look upon your face except to spit on it. But if you call off the sacking…then I'll do whatever you ask."

"You think it's an easy choice for me? On the one hand are all my feelings…for you, for my visions…and on the other, my duties to my tribe, who are just as deserving of this world's pleasures as any rich Alanyan." He ran a hand through his hair, exasperated. "Last night, I was praying. Praying to *you-know-who*. I sought guidance, but I'm more confounded than ever. Those visions I saw in the Palace of Bones…they've all come to pass — except one. Part of me wants to see this out, another to run away. And yet…I wonder sometimes if I still have a choice."

"What's left? What did you see?"

"I saw…you and me…holding hands in the sand…amid a deluge of smoke and blood. And in the sky above, I saw Lat with peacock wings, holding a magnificent gold scepter. And then I saw you and me…sitting on that golden divan…together." He chuckled somberly. "Can you imagine that?" He swallowed a lump. "If ever you thought I wanted such a thing, you're mistaken. I came here to help Mansur and get paid for it. That's what you asked your Ruthenian plaything to find out, right?"

I nodded. Nice to be honest, for once. "You've no higher ambition?"

"Mad dogs don't belong on thrones. Even I know that. So what you're asking…to defy Kyars, without Mansur or another Seluqal on our side…we would be fighting the greatest dynasty the world has ever known. And if we triumphed, we'd have to create a new dynasty, a new kingdom." He poked himself in the chest. "I'm a destroyer, not a creator."

"Then let me do the creating." I couldn't believe what I'd said. Was this what I wanted, or the best among many awful choices?

I took his hand and massaged his harsh fingers. "Here's the first thing to consider — if you sack this city, you'll be killing the mare. Instead, we ought to milk it, like the Seluqals do."

"I don't know much about…milking." Seeing his befuddled expression, I wished I'd conjured a better analogy.

"I know a thing or two," I said. "I've been living with them. Tamaz treated me like the daughter he never had. I know the game they play here."

"You do realize, if we succeed, all of Alanya will rise in rebellion. Sirm and Kashan will march their armies here, eager to fatten their own kingdoms."

"Then we'll ally with their enemies. The first few years will be a mess, but ask yourself — would you rather run back to the Waste? What's waiting for you, there? You'd be caught between the Sylgiz and the Alanyans. It's endless war for you, either way, but at least here there's a prize worth fighting for."

That was likely my best argument. But was I really going down this path? Was I ready to commit everything?

"I'll go call off the looting. In the meantime, go talk to Khizr Khaz and fulfill your end." Pashang clasped my hand. "Say it, now."

"Say what?"

"What you used to call me, when we were children."

I chuckled. Of all things. "How about when you get back?"

"All right — but I'm holding you to it." He went downstairs. I returned to the Sand Palace to speak with the Grand Mufti.

THEY KEPT Sheikh Khizr under guard in one of the guest rooms. When I entered, he was praying, his hands outstretched. I let him finish. Afterward, he sat on the floor and poured out two cups of tea.

"I noticed you in the great hall," he said, "turban and all. I see you found your sword. There's naught Pashang couldn't slice, so well done."

"Sheikh…" I didn't know what to say. Didn't know how to

describe my shame, so instead asked about his: "Why did you support Mansur and then turn your back?"

"For us old men, Mansur will always have the better claim. I was there when Shah Haran made his sons swear the oath — Tamaz to rule first, then Mansur after him — atop Holy Zelthuriya." He sighed. "But this country isn't for old men anymore. Truth be told, I don't know who it's for."

I didn't share his reasoning, but he seemed genuine. Seemed to be speaking from the heart…and perhaps that was why he'd lost.

"Whatever happens, I'll vouch for you," I said. "Like you vouched for me. You're a good man…one of the few I've met."

"Thank you, sultana. Your kindness is a breeze on these old bones. I believe we both wanted to set things right but got mired in the means. How sad that just ends can only be served by wickedness, by deceit, by treachery. By blood and blades. It's why we are only saved through forgiveness — forgiveness from those we've hurt and from Lat herself."

To see such a pious man — a living saint, as some believed — stuck in the same dilemma as me made me feel less alone. I only wanted things to be wonderful for myself and everyone but always had an awful choice to make. Even now.

"Sheikh…I have a request."

He sipped his tea. "Tell me, my dear. I am for you."

"To spare the city a sacking, I've agreed to end my marriage to Kyars. To burn that bridge…so that Khagan Pashang can take me as his wife, if he wants." I sobbed from the weight of it all. "Only a judge can terminate a marriage without the husband present, and you're the highest judge in the land."

He nodded. "I understand. That must've been a harsh decision for you, but you've taken the straight path." The straight path… no…I was farther from it than ever. "Cyra, that's what faith is about — sacrificing your desires for the good of others."

"I've always done the opposite — all my life." I sobbed some more. "I'm not the good woman you think I am."

"I know, Cyra." He put his hand on mine. "I know what you're hiding, and it doesn't make you wicked, nor does whatever you've done. It's what you do now — only now — that matters."

Did he really? "You couldn't possibly know."

"I know what's behind that eyepatch."

I gasped and pulled my hand away. How did he find out?

Sheikh Khizr took a long sip of tea, the cardamom wafting into my nose. "If there's one thing I want you to learn from me, it's that whatever you've done, whatever you've become, you can always choose to be better. You're never too far for forgiveness, so long as you show remorse, so long as you return to the straight path. You understand?"

I nodded. But I wasn't sure if I felt genuine remorse or if I wanted to feel better about myself. Did I even deserve forgiveness if I wasn't willing to right all my wrongs? "I'll treasure your words, sheikh."

I led him to the great hall. Whatever viziers remained in the Sand Palace were already there, discussing matters among each other. Someone had to govern amid the chaos, I supposed. But like Ozar and Hadrith, they must've been pressed to preserve their own power and wealth amid the turmoil. Or perhaps I was too cynical, perhaps some had purer motives, like serving the city, ensuring the markets were stocked, that people wouldn't starve, that trade continued, that crops were planted and watered, that justice was carried out.

They all glared at me. For the first time since Tamaz's death, I entered the great hall without a disguise, aside from my high-collared caftan and eyepatch. I couldn't hide myself any longer, given what Pashang and I were about to embark on.

Khizr Khaz faced the audience, snapped his fingers at a scribe standing in the corner, and cleared his throat.

"By my power as Grand Mufti and as a judge, I hereby terminate the unconsummated marriage between Kyars, son of Shah Tamaz, and Cyra, daughter of Khagan Yamar."

A thorn pricked my heart. I wanted to shout and stop him. The greatest thing I'd ever gotten…gone. My position, my power, torn to shreds…for what? To save pashas and peasants who cared nothing for me?

Khizr Khaz continued, "May you all bear witness to this termination — in the sight of Lat, the marriage is void. In the sight of Lat, Kyars son of Shah Tamaz is once more a bachelor, and Cyra daughter of Khagan Yamar is once more a spinster. A document will be rendered and stamped by me, the officiating judge, to finalize the divorce." He clapped once. "That is all."

How could I have let this happen? Now I had no choice…no path but that of winning it all. We had to destroy Kyars, and for that, we had to be strong, and for that, we needed allies — all the allies we could get.

I studied the viziers, who glanced at me with sweating foreheads and gulping throats. Would they ally with Tamaz's killer against Tamaz's son? Surely not. By Lat…what had I done?

I turned to see Eshe standing near the big double door. I went to him while Khizr Khaz waited for the scribe to finish writing the document that would certify my marriage's end.

"Pashang promised…that if I agreed to it…he wouldn't sack the city," I said. "I didn't want that on my head."

"I know. I'm sorry." Eshe beamed. "But now that you're a spinster…"

"Your mind's already swimming in the gutter?"

He chuckled. "What makes you think it ever left?"

I laughed too. Although it still hurt. Hurt like the day I watched myself cut my own throat. My one restitution was Kyars accepting me. Somehow, in trying to right the wrongs, I'd been forced to find new hopes.

"Kyars would never have loved me, anyway. It would've been an awful, frigid, bitter arrangement. Not that I didn't know that, going in. I think I've spared quite a few wine glasses that would've ended up shattered against walls, at least."

"Right. You seemed so eager to be unhappy."

"I suppose I didn't mind being unhappy and loveless, if I had a purpose, if I could make a difference. Truth is, I don't think I'm all that lovable. People have always wanted me for every reason that wasn't love, so searching for it seemed pointless."

Eshe sighed, sharp and annoyed. "Are any of us lovable? Take this room for a start." He pointed at the chatting viziers, as well as Khizr Khaz and the scribe. "We've all done awful things. Anyone here walks through a garden, the flowers would wilt and the fruit would rot. And yet, among us is the Grand Mufti, a former Disciple, the most powerful viziers in the land, and you, the Sultana of Sultanas…for a few more minutes, at least."

"I don't see your meaning. What does that have to do with love?"

"We didn't attain our positions despite our flaws, we did so because of them. And whoever loves us, it won't be despite our flaws, it'll be because of them."

I tried to understand it…perhaps I didn't have the wisdom to. "I don't know. I don't think I could ever love myself the way I am. Even when I make good choices, like this one, it feels so wrong."

Eshe put a warm hand on my shoulder. "Stop punishing yourself. Don't forget — Zedra's still out there. She caused all of this, not you, and she needs to be stopped. You merely picked up the pieces and made what you could of it."

He was right. All this time…and I still had no idea why Zedra did it. Why kill Tamaz? Why use me to do it? What was her agenda? Just to cause chaos?

"Eshe…do you know what a starwriter is?" I fingered my eyepatch.

"A starwriter makes a bloodwriter look like a scribbling child. Aschere was one. She conjured abominations from the Blood Star itself. For the power they possess, they are an absolute danger."

Oh Lat, that wasn't the answer I sought. But I wanted to bare myself. I had to. I'd shown everyone here my presence, now let them see what I truly was, Eshe included.

"Couldn't...a starwriter use her power for good?"

Eshe shrugged. "Perhaps. Any power can be used for good, for evil, or for the vastness between. But one thing is certain — power corrupts, and a starwriter's power is beyond obscene."

Had I been...corrupted by this power? Surely not...I was the same misguided Cyra, just...things were more complicated, and choices harder. But Ahriyya wasn't whispering in my ear, telling me to do awful things. I was doing those awful things on my own accord.

Eshe said, "If ever you suspect someone to be a starwriter, tell me, lest a calamity befalls us all."

"What if...what if I were the starwriter?" I watched his eyes grow wide.

He chuckled, releasing his tension. "Don't scare me like that."

But I remained serious, hoping he'd figure it out, hoping he wouldn't force me to say the words. But as he looked away and fidgeted, it seemed I hadn't been plain enough.

"It's really not something to jest about," he said, refusing to look me in the eye. "Anyway, we should get to work finding Zedra. We have to be—"

Someone shouted in the hallway, just outside. Everyone in the great hall silenced and turned their attention to the double doors. Steel clanged in the hallway — then more shouts and more clanging steel. Sword fighting? A gunshot sounded, and every vizier in the room gasped. Eshe grabbed my hand, and we ran up the dais and behind the golden divan as more shouts and clanging steel resounded from outside the double door.

Three gunshots. By Lat, what was going on? Who could attack us without the guards alerting us, first?

"Sometimes in the stories, there's a secret back exit," Eshe said as we trembled behind the golden throne. "Well?"

I shook my head. Only one way in and out of the great hall that I knew of.

The doors burst open. Gilded gholam marched inside, ornate matchlocks drawn in every direction. All the viziers got low, as did Eshe and I, as gholam swarmed the great hall. Khizr Khaz was standing in the middle of the room, holding the document that voided my marriage to Kyars.

Among the gholam, an obvious face trotted forward: Kato, helmeted and shining. Of course, he'd escaped from the shrine and found a way into the Sand Palace while the Jotrids were out looting. How foolish of Pashang to leave this prize so unguarded!

Blood flecked Kato's golden chainmail; he strode up to Khizr Khaz and grabbed the paper from his hands.

"My good sheikh, your rescue is here." It seemed Kato hadn't noticed Eshe and me huddling behind the divan.

Khizr Khaz said, "And here I thought you a craven, the way you ran from the Jotrids as they charged the shrine. I assumed you'd be miles from the city by now."

Kato didn't bother to read the paper and tossed it on the floor. "I've been called many things — craven is not one."

"You do know Khagan Pashang is on his way back? You've not the numbers to hold this place. What are you after?"

Kato wagged his finger at the sheikh. "For such a faithful man, you've so little faith. I didn't come alone." Tens of more gholam marched into the room. "Oh, and you can tell the fools huddling behind the divan that if they don't stand with their hands raised, I'm going to toss a bomb at them."

And blow up the throne? There was no use hiding, anyway, so Eshe and I raised our hands and stood.

"The one-eyed she-devil herself," Kato said upon seeing me. "A blessed day to catch all the rats at the roost."

It seemed we were to be his prisoners, at least until Pashang returned. How utterly disappointing that we hadn't considered this — did Pashang leave so few defenders that Kato's small force had overcome it so easily? If so, I'd made a poor choice believing in him — one I hoped I wouldn't pay dearly for. And what about Mansur's household guard; where were they?

Ugh, nothing could be worse than falling into the enemy's grip now. I could scarcely believe it…after coming so far…just as we were making real progress.

The gholam lined up on either side, then stomped their feet, matchlocks raised…as if a royal procession were coming.

More gholam marched into the great hall. One held a spear aloft, and at the tip of the spear was…a head! The head of an old man, his gray hair dyed black. The spear tip jutted through his left eye. I'd never seen this face but, given the circumstance, suspected that Mansur had lost his head.

So that was how Kato got in; Mansur's men were guarding the palace gate, and they must've surrendered upon seeing their master's head on a pike. Kato must've captured him, and that meant Zedra was behind this!

A man wearing golden plate emblazoned with the simurgh strutted into the great hall. It took a moment to recognize him; he was bigger than last I remembered. Fuller. He passed by the gholam; they bent their necks, as did Kato and Khizr Khaz. As did I.

Kyars climbed up the dais and dusted his throne with the flat of his blade. Then he looked upon me and said, "Cyra. Heard you've been rather busy."

Three women walked into the great hall — in front, a red-haired Karmazi I didn't recognize, wielding a recurve bow, behind her Celene, looking rosier than I remembered, and finally Zedra, clad in a breezy black caftan, her eyes stuck on me.

"You think I've been busy?" I chuckled bitterly and pointed to the woman who'd taken everything from me. "Why not ask the soulshifter what she's been doing?"

24

ZEDRA

As feared, Cyra knew. There she stood, behind the golden divan, pointing at me and repeating some combination of "soulshifter" and "bloodwriter" and "Tamaz's killer" while Kyars let her chitter instead of smashing her teeth with his golden hilt.

I'd had enough. "It pains me to say this about a once dear friend, but she murdered my beloved father. She helped the Jotrids over the city walls. She pulled her silks over our eyes. And now, this sorceress wishes to bewitch our ears, too. It seems I've become the target of her malice, which no doubt is inspired by Ahriyya's own, but next may be one of you. Our only safety is her death."

I turned to everyone. To Kato, Khizr Khaz, Kyars, the viziers, the gholam — anyone with the steel to bloody a girl. "Kill her. For the sake of this kingdom, kill her!"

Kyars, his scimitar brandished, said, "Oh, I will. I learned in Sirm not to suffer a sorcerer." My beloved wound his sword arm.

The Himyarite standing beside Cyra pushed in front and shielded her. "You don't know me," he said as Kyars paused mid-air, "but I was a Disciple of Chisti. I hunted sorcerers. And it's true — Zedra is a soulshifter! She killed your father, not Cyra!"

"How dare you accuse the mother of my son? You'll die too!"

In a flash, Khizr Khaz pulled a scimitar from a nearby gholam's sheath and wielded it in Kyars' direction.

"You may be the Shah," he said, "but I am the Fount, and I'll not suffer more murder in this palace! It is so — Zedra is the soulshifter!"

Kyars turned to him. "You dare raise a blade against me?"

Kato strode up and put a matchlock to Khizr Khaz's nape. "Drop the steel, old sheikh. The bitch isn't worth dying for."

"I live and die for Lat's justice alone. I serve naught else. There's truth buried beneath the lies, and if you start killing, we'll never uncover it."

I knew how to reveal the truth. Or at least, the truth I wanted. "Take off that eyepatch!" I shouted. "Show everyone what you really are!"

Cyra glanced at her Himyarite companion, then at the floor.

"Take it off, or I'll come up and rip it off!"

She shuddered, then pulled off the eyepatch. A glossy black marble shone where an eyeball ought to be.

Everyone gasped, myself included. Even the Himyarite aside her gaped and stepped away.

A righteous jinn from the Peri tribe who lived and died six hundred years ago once told me about such horrors: the eye of Ahriyya. A way to see the light of dead stars, and to pull them into each other's orbits, thereby writing on heaven itself. How could Cyra have gained such power? Given that I'd gouged out her eye, was I somehow responsible?

"As clear as the desert sky," Kyars said, "the sorcerer unveiled." He brandished his scimitar at the Himyarite. "Why the surprise? Were you fucking my wife without knowing what she was?"

The speechless Himyarite lowered his gaze.

Cyra dropped to her knees, shivering. Poor girl. I'd done this to her, hadn't I? Instead of accepting a quick death, somehow in her rage, she'd turned to the gods of the void. Names I'd learned but blocked from my mind because even thinking them could awaken something you didn't want gazing in your direction.

"Kill her!" I shouted. "Before she uses her power against us!"

But she wasn't trying to use her power — no, she was a young woman, shivering at the thought of death, despairing at being abandoned by everyone she loved. She would die, like my daughters, undeserving.

"Kill her!" I screamed.

Kyars wound his sword arm.

"He said I was the daughter Lat had taken away."

Kyars stopped at the skin, an inch from her life. Cyra didn't shudder from the edge on her neck.

"That's why he—" Tears streamed down her cheeks, even from her black eye. "That's why he ran to me when I cut my eye out. Because I was hurt, and he didn't want to lose another daughter. Not again." She pointed to Kato. "You were there. You saw the way he held me. Do you think I'd hurt the man who was a better father to me than my own? Who had just given me everything I ever wanted?" She looked Kyars in the eye. "Who'd just made me *your* wife? The Sultana of Sultanas?"

The sword rattled in Kyars' jittery hand. "Why, then?"

"I don't know why anyone would hurt Tamaz. Why anyone would choose war over peace. Why…I'm not the one to ask because I truly don't know."

She'd made a puddle with her tears. And now Kyars too — his eyes were well watered.

He sheathed his sword and turned away.

"What are you doing?" I shouted. *Calm*, I told myself, *calm*, lest I reveal too much in my anger.

"I've made hundreds of girls cry, heard hundreds of girls lie." Kyars shook his head. "She's not lying." He gestured to Kato. "Keep her and the Himyarite under guard." He walked down the dais and passed me without even a look.

"My love, where are you going?" I reached out my hand.

Still, he wouldn't look at me. "Your story and her story are irreconcilable, and neither seems whole. Sheikh Khizr is right. Truth matters...but so does winning." He gripped his hilt. "Eventually, I will get to the root of this. But for now, I'm going to go kill Khagan Pashang."

I turned to Cyra; gholam surrounded her and bound her with rope. Same with the Himyarite and Khizr Khaz, too.

The three knew, and so the three had to die.

TIME TO SIT in my closet, soulshift into a gholam, and kill them. Though it risked revealing me, their mouths flapping in front of Kyars was a worse danger. I asked Celene and Sadie to guard my door. A relief to see my room as I'd left it — empty fruit bowl in the corner, bed smooth and undisturbed, pillows leaning against the wall at the precise angle I'd left them. I plopped into the closet, pictured the bloodrune I'd written in the palace hallway, and pricked it with an imagined fingernail.

Nothing happened. I'd written the bloodrune with seeker's blood, which was so common plenty of gholam must've possessed it. Perhaps I needed to relax?

I breathed deeply and focused on the air going in...and out. Again, I touched the bloodrune, but again, nothing happened. I tried bloodrunes I'd left in the solar and antechamber, to no avail.

They weren't working, for some reason. Lat only knew. I banged my knuckles on the floor and growled. Had Cyra done something with her starwriting?

If so, I'd have to ask someone to kill them. If Kyars returned after defeating Pashang, and those three still breathed, they might convince him of their *truth*. Khizr Khaz, especially, was not known to lie, and I didn't know what to expect from the Himyarite. Worst of all, none could deny the sincerity in Cyra's tearful pleading. A few well-earned deaths would solve these problems.

Another idea: my soulshifting bloodrunes didn't work, but

perhaps I could write other bloodrunes that would. No…using sorcery to kill them would risk exposing me. I needed a killer. A brave soul who'd do my dirty work. Kato…Kato had always been by my side.

But if Kyars was going out to fight, then doubtless Kato would be beside him. By now, they'd both be going after Pashang. Who, then? Who would kill for me?

I beckoned Celene and Sadie into my room. Shut the door behind them. We sat on cushions around my wooden tea table.

"I'm so close," I said in Sirmian *while tap-tapping* on the wood, nervous and barely knowing what I meant to say. "So close…to peace." Though I wanted war. "Celene…I'm going to put you on the next ship for Crucis."

She gasped in relief. "R-Really? Now that you have your son back, that's all I want."

"Sadie, I ought to give you something, too. What do you want?"

She snickered. "Another bottle of ginja. I rather liked it."

"No, dear. What do you *really* want?"

"You…can't give me that."

Celene folded her arms. "You'd be surprised, the things she can give you."

"No." Sadie shook her head. "What I want is…to be with my mother and father again, and with my friends and tribe and the man I love, and just…live life until I grow gray. But it's impossible, and so I'm here, with you two, doing all I can to distract from the longing."

I could give her that fantasy, for mere moments, but then it would dissolve and leave her with an even more bitter longing. Considering how she piled up those ginja bottles, she was the type to become addicted, and I wouldn't do that to her. No, I wouldn't be so cruel.

But in truth, I'd been unbelievably cruel to Cyra. She didn't deserve what I did to her…and yet, she had to die. It was her or me, and I had to raise Seluq into the Padishah of the Final Hour who would save mankind from the Great Terror. My cruelty toward her, as things stood, was justified.

And yet...all I fought for seemed so distant from *this* day, *this* hour. Seluq was just a baby. These girls were just girls. I, too, was just a girl trying to kill another girl.

"You girls stay here. I'll be back." I got up and left the room.

Perhaps I could talk to Cyra. Convince her to shut her mouth and go away, back to the Waste, where she belonged. That would be just, wouldn't it? Else, she'd bear my full rage, and surely she didn't want that.

So submerged in my thoughts, I crashed into someone while turning a corner in the hallway. He grabbed my arm and kept me from falling. It was *him* — the fair-haired, light-eyed, jelly-chewing man. The man who'd taken my baby and brought him and Mansur to Kyars that night.

"You..." I said.

He stared into me. "I've seen those eyes. Heard that voice. A mother's eyes. A mother's voice. *'Khizr Khaz, now!'*"

By Lat, how could he know?

"What are you talking about?"

"I know an actress when I see one because I'm an actor, unrivaled in the west, unrivaled here."

"Aicard," a voice shot from behind me.

It was Sadie, and she was talking to the man.

"Sadie," the man named Aicard said. "My apologies for the seeds, but they are so calming."

I recalled Sadie talking to him before they stuffed seeds in our mouths, as if she knew the man. But more worrying, the man knew me. Perhaps my ruse was over. Perhaps I ought to take my son and flee.

"You're far from home," Sadie said to Aicard.

"I always am, no matter where I go in this world."

"Why are you here?"

He sighed with satisfaction. "I told your lover, not long ago, that

I'm on the side of man. And in this country, the gods toy with man like nowhere else. Kyars knows what I speak of — he saw the Archangel, a sight I was spared. When he came to root out the Ethosian pirates, I opened the gates for him, spared him a fight. Even got him the ships in the harbors, so he could sail back here at speed, unbeknownst to all."

So…that explained Kyars' sudden and timely appearance. It seemed my beloved trusted this man, but what was he *really* after?

"You're right," Sadie said. "The gods are meddling here. They meddled in Sirm and in my life, too. But they're gods, and we're not, so what could we possibly do?"

"We can start by not letting them manipulate us," Aicard said, looking at me. "By freeing ourselves of their requests, by disavowing their promises. We're a spectacle for them. A game by which they compete. They don't love us, they don't hate us, the same way you don't love or hate the sand you step on. But they step all over us — you can even see their boot prints across our necks."

Had he prepared that speech? I'd heard a Philosopher once spout such nonsense.

"Thank you for aiding my beloved," I said. "Doubtless, you are his trusted friend. I'd love to speak with you more, but I've tasks waiting."

"You think you know the enemy," he said. "But the enemy has always known you. Sorcery is not of this world…no matter its kind. Stars, blood, and souls."

I ignored him and continued toward the guest room, where they kept Cyra. It was too lovely for her; someone had opened the golden drapes, letting the sun kiss the silk sheets she was reclining on. As soon as I entered, she stood and backed against the window. Her hands were still bound — good; she was taller than me.

"Out," I ordered the gholam in the room.

"Shah Kyars ordered us to remain with her, at all times," one said. Khizr Khaz had ordered his men to stay with me, and it didn't work out for them.

"Out!" I ordered again. But instead, the gholam moved to stand between us. I couldn't speak to Cyra plainly unless we were alone.

"Afraid they'll hear you slip?" Cyra said. "Admit your crimes? You're a deceiver. A murderer. Worse than Ahriyya himself!"

"You have no idea! No idea—"

"Why'd you do it? Why kill Tamaz? Why use my hands? Why gouge out my eye? Why slit my throat?"

The gholam looked on, grips on their matchlocks.

"Out!" I shouted again. "I am the mother of the Crown Prince! You'll obey me!" But they just stood there, in the way.

"Haven't you realized, Zedra?" Cyra sniggered. "You're nothing. A slave, like them. A glorified womb. Were you jealous that Tamaz chose me for his son? Is that why you did it?"

Clueless girl. She could never understand how base her motives were compared to mine. Of course she'd think me as petty as herself.

"Cyra, your death would be a mercy, for yourself and all. But I'll give you the chance to go away. Far away, wherever you want. Anywhere, but here."

"I used to love watching rabbits play when I was a child. Know how they mark their territory?" She spat on the ground. "Want me gone? You'll have to put me in a funeral shroud." She presented her bound hands. "Why not untie this? Pashang and Kyars are out there, fighting. Let's do like and see who wins."

"So you can write my death on the stars?" I let out a poisonous chuckle. "Do you know you serve evil?"

"And are you serving something so wonderful?"

"I'm serving Chisti. I'm serving Lat."

"You served the good by killing a good man? By lies? By blood? By ruining lives — mine most of all — and bringing war?"

Was she right? Why did she sound so right? "You got in the way," I said, admitting it. "You weren't supposed to get hurt...but you got in the way, with your schemes, with your marriage, with the tender spot you'd tended in Tamaz's heart."

The gholam had heard. Yet another tiresome, dreaded, inescapable complication.

"Wonderful." She leaned forward. "To think…you were my friend. My only friend." Her eyes watered as she grinned. "Your palace of lies is crumbling, Zedra, and you know it. Everyone will see you for what you are. Fine — I'll die, but at least I dragged you down with me." Her high-pitched laugh grated. "They'll hang us both for the witches we are."

Perhaps they would. I'd come so close to succeeding…and yet, it was all slipping from my grasp. If Cyra and Khizr Khaz knew, how many others did, too? Ozar, Hadrith, and Lat knows who else. With Hadrith in the wind, who knew whom he'd told, and whom those he'd told had told, and on and on. Staring at Cyra's smug, tearful, grinning face, I realized I'd likely failed.

"You're ending the world, Cyra. Do you realize?"

She didn't seem surprised or upset and just continued grinning. "A world this wretched should end."

"You think the one coming after will be better?" I shook my head. "You have no idea. We will all be remade in fire."

"Wonderful." Her black eye bulged like an oil-soaked bead. "Let everyone feel the hell I've felt. Misery adores company."

"You think you've had a hard life? I watched as everyone I loved was laid prone at the edge of a river. I watched as their heads were pushed into the water until life had left them. Don't talk of misery, you bitch. You've not even sipped it."

She laughed. Laughed at what I'd suffered! The cold-hearted bitch put her lips together and said, "Wonderful."

"Is that all you can say?"

"What's left to be said? Out there, they'll be bathing in blood. Pashang or Kyars, only one will triumph. I'm confident in my prayers. Are you?"

Father Chisti had saved me. Had brought me here. Had given

me a son. I couldn't lose hope, not now. I gritted my teeth. "I'm with the light. With the good. With the truth. Pray to the dark sky all you want…but one day, the light will scathe everything."

Her smirk was as dark as her eye. "One day, perhaps. But I have a good feeling — today is a day for darkness."

25

CYRA

"*A day for darkness*"...how the hell did I come up with that? But it upset Zedra enough — she wasn't in control, which was a relief, and now glared at me in silence. Kyars...he'd heard me. He'd see through her veil of lies in time and see that I was innocent. Though our marriage was ended, I could at least hope he'd know it wasn't me.

But what a fool I'd been for clinging to our marriage: my black star-seeing eye had thoroughly disgusted him. As if I were not human. Even Eshe had looked at me with a terrified gape. But this eye didn't make me evil. I wanted to tell them that, though, how could I? I'd hidden it, and the innocent don't hide their eyes.

Zedra was still glaring at me. If not for the two gholam standing betwixt, she'd likely wring my neck. That murderous look...the way red poured into her sand-colored cheeks and how her nutmeg eyes grew so round...she was not the friend I knew. As if that friendship of memory was between two other people.

"You're still here?" I said to annoy her. "Don't you have better things to do than stare death into me?"

Her lips trembled, and she huffed. Seemed she was struggling to form words.

I got on my bed and reclined. In a way, I'd already won. All I'd wanted was to go home and expose the truth. Whether anyone accepted it was out of my hands, and perhaps, knowing that, I could be at peace.

But then what was this pain boiling my heart? Eshe…was he all right? Did he hate me? In a better world, we could've been friends. I would've visited his throne, each morning, for those sordid verses. Maybe Zedra would've come along to feel the thrill of debasing yourself. And on the way to the palace, we could stop to smell Ozar's spices, then pray with Khizr Khaz at the shrine, and see what schemes Hadrith was stirring.

All another lifetime, now. So far gone…but it was home, once.

Zedra pointed a shaky finger at me. Then she grabbed her forehead, closed her eyes, and fainted forward into the arms of a gholam.

He carried her out of the room on his shoulder and ran down the hall, probably to the healer. How stressed she must've been to faint like that in front of her enemy. "Wonderful," I said to myself.

Now only one gholam guarded me, though an uncountable number waited in the hallway. Were I the fearsome starwriter they believed me to be, perhaps I could erase them from existence. But I was just a tired, miserable woman who had lost everything. Too tired to even pray…so I closed my eyes and drifted…

I dreamed of fluttering and flying. Of sipping a warm cloud. Of being a feather blowing in a sandstorm.

Until someone slapped me awake; he wore a golden sword, glimmering chainmail, and calligraphy-covered plate. A gholam, obviously…but why did he have Eshe's lovely face?

He slapped me again, then pulled me up. "Let's go! Now!"

"Eshe? You came for me?"

He unsheathed the sword — bloodrunes covered the blade. The

gholam in the room stood like stone, perfectly still, eyes bulging and forward.

"They're tranced," he said. "Come, follow me."

I pinched myself — this was no dream within a dream. But could we really escape the most fortified compound in the kingdom?

Eshe peeked into the hallway. The *stomp-stomp* of boots on marble resounded, as if gholam marched through.

He took out the tiny perfume bottle of my blood that he'd collected earlier. On tiptoes, he wrote a bloodrune atop the door's threshold.

"Help!" he shouted into the hallway. "Help!" The gholam ran toward us, vibrating the floor with their bootsteps.

As they entered the room, they all swayed, obviously dizzy, then collapsed against the furniture, causing a plate of berries to spill.

Astounding...

"Close your eyes when you go through the door," Eshe said.

We stepped over their bodies and into the hallway — he'd tranced the guards outside our door, too. Eshe was so good; they should've feared him, not me.

"What about Khizr Khaz?" I said as we hurried toward the exit.

"I've no idea where he is."

"He stood up for me. He pointed a blade at Kyars. They may kill him for that!"

He took my hand but could barely look at me, even though I was wearing my eyepatch. "I'd risk my life for you, Cyra, and far more. But I won't lie — I wouldn't risk it for that old sheikh."

He'd risk his life for me? Why? No time to ask or think. I didn't want to leave without the sheikh, but I couldn't force Eshe. Perhaps if we were free, we could help him later.

We hurried through the archway toward the simurgh statue. Two guards drew their scimitars upon sighting us.

"It's them!" one shouted.

As they charged us, blades forward, Eshe slashed his scimitar in their direction. Snow appeared to fly off his blade toward them; the snow hit both guards, and their skin turned blue, and icicles grew from their limbs and encased them whole. By Lat…

Goosebumps erupted on my skin, and every hair stood. I didn't want to go near anything freezing and hoped I'd never, ever be targeted by such magic. How distressing…that my blood could turn things to ice.

Eshe grabbed my hand, and we ran by the simurgh statue toward the garden that led to the palace gate.

We darted around the corner of a hedge. The red-haired woman I'd noticed earlier with Zedra was standing amid red tulips, a recurve bow on her back and a bottle in her hand. Soon as she eyed us, she grabbed the bow, nocked an arrow, and shouted, "Stop!"

Eshe sliced in her direction; she dove and, by an inch, dodged the flying snow. It hit a palm tree; icicles erupted. A sound like steel clanging on steel pierced the air as the ice surged upward, so high that even the birds perched on the branches froze, their wings spread in failed take-off.

Prone, the girl loosed an arrow. Eshe swiped at it, and the snow hit the arrowhead. Ice engulfed the arrow, forming a block around it, which remained stuck in the air, as if floating. Eshe was about to swing again when an arrow pierced the floating ice block, shattered it, and surged toward him.

I smashed into him, causing us to tumble behind the hedge, as the arrow kissed my hair and flew into the distance. Thankfully, that floating ice block shattering had given me enough time to react, but I was too close to death.

As soon as I rolled off Eshe, an arrow arced over the hedge and pierced his chainmail. By Lat…how? By what magic had she arced an arrow like that? Blood gushed as Eshe grabbed his erupting belly wound and wailed. She'd meant that arrow for me!

Running steps sounded from the palace entrance. Gholam were

coming. I pushed on his wound to stop the blood, but it seeped through.

"I gave it my all," Eshe said. "I'm sorry."

"You'll be fine." I already tasted tears. "You'll be fine."

The gholam' bootsteps quickened. In seconds, they'd surround us. I'd go back into captivity, but Eshe…Eshe they'd surely kill. How could I have let this happen?

"You saw my eye," I said. "You know what I am…you know I'm the very thing you despise…so why did you risk your life for me?"

He brushed my cheek. "Because…I think I'm just foolish enough to love you."

I grabbed his hand, squeezed, and prayed. Prayed for Eshe to live, prayed that he'd be saved, like he'd saved me.

The red-haired woman stepped forward, arrow aimed at Eshe's head. The gholam breathed on my back. I pulled off my eyepatch. Daytime stars covered my sight, burning in blue and red and green and gold. They hymned in unison, low-pitched and somber, like an Ethosian choir.

"Help me," I said to them.

A star on my left vibrated; I touched it, and it hymned a solo, then I drew lines to so many vibrating stars above and below and to my left and my right until the pattern resembled the…the sigil of the Seluqal House of Alanya?

"Kill the man," a gholam said. "Return the girl to her room, tie her up this time."

I collapsed on Eshe, shielding him with my body.

Everything rumbled as if an earthquake struck. The Karmazi girl looked toward the palace entrance, gasped, and dove into a thorny hedge. Each gholam turned, then dashed aside. Something huge was…running through the garden…toward us. Shaking the world and shattering stone with every step.

Red eyes on a giant wolf head! I could scarcely believe as a falcon-winged simurgh launched into the air, dove, and grabbed Eshe and me with lion claws larger than a carriage.

The thunder of its spreading black wings popped my ears. It tossed Eshe and me onto its back as it soared, each flap bringing a storm. We clung to its feathers, though it didn't seem necessary, as a force adhered us to it. It climbed the sky, higher, higher, bursting through clouds and approaching the stars. Qandbajar shrank, its buildings and walls and domes like toys I could step on and crush. Dizziness swam through my throat and chest, and cold poured through my veins. Oh Lat, anything but cold.

I let go of the feathers and took Eshe into my arms. To ease the bleeding, I cupped my hand around the wooden arrow jutting from his belly. His body warmed me, and so long as there was warmth, there was life. When we landed — if we landed — he'd have to write a bloodrune to save himself.

"Did we…die?" he said, breaths tense and heavy. "This our carriage to Barzakh?" I had to strain to hear him over the scathing air. We hadn't died, yet, but everything in my mind and body screamed that we were about to. I pressed my lips on his — kissed him — the first time I'd ever kissed a man. I tasted blood on his tongue — oh Lat.

The simurgh broke through what must've been a higher heaven: only a cloud ocean below and the sun and moon and a starry sky above. For a second, it stilled, and we were as gods.

Before I could even smile, it dove beneath the cloud ocean toward shimmering orange land. My stomach churned; I'd have retched if I had anything in me. I'd dreamed of falling before, but this was worse — panic engulfed my senses, and I could no longer think or feel anything but terror, which surged through me in rippling waves as we descended through clouds that left me wet and shivering. Gazelle in the distance were ants, but as the desert-scape surged toward us, they grew. Then the simurgh fluttered its wings against the air, jolting my heart into my throat and slowing its descent. It glided sideways; whatever force was adhering us to it released, and we fell — screaming — onto a dune.

Eshe was still screaming. The fall had twisted the arrow inside him, and blood flowed and bubbled. I shuffled off my back and onto my knees, crawled toward him through the sand pile, and pressed my hand on his belly. "You'll be fine!"

"If this is Barzakh, why does it still hurt?" he screamed. "Isn't death supposed to be peaceful?"

"You're not dead! Listen, you need to write yourself a blood-rune. Stop your bleeding!"

"So you're telling me simurghs are real?" He laughed hysterically. "My blood is the wrong flavor. I need yours, and the bottle fell out while we were flying."

What to cut with? I bit down on my lip — as hard as I could — until I tasted blood. Then I took Eshe's hand and squeezed my lip so the blood tinged his fingers.

I ripped his shirt open where the arrow had pierced.

"Pull it out first," he said.

I squeezed my hands around the arrow and pulled. Eshe cried. Blood gushed from the weeping hole.

With my blood, he wrote the same rune he'd written on my neck, then mumbled the incantation. It glowed. I gaped as the weeping blood dried and a scar erupted to cover the hole.

"Did you — really kiss me — while I was bleeding out — on the back of a flying simurgh?" He heaved between words. "You have — the worst timing."

I kissed him again — only on the lips — since there was still blood in his mouth. That left a bloodstain from my bleeding lips on his. "I thought I was going to die, and I didn't want to die without kissing a man. It wasn't what I expected, though." It wasn't any different from kissing a girl.

"A creature that every Philosopher agrees never existed — and those bastards can't even agree that east is east — just took us for a ride, and that's what was on your mind?"

"Death was on my mind. Do you recall what you said when it was on yours?"

He grinned, flush. "Well, you know, I really thought I was going to die." He let out an ecstatic sigh. "Life — I'll never take you for granted again!"

It seemed his veins were surging with the same lightning as mine. After what we'd been through, it was entirely appropriate.

"You said you loved me, and you used the word *love*, as in rising romantic love, not one of the ten other words you could've used."

He rolled over, as if trying to powder himself in sand. "Don't rub it in. Oh Lat, I need some date wine. Think you can use your starwriting to summon a flask? Or how about a bath of the stuff? I want to soak in it. *Fanaa* into it."

He already seemed drunk. Or somewhat delirious, at the least.

Gallops sounded in the distance: riders dotted the horizon from the direction of the city. Oh Lat. If they were gholam, we couldn't outrun them. But considering a simurgh came to life just to drop us here, I had a strong feeling they were Jotrids.

"Are you...at all upset?" I asked.

"Truth be told, I felt betrayed at first. But I know why you hid it. You thought yourself evil, like Aschere. But when you took my hand, I saw the Morning Star. It's the same star that I invoke when bloodwriting. It's not the Blood Star, Cyra, and that means you're not like Aschere."

What a relief to hear. And yet, I'd gained this power from the Palace of Bones, where I'd floated for thousands of years. I'd watched as stars danced around each other and merged in a cataclysm. "Does that mean I'm...good?"

Eshe winced as he tried to sit up. "Oh Lat, when I move, it screams." He lay back in the sand. "That doesn't make you good... it makes you not Aschere."

"Well, I already knew that." Did I, though?

As the riders neared, I breathed in relief: they wore leather vests over fur-lined blue caftans and hard caps with argus feathers, Jotrid outfits. They surrounded our dune, kicking up sand.

"Cyra." The thin-limbed man was Tekish, face gritted and soot-stained. "Thought it would be you."

"He's hurt," I said, pointing to Eshe. "Please help us."

Several riders dismounted and climbed our dune. They handed us both fuzzy waterskins. I drank deep, relieved to be among allies again, though it was still strange to think of the Jotrids as such.

Tekish's wife, blood flecks on her vest, came to my side and asked, "Was that...really...what I think it was?" Her short hair, though odd, suited her, and she had such defined cheekbones and chiseled arms. My mother had a similar build, in her prime as a huntress, and lamented that I remained soft, uncoordinated with the bow, and more interested in playing with rabbits than hunting them.

"It was, indeed, a simurgh." Of course. I'd passed by that statue a thousand times. The same simurgh emblazoned the fronts of coins and mail plates and all manner of banners and carpets hanging in the palace and elsewhere in Qandbajar. "Sorry, I forgot your name."

Her annoyed resting face, too, reminded me of my mother. "Elnur. Come on, now. We should get back to camp."

A relief to hear we still had a camp. I sat at the back of her saddle. Eshe could hardly stand, so Tekish strapped him to his back.

"What happened in the city?" I asked Elnur as we rode by a bulging acacia tree, which looked like a giant cauliflower in a bed of saffron rice. Lat, I was hungry.

"I'd filled seven sacks with brocade after ransacking some rich cunt's house. Then Pashang ordered us to stop. Said you convinced him. So...thank you."

"*Thank* me?"

"Thank you...because had we not stopped looting and drinking and rutting, formed up, and returned to discipline, we would've been on our backs when the gholam attacked, and that would've been it." She sniggered. "My husband was dragging double his weight in gold when a gholam bomb exploded the stable holding his mare. He barely crawled out."

I scratched my head. Seemed I'd done some good. "You're welcome, I suppose."

"I say we leave. There's no reason for us to fight so many gholam. This isn't our home."

No, it was mine. And I needed them to stay. "You don't think there's a reward that could be worth it?"

"What reward is worth our deaths?"

True enough.

THE JOTRIDS still held the southern and eastern walls, as well as the adjacent city quarters. I met Pashang alone in his yurt, which was just outside the wall. When I entered, he was shirtless and…meditating, his back straight, legs crossed, and eyes shut.

I stomped my foot. "How could you do that to us? How could you leave the palace undefended?"

He groaned. "I left it well defended, but Mansur's guard lost their will to fight. Want to know why?" He gestured to a bloody sack on the floor.

I gasped, recalling the heads my brother had once emptied at my feet, all from a bloody sack just like it. "I saw them parading the head around. The rest of him is in there?"

Pashang nodded. "His body is covered in burns, fingers cut, bones broken in all the wrong places. He didn't go peacefully into the next world. Regardless, his children deserve to plant his shrine with what's left of him." He snickered. "Cyra, this might be a lost cause."

I overcame the fact that we were sharing this yurt with a headless body and said, "Pashang, have you forgotten our promise? I burned my only bridge. My marriage is ended. This is my home, and I'm going to fight for it."

"I knew you'd say that." He stood and paced between the stand where his mirror armor hung and a — sadly — empty meat pot. "The gholam…we can't defeat them. Their matchlocks fire four times faster than ours. Their gold-plated armor laughs at our arrows, the way the sun laughs at the birds flying by. While we held the palace, we had a defensible position. But now—"

"But now?" I shook my head, utterly disappointed. "So it's true — all you're good for is terrorizing the downtrodden. Those who can't slap back. But come against a proper host, and you're as terrified as those you once cut down. Why don't you just piss yourself already?"

He laughed. I didn't want him laughing. I wanted him in tears!

"Tell me, then. How do we win this battle?"

I never claimed to be a strategist. A general. A vizier. What the hell did I know about winning battles?

"I prayed…and a being that only existed in children's stories came to life and saved me. Don't you see, Pashang? With our prayers, how can we lose?"

Now his eyes went empty. "I saw three visions, years ago, and since then, nothing. Only when I met you did I feel that connection again. The connection…with something up there." He pointed at the hole in the yurt's center, through which shone the dark sky.

"Zedra said it was the darkness that we prayed to…are we heathens, Pashang? The bedrock of our faith is to worship only Lat, and yet we…"

Pashang lit a fire in the stove. The waft of burning wood and coal filled the yurt. "We are on a different path, but it's our own path. We aren't forcing anyone else on it, the way everyone else does."

I nodded, though I didn't know what to believe. The only god that had ever helped me was not the one my parents raised me to worship. Eshe had said we invoked the same star, but what was the difference between *invoking* and *praying*? I'd have to ask him, sometime, because what I was doing felt so…sinful.

Pashang, it seemed, had gone in deep. Was worshipping whatever spoke to us, turning his back on the straight path to Lat entirely. "Pashang, how can we lose?"

"Don't forget — they have a sorceress on their side. Our magic against theirs, our god against theirs. It's almost poetic, and yet... despite all I've seen...I fear the men the most. In the grip of battle, everyone is praying, and yet everyone is despairing. Everyone is brave, and yet everyone is afraid. One man charging forward or running in fear can decide it all. What could these gods know about a wavering heart?"

"Pashang..." I began to like the sound of his name. Perhaps because he and his Jotrids were my only hope. Even my own tribe had abandoned me the moment my brother died. My own tribe... "Pashang, what if we get help from the Sylgiz?"

He guffawed as if I'd told his favorite joke. "You mean the same Sylgiz who've been my tribe's blood enemies for generations?"

"*Blood enemies* is a tad much. We had good relations for a while. You even lived with us!"

"I was more or less a hostage, Cyra. And the day I returned to my tribe, we were at war again. There's no trust, and the Sylgiz being Path of the Children doesn't help either."

"But now we have the same enemy — the Seluqals." I stroked my chin, almost wishing I had beard hairs to pull. "It would help if we had the same path, too. Which gives me an idea..."

Pashang sighed and shrugged. "Those wheels in your head never stop turning, do they?"

"I asked my brother to convert the Sylgiz to Path of the Saints, in order to solidify an alliance with Tamaz, and he agreed. Now... what if...the Jotrids converted to Path of the Children, to solidify an alliance with the Sylgiz?"

Pashang fell down laughing. I — lightly — stepped on his hand to silence him.

"For Lat's sake, stop laughing! I'm no fool! Think about it — the Alanyans champion the Path of the Saints and persecute Latians on a different path. What if we, in an alliance with the Sylgiz, championed the other side? Do you know how many still revere the Children but are forced to hide their faith? If we show them our strength — that we are for them — they'll rise up with us!"

Pashang concluded his laughing fit with a long sigh. "If the Sylgiz were so willing to convert, then they aren't serious about their faith."

"No, but they're serious about power, just as you are. Just as I am. And that's why…that's why you and I have to get married. I'm the daughter and sister of khagans, and you're a khagan — can you think of a better way to unify two tribes?"

He sat up and nodded. Seemed I was finally making sense to him. "All right…it's an idea. But one far removed from the current dilemma — the ten thousand or so gholam bearing down on us. And that's not even the full force — more will arrive in days, by ship and land. What do we do about them?"

I didn't have all the ideas! "You're the warrior, not me."

"And as *the warrior*, I know we can't win without a defensible position."

"Can we hold, at least? Why not station our soldiers in the houses, hovels, and villas, instead of in this wide-open camp? Force Kyars to attack his own people if he wants to win."

"We can try that, but prolonging things is to their advantage. Unless…" He stared at the hole in the yurt, his eyes bright.

"Unless?"

He stood, got on his toes, and reached for the stars shimmering through the hole. "Tell me, how'd you like to visit our old friends, the Philosophers?"

WHILE PASHANG WENT to consult with Tekish and others about our next maneuver, I checked on Eshe. He was snoring on his side, which was relief enough for me. The moment when that arrow pierced his belly…among the most panicked of my life. I'd put him in danger throughout this ordeal…for what?

I caressed the bandage covering the scar on his belly — no blood, thank Lat. Whatever power my blood possessed had healed him. Perhaps rest was all he needed to feel like his old self.

"You're doubtless a fool," I said, recalling what he'd admitted after being shot by that Karmazi woman. "But…thank you for not abandoning me. I won't abandon you, ever."

"You sound like me," a man's voice said from behind.

I spun around. In the yurt flap stood a man with curly yellow hair. As he walked forward in the candlelight, I recognized his more-than-pleasant face.

"K-Kevah?"

"Cyra," he intoned so dismally, followed by a bitter swallow.

"We were worried about you. Thank Lat you're all right."

"But you're not *all right*, are you, starwriter?"

I stood and fingered my eyepatch — it was well on. How'd he find out? "I didn't ask for this. It just…happened."

"I didn't ask for this mask, either. Don't you see? We are but playthings for the gods. They dress us up and set us against each other." Another bitter swallow. "Once, I served a shah — I was his plaything, as well. But I served, and I serve, because we all have our roles to play for the shahs and gods above."

"I don't want anyone above me. Why should I serve? One day, maybe I'll be a shah. Maybe I'll be a god, too."

He shook his head. "Full of dreams. I was, too, at your age. But you've not seen the monsters. The screaming angels. The—" He clutched his head.

"I've seen them. I saw a palace made of screaming mouths and bleeding, bulging eyes." I pointed to Eshe. "He saw things, too. So did Pashang. We've all sipped it…whatever it is…"

"It's our future," he said. "The Great Terror. The hatching of an egg — the egg upon which we stand. The soil which we were born from…all it needs is a little heat…"

Kevah seemed so different from the jovial fellow I'd met in Zelthuriya. What had happened to him? "Last I saw you, you were staring up, saying you saw something…you said, 'her wings are the span of clouds.'"

"The veil has lifted for you, but by covering that eye, you're not seeing." He sighed, sharp and weary. "I wish it wasn't like this. Remember how I lamented that I'd not attained the allegiance of a single jinn tribe? It seems hundreds of days fasting in the caves of Zelthuriya did progress my *fanaa*. Or maybe, it's because I was willing to risk my life to save this kingdom and help you. Either way…Marada, sultana of the Marid, believed me worthy of her power and submitted to me." He pointed at the ceiling. "Want to see her?"

I shook my head, not wanting to see more terrors. "Are you my enemy, then?"

Kevah nodded. "Not just your enemy. I am your end. And the end of your god — the end of the Dreamer and the Blood Star and all those names from the void. They'll never look in our direction again once I'm through with them."

Words said so coldly, yet with utter confidence. I didn't want to be his enemy…I didn't want to serve some god from the void…all I ever did was pray…pray to have food, to have warmth, to have love. I wasn't evil. And Eshe had said it was the Morning Star, not the Blood Star he saw when we held hands. So why was Kevah saying different?

"Kevah…" I could do nothing but sob and crush my tears with my eyelids. "I don't want to fight you. It's Zedra I want to fight. She's the one serving evil!"

Kevah turned his back. "Zedra…she's wearing a mask, and I'm meant to wear them all. So…you see what I'm saying?"

"You're going to kill her?" I asked with hope.

"Then after I kill her, I'm going to come back here and — if you haven't gouged that eye out — I'm going to kill you."

I gasped, holding in my tears. "So…all I need to do is gouge it out? Right? Will that…get me back on the straight path?"

"I hope so. Because I don't want to hurt you. You remind me of my daughter. She was full of ambition, too. I'm not stopping you from that…magi aren't supposed to interfere in power struggles, because whenever they do, it attracts *other* things. But don't rely on the void to win…that's how it begins. Take it from a hashish addict. The first few times, you think it's serving you. Making you feel better. Eventually, you'll be serving it, and you'll be hollow inside."

What a strange analogy…but it made sense. "I don't want to serve anything evil. I'm a Latian." I sounded so different from when I was with Pashang, moments ago. What was the truth, then? "But…if it weren't for this power, he'd be dead." I looked at Eshe, who still snored. How deep and restful that sleep must've been — I was almost jealous.

"As I said, I'm going to kill Zedra, and when I get back—"

"I know what you said." I made a fist. "I…I'm not scared of you. I'm not scared of Zedra. I'm not scared of anything! I'll make whatever choice I want!"

Kevah chuckled and pointed at the hole in the yurt's ceiling. "Fearlessness is for fools." He walked out the flap.

What was so terrifying up in the sky? If I wanted to be as brave as I sounded, if I wanted to lead the charge, I had to see it. I slid my eyepatch onto my cheek and stared up…no stars. No sky, either. Something solid blocked all sight.

I pushed through the yurt flap, keeping my head on the sky. What I saw made my jaw hang: three heads, each bigger than a city, crowded the clouds. Each head had six eyes — balls of sun — and the creature's wings…they were white and feathered. Unlike a bird, it didn't need to flutter its wings to perch; rather, it seemed to float, to glide with the clouds. I'd call it a dragon of some sort, but the worst thing was the snakes coiling through its skin. Or perhaps, those snakes were its skin — constantly coiling and twisting and squirming throughout its body and three necks.

I could only gasp, shut my eyes, and slip on my eyepatch. Back in the yurt, I cried. Kevah had made plain he would kill me…and with that thing having submitted to him, what chance did I have?

Did I really have to give up my power, the only thing that made me strong?

Throughout, Eshe had remained asleep. "Truth is," I said, "I'm as much a fool as you." I brushed his head hair, happy that we could at least have more moments. Perhaps, no matter what happened, that was all that truly mattered.

THE GHOLAM LAUNCHED rockets at the Jotrid camp all evening. They flickered through the sky and rained like fireworks, though always landed on empty scrub. Now bushfires lit the night. I hoped Pashang would heed my advice and move us into the houses of the city folk; would Kyars shoot rockets at his own?

In response, the Jotrids loosed arrows, but without high ground, they couldn't go far.

Kyars and Kato must've believed it was their advantage to wait: they controlled the palace, the river, the largest sections of the wall, and most of the city. And their numbers would only increase, with most of the gholam host yet to arrive. While I'd convinced Pashang to fight on, it was harder to convince myself that we could win against such odds.

Pashang sent riders to the Sylgiz with our offer. My tribe had only recently departed — it hadn't been long since Tamaz's murder — and so we could catch them on their way to the Waste. Offer them the keys to the kingdom, not some far-flung province. But would they join their enemy to fight their enemy? Would they believe it possible to overthrow a dynasty that had stood for six hundred years?

I didn't believe it, but I didn't have to. Unlike them, I didn't have a choice, and so when Pashang suggested — of all things — we attack the Tower of Wisdom, I nodded as if it were a good idea. While it could contain some knowledge or invention we could use to even the odds, no one wanted the Philosophers as an enemy. They'd stayed out of this conflict, and by attacking their sanctuary, we'd be forcing them to take a side — the enemy's side, surely.

So in the middle of the night, with a hundred of Pashang's best, we rode to the Tower, dismounted at its thick stone doors, and tried to pull them open.

"Not budging," Pashang said as he pushed and pulled against it.

"Blow it up," said Tekish.

I approached the door and brushed it with my hand. Beneath a layer of sand, shown an emblem: a circle — the earth — and above it, a throne, stars dotted around it. I'd never noticed this emblem, despite walking past this place for so many years.

I wished Eshe were here — he seemed to know everything — but he was at camp, still resting.

"Bomb bomb bomb," Tekish said. "Stone won't stand against the fury."

Pashang gestured for his sapper to set a bomb at the door. "A few more seconds for someone cleverer than my fool brother to give me an idea," he said to the sound of grumbles. "All right, then."

The sapper — a short, muscled man — put a powder-filled clay pot at the door. We all backed away. Pashang stuck his arrow into a torch, setting it alight. Then he nocked it and loosed upon the clay pot.

The blast shook the Tower, shook the plaza, shook me. Chunks of stone flew in every direction. But when the dust and smoke cleared, the way inside lay open, behind a mound of broken stone.

"Onward," Pashang said. "First to the top gets a palace!"

26

ZEDRA

After I'd woken from fainting in front of the last person I ever wanted to show weakness to, I pricked my finger with a sewing needle and painted a bloodrune on a parchment. I invoked the Morning Star, and it glowed. I breathed deeply: I was to do something I'd resolved never to do.

I was to go back.

Because I needed it. My anger was in charge, and it'd made me shout my truths in front of Cyra and Kyars' gholam, and it seemed the stress caused me to collapse. My son once said, during a sermon, *"Patience in a moment of anger prevents a thousand regrets."* If I could go back, for half an hour, and be with my sons and daughters, then perhaps I could steel myself. Like the taste I'd given Celene while we were in the bath, this rune would transport whoever touched it home, though it would be a mirage. Still, a mirage inspires the journeyer to tread on, and I needed that hope.

So I tucked myself in my blanket, placed the parchment under my pillow — so none would see — and tapped the bloodrune.

. . .

THE VOGRAS RIVER once bore an altogether different course through the earth. Though, ironically, it still passed downstream through Qandbajar, as if the city and river were destined to meet.

Upstream, we Children lived off the river in our home at the base of the Vogras Mountains. To say it was our lifeblood was understating it: we bathed in it, washed our clothes and all else, and drank of its sweet flow. It fell from the snowy peaks, which themselves touched heaven — no doubt, the river was from Lat herself. A gift to her Children, who blessed it with their touch and let the holy water reach even the most ungrateful of Lat's believers.

This was the moment the water turned from holy to cursed. From blessed to blood.

I was kneeling at the riverside, knees red and aching. The birthmark beneath my ring finger told me I'd inhabited my granddaughter Najat. She was seventeen. From our conversations and the silent moments I'd spent watching her, I'd gleaned that despite how bright and cheerful she seemed, she carried a darkness within that fogged even the most pleasant moments. More than once, I'd passed her my wisdom: *"As you get older, you'll shed that restlessness, and you'll feel purer. Your pain will lose its edge."*

A mother plants wisdom, hoping it flowers. But those seeds would be ripped out. Everything ripped out.

I looked up; *he* was standing over me. Small almond eyes, ball-like cheeks, and a crescent mustache.

The man had never impressed me. He resembled the thugs who raided pilgrim caravans headed for Zelthuriya. A warrior of few words — at least ones I could understand. But I'd understood him the other day when he prostrated, kissed my son's feet, and asked for the blessing of Najat's hand.

The Sixth Chief, my great-great-grandfather, once lamented, *"Telling the truth left me with no allies."* Only in hindsight could I lament: we ended the world by saying no to Seluq the Dawn. I'd enough daughters and granddaughters to forge alliances with every tribe and kingdom in the east, but the Children weren't known for our prudence. We were known for our purity.

Najat, herself, was not pure. Her mother was a slave my son had captured after a battle with an infidel tribe. Still, I thought of her children, of how watered down their god's blood would be if she married him. Truth is, if only we'd not been so prideful, this one time, our tribe could've lingered on.

Wait…what was I doing here, anyway? So many thoughts, and yet, a moment ago, I was…in a bedroom…in a palace, lying on silk, drawing with blood on paper. Now, I knelt on this riverside, and everything was…frozen. Stilled. As if I were in a painting.

But this wasn't what I wanted. This wasn't what I wanted to go back to. Not this moment. Anything but this moment!

Something dead floated by me in the river: Eglab! A four-hundred-year-old righteous silat jinn with white eyes, backward feet, and the beak of a stork. He'd once told me, *"Lat has decreed that you have many daughters and one son. After that son, you shall have no more children. It was the same for your husband's mother and will be so for your son's wife."*

But he was wrong. I had another son. I had Seluq.

His namesake grabbed my head. I glimpsed the sky, or rather, what had replaced it: Marada, sultana of the Marid. Its body was all snakes, its neck taller than the Vogras, and its heads…if one were to fall, it would flatten Qandbajar. Each eye was a ball of fire brighter than the sun.

The jinn of the Marid floated down from it: clouds of whirling smoke, with hands that reached out only to grab and kill. They would bring an end to the righteous Peri jinn tribe that had taught me how to bloodwrite and soulshift.

To my left and right: daughters, granddaughters, great-granddaughters. Some with gray hair, others who couldn't yet walk. All were forced to kneel at the river's edge, one of Seluq's savages at their backs.

"Don't do this," I said to Seluq. Why even try, though? Nothing could change what had happened. History would flow, like this river, to wherever it was destined. And yet, I wanted to spare myself pain. Spare Najat pain. "Your horde will destroy the dynasty of the saint-kings, and for six hundred years, your progeny will rule three kingdoms. Your name will blaze in red and gold across history's pages. But that glory will never erase this sin. Don't do this!"

I was screaming at the deaf; his face remained plain, as if he were here to wash out his clothes, not our bloodline. *The blood of Chisti shall never mix with soil* — a commandment he would follow.

Seluq the Dawn pushed Najat's head — my head — into the river. Send me back to my room in the palace! Anything but this!

Holy water filled my eyes and nose and throat and lungs. I yearned for air, but gasping brought more water. The fear of death replaced thought.

I flailed, pushed my head up, but water filled everything. My eyes turned to ice, my screams to silent bubbles that popped in the darkness. And even my fear, as much as it became my existence, returned to the depths of a still, soundless, void sea.

I was heavy with water, bursting, pressure exploding my eyes and heart and belly.

Ruptured, hopeless, dead, dark — I stilled.

My mind emptied. I resigned to die. All pain, without name or reason.

A thought struck like lightning: *I DON'T WANT TO DIE.*

I raged, flailed, screamed, choked, pushed all I could. But the water flooded in, filling me with death, bloating my core. Chilling my hope. Freezing my bones. *I DON'T WANT TO DIE* would be my last thought before I sank into the abyss.

Hopeless, I stilled in a silent, unfeeling dark.

And then, I finally died.

A FAMILIAR CEILING. Surrounded by silk, in my bedroom, in the Sand Palace. Oh Lat, such a relief to not be drowned and dead.

Too real…and yet, I'd wanted to taste the past, though not *that*. Had Najat truly suffered so? It made my suffering seem so…tepid. Curse all water! Cold, tepid, hot — perhaps I'd never bathe again. How could what gives us life destroy us so? Annihilate…so thoroughly. No light, no sound, no air — water was the abyss we feared. I could still feel its torrent in my throat, its bursting pressure on my belly, its ice in my eyes.

Footsteps from the balcony snapped me from my thoughts. I gasped as a man entered my room. Light skin, curly yellow hair, youthful. He gave me a chill glare — a death look. If water was bad, then so were we humans. All of us, killers!

Behind him in the sky…something filled it. Dreaded, demonic. Those heads…three of them, each with six sun eyes. *Marada*. The Sultana of the Marid jinn tribe.

Water, men, jinn — it seemed everything wanted to kill me. By Lat…if Marada was with him, then he must be…

"Are you Kevah?" I asked as I pulled my blanket over my shoulders, as if that would save me.

He walked to the base of my bed, eyes as forlorn as I'd seen.

"What do you want?" I shuffled backward, into the wall. "Help!" I screamed, wishing this were still a mirage.

I wanted to bloodwrite. Do anything to save myself. But the man stepped onto my bed, bent down, and put his hands around my neck.

"The blood of Chisti must never mix with soil," I said.

"What?"

"The blood…must never…" I trembled and cried. "Never…" Of course, Father had warned me that Kevah was coming. My meddling hadn't gone unnoticed by the Disciples and the Order of the Magi.

"I'll make it quick."

"But I don't want to die." I'd only just drowned. Suffocation seemed little better. Both were airless and stretched the agony, pain compounding each second. Bloody deaths were a mercy…a quick beheading best…what a curse they wouldn't kill us that way. "Kevah…" I gripped his arm. "Don't do this."

Unlike Seluq, Kevah heard; hardness left his cheeks. He took his hands off my neck, brushed my hair, and slid his palm down to my chin, eyes crossed and bewildered. "You're not wearing a mask," he whispered.

"What?"

Kevah raised a finger; it turned to ice. He thrust it into my forehead.

I AWOKE GASPING. No one in my room, and nothing in the sky outside my balcony — just myself and a barrel's worth of sweat all over me and my silk sheets. So…it was a mirage. A mirage within a mirage — rather like a dream within a dream. I'd had a few of those, especially during anxious times in my long life.

As quickly as it'd come, the soaking terror of Kevah's hands on my neck evaporated, and the equally terrible reality flooded my mind.

Truth is, sometimes I barely believed the story my memories told. So perhaps it was good that the horrors were burned onto my mind once more. But, somehow, I felt the sweet remembrances, too: the joy of my grandson's tender hug, the laughter of my great-granddaughters as they played amid flowers, and even the smile of strange, white-eyed Eglab as he dove in the river and snapped at fish with his stork beak. I recalled my son's hope the day he left to fight with Seluq, to take back our inheritance, our kingdom from the saint-kings…a sad thing, to be betrayed, in the end. Perhaps as sad as the hope I clung to, on this day.

I crumpled the parchment with the bloodrune. It shouldn't have sent me into such terror — rather the opposite. And why had I inhabited Najat rather than myself? Perhaps, in the end, it was better to be reminded of the awful truth than poison my mind with wonderful lies.

I sat up in bed and threw off my sheets. I still needed to do much: kill Cyra, kill Khizr Khaz, kill that Himyarite, and kill everyone else who stood in my way. I gritted my teeth and filled myself with the rage and sadness of the day Seluq the Dawn destroyed my home.

THE SIMURGH STATUE...WAS not here. And as I stood beneath a thin, cloud-covered crescent on the platform where it once was, I could scarcely believe what Sadie said.

"It turned from stone to flesh and whisked them away, like in the stories."

The gholam nodded and repeated the like. If true, starwriting was more powerful than I'd imagined.

And yet, unlike the gholam, who couldn't stop recounting how the simurgh took to the air, Sadie's face remained plain — bored, even. She'd seen greater wonders, no doubt. Perhaps one day, when I had no one left to kill, we could sit over coffee and learn from one another.

"You said you shot the Himyarite? A killing blow?"

She tensed up. "Well...a slow death, I imagine."

I shook my head. "Slow deaths are not good enough. Imprisonment isn't good enough. Nothing but still hearts will win us this war!"

I clutched my forehead again, lightheaded. Sadie gripped my shoulders to steady me. Why was I so frail? What was happening to me?

We went to the room Cyra had escaped from. A fresh rune in conqueror's blood lay atop the door's threshold. It was the same one I'd painted in the harem bath. For thirty minutes after the bloodrune activates, all who crossed below would fall asleep. But Cyra was no bloodwriter.

I asked Sadie, "You said the Himyarite flung ice at you from his sword?"

She nodded. I knew that rune; you could write it with conqueror's blood, as well as two other rare flavors.

"So…he's the one." The two gholam he'd frozen had thawed, though their hearts would never again beat.

A thought blazed: the Himyarite must've written bloodrunes to block my soulshifting. If so, this palace was a prison. I couldn't win us the war from here.

In the great hall, Kyars was sitting upon his gilded divan and deliberating with Kato and his other generals.

"My Shah," I said to Kyars. "This palace is not safe. That Himyarite sorcerer has written his bloodrunes everywhere. Do you not see? It was him who bewitched Cyra, who turned her to evil. Everything makes sense, now."

"My love," Kyars said, "this palace is the only true defensible position in the city. If it's not safe, then nowhere is. And you…you should be resting."

"If you want a lover who'll do naught but rest, then why not dig up a corpse? I'm telling you this palace is not safe, and I'll not stay here another moment!"

Sadie clutched my shoulders as if to steady me. I hadn't noticed my tilt. Why was my young body swaying like an old woman's?

"You're upset, my love," Kyars said. "And yes, it is upsetting that they escaped. But…perhaps it's better if they go — all of them, Pashang included." He looked to Kato. "We had a chance when they'd turned their backs and fixated on booty, but they've since formed up. A battle now would devastate this city, and I'm its protector, not its destroyer."

"Are you so cowardly?" I clenched my fist. "You can't allow two sorcerers and a khagan who supported your usurper to live. This city can drown in blood, but they must die!"

"The moment the Jotrids entered the walls, they had us. I'm not just a shah, I'm the beating heart of this city. I won't let them harm it, nor harm it myself." Kyars stood. "I've already sent word to them, along with my uncle's pieces. This is their chance to do the right thing — to go away. Pashang has no Seluqal, and thus no rallying cause to fight me. If he's of sound mind, he'll see that and go."

I understood. Kyars cared about his people, or at the very least, the taxes they paid. He wanted to save them; convincing the Jotrids to go was the only way to prevent blood from painting the streets. But, like I once did, he underestimated Cyra; she was keen on some mad cause and had to die.

A dreadful knot twisted in my stomach. If reasoning wouldn't move Kyars, perhaps harsher appeals would. "Are you really so meek? Craven? Just like…just like your father! He let the enemy linger in the city, and they killed him! Are you so intent to join him in that sepulcher?" I sniggered. "Where will you sleep, to the right or left of Saint Jamshid? Seems you'd rather spoon him than me!"

Kyars stepped down the dais, face to face with me. "You're restless. Poppy seeds would do you good." He gestured to the gholam on guard. "Take her to her room."

Why was I so utterly incapable of convincing anyone? I wouldn't mind going to my room if I could soulshift, but thanks to the Himyarite, that wasn't possible.

"Wait," I said, "take me to my son. I need to see him. Then I'll feel better."

Kyars sat back on his throne, sighed, and nodded. "Of course, my love. You can both rest in my chamber." He smiled at Sadie. "Cousin, look after her."

I WASN'T SURPRISED to see Vera in the chamber, rocking Seluq's crib. Her smile upon seeing me was so false. Fear lay behind it, made plain by her twitching strawberry cheeks.

"Sultana." Her eyes watered. "Thank heaven you're safe."

Would I just forget, like the others, how she'd stoked Mansur's ego? How she'd rendered a false confession against me? I knew she did it to survive. I knew she took motherly care of my son; even so, anything but absolute loyalty from those who served was a danger — to myself, my son, and thus to mankind.

"Vera, I feared you'd been harmed. When I heard Mansur forced you to call me a whore, I imagined he'd beat you, burned you, pulled out your nails. And yet, here you are, more radiant than the reddest tulip."

She got on her knees, crawled to my feet, and kissed the base of my caftan. "Forgive me, sultana. I was weak. I said truly awful things. I take it all back."

Of course. But if Mansur or Pashang still controlled the palace, she'd be groveling to them instead. Such a wretch!

"What else did you tell them, I wonder?" I stepped on her hand, pushed down hard as I could. Vera yelped, tugged her hand out, and crawled backward.

"Sultana, I'm sorry! Please forgive me. I didn't mean you any harm. I was afraid!" Tears ran down her cheeks — how sickening. How utterly insufferable.

Why weren't traitors being drowned, strangled, noosed? Why weren't their heads decorating our walls? Why were so many vile hearts still beating in this city?

Perhaps we could start with her. With someone weak. I could hang her lovely head on the palace gate, show everyone what happens to traitors!

I glanced around the room for something to bash her head with. But this was a pleasure room, so there was nothing but pillows, jewels, and silks. Perhaps I could just beat her head against the wall until her teeth shot out and her brain bled.

I cornered her against the wall. She screamed. I knelt and put my hands on her neck. Dug my fingernails into her soft skin. Then I squeezed. Squeezed. She squirmed. Grabbed my arms and flailed. But I squeezed. Squeezed as those pink cheeks turned blue. I banged her head against the wall and pressed my body on hers to keep her still. Squeezed as she screamed silently, without breath.

And then she stilled. I shut her wide eyes, closed her hanging mouth, and cradled her in my arms. I could not help but cry. If only I could have held my dead daughters like this. I dried the tears and slobber from her face with my caftan, letting her seem at least somewhat at peace.

In a better world, Vera could've been a daughter to me. Someone worth loving, like Najat, despite her base blood. But this was not that world. And still...it was my task to save this...this wretched existence we shared from being remade in fire.

Baby Seluq cried out, as if he knew his caretaker was no more. Who would look after him, now? Did Celene know how to rock a baby to sleep? Was her kiss as sweet as Vera's? Could Sadie hold a baby the way she held that bow?

SADIE AND CELENE watched in the hallway, mouths agape, as gholam carried Vera's corpse out of the room.

"Send that to Cyra," I said to the gholam. "Fire it from a fucking cannon."

I'd done some good. But more good was needed to win. Khizr Khaz had to die, too, and he was here, somewhere. As for Ozar and Hadrith, they were a two-headed snake licking the asses of two masters at once. I'd have to sever both heads. These traitors were no better than Seluq and his horde, bowing to us one day and drowning us the next.

Sadie said, "Y-You killed her!?"

I nodded. "Someone has to clean up this place, dear."

She covered her mouth and swallowed. "Why? How could you be so cruel?"

"Nothing cruel about it. It was justice, carried out deftly."

"Justice?" Sadie scoffed. "Then where's the judge? Was he in there, with you? Did I miss the trial?"

"Don't let appearances fool you. She was a traitor. We're in a war with blurred sides — there's no time for trials. Each of us must fight for the good on whatever battlefield we can, whether out there or in these halls."

She chuckled, as if she found it all so absurd. "I…I don't want to be a part of this."

"You don't want to help restore this kingdom?" I took her hand, but she yanked it away. "Sadie, dear, that girl aided the enemy throughout. Lat knows what she would've done had I let her live. She was a danger to us all, and to my son. I couldn't suffer her any longer."

"You're not who I thought you were." She shook her head and glared at me in disbelief. "I came to Qandbajar for an archery tournament, not to abet the murders of young girls. I won't stand with you."

Just as well, then. I didn't need her. Didn't need anyone. I couldn't rely on these saint worshippers — I'd have to do everything.

"Go, then." I smiled. "Go be with all the unsoiled, bloodless hands. The true saints. Prepare for a long journey — you won't find them within a thousand miles of here."

She turned her back and walked away.

"Some parting advice," I said. "Want to protect what you love? Shoot to kill. The wounded come back for vengeance."

Celene came to my side. "You all right?"

I nodded. We watched Sadie walk away, bow on her back and fist clenched.

"I know…firsthand…the danger traitors pose," Celene said. "They forced me to marry one. I won't question why you did what you did."

This girl had more history than I realized. "I didn't know you'd been married."

"To Micah the Metal himself. But we never consummated it, thank the Archangel." She let out a relieved sigh. "Zedra, what's going to happen now?"

I let myself breathe, then said, "Only what we make happen, dear."

I CAUGHT Kato on his way out of the great hall. He wore heavier armor than usual and sweated more, too. But the calligraphy-covered gold plate across his chest and shoulders suited his hard build.

"I don't feel safe here," I said. "Lat knows where that sorcerer put his bloodrunes. Cyra must've helped him sneak into the harem and put runes there, too. We know not their purpose — you must convince Kyars!"

He rolled his eyes. "Am I in charge of your security, too? Here I thought I was a general, yet you seem to think me a glorified sentry bent on your will."

"You're a gholam. Your only job is to protect my family!"

"Indeed." He pointed toward the exit. "There just happens to be a man out there devising a thousand ways to end your family. Now, if you'll excuse me, I'm going to chase him away, and if that doesn't work — well," his voice turned melodious, "Qandbajar, O' Qandbajar, you were lovely once!"

"The house you mentioned," I said before he turned away, "in the Glass District. Perhaps I'd be safer there."

"I agree. You likely would be." He hunched his shoulders. "Now go convince the man who owns us."

Kyars was in his chamber, rocking Seluq's crib. I entered and shut the door behind; he turned toward me, teeth clenched and eyebrows zagged.

"You killed Vera?" He shook his head in disgust. "Why?"

I snickered. "Miss your little plaything?"

He marched over and backhanded me across the cheek, bells exploding in my ear.

"You can't just kill whoever you feel like! This is not some patch of shit and dirt in the Waste! Only me," he jabbed his own chest, "only I decide life and death here!"

I rubbed the sting. "You're weak. Mansur was weak. Tamaz — your father — was so weak a slap like that would've made him cry."

He smacked me again. Oh did it shock my jaw.

"Remember your ancestor, Seluq the Dawn?" I rubbed the bruise and snickered. "Now there was a strong padishah who did whatever was needed to win. May our son be like his namesake and nothing like you!"

Kyars looked nothing like his ancestor: round eyes, rather than almond-shaped, slender cheekbones, not the bulging things that flanked Seluq the Dawn's flatter nose. After Seluq wiped out the Children, the Vogras Mountains were settled by sheepish Waste tribes who dared to call themselves *Vograsians*. Kyars' mother was from their stock, and so were his great grandmothers on both sides. Gorgeous faces but weak blood.

When the Sylgiz conquered the Vogras, a year ago, I joined a caravan of those they'd enslaved and sold to the Alanyans — that's how I ended up in Kyars' harem. Of course, this was just after Father saved me from Seluq and brought me six hundred years forward to this time.

Kyars shook his head as if in disbelief. "Zedra, what is wrong with you? Was it weak the way I beheaded my uncle and sent his pieces to Pashang? There's a difference between strength and cruelty. Killing a slave girl who was only trying to get by...who took loving care of our son...that is cruel! And I'll not allow it."

"And what of Cyra? You had every chance to end her, and you let her go! And now she's going to kill us all with her star magic!"

He wound up to slap again, then caught his own hand. "So you punished Vera for the crimes you accuse Cyra of, is that it?"

"They're going to kill us, the way they killed your father. They're going to kill our son!"

"Mad fucking woman," Kyars said under his breath while tightening his chainmail. "Stay with our son. Take care of him. That's your *only* role, your one job, you hear me? You are not to step out of this room."

Curse the saints — the last thing I wanted was to be stuck here, where I couldn't soulshift. Once again, I'd exploded in anger and set myself back. If only that bloodrune had given me a sweet mirage, perhaps I would be calm. Instead, my whole body sipped of Najat's bitter, drowning death.

"Everyone just wants to lock me up," I said, my throat sore. "Mansur locked me up. And then Khizr Khaz. And now you."

"Speaking of Khizr Khaz…" Kyars glared at me, hesitant. "He says Cyra's story is true. That you're the sorcerer who killed my father, not her."

"And are you fool enough to believe that?"

"Khizr Khaz is many things, but not a liar."

"Have you forgotten? He backed Mansur's claim before switching to your side. If not a liar, then a traitor!" I didn't want to shout, so tried to chill my temper. "Why don't you ask Kato what he thinks? He's the only one who remained loyal. Your gholam are loyal. I am loyal. We're your slaves. We're only for you. Unlike Cyra, I'm not the sister or daughter of a khagan. All I have to uplift me is your glorious name. It's the same for Kato. Save those who stood for you — unwavering — and kill the rest."

"If I kill everyone who wavered when my father died, who'll be left? Rather, I'll give them a chance to show loyalty and kill those who insist on standing against me. Saint Chisti forgave those with hearts like a shifting sea, and I'll do the same."

I glared at him as bitterly as I could. "Are you suddenly filled with faith, now? How convenient — but faith is not a cloak for your weakness."

"Easy for you to say. But I have to think of the kingdom *after* the battle, not just about settling scores."

"Win the cursed battle first!"

He shook his head and looked upon me with a pitying smile.

"Zedra…you are a killer now, you realize? And you talk like one. But I don't see it. There's no evidence that you're a sorceress, that you're at all clever in what you do…rather, it's just rage in you." He sighed. "Khizr Khaz, it seems, was deceived by Cyra — as I was. I'll accept the blame for her escape. But killing the undeserving is no way to win."

He knew nothing — nothing! — about who deserved to live and die. If he wouldn't win this, then I'd have to. I'd have to soulshift and kill Pashang and Cyra. Ozar, Hadrith, and Khizr Khaz I could get to later. And finally, Kyars — *oh Kyars, don't think you're not on my list*. Perhaps I could spare Kato; he listened to me whenever he could. He was faithful.

"I need some air," I said. "Let me stroll in the garden. Please."

Kyars sighed. His expression softened. "All right." He always relented to me in the end, at least in small matters. "I'll have a girl from the harem watch the baby. Don't kill this one."

SADIE WAS THERE, in the garden, chatting with Aicard as fireflies and locusts flew about beneath a sickly crescent. Kyars had assigned me a gholam escort, and they kept Celene and me surrounded, so I'd have to watch my words.

"You're still here?" I said to Sadie.

"I'm not leaving," she said. "I'll fight for Kyars, but I want nothing to do with you."

Aicard smiled. "I convinced her to stay. But failed to convince her you're a victim, Zedra."

I didn't want to suffer more of this fake philosopher's nonsense, but I'd never been called a *victim* before. "I am a victim. How profound. Too much cruelty have I suffered."

"And she's a victim." He pointed to Celene, then at himself. "As am I. As is all mankind." The nonsense finally spewed.

"Tell me, Aicard," I said, "when you're smoking hashish with my beloved Kyars, is that when your *best* ideas come to you?"

"Mine is not an addled mind. I spent much of my life deceiving others. But nothing I did can compare to the deception of the gods. Tell me — who is it you believe to be fighting for?"

What did he think he knew? And had he really figured out that I'd soulshifted into Mansur that night? If so, I'd scrawl his name on my list.

Celene whispered to me, "That man was Micah the Metal's spymaster. Whatever you do, don't trust him."

I wasn't about to trust him, in any case. But what was Kyars doing with a dead Crucian general's spymaster? Oh, I understood that he'd helped Kyars retake our western coast at lightning speed, but what was his true aim?

"You talk a lot," I said to Aicard, "and yet, say nothing. If you hadn't noticed, we're at war, and here you are, dawdling in the flowers. Why not use your skills of deception for some good, hmm?"

Aicard raised his hands, palms up. "I've been telling Kyars — we need to sit down with them. Find a way out that doesn't cause this city suffering. I'd be most useful in a negotiation. You see, I'm very convincing."

I didn't see. "So you're the one whispering this nonsense in my beloved's ear?" I really did need to add him to the list. "The Jotrids aren't reasonable. We just barely stopped them from ravaging the city." I stepped closer to Aicard and Sadie, trudging over the dew-covered flowers, and whispered in their ears, "Kill. Them. All. Does that sound like the words of a god? You're so busy fearing the sky when truly, it's all on us down here."

Sadie shook her head. "You remind me of my father. Kind and nurturing one moment, screaming for blood the next. I've felt those yearnings too…they can never be quenched."

What did this irksome bitch know? Did she think I was a child? I'd lived longer than the two combined, possessed more wisdom than they'd ever attain — I wasn't *yearning* for vengeance. I just wanted a good, clean victory, and nothing's cleaner than your enemy dead and buried.

My sigh was tinged with remorse. I'd wasted enough time on these fools. Aicard and Sadie could rot, for all I cared.

I needed a way out of here, and that meant losing my gholam escort. And yet, I couldn't use my bloodrunes — that would expose me further, perhaps beyond hope. Worse, I no longer had willing allies. Why was I so intent on antagonizing everyone? I needed to be far more clever, cool, and in control. But I still felt like I was drowning, and so I flailed.

The palace wall stood two stories high. How could I get over that? With thousands of gholam everywhere? Was I truly stuck?

I walked across the garden toward the palace gate. As soon as I arrived, an arrow arced through the sky and landed just inside the gate. A young man in the white and blue garb of the Archers of the Eye picked up the arrow and pulled off a paper that was pressed around it.

"What does it say?" I asked him.

He ignored me and handed the message to a nearby gholam, who then ran toward the palace. Whatever it said, he was in a hurry to relay it.

"What did it say?" I asked again. Perhaps he didn't know who I was. "I am the mother of the Crown Prince! What did that message say?"

The young Archer gulped, then said, "The Jotrids have entered the Tower of Wisdom. That's all it said."

The Tower? If you stood several paces away from the palace wall, you could even see its tip kissing the sky. By Lat — what if the Jotrids hauled cannons up there? They could fire down at the palace! Perhaps this was the perfect reason to convince Kyars to let me stay elsewhere.

I smiled, satisfied. I knew exactly what to do. I had to act fast on this fresh knowledge, lest the opportunity slip.

27

CYRA

I'D NEVER BEEN INSIDE THE TOWER OF WISDOM BEFORE, SO I CLIMBED the winding steps with an excited smile. First, I noticed that, though there were no lamps, moonlight shining through the windows lit wall mirrors that caused the whole stairwell to glow. The palace had something similar, but the light was brighter here.

Our footsteps echoed as we climbed, as if it were hollow. Then we came upon the first floor.

The massive, circular room had walls covered in book niches… all empty. Not one book, not one Philosopher. I expected resistance, not this tidy emptiness.

Divans stuffed with blue pillows were arrayed around the room, perfect for comfortable — even luxurious — reading.

Eleven more floors to go.

And they were all alike: tidy and echo filled. Seemed the Philosophers had taken their books and escaped. How? And where?

A back room near the top contained something so large they couldn't carry it: a miniature great hall, complete with a golden divan, pillars, and mechanical dolls in the likenesses of viziers and

Tamaz himself. With the pull of a lever, water coursed through the contraption, and everything moved. Dolls wearing the high felt hats and blue caftans of the Philosophers, holding sitars and flutes and tambourines, sprang up from behind the divan, their melody utterly lifelike. As they played, the viziers and Tamaz danced — which, to me, was the strangest part. You could even press a switch that changed the song and dance being played, with up to four settings, ranging from exciting to tranquil.

Now, in actuality, I'd never seen Tamaz or his viziers dance, no matter the melody being played. And given that the Philosophers hid this contraption in a back room, I wondered if they wanted anyone to see it, and something about how lifelike the dolls were filled me with more dread than wonder.

Aside from that, they left another massive contraption, consisting of a lever that, when pressed, sent water through a spinning wheel which caused these giant hammers to mash down on a white liquid bubbling in big buckets. The finished products were hanging on the ceiling: layers and layers of smooth, white parchment. In an adjacent room, printing presses were set up; they resembled giant stamps attached to strings and switches and rollers. The finished products lay neatly on high tables spread across the room — papers with gleaming ink that still needed to dry, which was likely why the Philosophers hadn't bothered to take them.

At the very top of the Tower, we came upon an empty room with a high desk of glass and wood. A book sat upon it, as if welcoming us. Pashang picked it up, then handed it to me.

Melody of Flowers was written on the cover. Flowers…was this the book they made Eshe transcribe? Why'd they take everything and leave it here?

Jotrids filled the room, inspecting everything, though there was naught else betwixt these rounded corners. Whatever treasures they'd kept here, whatever invention we could've used to turn the tide, they were smart enough to haul away. But the real treasure — the Tower itself — they couldn't bring.

"The Tower is ours," Pashang said. Jotrids cheered and hollered and ululated. A small victory with a hopefully large outcome. "Let's make holes in the walls and haul up those cannons."

"Pashang," I said, "no one ever reported the Philosophers carrying out books in mass."

He hunched his shoulders. "True…but they did. We must've missed it."

"Missed it?" I shook my head. "Since we came here last, we've held this part of the city, right?"

Pashang nodded.

"Then how could we have missed it?"

"What are you saying? Did they fly away, like you?"

"Of course not. We would have seen that. And why did they leave that one book? What the hell is going on?"

He rubbed his head and sighed. "All good questions. You think on it while I work on bringing Kyars and Kato an early *bright morning*."

I searched every floor. Aside from the back rooms with the large contraptions, they really had cleaned up — not a parchment, a drop of ink, nor a hair to be found. Just divans, wooden stands for reading, pillows, and empty niches.

Back at ground level, I was so tired I collapsed against the wall, breathing heavily. That was when I noticed it.

Most of the concrete here was worn from being tread upon, but in the corner shone a fresh patch. I tapped my feet on the worn concrete — a dull, matted sound. Then I tapped my feet on the fresh patch; a thud echoed below, as if allowed to breathe. The floor was hollow.

I went to Tekish and said, "We're going to need another bomb."

28

ZEDRA

KYARS WAS INTENT ON SENDING US INTO THE CISTERNS; I PLEADED THAT the dark, damp air would be poor for our child. But it was Kato who stood for me, who finally convinced Kyars to move his harem and heir from the palace and into the Glass District by reminding him that *"cannons care not whom they shred — man, woman, or child — it's only flesh."*

Perched on a hill and surrounded by a short wall, the Glass District had some protection. But our best protection was not being known; Kyars moved us quickly and secretly, out of fear that the Jotrid cannons doubtlessly being perched onto the Tower of Wisdom could fire at any moment.

Kato's mistress was a woman of skill. A merchant, it seemed, who bought and sold perfumes from as far as Abistra, given the language on the bottles I'd noticed sprawled across her foyer. She was polite when addressing me — I wished she'd teach Kato the same — and wanted to tour us through her mansion; I insisted on sleeping, so she took Celene and me to our room.

It had a closet. Perhaps Lat was starting to smile upon me.

Unlike the one in the Sand Palace, there was no hole, so I kept the door ajar. Celene sat next to it, content to guard me.

"Once you end this war…that's it, then," she said, somewhat jittery. "I can finally go home, right?"

I poked my head out. "Celene, dear, of course you're going home. You know I'd never betray that." I stroked her hair. She'd kept loyal and deserved to go home. "You deserve happiness. That mirage we shared — you deserve that and more."

She gulped hard. "I bet everything on you. And, even though it doesn't concern me, I want you to triumph. Want you to be happy. So please don't…please don't be lying."

She could have played games, like the others. Hedged her bets. But she stood by me, even when all seemed lost. And if I couldn't reward that, then I truly was wretched.

"You're like a daughter to me, dear. I won't suffer your loneliness. You'll go home. I promise, on my life."

She nodded. "Marot forgive me."

I huddled in the closet and pictured the rune I'd scrawled beneath a divan on the tenth floor of the Tower. I *pricked* it in my mind, and it glowed with the light of stars.

I WAS STANDING on a familiar spiral staircase, surrounded by Jotrids. I looked down. Breasts. It would've been better to be a man with arms chiseled like diamonds, but a woman could be less assuming, could get closer to Pashang or Cyra. I was young, given how smooth my face felt, with small-and-rough rider hands. I brushed my short head hair, then felt a bone bow clinging to my back. That wasn't all — two daggers, one on each side, and a scimitar in a leather sheath hung on my belt. This Jotrid bitch was truly armed.

"Heave!" They took deep breaths. "Heave!" A troop of Jotrids pulled a cannon larger than a horse and *heaved* it up the stairs. Oh Lat — to think they'd unleash such a monster on the palace…good thing my son and I weren't there.

I asked a man with a spotty beard and reed in his mouth, "Where's Pashang?"

"Your brother-in-law's at the top, of course."

Brother-in-law!? Was I…his brother's wife?

"And is Cyra with him?"

He shook his head. "Last I saw, she was setting up a bomb downstairs."

A bomb? What? Were they going to level the Tower? Obviously not, if they were hauling cannons up it. Just what was she up to?

I peeked into the tenth-floor reading room: empty. So…the Philosophers had departed…but when? And to where? And how? No one had seen them leave — surely we would have heard about it at the palace.

Add it to the pile of mysteries hidden behind the fog. Now, I had a choice: climb two floors and kill Pashang or descend ten floors and kill Cyra. I could only kill one before being caught. Killing Pashang could end the war, but he had a brother, it seemed. Wouldn't the brother just take over his command? And considering Cyra had brought a simurgh to life, she was surely more dangerous than some khagan.

Someone brushed by me while I was thinking:

"Whoa, sister," the tall, brown bearded man said, "in a bit of a daze, are you? Come, let's see what Cyra's found."

Pashang! I could stab him now, but if they were together downstairs, I could stab them both. So I followed Pashang down to wherever Cyra was.

"Still mad at Tekish?" he asked. "The idiot never remembers my birthday, either."

Tekish was…my husband and Pashang's brother?

"You're right," I said. "Such an idiot."

He stopped, his eyebrows raised. "You know, I think that's the first time you've ever agreed with me." Oh Lat, was he on to me?

I clutched the dagger on my right side. Perhaps I ought to slit his throat and not risk failure.

He put his hand on my shoulder as I lifted the dagger, ever slowly, from its sheath.

"I know this whole thing's been rough on your marriage. But…Tekish loves you, and only you. I even saw him writing you verses the other day, poetry book in one hand and quill in the other."

Pashang turned and trod down the stairs. I breathed in relief and pushed my dagger back into its sheath. I should've just killed him, but one thought kept me from it: Cyra must die.

The Tower rumbled and shifted as an explosion sounded downstairs. I ducked, arms covering my face, while Pashang quickened his pace. Just what was Cyra doing?

I bolted down to catch up, coughing from the smoke. Finally out of the stairwell, I saw Cyra in the corner of the ground floor, a smoking hole beneath her.

"Stairs!" she exclaimed, pointing at the hole. "This is how the Philosophers escaped!"

Jotrids gathered around — by Lat, they stunk. Of horse, sweat, horse sweat, and various kinds of grasses and shit. It reminded me so much of Seluq's horde that I wanted to spew.

I pushed to the front of the crowd; the hole Cyra had made lay before my feet: an iron staircase, covered in shattered concrete, leading into the darkest tunnel I'd ever seen, as if it were steeped in black fog.

Footsteps. From the tunnel. Faint, but they neared. Pashang moved toward Cyra; now both stood in front of me. Everyone focused on the footsteps coming from the tunnel; whoever was making them neared. Good.

I unsheathed both my daggers. One swipe at Pashang's neck and one swipe at Cyra's was all I needed to end this. To win. I stepped closer to them, as the footsteps from below ceased.

"You…" Pashang said. "I knew it would be you!"

Who? Instead of jumping for their necks, I turned to see a man standing at the bottom of the staircase, murky in the black fog.

He wore a tulip-patterned cloak, hood off. His hair was combed almost over his eyes, and what dead eyes they were.

"Father?" I said, regretting it immediately. What was he doing in the tunnel the Philosophers had supposedly used to escape?

I looked up to see Pashang glaring at me. Curse the saints. He knew.

I lunged at his neck. He sidestepped and elbowed me in the cheekbone, sending stars through my vision as the daggers flew from my hands.

"Elnur!" another Jotrid shouted. Pashang wrestled me down.

"Elnur's not in there!" Pashang cried, pinning me. "Zedra is! Get rope!"

"Father!" I screamed. He was just down those steps. He had to help me. "Father!"

Pashang twisted me onto my stomach, then tied my hands tight. I could do nothing but flail my legs and scream for Father's help.

Footsteps on iron. Father was climbing the stairs. Coming to save me. As he did, the Jotrids made way, as if fearful. He emerged and looked upon me...with a stinging pity.

"You know what?" he said to Pashang. "I think I forgot a book upstairs. Did you happen to find it?"

A...*book!?* Your flesh and blood was crying at your feet, and you asked about a book!

"Father!"

"Why's she calling you that?" Cyra asked. "Who are you?"

The Jotrids raised their matchlocks as Father stepped toward me. Pashang stuck his hand up, gesturing for everyone to lower their guns. Perhaps by some prior experience with Father, he knew weapons couldn't harm him.

Father would save me, surely. But unlike the day Seluq came, I didn't need saving. I wasn't *really* here. They weren't about to kill Pashang's sister-in-law, and this cycle would end soon enough. I needed to calm down and let it play out.

"I hoped for more from her," Father Chisti said. "But she's turning out to be such a disappointment."

Why was Father telling them that? How could he be so cruel?

Father sighed, then crouched near my head. "Zedra, you know what you must do. Use the bloodrunes from *Volume Two*. That will end this war, not this pathetic attempt."

"Just what are you telling her?" Cyra shouted, as if ready to punch my father with her bony fist. "And where does the tunnel lead?"

"You're welcome to come and see."

Pashang stepped forward, face to face with Father Chisti. "That day in the Red, you led me to the Palace of Bones. Why? What's this all been for?"

What? Why would Father Chisti lead Pashang to that cursed place?

Father shook his head, then looked down at me. "You're not desperate enough, Zedra, is that it? You have the key to the kingdom in your hand." He turned to Cyra. "She's in the Glass District. Aim your cannons there, specifically at a cluster of houses just east of the unbreakable statue of that wonderfully named saint. One good blast, and all the glass will fly. Mayhap a stray shard will cut that son of hers across the cheek."

Curse the fucking saints! How could he reveal where I was!? Where baby Seluq was!? I screamed and flailed against the riders holding me down.

"Our son!" I shouted. "How could you endanger him? Why?" I writhed and cried, but to no avail.

Father turned away. The Jotrids let him walk down the steps. He gave me a final, disappointed glare before disappearing beneath the black fog.

"Don't walk away!" I screamed. "All I did was for you! For your Children!"

But he was gone. A Jotrid, who resembled a twig-thin Pashang, knelt over me.

"Elnur…are you in there?" he said.

No, Elnur wasn't here, unfortunately. I wanted out as much as they wanted her in.

Cyra stood over me, a black patch covering her profane eye. "Let's attack the Glass District, like he said to."

I wanted to bite her shin but couldn't break free of the Jotrids holding me down.

"Who are you, Zedra?" Cyra asked. "What was this…this game…all for?"

"It's not a game!" I screamed. "Everything depends on me!" I let myself breathe. "On me…always on me…"

She bent down and brushed my cheek with her smooth fingers. "You invaded my body, killed my father-in-law, and then slit my throat. Don't you think I deserve to know why? Is there no justice in you?"

Justice? What did this bitch know? What did any of them know? "Was there justice, the day Seluq murdered three generations of the Children?"

Cyra shuddered, then shook her head. "Seluq…the Dawn?" She gasped, as did the Jotrids around still listening. Understanding dawned on her face. "*The* Children," she said, covering her mouth.

"I am the last of them," I said. "Me and my son. Please…Cyra… I'm sorry…I'm sorry I hurt you the way I did…but I had to…I had to…the Children must rule again…must rule…or else…the Great Terror…"

"Will remake us in fire." Cyra shut her eyes, but the tears leaked anyway. "That's why you did this?"

"Father Chisti said it was the only way."

She glanced at the hole in the ground that led to the fog-filled tunnel. "Chisti? Are you saying *that* man was him?"

"He is the father of our faith, the father of the Children."

"Zedra, have you ever considered that maybe he was lying to you? Father Chisti lived and died a thousand years ago." She shook her head. "I stood at his sepulcher. I saw his shroud. That can't be him. You've been misled all this time."

Dull girl. The truth is, I'd prayed to him, and he saved me. Brought me to that cave, which brought me to this time. Only Father Chisti could do that, would do that.

"I lived six hundred years ago, and yet I'm here. I don't expect you to understand." I swallowed the pool of spit in my mouth. It tasted just like my own. "Cyra...Pashang...if you don't stop this, it won't end well. I will do what I must to win. There's going to be calamity. I don't want to...but you're forcing me by being so obstinate. Just go away, all of you. Kyars has given you time to go away — that's why he hasn't attacked and finished you all off. Don't think hauling up a few cannons will win you this war. You can't win. Just go. Go away, far away, to the Waste, a world away. Never come back here. If you don't heed these words..."

Cyra shook her head while the surrounding Jotrids grumbled. "Wouldn't that be nice, if all your problems just ran away? I've thought about it, I really have. I didn't have to come back to Qandbajar. The world is vast. I could have gone anywhere else, cherishing my life, after what you did to me." She paused, as if in reminiscence. "Perhaps I should've. What is there for me, here? You took everything that mattered. But I've thought about it." She sniggered. "Bring your calamities. Throw at me, whatever you can muster. It won't stop me. You're descended from the Children... good for you. I'm descended from khagans, from conquerors, and I won't back down."

Why? Why did it have to be her? Was this the curse of the Blood Star, choosing the most stubborn bitch on earth to stand in my way?

I laughed. "All right, Cyra. See what happens now. You chose this, not me. The suffering, the torture, the screams — you're going to bear it, not me. I gave you the chance to turn away, but you chose this path, so I'm going to do what I must. This is the end."

• • •

My soul returned to the closet. What else could I do but cry? I dried my nose on the dress hanging above my face, then pushed open the closet door.

Celene was still there, sitting against the wall. "You all right?"

"I failed again." I trembled and sobbed. "I always fail."

Our room had one small window near the corner. I'd put Seluq and his crib just beneath so he'd get fresh air and light. I picked up sleeping Seluq, handed him to Celene, and pulled the crib into the other corner, as far from the window as possible.

"Stay away from the glass, dear," I said, after putting Seluq back in his crib. The baby cooed. Soon, he'd be crying.

I sank against the wall, tasting bitter tears. How much longer did we have? Where else could we run if they attacked? My enemies were everywhere, and I made more every hour. Would Kato and Kyars turn on me soon, too? It wasn't supposed to go like this!

"What happened?" Celene got on her knees in front of me.

"They know I'm here," I said, "and they're coming for me. I'm so tired. So tired of running."

Celene took my hand. "Running is good. It means you're still free. It means there's hope, right?"

Hope. The bitterest thing in the world. Sometimes I wished Father had just let me drown with my daughters. Let my hope and the hope of this world end.

"Celene, dear…you shouldn't suffer with me." My arm began shaking. "Celene…I've been lying to you…" And now my leg. "I can write a rune that will…" Even my words shook. "…really take you home."

She looked at me sideways. "What? Then why…why didn't you, all this time?"

"Because I needed you…but now…you should go. This isn't your fight. You've served me well, and, more than that, you've been a dear friend. You deserve all the good in the world." How could I do this to her? She'd been loyal. She'd stayed true. "I'm just…going to need some of your blood…to write the rune."

They would come soon. Come for Seluq and me. They'd launch their cannonballs at us any moment. I hadn't the time…the time to reason with myself. To justify what I was doing.

"Why are you shaking?" she asked.

"Because…I'm scared. Scared of what they're going to do to me, to my son, to my family. But you need not be here. I'm going to send you home…it's the least I can do."

"Is it so?" She pushed closer to look deep into my eyes. "I can go home…just like that? But if you're so powerful, why not send yourself away, too?"

"And go where? This is my home! My son is the heir to this kingdom. I've nowhere to run!"

Celene touched a finger to her chin, as if to ponder.

"Dear…" I threaded my hand through her hair. "I would never allow anything to happen to you. Just a bit of your blood…that's all we need."

Celene nodded. "All right…I saw a needle in the closet. Will that do?"

"Yes, dear. I just need a few drops."

So she pricked herself with the needle; I wet my finger with her blood as it dripped and wrote a bloodrune on the wall: it resembled a throne.

"Think about your home really hard, dear," I said. "Picture it in your mind. How it smells. How it sounds. The people who make it warm." I heaved and swallowed every bitter feeling. "Don't stop thinking about it. Now…close your eyes."

"All right," she said, smiling. "Is this goodbye, then?"

I brushed her cheek. "No, we'll see each other again, I'm sure of it." I kissed her forehead, then hugged her. She held me tight, warming me.

Celene said, "Ever since I boarded that ship with the Patriarch, bound for Kostany, it's been hell upon hell. Between three kingdoms, you're the only one who was good to me."

A whine came from the window, as if the sky screamed. Then thunder struck, and with a rumble and *screech* all the glass in the Glass District shattered and flew, including the small window in the corner of our room. Glass peppered the floor.

Baby Seluq filled the air with wails. I peeked into his crib; he was fine, thank Lat.

"They're coming," I said. "We have to hurry, dear." I took her hand. "Give my greetings to Adonia."

Celene nodded, closed her eyes, and smiled the smile of home. Such radiant joy — she must've been thinking of her father and Adonia, so eager to hug them and laugh and be happy again.

I pushed her finger into the rune. She collapsed in my arms.

I finally let the tears flow; they trailed down my cheeks and onto her forehead. She was only asleep...for now. Father was right...I hadn't been desperate enough...but now...now that I knew they wouldn't stop...I had to do this.

I locked the door. I pushed the mattresses against the wall for space to paint the bloodrune. A massive one, larger than I'd ever made. It would require every drop from her body.

I pulled Celene into the center of the room. How serenely she slept. How could I? How could I do this?

With her head in my lap, I unsheathed the dagger I'd been concealing. My tears dripped onto the blade; I wiped them off, polishing it. An old woman looked back in its sheen. An evil woman. Driven to hateful things by hateful people in a hateful world.

I squeezed the hilt, ready to slick the blade across her beautiful neck.

Wasn't there another way? Was Cyra right about me? Had I been deceived all this time? Was Aicard right about god...was I a victim of her schemes? I'd never been so unsure of myself, and yet, I had to save my son. They were coming!

Another cannon blast shook the earth. And more rumbling — the endless rumble of hundreds of horse hooves. The Jotrids neared, and though gholam guarded the district, who knew what Cyra would do? She'd summoned locusts and then a simurgh... what monster would she conjure next from the depths of the Blood Star? I had to act before she did. I had to conjure my own monster, and this was the only way.

A knock sounded on the door. "Sultana, are you all right?" It was Kato's mistress.

"We're fine," I shouted back. Baby Seluq was still crying. Perhaps I ought to calm him first.

I picked up my son and cradled his head over my shoulder, his cheek tucked into my neck. I rocked him, as jittery as I was. But he wouldn't stop crying.

Another cannon shot quaked the district. Then, more cannons sounded — but these shots came from the palace's direction. Was Kyars firing back? I could only pray he would level that fucking tower.

Amid all the blasts and shattering of glass and stone, my son would not cease wailing. So I settled him in the crib and turned my attention to Celene, who remained sprawled across the floor.

I cradled her head in my lap once more. Put the blade to her neck, my hand too jittery for a clean cut. So I breathed in...and out. In...and out. The death-giving cut was the hard part; I just needed to get it over with. In...and out. She wouldn't feel pain; she'd go to hell with the other disbelievers; or, perhaps, go to her god, if we Latians were the cursed ones. Either way, a small comfort that her ultimate fate wasn't mine to judge.

I held my breath to still my thoughts. One slice, just like I'd done to Cyra. I was fearless then, and this was no different. Just another girl who needed to die for the sake of the Children, for the sake of mankind.

29

CYRA

ZEDRA...HOW FOOLISHLY SHE'D BEHAVED. HAD SHE KEPT SILENT, WE wouldn't have been certain where she was, but by writhing and screaming at her *father*, she confirmed that Kyars had sent her and the harem to the Glass District in anticipation of our cannon barrage. It was too sweet a target to ignore, so Pashang and Tekish and hundreds of riders had gone to charge it whilst our cannons gave it an early *bright morning.*

It made me a little sad. Sometimes, when I thought of Zedra, I still felt the friendship of a girl who loved the adoration of Laughter Square's poets. Who doted endlessly on her innocent son. Who would eat too many jelly sweets, then cry about the extra pound on her hips. Who could imitate the harem dancers almost too well. Was that really our life, once? By Lat, what had happened? How could it have come to *this?* Though I still wanted to smash her eye out, there was a deeper menace behind it all, and I couldn't rest without knowing.

Kyars, predictably, had fired his cannons at the Tower of Wisdom. It wasn't easy to hit: though tall, it stood rather narrow, and so his shots, which fired from atop the walls under his control, missed and exploded the houses of the people he was supposed to protect. A fire now raged in the shanties and tenements behind the Tower, and droves of Qandbajaris ran from their homes and stampeded toward the city gate. Some dragged wagons of their belongings, others cradled children at their chests, and yet more departed with only the clothes on their backs. It made me sad, what Zedra had done to them.

The Tower would eventually come down, so only a few brave warriors remained within to fire cannons at the palace, and of course, at the Glass District.

In the meantime, I wanted to know more about the black tunnel, so I asked a rider to awaken Eshe and bring him here. I waited outside by the entrance and watched the rising sun streak red across the clouds.

This was my home, and now war engulfed it. I couldn't help but feel for everyone huddling in their hovels, hoping it would soon end. The same folks I saw every day for the past eight years. And yet, it wasn't just Zedra making them suffer. By fighting back, I too was guilty, though I hoped to spare them whatever catastrophe she'd planned.

What was the alternative? To run away? I wouldn't, ever. Qandbajar was mine as much as anyone's, and I was here to stay. This was my home, and I resolved to die than be chased out again.

Eshe arrived on horseback, a kabab skewer in his hand. He munched it upon dismounting. When was the last time I'd eaten?

"You better?" I asked.

He nodded, mouth full. After swallowing, he looked up at the Tower and said, "Didn't I tell you *not* to kick this bag of scorpions?"

"Wasn't my idea…but I can't say I protested much. Telling me not to do something is a sure way to make me do it."

"You're self-aware. I like that." He wielded the now bare skewer like a sword. Jabbed my shoulder with it.

I raised my hands. "I'm unarmed."

"Are you?" His mischievous smile warmed me. From his

pocket, he took out another skewer, the heavenly scent of mutton, onions, and cumin wafting off the kabab within the wrapping.

I grabbed it, threw off the wrapper, and took a meaty bite. Tender, juicy, and filled with flavor — just like how they made them at the Grand Bazaar. "This's a Sirmian kabab," I said, mouth full and dripping. "Where'd you get it?"

"Saw a few open stalls on the way. People still have to earn and eat. War and all. Paid twenty times the usual, given what your locusts did to the crops and grazing grass."

"It's damn good." After devouring it, I ran my fingers over the empty skewer and licked the juices off them.

He raised his skewer to eye level and wielded it straight at me. "We going to duel, or what?"

I chuckled. "You're in a good mood." Was he still feeling the lightning of our near-death flight?

He lowered his skewer and scowled. "I shouldn't be, though. Look around. This city...the people...it's just getting worse for them, isn't it? The Disciples have a saying, *help others and you won't need to help yourself.* But now...it's like we've turned that on its head."

"I want to end this awful trouble, too. Which is why...Eshe, there's something you need to see."

I'd left the book — *Melody of Flowers* — near the Tower entrance. I picked it up and handed it to him.

He shuddered. "This is what I transcribed, from memory, for them. Though, I don't recall *this* being its title. It was much dryer — *Flowers and their Properties by Tamor.* I rather like this new title. *Melody of Flowers* — so much sweeter. Anyway, why, of all things, did they leave it here?"

I hunched my shoulders.

Next, I showed him the iron staircase that led to the tunnel of black fog. None of us had gone down yet, the Jotrids remarking it was home to cursed tribes of jinn.

Eshe's eyes widened. "Labyrinthos. The gateway to hell."

"Gateway…to hell? But the Philosophers took their books and inventions and marched through there, to wherever it leads."

"I read a book, once, about a man who claimed to have charted it. According to him, it has openings throughout the earth, and once you learn to navigate it, you can cover a month's journey in an hour." He shook his head. "But the dangers…the jinn down there leech on men's minds. If you can't find your way…the suffering is untold."

I shuddered at the thought. Perhaps the man whom Zedra called Father Chisti knew the way through and so guided the Philosophers to some other place. "So I'm guessing you don't suggest we go inside."

"Well, I won't tell you *not* to go inside because then you just might."

I gave him a wry smile. "I'm not that foolish." I recounted how Zedra soulshifted into Elnur's body and how she called the man in the flowery cloak *Father Chisti*.

Eshe laughed…too nervously for comfort. "The bitch is howling at the moon."

"She must be crazy. You're right. But still, by manipulating her, that man is responsible for all this. For what happened to me. For what's happening to my home, as we speak. He's responsible, and he needs to be stopped."

"But we don't even know who he is. What he's capable of. When the Philosophers brought me here, they showed him so much reverence. Wouldn't look him in the eye, would keep their heads bowed and never show their backs, as if he were their king."

I sighed. It all seemed so strange. Litani was the Grand Philosopher, so how come they had a king that even he revered?

"Eshe, when you got arrowed in the stomach, do you remember when I took your hand?"

He shrugged, all jittery. "I was in tremendous pain. All I remember is seeing the Morning Star."

"I took Pashang's hand, the night we rescued you. I think…

when I really want something, the Morning Star hears me. Or rather, when *we* really want something."

"I don't know how starwriting works. Had I known, perhaps I could've stopped Aschere." He smiled at me. "All I know is, you're not like her."

I wasn't so sure. "In what way am I not like her?"

"She led a Crucian army into a Latian city," he pointed at the black fog below us, "through Labyrinthos, might I add. She caused untold suffering, indescribable slaughter."

Through Labyrinthos…if she could navigate it, then why couldn't I? "Eshe…are you so sure that I'm not like her? That I wouldn't do things that lead to suffering and slaughter?"

He shook his head. "I don't see you that way. I…" He hesitated.

"Maybe…maybe your love for me blinds you…to what I truly am?"

He shook his head again, more vigorously. "No…you're kind. When the Philosophers took me, you joined with your enemy to save me. When I got shot with an arrow, you shielded me with your own body." His eyes watered. "Bloodwriting, starwriting…some of us are cursed with these powers. It's not the power that's evil, it's what we do with it."

But…what *wouldn't* I do with it? Did Eshe not see what I saw in myself? I was indeed self-aware, like he'd just said, and so knew how impetuous I could be, how disdainful. Perhaps that was why the Order of the Magi required *fanaa* from seekers of their power.

I slid my eyepatch off, then held out my hand. "Let's try. Let's see if we can light the way."

Eshe smiled at me, nodded, and took it. We held hands. It was…nice.

"Is something supposed to happen?" He stroked his beard. "Or do we just wait?"

No…I'd forgotten…I needed to pray. I hadn't even told Eshe who I was praying to, that I was committing the worst sin of our faith that would undoubtedly doom my soul.

Perhaps that reveal was for another time when we weren't trying to enter *the gate to hellfire*.

I pictured the black sky — the darkest thing I could — and prayed for it to light the way.

Something twinkled by my ear. At first, I thought it a green star, but it had tiny wings that buzzed: a firefly. It flew into the tunnel and, where its light went, the fog seemed to clear. More appeared, coming from the air itself and streaming into the black cave.

Eshe's jaw hung. I, too, couldn't believe what I'd just summoned. Couldn't believe how easily my prayer was answered.

"Let's go?" I asked, looking into Eshe's wide eyes.

He gulped, his palm suddenly sweaty. "Not going to lie. This is pretty fucking terrifying. We're relying on insects to guide us through the gate to hell."

"Insects brought us through Qandbajar's wall…"

"Good point." He rubbed his cheek. "We've watched so many suffer, for what? What was Zedra trying to do? I suppose…all the answers are in there, with that man, and we need those answers as much as we need breath."

Full agreement. I had to know what all this senselessness had been about. Why I, and so many, had suffered.

We gave *Melody of Flowers* to a Jotrid on guard, instructing him to give it to Pashang for safekeeping. Then we clasped hands and took the first step down. Cold air engulfed my feet. Oh Lat…it was not only dark but freezing.

Above, a cannon shot screamed through the air, whizzing by just outside. Kyars had resumed firing on the Tower.

"If they succeed, the Tower will fall on this entrance," Eshe said. "We may be sacrificing our lives for these answers."

Worse than that, I didn't want to be cold. Not now. Not ever.

"We need to see this through," I said. "If we go back out there, to the war, we won't know why we're fighting. *Who* we're fighting. That man…it all leads to him."

Eshe sighed. "You're much braver than the girl who came to my brass throne, in what feels like forever ago."

I could only smile at the memory.

"But," he said, "it could be a trap, couldn't it?"

"Wasn't it a trap, also, to come back to this city? We could've stayed in Zelthuriya or gone anywhere else and just moved on from what happened."

"But Cyra, they say getting lost in Labyrinthos is a fate worse than death."

"Never knowing is worse than death, too. Zedra was my friend, once. That man tricked her. Turned her against me. Made her murder Tamaz. Then he tortured you." I clenched my fist. "I'll not have it!"

The fireflies floating in the cavern seemed like green stars pulsating against an oppressive black sky.

Eshe gulped. "What if…what if he has something to do with Aschere, too?"

"Unless we find him, we'll never know."

A firefly landed on my shoulder. Then more on my head and across my arms and legs. They did the same for Eshe, and, with their somber glow, they warmed us.

We shared a resolute nod. Together, we descended until we stood in the cave itself, surrounded by what looked and smelled like tar.

Eshe touched the cave wall and came away with stains. I shivered as frigid whispers scathed my ears — the fireflies could only warm me so much. But we were inside now, and I resolved not to turn back.

So on we went through the cave, guided and warmed by the green bugs. I wouldn't let go of Eshe's hand, and he wouldn't let go of mine. Until we saw something: a wood-bound book lying on the ground.

Eshe picked it up and dusted it. A firefly landed on the cover, illuminating the title: *The Melody of Nora.*

I touched my chin. "Another melody? Did the Philosophers, perhaps, drop it while they were escaping?"

We flipped through it together: empty page after empty page, until we came upon a picture of seven stars surrounding a single eye — written in blood.

Eshe gasped. "By Lat...this can't be what I think it is."

"Something wonderful, I hope?"

He shook his head. "This is a memory rune. It transfers memories between people, replacing your own. Entire lives of memories. In Tinbuq, the now blood-flooded capital of the Golden Kingdom, the Philosophers would use these runes to inherit lifetimes of knowledge. And worse...it can only be written with saint's blood, angel's blood, or god's blood. Three of the rarest flavors."

"So...I assume we shouldn't touch it."

"We don't know if it's active or not, so we shouldn't...unless, you know, you hate yourself and wouldn't mind being someone else...whoever's memories are baked into that rune."

I rubbed my forehead; a headache was coming on. "But whose memories are they?"

"Nora, I suppose...whoever that is."

"Nora...as in Saint Nora? From the unbreakable statue in the Glass District?"

"Obviously not her. I've met dozens of women named Nora. Nay, hundreds." Sure he had. "Common enough name."

Eshe flipped to the next page. Another bloodrune lay on it, but this one had four stars, and the eye was sideways. "All right, this is peculiar — also a memory rune, but this one is less powerful. It makes you experience a particular memory and doesn't erase your own."

I scratched my head. "So...it's safe to touch?"

"No, not at all. When that man tortured me, he used the same kind of bloodrune. He was showing me a memory...and making me live it. This could be a trap for the curious."

It was all so utterly unbelievable. We flipped through the rest of the book, but the pages were bare. Best not to linger in the gateway to hell, so Eshe tucked the book into his caftan, and we moved on. Finding that was a good sign we were getting somewhere, at least.

The ground declined and turned moist, as if we were stepping on a thin mud layer. We slowed and tightened our handhold, wary of sliding.

"Whatever happens, we can't get separated," Eshe said. "In all the stories I've read, that's when it goes badly."

A bird squawked and fluttered by, making us duck. Black feathers: a drongo. Did birds really live in this cursed place!?

Eshe said, "Y-You know, they say the jinn who live here have daggers for nails. They take the form of birds, sometimes."

Could I see them if I removed my patch, like I'd seen Marada in the sky? I didn't want to find out, but I had to know, so lifted it slightly…

Faces formed in the tar. Big, twitching eyeballs. Wide mouths, silently screaming. Above, to the right, to the left: eternal pain surrounded us. This wasn't a gate to hell…this was hell!

I tugged on Eshe, but he didn't seem to notice.

"What?"

I pointed to the wall, then realized only I could see them. I slipped the eyepatch back on, and the faces disappeared. The curiosity hadn't been worth it.

After I caught my breath and sanity, we continued through the tunnel and reached an open area. A black sky stretched above, with rocks and hard stone beneath our feet. Were we on a mountain…in a cave?

We followed the green fireflies toward a cliff's edge. I stepped on something hard and ball-like. I picked it up and brought it to my eye: a bullet ball casing. More were scattered about. By Lat, had a battle happened here?

Eshe tugged my shirt.

"What is it?" I asked.

"I see something." He pointed it out.

A thin rope dropped from the sky in the distance. As we got closer, the fireflies perched upon it. I could scarcely believe it: a ladder rope was hanging in the air, leading up to…something so high, we couldn't see it.

"Gate to hell…" Eshe snickered. "Ladder to heaven."

"We can only hope."

An icy gust blew by my ears. Cold crept through my arms. I wanted out, and that ladder seemed the way. The fireflies climbed it, as if goading us.

Eshe rubbed his hands together. "Thanks for sweating all over my hands."

"Certain it wasn't you sweating all over mine?"

He squeezed the rope ladder. Pulled it. "You find this quality of rope on hastily built reed boats."

"So…you first?" I grinned. I wasn't the best climber; perhaps him going first would help my confidence.

"Right, me first." He stepped on the first rung, then heaved up. The rope barely shifted with his weight, which was a relief. He climbed several rungs, then gestured to me.

I took a resolute breath and followed him. Seemed I was stronger than I thought and could balance my bodyweight. But how high did this thing go?

What the hell were we even doing? Surely coming here was one of the worst ideas I'd ever conceived and among the poorest choices Eshe had made. But those weren't comforts waiting for us in the world above. Besides, when had my prayers led me wrong?

"Oh, some advice," Eshe said, pausing momentarily. "Don't look—"

"I know!" I used to climb hills with my mother as a child, so wasn't entirely unused to heights. "Don't stop!"

As we climbed, the fireflies surged upward and sat on…the sky? No, a roof. They formed a circle, as if blazing a way through. Though I yearned to hurry into the sky, I had to be careful; falling now would certainly be the end.

Chirp-peep. I turned to my left; wings fluttered past my right ear. *Peep-chirp*. Black feathers.

A little girl giggled below.

I swallowed. "Eshe…you hear that?"

"You too? Did someone's daughter get lost in here?"

More flutters. I swung my head left and right: nothing but shadows. Shadows in the form of birds, swirling around us.

"Hurry up!" I said, my palms sweaty. So, it was me.

"I'm going as fast as I safely can!"

Finally, Eshe reached the circle of sky where the fireflies blazed; I pulled just below his feet.

"Push it up," I said. "It might be a hatch or something."

He pushed against it. A blinding light scathed my eyes; I shut them, but the light poured through my eyelids.

Eshe continued climbing. I followed, blinking at the intense, milky light.

No more rope to grab. Eshe stood next to me, on solid ground. I pushed off the wood floor and onto my feet.

Strangely, that brightly burning light was gone. Instead, the fireflies throbbing around provided sight. Piles of books sat around the room. Eshe grabbed one while I looked for a door.

"What the hell?" He showed me the spine.

Angelsong was written in Paramic. "The Ethosian holy book?"

Eshe nodded. "Didn't see too many copies of these in the Tower. If it's in Paramic, it must mean we're still in Alanya."

"Do you think we're still in Qandbajar?"

"No way to know aside from exploring wherever we are."

We stepped toward a door on the far side. A faint melody from above graced my ears: hymning. Somber and low, like the hymns of the stars I touched.

"Ethosian hymns," Eshe said. "In Paramic, too."

We opened the door and entered a stone corridor. The fireflies whizzed by toward a staircase. I grabbed Eshe's hand and stayed behind him as we followed the fireflies up the stairs. The hymns loudened with each step.

And the angel said,

We are only a trial, so do not disbelieve.

How terrible the price for which you sold your soul.

Beneath the light of Aurora — the dead star of morning.

At the top of the staircase, the hymning stopped. We entered a vast room with rows of ornate wooden benches. They faced a dais, upon which stood a statue of the Archangel; I'd seen Ethosians buying small likenesses in the Grand Bazaar. Strangest of all...the pews lay empty...no choir.

Except, a man sat in the foremost pew. *Father Chisti,* wearing a flowery cloak, his thin hair almost covering his ice-dead eyes.

"You really were brave," he said as we stood before him, "to follow me here."

"Where is here?" Eshe asked.

He gestured to the Archangel statue. "Never been to Basil's Cathedral?" He shook his head and clacked his tongue in disappointment. "Eshe, my dear, it's just down the street from your house. You ought to see new places, try new things — why else be alive?"

I'd walked by Basil's Cathedral hundreds of times — a castle with four spires and a dome, at the edge of the Ethosian Quarter, just outside the Glass District.

"Why did you ask Zedra to do those awful things?" I clenched my fist. "Just what kind of game are you playing?"

"*Game*...oh, this is no game. At least, not for us. It's not a game when *you're* the die being thrown, the card being drawn, the pawn being sacrificed." He sighed, melancholic. "I wish this were a bit of fun. But the truth is, like you, we Twelve are pushed and pulled from above."

"Twelve...Angels?" Eshe said. "Then...which of the Twelve are you?"

The man crossed his legs, then put his hands behind his back. "I gave man a choice, knowing full well his nature. Bloodwriting, star-writing, philosophy, science. Ultimately, it's all dangerous, it's all knowledge," he spread out his hands, cards between his fingers, "and I am the teacher."

"Now I see." Eshe's eyes lit up as he gaped. "If you're one of the Twelve, as you say, then you would be Marot!"

Twelve? Marot? "You still haven't told me why!" I stomped my foot.

He threw the cards — they never landed, vanishing into the air. "Servants aren't told *why*." His laugh echoed through the empty hall, like the plucking of broken strings.

"We're not your servants!" I said.

Marot shook his head. "Such folly. I'm not talking about you, I'm talking about myself. *They* don't tell me why. Truth is, I've never asked. I find it rather invigorating. When you've lived long as I have, in a formless void, it's nice to be put to use — I'm sure you can relate, eh, Cyra?"

"Was it *invigorating*, destroying my life?" I wanted to plunge a dagger through his heart...if he had one. "And Zedra? Why her? Why?"

"'Why why why'," he imitated me and made a crying motion with his hand. "A better question would be — *what*." More laughter. "Just what comes next, hmm? Step outside those doors, and perhaps you'll learn what a girl-sized portion of angel's blood can do."

None of it made sense. He had to have a better reason.

"If you're Marot," Eshe said, "why are you with the Philosophers?"

He sighed in disgust and shook his head. "You two need to learn how to listen. The Philosophers seek knowledge, and so I give it. I am the reason you can make fire, carve a wheel, blow glass. I taught you how to forge a sword, and what to do with it. I made you thirst for gold, though it be mere rocks. How to write with blood and on the stars — I tempted you with these gifts, and you succumbed. In the end, knowledge is one, whether of the arcane or the obvious." He sniggered. "What's the matter, dear Eshe? Did you think mankind figured all that out on their own? Without our guidance, you're naught but hairless apes."

"Then that would imply purpose," I said. "That doesn't sound like something you'd do blindly."

His smile made me shudder, as if worms crawled across my shoulders. "On the contrary, chaos is blind. Though, I didn't have to do much to set you against each other. You were already predisposed to hatred." He pointed to my eyepatch and laughed. "Do you think it was *only* Zedra I shepherded?" He clacked his tongue in disappointment again. "Who do you think brought you to the Palace of Bones?"

He stood. His limbs made a nasty cracking sound and…they stretched. Eshe and I backed away, mouths stuck in horror, as the man's neck bent and lengthened along with his arms and legs, which now had too many snapping joints to be human.

"Remember me now?" His voice came from everywhere.

"You were there," I said, terror in my throat as I recalled the desert snowstorm that led me to the monstrous man who'd warned us of the Palace of Bones. I couldn't help but say, "Why?"

"I told you, that's the wrong question. *What* will she do, and *what* will you do? Hmm?"

"Who is Nora!?" Eshe shouted as the thing's limbs mangled like tree branches. "What are those bloodrunes?"

"Nora-Nora-Nora." More dark and discordant laughs. "A lovely name, like a stroll for the tongue."

The thing kept growing until its eyes dangled from its sockets and its head cracked the ceiling. Limbs stretched like roots across the pews and stone floor.

Eshe grabbed my hand. We ran by the pews toward the double doors, which had sunshine leaking through.

Outside, a hot day strained my eyes. The empty thoroughfare, just beside the Glass District, almost seemed peaceful…if it weren't for the arrows, bullet ball casings, and char littering the ground.

We crept through the streets, hurrying to put distance between us and the monster in the cathedral, yet wary of gholam, too.

Pashang had charged the Glass District after we learned Zedra was hiding there. But did he win, or did the gholam hold?

"My house is five minutes," Eshe said. "You think we should go? Or try to get back to the Jotrid line?"

"I want to talk to Zedra," I said. "How much of a stupid bitch is she? How could she fall for that monster's trick?"

"Tricked or not, you're still on opposing sides, and she'd sooner kill you. Anyway, no-man's-land is not the place to digest what happened. Let's see if we can make it to my place."

Eshe unsheathed a dagger and showed me the flat of the blade.

"You need my blood, don't you?"

"Might have to freeze a gholam or two, to get us to safety."

I sighed, held out my finger, and closed my eyes. With a prick of the blade's point, my blood dripped. Eshe let it land on the flat of the blade; he drew a bloodrune on it, mumbled some words, and made it glow.

"I've been wondering," I said, "what is it you say, each time you draw one of those?"

"It's an incantation to the Morning Star."

"So, then, it's like…a prayer?"

He shook his head. "Absolutely not. It's an incantation. Praying to a star, no matter its power, would be worse than heresy. Aschere had prayed to something other than Lat."

If only he knew what I prayed to. "Let's go." I reached for his hand.

We crept, staying low, down the thoroughfare and toward the colorful arches that decorated the entrance to the Glass District.

We hid in a nearby alleyway and observed: a column of gholam guarded the archway, which ascended upward, and they'd placed sandbags across it. Bullet-ridden Jotrids and horses lay across the inclined street; a breeze brought their nauseating death-stench to us.

Obviously, the gholam had held. If the Jotrids couldn't take the Glass District, even with those cannons firing at it from above, what hope did they have to take the Sand Palace?

"Even with my bloodrunes, we won't get through that," Eshe said. "However, there is a back way in."

"Won't they be guarding the back way, too?"

"Likely. If Kyars is keeping his harem and heir there, the place would be a fortress." Eshe stroked his beard. "The Jotrids must've had a terrible time charging up that hill. This is foolish. We should go back to camp."

I rubbed my arms, just wishing to be out of danger. And yet... "Zedra is somewhere there. If we go back, we'll just be sitting around until this war plays out. Until Pashang or Kyars emerge victorious...or until Zedra," or I, "does something truly desperate."

"What makes you think she'll understand? If Pashang wins, first thing he'll do is kill every Seluqal he can get his hands on, her son included. She'll do whatever she must to save him, like any mother." Eshe sighed and shook his head. "'A girl-sized portion of angel's blood,' Marot mentioned. One of the rarest flavors. I wonder what he meant by that?"

A thought struck: how cruelly he'd manipulated us! "Every time I do something desperate with my power, in response, Zedra does something desperate, too. I summoned those locusts, bringing the Jotrids into the city, which made Zedra soulshift into Mansur to try to save her son." The fog in my understanding began to clear. "And I only summoned them to save you...after *he* kidnapped you! And now...Lat knows what Zedra is going to do...or has already done... to save herself and her son...after he goaded us into attacking the Glass District!" We needed to stop her. If we turned back... "Eshe, we have to get to her, lest she do something calamitous!"

Whizzing thuds and popping sounds, in rapid succession, followed by the *shh* of pouring sand brought our attention back to the gholam and their sandbag wall. Arrows had just landed and now jutted from the sandbags, leaking sand onto the street. The gholam higher up the hill were crouched, golden shields raised.

"The Jotrids are still attacking?" I said. That meant they were somewhere behind us.

"Mellow arrow rain. Pashang's keeping the gholam awake, seeing if they can pick off a stray one here or there. I'm surprised Kyars hasn't struck with full force."

"What are you, a strategist, now?"

"I've read a few books on strategy." He puffed his cheeks. "I think I'd make a great general. Calm, cool head. Predisposed to brilliance." He pointed at me. "You, though, would be beyond awful."

I didn't care enough to disagree — though I had a few ideas I'd like to try.

The ground rumbled. Riders. We crept deeper into the shadowed alleyway as an uncountable amount of horses galloped by, each mounted by a gleaming gholam. They torrented up the inclined street, around the sandbag wall, and into the Glass District. After them came carriages — twenty or more — with lion-patterned housings and thick wheels.

"Carriages," I said. "You think he's sending his harem back to the palace?"

"With the Tower still standing, I doubt he considers it safe. And do you really need an escort that large, and wheels that big, for the quick journey to the palace?"

I gasped. "Then the harem is leaving the city! Unless we go now, we'll lose our chance."

"There's no way we're getting into the Glass District. We ought to go back to camp."

No, I wouldn't go back. "Eshe...what if you take my hand again, and we—"

"Are you mad? Didn't you hear what Marot said? He gave you this power to set you and her against each other. There's no telling what will happen if you write on the stars. Like you said, every time you do something desperate, she does something, too. You'd be playing his game!"

He was right. And so, we did the only thing we could: we crept toward the Jotrid line. The whole time, I only hoped I could find a way to reach Zedra, to convince her — and myself — that perhaps there was some way to end this war.

NOW IN FRIENDLY TERRITORY, bow-wielding Jotrids crouched atop the house roofs that lined the thoroughfare. My idea, it seemed, had been useful in keeping our soldiers alive. Perhaps Eshe was wrong; perhaps I would make a good general, after all. Meanwhile, the common folk sat by their windows, dismal-eyed because we'd turned their houses into our shields. Well, winning did have its costs.

Despite the dangers of being outside, we passed by men and women going about the city, mostly carrying water pitchers and sacks of fire-roasted locusts. People had to survive, war and all. The Jotrids had set up check points to prevent spies from getting behind our lines, and we passed through several on our way to Pashang.

To our astonishment, it seemed Pashang had taken the Grand Bazaar and was now hauling cannons up the pyramid, too. Eshe and I climbed the inner steps to the top, which was normally an open-air office for the viziers who ran the place.

Our khagan sat amid silk carpets and piled pillows, along with his brother. A day or two of not trimming made both their brown beards unruly, which suited them. Elnur's head was in Tekish's lap; he stroked her hair as she waved at us. Good to see she'd recovered.

A hookah pipe sat in the center, as if waiting. A breeze blew through from every direction. Qandbajar itself sprawled out before us.

I went for a pink, powdered jelly delight sitting on a brass plate.

"How the hell did you take the pyramid?" I asked while chewing the goopy, pomegranate-flavored treat.

Pashang's wide smile and nod reminded me of when he'd once downed an eagle with a slingshot. His teeth were still these big, discolored, blocky things. "When I charged the Glass District, they moved most of their forces from the Grand Bazaar and the riverside to defend it. I distracted them with arrow rain and sacrificed some brave men and women in the assault, so they'd believe we'd committed to the attack. Meanwhile, we attacked where they'd withdrawn from and lined the houses with our soldiers — like you suggested — so they'd be reticent to counter. A simple feint, but well achieved."

How self-satisfied he sounded. I supposed he'd earned it. Doubtless, Pashang was a good general.

"Well done." I ought to have been happier, but given what we'd learned from Marot, a hollowness ached within. "Didn't realize you were so clever."

"That's how I prefer it." Pashang puffed the hookah pipe, bubbling the water at its base. "Low expectations, overwhelming results."

Eshe sat next to him and gestured for the pipe. After taking a hit, he flipped open *Melody of Nora* to the page with the bloodrune of four stars and a sideways eye, careful not to touch it.

He mumbled his incantation, and the bloodrune shimmered. "Oh Lat...I activated it. How peculiar. Normally, you can't activate a rune you didn't write. Unless whoever made this wanted someone else to do so."

Tekish peered over. "The hell is it?"

"I think...the memories of someone named Nora," Eshe said. He held the book out. "Do we have any volunteers?"

Tekish shuddered. Elnur winced. I glared at the page with disdain.

Pashang, though, grinned, "You're telling me that if I touch that bloodstain, I'll experience the memories of some girl named Nora?"

Eshe shook his head, slowly, and let out an uneasy chuckle. "I'm not telling you anything. It could be the memories of a fish that got swallowed by a whale and spent the next four days being digested, along with all its friends from the local reef." He shuddered as if speaking from experience.

Eshe had described how Marot tortured him with a bloodrune. And Eshe had himself tortured Ruhi with one. Remembering that chilled my curiosity.

"Close the book," I said. "This is a bad idea. Given where we found it, I don't think we need to know. Marot left it there for a reason, didn't he? It can't be a good one."

Eshe's eyes widened as he fingered the parchment around the bloodrune. "You're right...and yet, when I gaze at the blood, it whispers to me..."

"We have other things to do," I said, turning to Pashang. "We saw big carriages riding into the Glass District. Since you've taken the riverside, they can't travel by ship, so—"

I stopped because Pashang wasn't listening. He was staring at the bloodrune, along with Eshe. He put his hand over Eshe's and pulled it off the page. "Not you," he said. "Me. I need this. I've been craving...more...since the Red..."

"No!" I got on my knees, reached over, and grabbed at the book. Eshe whisked it away. "It's too dangerous. You could lose yourself. Give it to me!" I shouted. "What's wrong with you two?"

Pashang and Eshe eyed each other. Both wanted it, but while fear filled Eshe's eyes, Pashang's were wide and expectant.

"I'm doing it!" Pashang stabbed his finger on the rune, then collapsed on the pile of pillows.

30

NORA

I awoke with lava churning in my stomach. I expected queasiness but retched my insides out that morning, and it wasn't even me getting married.

Meanwhile, my sisters were awake and practicing. Grandpa made music with his tambourine, clicking tongue, and throaty song. They were by a stream, of course, where the air stayed cool during a strangely hot flowering season.

Once I'd washed my mouth with water and lye, I joined them. Only to watch. While Disha spun slowly on flat feet as a girl ought to, Diyne jumped on tiptoes, rotating around her, playing the boy.

Grandpa sat on a stool so small, he might as well have been squatting. I came to his side and clapped my sisters on, finally feeling some joy.

The music, the morning breeze, the seeping dawn — a perfect, deep, ever-brightening memory.

"Nora, one day you'll be a gray, old bag like me," Grandpa said, "and days like this will be a mug of mare's milk, fresh from the fire pot."

460

I faked a smile. Said nothing. I liked to hear Grandpa talk, and my smile said *continue*.

"Three things are unlike all else." He held up three coarse fingers. "Hunting on the first day of the thaw. A summer rain. And the joy of watching someone you love find someone to love."

I sweetened my smile. While I'd never hunted, those summer rains felt good. I wouldn't say I loved my cousin Shireen, but I probably loved Hamet and felt no joy in watching them *find each other*. Just the opposite.

Afterward, I grabbed the book I'd stumbled upon yesterday and went into the forest to pick flowers. Perhaps I could find the ones drawn so beautifully in the book. I couldn't read their names — couldn't read at all — but I'd never seen such beautiful pictures before.

I could, begrudgingly, make a flower bouquet for Hamet and Shireen. That was what I told Grandpa I was doing. Last night, I even dreamt I was skipping in a flower bed, and the forest had so many.

I wouldn't go in too deep. Leopards, boars, bears, snakes — they stayed away from the tree lines near our tribe, but if you strayed into their territory…well, I didn't feel like dying today.

The flowers grew upstream, where I once saw the fattest rat ever — but unlike most rats, it didn't have ears, and its face was flat. Grandpa said it was something called a *lemming* and that he'd seen them up north, where it was colder and more forested. It seemed our summers were becoming so hot and winters so cold that strange creatures were making a home here. I didn't mind if they were all cute like the lemming.

I hoped to see one today. I went into the thick, where the ground turned muddy, and the sun painted leafy shadows on it. A stream cooled the air. The sweet sound of its gush mixed with the chirping of birds fluttering between trees.

There! A flower I'd seen in the book! By Lat, it was purple! I bent down, muddying my dress, and caressed its edge. Near the bud, the purple was a bruised sky, but approaching the edge, it lightened like cold lips.

I fingered the bud: soft and wilting. Hard leaves decorated the stem, which reached my head while I crouched. I opened the book and flipped through to the page with this flower. Whoever the creator was, he'd drawn it perfectly! He'd also written much beneath the picture, in these block letters that definitely weren't Vograsian — if only I could read it. I wanted to know this flower's name, where it came from, what you could use it for — everything!

Footsteps on mud sounded behind me. I spun around, book in front like a shield. A man stood in the distance beneath a twisted tree, his hands in his pockets. He wasn't wearing a turban, nor any hat, and his thick cloak was tulip-patterned and foreign.

"I don't mean to startle you, girl." He pointed to the book. "I see you found my work-in-progress."

Now I hugged the book, not wanting to give it back. Yesterday, I'd found it in a pile of leaves nearby. I knew it wasn't mine but loved it so much, I didn't care to ask for its true owner.

"Can I keep it?" I asked, swallowing a mound of guilt. "Please?"

He wore his hair so strangely: combed forward, strands over his eyes, as if he wanted to hide them. I could still see his pupils, gray and bleak. But when he smiled, I sensed kindness. "I toiled to create that. Tell me, do you like it so much?"

I nodded as fast as I could. "I love it!" I could scarcely contain my excitement. "Are you the one who drew these pictures? They're incredible!"

A strange man in the forest ought to have filled me with fear, but surely whoever made this book couldn't be bad.

"I'm a better writer than artist," he said, "but I'm thrilled you enjoyed the pictures."

"I've never seen pictures like it. It's as if I'm looking at the flower itself." I sighed with sadness. If he'd worked so hard, how selfish for an unlettered girl to keep it. It probably had instructions for those with knowledge, like a healer or alchemist. "I'm sorry, here you go." I held it out for him to take.

He shook his head. "Few things are better than being appreciated, and I can always make another. You keep it."

"No…that would be so selfish. I don't deserve something like this."

He came closer until he was standing an arm span away. Only then did I notice his towering height. He smelled of leaves, too, as if he'd been living in the forest. "You sell yourself short, Nora."

"I'm sorry, but how do you know my name? Do you know Grandpa?" I couldn't look him in those bleak eyes, so kept my gaze on his shoulder.

From behind his back, he took out another book. As he flipped through it, I noticed bloodstains on each page. My heart thudded into my throat; had I been wrong about him? Was he dangerous?

He stopped at a page: upon it was a series of pictures, all drawn in blood. One picture looked like a tower. He mumbled in a language I'd never heard, and those pictures glowed for a second.

He held it out for me. "I want you to appreciate that book to its fullest. Touch this."

Touch the blood? It seemed so wrong. And I swear…I heard whispers coming from the trees.

"What will happen?"

"Only good things." His smile seemed genuine despite his lifeless eyes. I'd only seen such eyes on the blind. "I promise it won't hurt. It will, instead, make you worthy of my gift."

"Worthy? How?"

"Trust me. I won't lead you astray."

Well, I wanted to be *worthy* of the book, whatever that meant. But trust some stranger in the forest?

I placed the flower book on the ground. "Please take it. I must be going."

He reached behind his back, then took out a red flower. From where had he plucked it?

"It's a red tulip." He sniffed it, eyes closed, breathing deep. "One of my favorites."

"Are you...a sorcerer?" How strange for a sorcerer to be wandering the forest, writing about flowers. I could only hope he wasn't a wicked one.

He held out the tulip in one hand and the open book, bloodstain forward, in the other. "I'm a teacher. And I want to teach you, Nora. Teach you something that will unveil a whole new world. But you have to want to learn. You can't be like the others, willfully plugging their ears, blinding their eyes, refusing to wake from their stupors."

I did want to learn. I wanted to learn everything. And I did think, in his own odd way, this man truly was kind and good. But those were bloodstains. I suppose, if he were an *evil* sorcerer, he could have killed or hurt me in some simpler way.

I took a breath, pushed my trembling finger up and onto the page, then slid it onto the blood.

Nothing happened.

The man pulled the blood book away and snapped it shut. "It's done." He smiled wide, showing a perfect set of smoke-gray teeth. "I'm so happy for you. You've taken the first step on an ever-ascending path."

He turned and walked away, his steps crunching on the leaves.

"Wait...I don't understand."

He held up a hand. "Open the book."

I flipped to the page with the purple flower. *Althea, an herb native to Ruthenia, the region north of the Siyah Sea, and the Vogras Mountains. Found on moist soil on riverbanks, salt marshes, and sand. Can grow up to six feet tall, averages three feet. Though many cultures use it for healing various maladies, experiments have yielded no healing properties aside from a palliative for sore throats.*

I didn't know what every word meant, like *palliative*, but by Lat: I could read!

I looked up from the pages; the man was gone. I wanted to

thank him, so rushed forward, darting my head in every direction, hoping to spot him. But he was nowhere.

INSTEAD OF PICKING FLOWERS, instead of trying on dresses for Hamet and Shireen's wedding, I spent the morning on my cot in our yurt, reading the words in the book. Grandpa and Disha and Diyne kept trying to pull my attention away, but I blocked them out, as if my book were a wall.

The flowers were so mesmerizing, and they grew in so many places I'd never heard of! As I read on, I became less interested in the flowers and more interested in the snippets about where these flowers grew.

Ruthenia, for example — so many wondrous flowers grew there! The book claimed Ruthenia held most of the world's forests, animals, and flowers — and yet it was mostly ice. And then there was this place called *Himyar*, where flowers wouldn't grow because of something called the *blood plague*, which had started as a puddle in the desert and spread until it poisoned the land.

But I could only ignore my family for so long. Eventually, I had to get ready for the wedding, so I pulled out whatever dress sparkled most from my clothes chest. A rather pointy hat with fluffy plumes sticking out the top came with the dress, which was thick and a shade lighter than gold. I tied the sash around my waist, tight as I could since I was thinner than when the seamstress had measured me for it last year, for the wedding of a cousin I liked much more than Shireen.

Staring at myself in the mirror, I resembled a yellow tulip. Just wonderful! According to the book, the Sargosans, who lived far to the west and sailed across the seas on ships called *galleons*, believed yellow tulips brought cheer. I'd never seen the ocean but now knew so much about so many things, all from reading about flowers!

The wedding would take place beneath the sky and within several palatial yurts on the plain. It started with the groom,

Hamet, leading a hundred men on horseback while the women ululated and banged drums. They'd decorated the horses with colorful, tapestried saddles, which I heard they'd bought from Abistran traders. Still, watching them ride around bored me, and I wished I were in bed, reading my book. Even the sight of Hamet high on his mare did nothing for me.

Strangely, it wasn't Hamet at the front. Another man rode at his side, a few feet ahead. I'd been to dozens of weddings and never seen someone ride ahead of the groom. That defeated the whole purpose, didn't it? I nudged Grandpa and asked, "Who is he?"

Grandfather smiled and said, "That's our tribe's new protector. That's Khagan Pashang."

"No way. *That's* Pashang?" I'd heard he was a great warrior who fought heroically against our enemy, the Sylgiz tribe. He'd even gained the favor of the Alanyans, and so held more power than any khagan on either side of the Vogras Mountains. But he was skinnier and less fearsome than I imagined. A neat brown beard covered his cheeks and chin, and his bright brown eyes seemed so mellow.

Grandpa nudged me back. "Step forward out of the crowd a bit. The man isn't married. He might notice you."

Other girls stepped out as he rode by, their gazes low and arms clasped at their navels. When the riders came near, they slowed, and the crowd threw flowers at them. Pashang and Hamet trotted toward us, so I stepped out.

Khagan Pashang stopped in front of me. I looked into his eyes, and he looked into mine. Perhaps I should've taken better care getting ready today. I smiled. He smiled back and trotted on.

"So…" I said to Grandpa after they'd gone far ahead. "Are we of their tribe, now?"

"Jotrids, you mean? In a way, I suppose. It's the only way we'll keep our land with those heretic Sylgiz encroaching closer each year."

We hated none more than the Sylgiz. They'd seized so much of our grazing and hunting land that we were forced to hug the mountains and forests instead of spreading across the plain. Although, I adored the mountains and forest, and their animals, like the red-horned goats that climbed the mountainside.

Now it was time for my favorite event: the unveiling! I finally put the book out of mind while grabbing at Shireen's veils and twirling. We pulled off twenty layers of veils. Twenty! Each was a shade of blue, starting with a dark sky and ending with a clear river. I was worried Shireen would suffocate under there, but the whole time she was giggling and laughing, and so were we.

The dance began, and my sisters did so well! The men stayed light on their toes, prancing around the women, even sword fighting with each other as they spun. The women swayed, slow and rhythmic. Someone played a flute from Kashan, which I'd never heard before, but by Lat, it was the perfect happy melody!

I regretted not dancing, regretted my bitter thoughts of Shireen marrying Hamet keeping me from something I loved. I'd never stop regretting it.

Finally, an Alanyan sheikh with a mesmerizing red beard administered the marriage. Hamet and Shireen signed some parchment — though neither could read nor write — while I swallowed the bitter lumps in my throat. While walking home, I realized the world was vast, and Hamet, despite his perfect nose, was just another boring boy from the tribe.

SLEEP DIDN'T COME that night as I lied between my two snoring sisters. Grandpa, on his cot across the yurt, was snoring too. But that wasn't what kept me awake. I was already dreaming about where those flowers grew.

Close by, in Alanya, red tulips jutted from the desert sand, said to be nourished by the blood of a war that raged five hundred years ago. In the jungles of Kashan, another red flower called *santan*, which resembled a pinwheel, could be eaten whole, its sugary juices gushing down your throat as you chewed. And in a land called Talitos, said to be across the sea mists, black birds called drongos would be eaten whole by *sundews*, crazy flowers that resembled, of all things, a snake with hundreds of slimy tentacles on its skin!

And this was only what I'd read in one morning — the book had much more to show me! I couldn't wait till sunrise so I could read. But the sun would never rise. Not for me, not for any of us.

It started with screams and the stench of burning. I pushed my sisters awake, then ran across the room and pushed Grandpa awake, too. He grabbed his sword, dagger, and matchlock, and we all rushed outside the yurt.

Fire, everywhere! Even the forest, with all its flowers, was just a massive flame. I'd forgotten the book, but when I tried to run in to grab it, Grandpa held my wrist.

"We have to get out of here!" he said. "Nora, Diyne, Disha, hold hands now and follow me!"

I took his hand, then Diyne took mine, and Disha took hers. The thundering of horses sounded from the burning yurts behind us. It was hard to see amid all the fire and shadow. Steel hummed against steel in the distance, creating a drumbeat for the gunshots and blasts.

Grandpa pulled us toward what had once been a river that descended from the Vogras but had since snaked a different way, leaving only a dry, crack-filled bed. It was near the ascent to the mountain, so perhaps we could hide there.

"Who is doing this!?" I asked, my voice a tremble.

"Khagan Pashang will help us. He'll help us. We just have to stay safe until the Jotrids arrive. Stay safe in the mountain."

We trudged through muddy grass at the edge of the dried riverbed, away from the burning tree line, toward the mountain's ascent. The red-horned goats usually grazed here, but at this dark hour, they must've been asleep. The hanging crescent and the distant flames provided enough light for us to avoid the boulders dotting the landscape, though I wished we'd brought a torch.

But why was this happening? Why were we running? Why was a fire burning the forest, burning the flowers? Not even a day after we'd been so joyous. What had we done to deserve this?

We didn't notice the three horsemen shrouded on the dark path to the mountain. They were sitting there, leaning forward on their mares, watching us. Those outfits…bear fur covered their shoulder pads and plumed hats. The hard leather across their chests was brown, too. Sylgiz warriors.

I tugged at Grandpa once I saw them, and squinting, he finally did too. I squeezed my sister's hand, and we turned around.

"Wait," one of the riders said in Vograsian, though he pronounced the word all wrong. "Stop, or I'll run you four down."

Grandpa stopped, so we all did. "Please let us go," he said. "These are my children."

He trembled. I'd never seen him so afraid; dread poured into my veins. I hugged my sisters to settle their tears, but I, too, wanted to bawl. Instead, I muttered the prayer for safety from the Recitals of Chisti.

O' Lat, protect us from what is in front, behind, to the right, left, and above.

The horsemen cantered toward us. The first one held out a lantern. "Ooh, forget about spices." I could scarcely see his face, but he sounded so excited. "How much will these three fetch, you think?" Then he muttered something in another language, probably Sylgiz.

The second horseman said, "Cihan told us to kill everyone here. Well, so—" He pulled out his matchlock, snapped the trigger. *Bang.* I ducked and covered my ears as Grandpa fell. He clutched the erupting burn on his belly and wailed.

"No!" Diyne screamed. I could only look on, frozen as a dead winter tree. Disha cried, "help!" with all the air she could suck in.

"I say we fuck them," the third one said. "I'll take the shapely one since I know you ball-lickers like them slightly underripe."

"No-no-no. My wife has been begging for new Alanyan carpets

for the walls. The little one's at least five horse loads worth." He pointed at Diyne, the youngest.

"Just let the poor things die," the second horseman said. "We don't have time. Cihan said this was to be a quick reprisal. In and out."

"I can *in and out* all three at speed, too!" the third said with a chuckle.

I realized, only then, that they were speaking Sylgiz, which always sounded so choppy and strange. How, then, could I understand them? Thinking on it, I didn't know what language that book was written in but could understand it, too. Frozen from fear, as I was, I could scarcely make sense of anything.

"Listen," the first said, "here's the right of it. There are three of us, three opinions on what to do, and three of them. We'll kill one, fuck one, and sell one. Fair?"

I wanted to grab my sisters and run, but ice wouldn't cease pouring into my veins, freezing my will. I wanted to help Grandpa but couldn't move my hands. I wanted to kill these awful men but didn't know the first thing about killing.

Disha was still screaming "help!" while Diyne held Grandpa's head as blood bubbled from his mouth.

"So we sell the youngest since she'll fetch the highest price."

"Let's fuck the oldest, then. Her breasts are like the Vogras. She'll be dry like the river when I'm done with her."

"So, bye-bye to the middle girl?" The man snapped his trigger. *Bang.* Disha's screaming ended, and her body thumped onto the grass. "Ah, by Lat, that scratched an itch."

"Curse the fucking saints! May I never, ever get on your bad side." The horseman cleared his throat. "So, to be clear, after we fuck the older one, do we just…leave her here?"

"Why not? One witness to carry this sordid tale, so hearts tremble when they hear the name *Sylgiz*. Besides, could be one of us puts a child in her, and she can rebirth her tribe!" They got off their horses, laughing the while. One held the lantern over my head. Finally, I saw their faces.

"You lucked out, girl," the third rider said as he pulled his pants down. "You'll have a gentleman like me taking your flower, not one of these two degenerates."

The three looked up, like they saw someone behind me. Fear filled their eyes, and then those eyes flew in the air, along with their heads, atop fountains of blood erupting from their necks.

The heads landed around my feet. I didn't scream. I was stuck like prey. Even the horses fled, whinnying the while.

Diyne put her trembling arms around me. I turned my head and looked at the man walking toward us.

It was him, the stranger from the forest. He dallied over, as if enjoying a moonlight stroll. Then he bent down next to me, a book in hand.

"They burned it, along with your yurt," he said. "The flower book. Such a shame."

What did that matter? Grandpa...he'd stilled some time ago, and I hadn't even noticed. Disha had stilled immediately, a burnt, bloody hole where her cheek should've been.

"In the end, Khagan Pashang couldn't protect you. *Tsk-tsk.* He's probably the reason your tribe is dead. You bet on the wrong horse, I'm afraid. Khagan Cihan is far cleverer. The battle was a good one, though the victor was obvious from the start."

There'd been a battle the night of the wedding?

The strange man took off his tulip cloak and put it around Diyne. I hadn't noticed the night's chill with how frozen I was within. I could feel my tears now, gushing hot down my cheeks.

"I never told you my name," he said. "Not as pretty as yours, I'm afraid. I'm Marot."

Marot flipped through the book. He settled on a page which, like the others, had a blood painting. It resembled a sun rising above a vast lake...the ocean, perhaps.

The first time I'd touched that book, it had taught me letters and languages. What would it do for me, now? I raised my hand, but fear kept me from touching the page.

"Nora-Nora-Nora — it's like a pleasant stroll for the tongue," he said. "There was a woman who lived here, long ago, before the river dried. She watched her family die, too. But unlike you," he brushed my hair, "she was rather powerful. A sorceress to fear, and a student of mine, though she never knew I was her teacher."

Why was he telling me this?

"Nora," the man continued, "this won't bring you happiness. It'll only add to your pain. But by it, you'll become something to fear. You'll become *her*. And then, you can avenge your tribe. These sins," he gestured at the pillars of fire behind us, "should be repaid."

Oncoming riders shook the earth. More Sylgiz. My sister's trembles turned unbearable, and my tears burned on my chin. Was this the end of my hopes, my dreams? My tribe, my family?

"I wanted to see where the flowers grow," I told Marot as I hugged my sister. "You wrote about such wonderful places. Have you really been to them all?" I don't know why I asked him such a thing in this horrific moment, but I'd wanted to know since reading the flower book this morning.

He chuckled. "Dear girl, this isn't the time. But if you must know — yes, I've been to all those places. And one day, you both might travel to some, too." He sighed, sharp and sad. "But not if you die today."

"You know, I was so stuck inside the book that I never read its cover."

"Cover?" Marot smiled with warmth. "Well, what do you think it ought to be called?"

I blurted out, "How about *Melody of Flowers*...because it was like a flute, whistling in my heart."

Marot nodded with a chuckle. "*Melody of Flowers*...I rather like that. So it shall be." He snapped his fingers.

I kissed my wailing sister. Marot was right. I had to protect her.

If I gained whatever power he was promising, perhaps we could go together to see the flowers, wherever they grew, all across the world. What other path did I have?

"Did you read about the red tulips?" Marot asked as the riders came into sight, their torches raised and fierce. "I've seen them growing in the gardens of the Shah of Alanya. Would you like me to take you there?" He held the book in front of his face.

I nodded and swallowed tears. As the riders surrounded us, I pushed my trembling hand forward and down onto the page.

31

ZEDRA

BEHIND THE *CLOP-CLOP* OF CHARGING HORSES AND THE *POP-POP* OF guns, the battle sounded like a long sigh. Kissing steel, arrow rain, bomb blasts — I heard it all. I cradled my son the whole time, nuzzling his forehead as he cried. Thank Lat none of the cannon shots hit our house — Pashang didn't have the exact location, after all — though they'd exploded stone and glass around us. Once the battle had passed, I went downstairs, carefully stepping over jagged shards to where Kato waited.

If the battle was a long sigh, then it was Kato's. Sweat, soot, and blood decorated his golden armor.

"Sultana," he said, voice cracking from tiredness, "Shah Kyars has ordered you and the heir to depart the city. I'm to guard you on the journey." Seemed he was a glorified sentry, after all.

I no longer had the spirit to resist Kyars' decisions, so I nodded and asked, my throat sorer than it'd ever been, "Where will we go?"

I was tired of running, but what other course was there? Nowhere in this city was safe, and I was, in appearance, just a girl with an infant son.

"We'll go west to Dorud — Grand Vizier Barkam and Prince Faris are there. It's the safest place, sultana."

How formal. Half a dozen other gholam stood in the room — my escort — and they were Kyars' own, so I understood why he watched his words.

Kato leaned against the wall and slid until he was sitting. "You and your Crucian handmaid," he huffed, "should be ready to leave in fifteen minutes."

"She won't be coming."

"Why is that?"

I swallowed a lemon. "She's not here. I sent her home."

Kato raised an eyebrow. "You sent her…to Crucis?"

I hadn't been carefully crafting my lies. I nodded. "I asked a rider to take her out of the city, to the nearest port with a ship bound for Crucis."

Kato's bewildered face showed he wasn't swallowing it. "All right, if you say so. Be ready to go in fifteen minutes."

"I'm ready now. I'd rather not wait a moment longer." I kissed my son's forehead as he cooed. "Let's go."

Outside, in the plaza of shattered glass, only the statue of that saint, whose name I could never remember, stood unbroken. A troop of Archers of the Eye stood in a line, wearing white dresses that only reached their knees. Among them, to my surprise, was Sadie — dressed normally, in chainmail and a cheap blue and rose caftan.

"Are they coming?" I asked Kato.

"We'll leave an Archer every quarter mile to form an array," Kato said. "Kyars wants messages on the hour, and we're not taking the obvious road to Dorud." He whispered, "Don't want those horse fuckers lying in wait."

Once Sadie noticed me, she pushed past the Archers and gholam in the plaza to my front.

"Where's Celene?" she asked. Just what I feared.

"I sent her home. With a rider. Bound for the first port with a ship to Crucis."

Kato gazed away from my lie as Sadie shook her head.

"No you didn't. I've been standing out here for hours. I would've seen it." Her eyes went wide. "Is she…did you…"

She must've read the guilt on my face. Oh, if only she could let me lie.

I didn't stop her from marching into the house. While waiting, carriages and riders formed up. Kato escorted his two mistresses and two children into a carriage. They'd be coming with us to safety. He then went about the plaza, inspecting his men and barking orders.

Sadie returned. In her arms, she held Celene, who breathed in the slow rhythm of the sleep I'd left her in.

In the end…I couldn't do it. I couldn't cut into her the way I'd cut Cyra. Couldn't sacrifice her to my vengeance, like I'd done with Vera. Couldn't kill another daughter for power, like how Seluq killed mine.

"Why won't she wake?" Sadie shouted. "What did you do to her?"

After lying to Celene, after telling her I was sending her home, how could I face her? I was a danger to her — had always been — and if she stayed with me, I'd be tempted…

"Sadie, she'll wake in a few hours," I said. "Take her and go. Go far from here. As far as you can. Get her back to Crucis. Get yourself back to Sirm. Be with your families. Because one day…death is going to separate you. They'll be in one world, and you'll be in another, and it'll be impossible to cross that threshold. Until that day…spend every moment you can, with them."

Sadie just stood there, tears in her eyes as she held Celene.

"Take her home!" I shouted. "And you…you go home! I'd trade this whole kingdom for a single second more with my family. But no trade can bring them back. So you…you and Celene need to be happy…for me, all right?"

She just stood there, holding her.

"Not for me, then. Truth is, I don't deserve even that. For yourselves, be with those you love. Even if it's hard, make it work, and always remind yourself that it could be much worse. That, at least, you have them, and they have you."

She just stood there, holding her.

"Am I speaking Paramic? Do you hear me, Sadie?"

Sadie nodded. "All right. I'll take her home." She sobbed. "I'll get her to Hyperion. On my life."

"No — your life is as precious as hers. You'll get her home, and then you'll go home, too. You'll kiss your mother and father and you'll tell them how much you love them, and you'll spend the rest of your days in their company, whether or not they or you like it. You'll learn to like it, no matter what. Take an old woman's wisdom. No more running, understood?"

I HELPED Sadie tie Celene to her back and get on a Kashanese mare. The gholam wouldn't open the city gate until they'd scouted ahead for Jotrids, so I waited in my carriage with my son and a young Kashanese handmaid from the harem. Skin the color of a walnut, big eyes, and thick, wavy eyebrows. Hayda was her name. I stared out the window at the sunbaked hovels of the commoners, as we made our way to the northwestern gate.

"Goodbye, Qandbajar," I whispered, feeling no affection for this awful, heaping pile of mud and lies. I wished I could say goodbye to the bitter remorse that stirred in my veins and poisoned my core. What awful things I'd done…only to fail because the forces against me were so onerous, mighty, and cruel.

I didn't want to think on it. I wanted distance for my son and myself. I'd watched him come out of me and so knew he was the only real thing. The only thing attaching me to this world, to this time, to this place. The only one worth fighting for. I'd have to protect him. I'd have to, no matter what.

But I wouldn't do it by hurting the weak. I wouldn't be like those who murdered my family. My soul couldn't take it. No more. There had to be a better way.

Men heaved and metal grinded — they were finally raising the portcullis, content that the way was safe, that Jotrids didn't lie in wait. Sadie and Celene could go home, and I could go away from this miserable war I'd started.

I watched as Sadie, sleeping Celene tied to her back, rode past my carriage, the *clop-clop* of her mare's hooves on the pavement getting fainter as she galloped through the gate and away. Thank Lat. Celene's blood…angel's blood…that rune I was seconds from slitting her neck for…it would have done something truly awful. Something that nothing could undo, for all of time.

I shuddered, not wanting to imagine it. Not wanting to imagine anything except a safe place for my son and me. I wouldn't do what Father Chisti asked, not anymore. I trusted him because he'd saved me, but now…I didn't know what he truly wanted. Because that rune he wanted me to paint…it would have won the war, but it wouldn't have done anyone any good, least of all my son and myself.

I handed my son to my Kashanese handmaid, intent on closing my eyes for a while. A long carriage ride awaited, requiring stops at several caravansaries along the way. Perhaps I'd feel better with distance. Once we got moving and passed the gate, I enjoyed a feathery relief across my shoulders.

Gasps sounded throughout the caravan, behind which was the cacophony of stone exploding. A rumble shook the carriage. I gazed out the window at the distant dust plume that had replaced the Tower of Wisdom. Finally.

That relief let me drift into sleep as the carriage rolled on the pavement.

• • •

KATO SHOOK ME AWAKE. "Zed, we're surrounded. And they're asking for you."

Before addressing him, I looked toward my baby. The Kashanese girl held him gently in sleep.

"What do you mean 'surrounded?'"

"A spy must've tipped them off. The Jotrids. They were lying in wait along the route, jaws wide open."

I gasped. How could this be? How could Kato be so foolish? "What are you saying? I thought you scouted ahead!"

"Fuckers were hiding behind a mountain." He gestured to the dry and sandy peak outside the window. "Only a bird could've seen them. Hours ago, scouts reported they'd sent near half their force in a different direction, toward the Waste. I assumed it to be a sign that the Sylgiz were entering this mess, striking at the Jotrids. Seemed that was a ruse, and they doubled back here." He sighed, tense and heavy. "From what I can tell, they've many times our number and the high ground. I've already sent a message to the palace, through the Archers. We need only delay till help arrives."

Outside the window, mounted gholam formed up across the road and in the scrub beside it. Spears, bows, guns, swords, hand bombs — they didn't lack for war's instruments. Men and women with dirty faces passed by, lugging sacks and holding children. We weren't the only ones absconding from Qandbajar into the enemy's jaw.

"Delay?" I said. "They want to kill me and my son, Kato. They want to end Kyars, perhaps end the dynasty, even."

Kato wiped his sweaty, soot-stained eyebrows with a kerchief. He'd just fought one battle and now another threatened. "Cyra is with them, as is Pashang, as is Eshe, the Himyarite sorcerer. They claim to just want to talk with you. So talk to them for as long as you can. Meanwhile, Kyars will send all we've got, and we'll smash them, here — under the open sky — where they can't cower behind the good city folk. We'll turn this desert into a Jotrid shrine. End this war today."

I gulped. Why me? Could he not see how weak I was? "I have nothing to say to them. Can't you go negotiate?"

"Zed, you're the best talker I've ever met. You could make a rat think he's a bird. So make them think they've won. Make them let down their guard. We won't get another chance like this. The rats have taken the bait!"

I knew what he meant. I knew he'd not intended this. But I had to say, "My son and I are not bait. We are the future of this kingdom. You'd do well to remember that."

"Listen, Zed." By Lat, why was he shortening my name? "I can't stall them forever. If you don't go out there and *talk-talk-talk*, they're going to smell blood. Your son's, especially."

"Kato…tell me…do you ever regret coming to Alanya? And everything you had to do, to get your position and keep it?"

"All the time. But so what? What's another fool with regrets?" He gestured to the carriage door.

Resigned, I took to my feet and went outside. Our caravan of horses and carriages and folks on foot spread into the distance toward Qandbajar. Puffy clouds provided shade from the declining sun, and a breeze drifted across the scrub. Along with Kato and twenty armored gholam, some holding shields and others matchlocks, I waited on the road just ahead of the caravan. A wall of mountains covered the landscape to my left, while to my right, an endless patchwork of grasses, dunes, and dreary fauna spread to the horizon, all settled on craggy, caked ground.

They came on horseback: Cyra, Eshe, Pashang, and a few Jotrid ilk. Were we really going to negotiate in the middle of the road?

Cyra, Pashang, and Eshe dismounted and walked the rest of the way. Meanwhile, Kato said, "Zedra, it'll be the two of us and the three of them."

No. I wanted to speak plainly. "I'll speak with them alone."

Kato shook his head. "Alone? That's not what I meant when—"

"Just shut up. They asked for me, so let me do this."

He rubbed sand from his beard, then nodded. Three gholam

approached their group first, patting each down to ensure they weren't concealing anything deadly, though they seemed shy to touch Cyra in certain spots. Afterward, the gholam guarding me stood aside, and I walked down the road to where they waited.

To my surprise, Cyra stepped forward, alone. We met in the middle, away from everyone's ears.

That eyepatch…was she going to wear it forever? Hide what she was, like I did? Perhaps I ought to share my wisdom: you can only hide for so long. Truth would claw its way out of the grave and expose you.

Now face to face, I waited for her to speak. This meeting was her idea, so what did she want? I resolved to delay by pausing, speaking slowly, and letting silences linger.

"It's just us," she finally said. "Do you have nothing to say?"

"Last we spoke, I told you to die. I said it all then."

Did she want me to say *sorry*? Sorry I destroyed your life. Maimed you. Killed a man you treasured and got your brother killed. I wished I'd never done it, but I couldn't hold that remorse. True remorse requires repentance, and true repentance requires justice, and if I were to face justice, then who would protect my son?

"I…" She kicked a stone, put her hands in her pockets, and gazed at the ground. Good. She was doing my delaying for me. "I…even after all you've done, Zedra, I've decided — I don't want to hurt you. And I don't want to hurt your son."

That made me smile. "Then why block our way?"

"Because I can no longer let you abuse your power. Your power to bloodwrite, to soulshift. You can leave with your son, but not with your sorcery."

What? Had she found a way to strip me of my sorcery? Impossible…but with her, it seemed nothing was. I swallowed a lump.

"Zedra…we were happy, weren't we?"

"I was never happy." I shook my head. "My pain…the pain of my tribe…six hundred years couldn't wash it away." Perhaps I ought to lengthen this story, get her to sympathize. "You were born and raised on the same path. The Path of the Children. You know our story, what we suffered. Don't tell me eight years with the saint worshippers erased your love for the Children."

Birds squawked overhead — vultures. How ominous...and clever.

"I haven't forgotten the Children," Cyra said, "but I never cared for the divide. What does it matter whether you believe in the saint-kings or in Chisti's descendants? In the end, we worship the same god, in mostly the same ways. But it was never about god — it was about power. I know it's not what you want to hear, Zedra, but it's what I believe. And I fear...I fear *that* man used your pain to control you. He's not who you think he is. He's not Father Chisti."

"I know..." I looked away in shame. "I could never understand why he was so different from the holy man I imagined. Why he'd been severed from Lat. And yet, I don't blame him for what I did. His motives might be false, but mine aren't. I *do* want what I want, and I'm still going to get it, but I'll do it my way, not his."

"That's all I've been wondering." Cyra's voice cracked. "What do you want, Zedra?"

The sad truth is, I could've just done nothing. I could've let Cyra marry Kyars, and the three of us would've raised my son into the eventual Shah of Alanya. Had I just let it be...but I wanted to make them suffer, more than I wanted justice and mankind's salvation. I wanted to destroy the saint worshippers and the Seluqals who championed their path, and I still did.

"Cyra, you're a fool for thinking we can resolve this. There's no world where you and I share a place. My son is going to be the Shah of Alanya one day, and you're going to be dead in a ditch." Curse the saints...that outburst wasn't helping. All this time, I'd let rage poison my words and deeds. I couldn't achieve what I wanted this way — I needed to grip myself the way a warrior grips a sword.

"Why?" She seemed to struggle to pluck her words. "What did I ever do to you?"

"Nothing! You did nothing!" I shouted so loud that those out of earshot must've heard, their necks steered in our direction. "You were innocent, and I know you earnestly tried to be my friend. But that's all shattered into a thousand thousand pieces, and we can't put it back together. And…you're right. It's all because of me — my weaknesses, my delusions, my wickedness." Perhaps if I showed remorse, she'd think her plan working, and we could continue conversing until help arrived.

"I can't accept that. Whatever made you invade my body and do what you did…needs to die. If it was that man who made you do it, then say so. I'll understand that he misled you…that you thought you were doing something good."

I sighed, wishing I could say that. Perhaps I ought to absolve myself. Put the blame on *that man* and his whispering. It would make her hate me less, perhaps even forgive me, if her tone were true. But I didn't want her forgiveness. I didn't care if she hated me. Eventually, for the safety of my son, I'd have to kill her, regardless.

"It was me," I said, hoping she'd appreciate my honesty. "I won't lie. I didn't feel bad stabbing Tamaz. He was just another evil man hiding behind a mask of kindness, sitting on a throne that his ancestor Seluq took by might. A throne that belongs to my family alone." Finally saying that to someone's face was like lifting a boulder off my chest. "As for you, Cyra…I never liked you, and maybe that's why I didn't feel bad hurting you. You think of us as friends, but I'm too old to be your friend. You were like a petulant child to me, and you still behave like one." I didn't expect honesty to sting so much. "That's the sincerest thing I can say."

Her eyes watered; she shook her head. "You say it so *matter-of-factly*. As if you're recounting an average day in the life of Zedra. Are you sorry in the least?"

Honesty seemed to be working, bringing out her emotions…as well as mine. "Why does it matter? You said you don't want to hurt me…well, I have a way out for you, too. Take your Jotrids and go into the deepest, reddest part of the Endless. Never come near this kingdom, and I won't have to kill you. We're only enemies because we're both trying to sit on that dais, just beneath the golden divan in the great hall. If not for yourself, then do it for Alanya, Cyra. My son is the heir, and as his mother, I can't get what I deserve, because if I did, they'd string me up, and there'd be no one to protect him from the machinations of the viziers and sheikhs and gholam and whoever else wants a piece of him. Stop only seeking justice for yourself — think about what's best for everyone. I need you to see beyond yourself, for once."

I couldn't have said it better, could I? Surely that was my best, sincerest, and most honest argument.

Cyra kicked another stone off the road. "You're the one not seeing. You're the one who brought calamity to the kingdom — I just reacted to what you did. For the sake of your son, I'm going to let you live. Bereft of your power. Alanya will be shaped by us, not the Seluqals, and not you." She huffed out an exasperated breath. Bearing these heavy words seemed to take a lot out of her, as it did me. "I'm giving you a way out, one that you don't deserve."

I chuckled at her overconfidence. Determination mattered, sure, but in that she'd met her match. "Lat herself gifted this kingdom to the Children. My grandmother, Safia, ran away because she had no power. She couldn't bloodwrite, nor soulshift, nor write upon the stars. I'm not so weak." I smiled as tenderly as I could. "Thank you for offering me a way out. You're right — it's more than I deserve. But I can't let you take my power. Understand this, Cyra. I'm not seeking justice — I am justice. Justice for the Children. I will destroy what destroyed them. I will restore their place upon the throne of the earth. You can be safe from my wrath, so long as you go and never return. It's really that easy, dear."

This conversation wasn't as worthless as I'd expected. So many doubts plagued me on the carriage ride, but Cyra had — unintentionally, I'm sure — reminded me of my gifts, my enemies, my purpose. Perhaps *that man* had fooled me, but the injustice suffered by the Children was no mirage. My ability to right those wrongs was real, and I'd already started down that path. Baby Seluq still had my blood, which made him the Children, regardless of whom his father was. I couldn't run away from what I'd started; rather, I'd have to return to Qandbajar, once my son was safe in Dorud, to finish it.

"Cyra!" Pashang shouted from down the road. He and Eshe raised their hands and ran over to us. Behind me, Kato and one other gholam did the same.

Pashang pointed toward the open scrub. "Someone's coming!"

I squinted to see a single horseman galloping toward us.

Kato stood in front of me, as if to be my shield. "This your trick?" he said to Pashang. "I'm sending a rider to intercept."

"No trick," Pashang replied, "unless it's yours. I'm sending one, too."

They both gestured their orders to their respective riders, who took off to meet whoever was coming at us.

"Let's go, Zedra," Kato said. "I don't like this."

I couldn't help but watch the Jotrid rider and the gholam rider approach the oncoming horseman.

"Zed, let's go!"

Pashang and Eshe begged the same of Cyra. I was about to follow Kato back to the caravan when the riders we'd sent to intercept suddenly…vanished. Into the air.

The oncoming horseman sped up. The ground quaked as he neared. By Lat…my throat tightened and my hairs chilled…it was him.

"Father?" I said as the rider arrived, not knowing what else to call him.

And he wasn't alone. At his back, bound together with rope, were Sadie and Celene. With one hand, he gripped the rope binding them, held them both up as they wriggled and screamed like trapped rats, and tossed them into the air. They landed with a soft *plush* in a pile of sand while the rest of us backed away.

Kato said, "Hurry back, now. We'll deal with him."

Gholam rode by, matchlocks forward, toward Father. I didn't want to watch, but I had to see. Had to see what he'd do.

Father drew a line in the air, as if the riders were a picture he was striking out. Heads flew off necks; blood erupted; their bodies dropped onto the road as the horses nickered and ran in fear.

"Fuck," Kato said, eyes stuck with terror.

"You're the one who needs to run. Go to your son and daughter — take my son, too — and get out of here!"

"I'll not leave you, Zed."

"He's here for me!" I grabbed Kato's shoulder plates. "You all need to go!"

"No way I'm telling Kyars I deserted the mother of his son. If I must die fighting some debased sorcerer, then so be it! I'll be in good company."

"He's not just *some* sorcerer!"

I pushed Kato away and ran toward Father. Father drew a square in my direction. Sand erupted into the air at my back, forming what resembled a waterfall…a sandfall. It grew and widened until it was bigger than a palace, cutting me off from Kato, the gholam, and my son.

"Stop this!" I yelled.

He drew a square in the other direction, and a sandfall erupted behind Cyra, blocking her from her allies. Then he did the same toward the mountains, and the scrub, until a deafening wall of falling sand enveloped us.

I knew what he wanted. Why else drag Celene and Sadie here? For the bloodpainting I refused to make. But if he were so powerful, why couldn't he just paint it himself?

Father climbed down his horse, then tugged off the rope binding Sadie and Celene. Free to move, they both crawled away. But there was nowhere to go.

Cyra approached Father, as did I. The air between us filled with sand blowing and roaring across the sandfalls. It stuck in my eyes and mouth and hair.

Sadie and Celene got to their feet and held hands. Cyra made a fist and glared at Father.

"Marot!" she screamed.

Marot...the angel who'd tempted men with magic. One of the Twelve revered by the Ethosians. I'd seen his mural in Celene's mirage, holding four cards at his front and ever more behind his back as he offered men the power to write with blood and on the stars. So that's who Father was.

"I failed." His voice came from above, below, everywhere. "I'm going to suffer for my failure, but not alone. You'll do what must be done."

Celene tugged on her hair, tears across her face. Sadie's arms shook as she hugged herself. Cyra glared at Marot with her fist outstretched.

I stepped in front of him, not even bothering to rub the sand from my tear ducts. "I won't do it. I won't hurt them. If you're so intent, stain your own hands."

Marot said, "That's not how this works. *You* have to do it. Because if I were to write a bloodrune that powerful...well," he pointed to the sky, "someone up there might notice. Perhaps my father, or grandmother. And if you think I'm bad, see what happens when *they're* looking our way."

I shook my head. "No! I won't! I won't ever. You're a greater evil than anything I've seen!"

Someone took my left hand; Cyra, her eyebrows ruffled in anger. She squeezed my hand, dampening it with sweat.

"What are you going to do?" Marot laughed. "Write me out of existence? That's not how starwriting works. The Blood Star loved the Morning Star — before they merged and thereby destroyed seventeen million worlds. Your handhold must love you too, Cyra. I'm afraid Zedra doesn't."

The Blood Star and the Morning Star had merged? As in, they were one and the same?

Marot drew a pattern with many points and sides. He stepped back, and a woman blinked into the spot in front of him. My Kashanese handmaid, and she was holding baby Seluq! Marot grabbed my baby and touched the terrified handmaid on the forehead; she screamed, and her body exploded, blood and guts splashing. I turned away, but it washed over my face, my caftan, and got in my eyes and nose and mouth, tasting sour and sweet and metallic. Fleshy and sickening and full of bile. Her innards must've covered Cyra and the others, too. But truly, all I could think about was my son!

I lost sight with the sand and blood blowing in my eyes. My son's cries, though, were a relief. I rubbed the blood and sand from my face, enough to see Marot cradling my son, his fingertip on the baby's forehead.

"Please don't!" I cried. "The blood of Chisti…must never…"

"He doesn't have the blood of Chisti," Marot said. "Nor do you. Chisti lives on in my memories, as Zedra lives on in yours."

What? What lies was he telling? "I'm Zedra, daughter of—"

"No. You're not. You're just a sad little girl with the memories of a sad, old woman who died a long time ago. That's why your blood is so base. But the blood of this little one," he rocked my son gently, "is my own. God's blood."

How could that be true? Impossible. And yet, just as bloodrunes could transport you into another's dreams, bloodrunes could pass on memories and lifetimes.

But…no…*I was there*. I lived that life. It couldn't all be because of some bloodrune! "Don't hurt Seluq. Are you so vile to harm your own?"

Marot laughed, utterly demonic. "I've baptized thousands with the blood of my children — without their sacrifice, there would be no bloodwriters. My father will likely sacrifice me, one day, for his own cosmic purpose. *We* don't share your base sensibilities. Ah, but that's what makes mankind so beloved to Lat, isn't it? And yet, where is she?" That demonic laugh sapped me of strength. So confident, so in control. "Where is the queen of the jinn, the fallen angel, the protector of this land? *Tsk-tsk-tsk.* I think it's quite clear — she has forsaken you."

A red tinge infected the air; the sand turned...bloody. I looked up to see a red sky, red clouds, and a red sun. Blood in everything.

Sadie stumbled toward me. She clutched my arm. "Zedra, if you must, then use my blood. I've already seen death, and I don't mind it. Just...don't hurt Celene."

I wiped an orange bit of flesh dangling off her cheek. "No, I won't do it."

"He'll kill your son. Your son is the heir. He's more important than me."

"He'll be the heir of nothing if I write that rune. They say the Golden Kingdom fell in a decade to the blood plague."

That made Marot laugh. "I was there." His voice burned in the air. "It was the Philosophers who succumbed to temptation in the Golden Kingdom. Their lust for power, for advancement, for ascendence brought it upon them. The rivers turned to blood, as did the rain, and even the water in men and beasts, till they exploded from the pressure! To this day, Himyar is a cursed land."

Cyra approached us, her arm around Celene, who still trembled.

"Why would anyone want that?" Cyra asked. "Why destroy?"

"You always ask 'why'. But what you really need to ask is — 'why not'. Leave your house unlocked, do you wonder why someone burgled it? If you must ask, ask it of your god."

Why, indeed, was any of this happening? My son! My anchor in the world. My love for him was my only certainty. Even if the blood plague destroyed this kingdom, at least I'd still have him. We could go somewhere else and just live...

I looked to Sadie and Celene. I could choose either. But it would have to be Sadie, wouldn't it? Sadie was willing to die again.

"I'm going to kill your son," Marot said from everywhere, "and then, I'm going to kill everyone here. There won't be a victor. Or, one sacrifice and the rest of you live. Millions will die from blood sickness, but did their lives ever matter to any of you? You who waged wars for your own sake?" That laugh again. "And yet, you think I'm wicked? What I'm not is a hypocrite, content to order death so long as I don't suffer."

"Marot!" It was Celene. She screamed, "is this the will of the Archangel!?" at him in Crucian. Of course…Marot was her angel. She was a heathen, after all. Perhaps she ought to die in sacrifice to her own god. Better her than my son. Better this kingdom than my son! Whether he was the Children or not, whether I was the Children or not, we were mother and son, and that no one could take away.

"All right," I said, glancing between Sadie and Celene. In the end, Sadie had left my side, while Celene stayed true. That ought to be the deciding reason. "Sadie…I'll do it with her blood."

Sadie's eyes widened. "No…if it's going to kill millions, then—" Her lips clamped shut, and a thread wound across them, tying them so she couldn't make a sound. Thread bound her hands, too, and a force knocked her to her knees.

Marot came to my side and put a dagger in my hand. "Excellent choice," he said. "This land will drink deep of her star's blood."

Black thread also bound the lips and hands of Celene and Cyra as Marot's magic forced them to their knees. Only I remained standing while my son wailed in Marot's grasp.

Perhaps this was justice. Or the closest thing. If the Children couldn't have this land, then no one should. Better it be cursed, for eternity.

"When it's over, will you do something for me?" I asked. "Take my son and me far from here. As far as you can."

"Fair enough. You and your son can live in peace, in the land beyond the sea mists, where the sundews grow."

Would his promise prove true? Did I have a choice, anyway? I approached Sadie. She stared at me with bulging eyes. Best slice her quick. Like killing and bleeding a goat, you don't want them to linger with death's terror.

I bent down, put the blade to her neck. Looked upon Cyra and Celene, who were just as terrified to watch her die. How weak we were, in the end, playing to the tune of some wretched angel. How sad that our own god didn't protect us, protect her land. Just as she'd forsaken her Children, she'd forsaken us. But today, someone's blood would mix with soil.

Truth is, we weren't worth saving, were we? Marot was right… we were hypocrites, goading others to die for our selfish ends. What did it matter if millions drowned in blood, if my son could live?

The blade trembled against Sadie's flesh. I grabbed my wrist to steady it. Tears dripped off her cheeks and onto the sand. In my hesitation, I'd failed to save her from the terror. But she needn't suffer any longer: I closed my eyes and pushed the blade in and across.

Yet still, I heard her tremble. And my hand…so numb…as if it were…frozen.

I opened my eyes. Ice encased my arm. Within seconds, the roaring of the sandfalls turned to a whimper, and the sand itself froze in the air.

Meanwhile, Marot's hateful eyes gazed upon someone at my back. I turned to see him: Kevah, the magus, his outstretched hand open and fingers pointing forward.

"So," Marot said, "someone is watching over the land. Torturing little girls was getting stale. But you," he chuckled, "you'll make for quite a thrill."

32

CYRA

Well, this hadn't quite gone as planned. Wasn't expecting Marot to grace us. Wasn't expecting Kevah, either, but thank Lat he was standing there, commanding his jinn to freeze the sand.

Through my star-seeing eye, those jinn showed as clouds of fire-less smoke — faceless and limbless. Where he pointed, they would whirl toward. And what they touched froze. One had whisked through Zedra's hand before she could stick her dagger into the Karmazi girl's throat. A larger, tornado-like one had spun across the sandfalls, turning them to frost. And now they headed for Marot.

Fear of the cold shuddered through me. I hated it more than having my lips and hands bound by threads and even this crushing pressure keeping me on my knees. When a smoky ice jinn veered off Marot and toward me, I feared it would freeze me to death. Perhaps Kevah was about to make good on his promise.

But instead, a smoky hand reached out of the whirling cloud, grabbed my wrists, and tore the threads binding them. A finger on the hand shapeshifted into a tiny blade, and it sliced across my lips, cutting the thread without cutting me.

Why me? How was I supposed to help? When I'd grabbed

492

Zedra's hand earlier and prayed for Marot to die, it didn't work. The daytime stars would not sing — was it as Marot said?

Did I need a loving partner? But everyone between these frozen sand walls hated me.

Marot's voice echoed from everywhere. "Kevah, you can't defeat me with the powers I bequeathed. I'm afraid you'll need someone *higher up*."

Kevah obviously couldn't be my partner; he detested my star-seeing eye and was busy staring down Marot while shouting orders to his jinn. So…I needed Eshe or Pashang, and that meant I needed out of this crucible.

The whirling jinn surrounded Marot. His form was…expanding, limbs snaking like roots, head tilted and inflated, eyes bubbling from his growing neck.

The ice jinn surged toward him, freezing his snaking limbs. Were we winning?

I kicked at the frozen sandfall; instead of cracking the ice, I nearly cracked my foot. I needed fire.

While Marot froze as the jinn coursed through his sprawling form, I ran to Zedra, who knelt on the sand, bound like I'd been. Her right hand dripped with ice, blue and stuck. I cut the thread binding her hands with a dagger I'd been concealing, in case Zedra tried to kill me, but her lips I left sealed.

"Can you make fire?" I asked.

She nodded, then pointed to Celene. Why? I helped Zedra up, and we ran to Celene. I got on my knees and cut her bindings. After, Zedra grabbed my dagger, pricked Celene's finger, and dripped blood onto the blade. The girl shuddered but could barely yelp from her bound lips. Zedra scribbled a bloodrune onto the blade's flat.

Unlike the ones Eshe had painted, it didn't glow. She pointed to her threaded lips in agitation. Of course, she needed to recite the incantation.

I clutched Zedra's head, put the blade to her face, and realized I could pluck her eye out if I wanted. Make things more even. But instead, I sliced at the thread binding her lips. She gasped and spat blood. My slice left a gash across her mouth and flowing blood, but she didn't seem to mind it and whispered her words.

The bloodrune on the blade glowed. I handed it to her, and we three ran for the nearest frozen sandfall. She swung the dagger at it; fire flew off the blade and onto the ice wall. It cracked the ice, hissing a chilling smoke into the air. Zedra swung at it again, and again, and again, until the fire blazed a large hole through the frozen sand.

"Go, dear," she said to Celene in Sirmian.

Celene ducked through, racing away from the monster at our back. But Zedra…she ran toward Marot. Perhaps she was going after her son. I turned for a last look.

Kevah's jinn whirled through Marot's stretched, root-like limbs, his towering neck, and even the sprouting eyeballs that resembled sacks of spider eggs. They'd almost fully encased him in ice. But was it so easy to freeze a god?

Sadie stood behind Kevah, cradling baby Seluq. Zedra had just reached them. Perhaps the magus didn't need my help, powerful as he was, and I could instead focus on getting safe. Getting to Eshe and Pashang.

I crouched and followed Celene through the burning hole, unafraid of the flames ringing it.

A horseman rushed at me! I rolled across a sandy patch as he and more gholam galloped by, their war cries heavy in the air. What the hell was going on out here?

I got to my knees; scores of mounted gholam with spears and matchlocks charged what looked like the Jotrid line, which was firing bullets and arrows back. How could I get through to Eshe and Pashang?

I shuffled away as an arrow landed where I knelt. The gholam charge was just in front, so a stray Jotrid arrow could hit me any second, or a gholam rider could trample me, or a bullet find my heart.

I had to get to the Jotrids, lest gholam capture or kill me. I stood — where had Celene gone? Maybe behind, toward the gholam line, where she'd be safest. I couldn't worry about her. Death gripped me, and I had to get out, had to go forward.

I ran toward the battling gholam and Jotrids as arrows rained. Gunshots and screams and clanging steel resounded. Riders threw spears, wrestled each other off horses, and tossed bombs that splattered guts and char everywhere. I couldn't account for every danger. My heart burned with crippling fear; it was too horrible to be real — a nightmare. I kept low, creeping forward, tasting sulfur in the sandy air.

Gallops shook the earth from behind me. I turned to see gholam charging, guns drawn, armor a blinding glint. So I stood and ran, knees nearly buckling from the purest fear. I stepped over a horse flailing from an erupting spear wound, around a gholam trying to pull an arrow from his own neck, and by a half-crisped Jotrid, prayers on seared lips.

Jotrids charged from left, right, and front into me and the oncoming gholam, surrounding the scape with sharp edges, arrows, and gunfire. I tasted death in my swallow. Could this be it?

There! I sighted Pashang atop his mare on a dune just behind the charging Jotrids, Eshe beside him. I ran faster than I ever had through the rushing horsemen, fear and hope pushing me, no longer focused on the death and pain and rot. Both noticed, their eyes lighting up as they scoped the battlefield and sighted me. They galloped down the dune, through the battling mass of riders, toward me. I had to—

Hands ensnared me, tightening around my neck, then my chest, whisking me up onto a charging horse. The rider dropped me on the saddle and pressed me against his armor — I couldn't see as my face scratched against his golden chainmail. Then he shouted and pulled the reins of his horse, steering it in a half-circle before he charged again. I'd been seized! By, by—

I tried to look up, but with a bulging arm, he crushed my face against his mail as my legs dangled awkwardly off the saddle. The horse jumped; I screamed and my teeth punctured my tongue.

His deathly arm squeezed my neck till I could neither inhale nor think. Blood from my tongue gushed down my windpipe, but his hold kept me from coughing it out. I drowned in my blood. My legs bruised and numbed from banging against the charging horse's sides.

Whoever it was halted with a sudden pull of the reins. He grabbed my collar and tossed me off, flipping me through the air; I crashed onto hard ground, a bone in my back burning. I coughed blood and blinked against the sight of the sky and dozens of golden gholam surrounding me, an overwhelming throb in every bone.

The rider who'd taken me jumped off his horse, threw his golden helmet to the ground, and grabbed my collar. He pulled me to my feet, though I couldn't stand. His arm well wound, he knuckled me in the jaw. My cheek tore against my teeth and a blood-soaked tooth ripped out my mouth.

"What did you do to Zedra?" he shouted.

I blinked and blinked the blurriness away until I saw Kato, his face lit with rage.

I could only whimper, "I didn't—"

"Fucking sorceress! I shouldn't have ever let you near her!" He unsheathed his scimitar, raised it.

"Zedra said you must not hurt her!" Celene's voice. She pushed through the gholam and crashed into Kato's chest, barely moving him. Then she stood between us and waved her hands. "If you hurt her, Zedra won't forgive you!"

To our left, the frozen sandfall towered, blocking us from the battle beyond it and within it. Even in my battered state, I realized Kato had sent his gholam around the sandfall to attack the Jotrids, thinking we'd created the wall to trap Zedra.

"Does anyone know what she's saying?" Kato asked his gholam. Seemed he didn't understand Sirmian.

One of his men translated. Kato yelled in frustration and sheathed his sword. He wouldn't go against Zedra's wishes, though I didn't recall Zedra wanting anything for me but death.

"Zedra's inside," I whispered, sipping my blood. "We didn't cause this. The angel did. You must believe me."

"Angel?" Kato spat on the ground. "We all saw him in Kostany, with his big wings and sword. In the end, Lat won, shattered him into a thousand thousand pieces. Same will happen here. We fear no angels, only men."

Gholam on foot, matchlocks forward, ran by our position. The jumble of crying steel and battle shouts and gunshots neared. The Jotrids must've been countering, hard. Were they coming to free me?

Kato picked me up by the collar, his sweaty knuckles jutting into my neck. "How do we get Zedra back?"

"I need to pray." I coughed on blood and agony. "I can pray for the death of the angel. My prayers are always answered, but I need a willing partner. Someone who…who loves me."

Saying those words, I finally understood. That freezing day in the Waste, when my brother and I were huddling within a moth-eaten blanket, our bellies filled with air, I'd taken his hand. I'd prayed for my father's safe return, for our bellies to be full, for the cold to end. And it all came to pass. Had I been a starwriter longer than I realized?

Kato snarled. "Who could love you but another monster?"

"Call it off," I whispered, barely able to because of how crushed my throat was. "Call off your attack."

"Our attack? You're the ones who attacked us!" He gestured at the arrows jutting out of the ground. So, the gholam were only countering the arrow rain when they charged. Pashang had tried to use Marot's arrival and the sand wall to his advantage. How clever.

"I can help. But I need—"

Kato tossed me onto the ground. Whatever bone had broken earlier stabbed my back muscle; I wailed and choked on pain.

"There're too many of them. We're all going to die." Kato glanced around. "You there, Archer of the Eye!" He pointed to someone that seemed to me a blurry white smudge. "Shoot a message to Pashang. Tell him I have his bitch, and that I'll smear her innards across this hellscape if he doesn't halt his charge."

Even in agony, I yearned to see beyond the sandfall — what was happening inside? Was Kevah winning? But I knew it wouldn't be so easy. Marot didn't seem worried when Kevah showed up, and that terrified me more than Kato ever could.

Numbness and nauseous pain took turns engulfing my body. *A fate worse than death.* Could this be it?

Celene knelt next to me, then wiped blood off my lips with her caftan.

"You probably shouldn't help me," I said. "They won't like that."

She shook her head and smiled with her cut-up lips. "They don't understand. They don't understand how important you are."

"Important?"

Her smile seemed…too happy. This wasn't the time to be smiling like a prince had just kissed you.

The thundering of Jotrid riders shifted the air. Steel sang, arrows whizzed, and gunshots roared. They crashed into the gholam line and melded together in a melee. With that momentum, the Jotrids should win soon enough.

"We were brought here for a reason," Celene said, her voice anxiously joyful, "by Marot, by one of the Twelve. We should not question his methods. All is happening by his design."

That made no sense. Worse, it terrified me. "He was going to kill you. I saw how scared you were!"

"Because, despite all I've witnessed, my faith is weak. I didn't want to die. But even firm faith is not enough for me to enter Paradise. Only deeds, only service, will save me. Marot said, while we were riding here, that you were the key to everything. He told me I'd never go home, that I'd die in the east, and that, as long as I lived, I should devote myself to you."

Why would he say such things to Celene? Was he trying to *shepherd* her, the way he'd tricked Zedra and me? To what end?

A pillar of light cracked the air, surging from within the sand wall until it hit the sky. It burned like the sun had crashed upon us, and I could scarcely look away as it lashed my eyes. The screams of the Jotrids and gholam fighting near the sand wall cut off, as if they'd been obliterated.

When I opened my eyes, the sand wall was gone — melted by the exploding light. Charred horses and men and black sand outlined where the wall once stood.

Before I could digest what happened, Kato ran over and pulled me up. He tossed me over his shoulder as if I were a gazelle he'd hunted, climbed his horse, then slid me down in front of him. With a kick, his horse bolted away from my hopes. My groin sat properly on the saddle this time, so at least it wouldn't bruise me. But that didn't help my back, which still screamed. I tried to make out Zedra or Kevah or even Marot, but smoke obscured everything, and we were galloping away. Away from the Jotrids, who emerged from the smoke and gave chase, fearless despite...despite something huge, winged, and monstrous in the sky.

I couldn't see it clearly amid the haze, but the angel had transformed. Its head was in a cloud, and its mountain-sized feet were dangling above the earth as its wings flapped with a thundering that drowned the sounds of battle.

But my present problem was earthly. I couldn't let Kato whisk me away. I wouldn't be his prisoner, nor anyone else's. I breathed deep, then lunged forward and smashed my head into his chin. He shouted and weakened his grip; I dipped to the side, fell off the horse, and—

Smashed onto sand. The impact sent me into the air, and I smashed again and rolled across the ground, blood blowing out my mouth, bones cracked and shrieking, stars blinking everywhere. The charging horses barely diverted, their hooves kicking sand into my face, but at least these were Jotrids.

I finally came to a stop, positioned on my belly to see what they were fleeing: a flying giant with hundreds of flapping black and gold wings. Its face was a mesh of eye sacks that dangled off each other, each pupil blinking sideways. It gripped swords in all its seventeen tentacles, and the blades shimmered like colored crystals, red and blue and green and so many hues between. Was that angel…Marot's true, full form?

Marada, the sultana of the Marid tribe of jinn, hovered across from Marot. Its three heads seemed eerily human and more horrifying than the squirming snakes that composed its body. Marada blasted the winged angel with an icy breath, but the angel didn't flinch.

Three swords — all with crystal-red blades — flew off Marot's tentacles and pierced Marada's body. Then Marot fluttered his wings at a hummingbird's speed, closed in, and swiped at Marada's neck. A head severed, and a wave of air pushed the clouds. The flying head painted blood across the sky and puffed into black smoke.

Celene must've been giddy watching her angel fight. Even to me, something about it was wondrous. It…comforted me…because no matter what I did, I could never be as horrifying as that jinn and that angel battling in the sky. And if such things existed, and we could witness and be influenced by them, then surely it wasn't all on us, the ants that we were…

Or perhaps the pain ringing every bone in my body as if they were broken bells had pulled me into a stupor of befuddled thoughts. Either way, if this was the end, then I could die watching wonders.

Familiar human shadows loomed over me. Pashang and Eshe crouched at my side.

"Can you walk?" Pashang asked, pulling me from my stupor.

I couldn't even shake my head.

"Healer! Get a healer!" Eshe shouted. "My bloodrunes can't fix broken bones!"

"We need...to help Kevah." I wondered if I'd even made a sound. Pashang and Eshe put their ears to my face. I said, "Help Kevah kill Marot."

A wail like the births and deaths of a thousand demons rent the sky. Another of Marada's heads flew off, splattering blood across the clouds and then withering into smoke as it surged toward the land.

"What the hell is that thing swinging at?" Eshe said. Of course, he couldn't see Marada. He could only see Marot. For whatever reason, the angel had unveiled itself while the jinn hadn't.

Pashang said, "There's something there. If you squint, you can see its outline distorting the sky." He put his hand under me; the pain from the broken bone in my back made me see stars, figuratively. I wailed, so Pashang set me back down.

"Take...my hand," I mumbled to either of them. "I think...I finally understand...how this works. We need...to pray."

Eshe shook his head, seething as if angry I'd even suggested it. "No, we need to get you on a litter and get out of here."

The rumble of oncoming horses shook and nauseated me almost to sleep. Why were the Jotrids now galloping away from the gholam, whom they'd routed? What the hell could make them run from a human enemy toward an angel?

Ululating? It loudened with the endless earthquake of riders, the shrill cadence for which the gholam were known.

Meanwhile, Marot's sinuous tentacle wrapped around Marada's remaining head, pulled it off, and tossed it a hundred miles. The jinn sultana's body turned to blood and smoke. Had Marot won? Was it over?

I coughed blood and spit. The gholam' ululations deafened, coming from everywhere. Kato had said they feared no angel, but they seemed to not fear us, either. Pashang's dismal gaze told me they'd surrounded us. We'd lost. Their reinforcements had arrived, whereas ours, the Sylgiz, were days away.

In the sky above Marot, a hole appeared, through which was a black, starry heaven. A woman with brilliant blue and green peacock wings descended through it, a scepter in her hands. Her long black hair reminded me of my mother's, last I'd seen her, eight years ago. More than that, just the sight of her soothed my pain.

"Lat with peacock wings, holding a magnificent gold scepter," was how Pashang had described his third vision. Was that truly her? The god?

She aimed her scepter at Marot; it emitted a blinding aurora, from which I felt balms for all the pain, hopes from a heaven of stars and rings of light, and pure, warm memories that weren't even mine.

The angel turned to crystal and exploded, waves crying through the air, shards raining in all directions. They fell like hail upon us: clear, radiant, bloodless diamonds. Even the guts of a god were beautiful.

By Lat, did this mean Marot was dead now, too? She'd eliminated him so easily, as a true god would.

The gholam ululated louder as the angel died. Kato was right — the same had happened here. Eshe, Pashang, and I looked on, mouths agape. It seemed we could all see her. Lat had shown herself, finally.

"This is my final vision," Pashang said, joyful. "This…it's her."

"Is it truly Lat?" I asked, shuddering once more from the stabbing feeling in my broken back.

Pashang took my hand. "Let's pray. It's all been for this."

Eshe pulled our handhold apart. "She's killed the angel. There's nothing to pray for!"

"Eshe is right," I said. "I think I've had enough."

Pashang banged his knuckles onto sand. "Enough of what, life? The gholam are about to slaughter us. Why not *ascend*, instead?"

Ascend? Something about that word seemed so…alluring. To

ascend, to be above this blood and death. As if we were clouds, scoffing at the humans shooting arrows at us. To be…as the jinn… as the angels…as the gods…

Pashang held out his hand. I reached for it, but Eshe swatted it away.

"It's better to die," Eshe said. "Cyra, have you forgotten? Marot gave you the power to starwrite so you and Zedra could bring calamity. You mustn't use it, and especially not in desperation!"

Pashang got in his face. "We're on a path you could never understand. I'm here to remove the obstacles off that path…I like you, but best you not be one, Eshe. With a single choice, this is defeat, or the ultimate victory."

Victory…I wanted it. How could I let us lose, now, when we'd come so close?

Arrows rained on us. The Jotrids around fell with shrill, endless, gaping death screams. Some charged at the surrounding gholam, perhaps hoping against sense to break through. Given the breadth and depth of the gholam' hollering, they'd need wings.

"No surrender!" Pashang yelled. "Fight till the sands sip your blood!" We were in a sea of dying horses and men. An ocean of sand and blood and fear. All the while, arrows hailed. Jotrids ran to us, holding shields above our heads, blocking out the sun and sky. The shields *thump-thumped* as arrows hit them.

Pashang reached out for a third time. "Take it, Cyra. We can be below the sand, or we can be among the clouds."

Eshe hit the ground, cowering as an arrow landed next to his leg. "Don't do it, Cyra! There are fates worse than death!"

A fate worse than death. That was our path, wasn't it? But I couldn't agree. There was no fate worse than death, than annihilation. So long as there was life, there was hope.

And you, Eshe, you I'd never let them hurt.

The gholam stopped ululating and yelled as they charged us from all sides. The sounds tortured me: bombs exploding horses, gunshots bellowing, the grunts amid screaming steel, the final cries of life. Worse were the smells: rot and bile and sulfur, each drenched in defeat. And yet, I could do naught but lie here, the screeching ache in my back keeping me still.

No matter how excruciating the pain, I wouldn't choose death. I recalled the burning sadness the day I was taken from my yurt in the Waste, toward a new home, and that freezing abyss when I'd said goodbye to my brother and Tamaz as I cried in some shrine in Zelthuriya. It's true, I'd wished for death, but that was then, when I was powerless and reliant on the promises of others. Now, with a prayer, I could change it all.

Instead of leading his men in this hellish last stand, Pashang was here, kneeling next to me.

"A fate worse than death," he said. "Well, this is already pretty bad. Maybe Eshe is right. Let's just die." Somehow, I heard him clear as a ringing bell amid the awful cacophony. Hopeless words. Even the feared Khagan Pashang had lost his resolve, turning from man to boy as the noose tightened.

Blood sprayed everywhere as the gholam began a killing frenzy. And yet somehow, somewhere, I smelled flowers.

Eshe crawled next to me, careful to stay low. "Wish I had some seeds."

How sad to give up. To go willingly into death for someone else's cause. Zedra had won, but only because we chose to lose.

A horse with a sizzling bullet wound almost fell on me; its rider crashed into Eshe, then rolled off him. The rider had pissed his pants and now stuck his bleeding head on the sand, waiting to die. One by one, those shielding us fell, each to gunshots.

Pashang, too, waited to die, no prayers on his tongue. He looked at me, and I looked at him. *Ascend*…that sounded much better than what we waited for.

I grabbed his hand. He resembled the boy from memory, who'd tripped into a ditch and broken his leg, with only me to help him out and tend his wound. I whispered what I used to call him when we were children, and we both smiled.

Together, we prayed to the dark, dreaming sky. Prayed to live. Prayed to be free. Prayed for victory, for home.

The stars shone, floating above my body like so many fireflies. I connected the flickering ones, pulling them into each other's orbits. Above me, to my side, and near my navel. The final star was the color of blood, and when I touched it, it screamed.

With the shadows of frenzied gholam looming over us, their swords and spears and guns and arrows bearing down, the sky turned to rust.

And then, as if it were a tarp, it tore. A sinewy hand pushed out the tear, attached to an arm covered in eyes. It grabbed the woman with peacock wings. She flailed in its grip, dropping her scepter, which landed in the distance. The eyes on the arm blinked sideways a hundred times a second, the pupils changing color all the while. And then it crushed her. Crushed her so hard that she burst bloody.

With its blood-dripping fingers, the hand wrote something on a cloud. It resembled a tree. All the while, Eshe and I looked on with horror. Pashang with ecstasy. The bloodrune glowed, and the giant hand receded into the tear.

The gholam bearing down on us exploded, their heads flying in a bloody eruption. Bile stench filled the air, and rivers of innards surrounded us. What the hell had I prayed for? Was this victory? Was this…ascension?

"I was wrong," Pashang laughed, every speck of him covered in blood. "This is so much better than death!"

And yet, one thought resounded: *Did I just kill god?*

33

ZEDRA

I BLENDED INTO THE STINKING MASS OF REFUGEES WALKING THE ROAD to Dorud, baby Seluq at my chest. We'd run clear of the battle, but it would be a tiresome journey through thorny scrubland that seemed to hate whatever lived on it. The high sun's scorch made me want to throw off my clothes and rush into the ice pool…but I was as far from the harem bath as could be.

It wasn't long until Seluq cried; he was thirsty. For whatever cursed reason, I never was able to lactate, so I begged for water or milk from a big, pockmarked woman who herself was holding two babies; from a man in rags, his face swollen; from a dirt-faced brother and sister who barely reached my waist — what had happened to their mother and father?

Not a drop of sustenance, among so many. Or perhaps they were saving it for themselves, as any hoping to survive ought to. If only my bloodrunes could conjure food and milk, like Vera's grandmother could.

The dirt-faced girl reached into her caftan and presented something to me: a locust, roasted to hickory. No, I wouldn't feed my son one of Cyra's abominations. So I suffered his cries. At the very least, we were alive.

I didn't know who won the battle, whether the battle in the sky or on the land. I hoped not to find out until I reached Dorud. Nothing mattered except getting there, to the safety of Grand Vizier Barkam. But I had to survive this trek first.

Perhaps I should've sacrificed Celene when I had the chance. True, it would've cursed the land, but better to be rulers of a cursed land than dead. I'd lost because I couldn't go far enough. Perhaps the Children were no more because we could never be as cruel as our enemies, and so they inflicted cruelties upon us, time and time again, until we ceased to be.

Baby Seluq's cries only heightened…but it was a relief to have his warmth bundled against me. Kevah…Kevah had saved him, whisked him from Marot's frozen hands into Sadie's, and she'd given him to me. So now…now all we had to do was keep going. Keep breathing. If we could get to Dorud, perhaps there was a chance.

The ground rumbled from oncoming horsemen, each *thud-thud-thud* filling my heart with dread. I turned to see Jotrids getting larger on the horizon. A faintness threatened to topple me.

How foolish to have hope.

IT WASN'T long before I was sitting in a carriage, a prisoner of the Jotrids who'd encircled my child and me. No amount of begging would change their minds.

They'd bound my hands so tight, I could scarcely feel them. No chance for me to bloodwrite. Across sat a short-haired woman, blood and soot caked on her face. She fed drops of mare's milk to baby Seluq from her fingers, which seemed to calm him. I recognized those lithe hands, the daggers at her sides, and even the shape of her breasts. Elnur, the woman I'd soulshifted to kill Pashang and Cyra.

Her deadpan eyes wouldn't leave me, even as she shushed and rocked Seluq. What could I say to make her help me?

"You have children?"

She shook her head. "Only a stillborn."

"I…had a few of those. It's crushing. Like an eclipse seizing your light." I swallowed despair. "You won't hurt my baby, then, will you?"

She hunched her shoulders. "I'll do what I'm told."

Do what she's told…by who else but Pashang? The cruelest man in the kingdom. I shouldn't have expected more from a Jotrid.

"I'm sorry," I said. "For what I did to you." But I was sorrier I'd failed to kill Cyra and Pashang.

Elnur snickered. "Sure you are."

"You're not so talkative, are you? These could be my final moments. Tell me something good. Anything. Please, don't make it so terrible for me." It felt real now, my end. Finally, death. My throat sored, and no matter what, I couldn't stop shaking my leg, *tap-tap-taping* it on the carriage floor. My final tremors.

She sighed. "We've just come from a battle, lady. A battle caused by you. Gholam guns killed four of my cousins. My younger brother lost a leg. The lovely girl I was trying to get him engaged with burned to death. So, why don't you tell *me* something good?"

The carriage door opened. A man climbed inside: Pashang, covered head to toe in bloodstains, a book in his hand. *Melody of Nora* was written on the cover. He flipped it open, then showed me.

A bloodrune lay scrawled across the page. A memory writing rune — seven stars and an eye — which could only be written in god's blood and a few other rare flavors.

"You have a lovely smile, by the way," Pashang said. What an odd greeting. He reached over and untied my hands. They tingled as the color seeped back in.

"You've never seen me smile and never will."

He caressed baby Seluq's cheek, which made me hopeful, which terrified me, considering how my hopes had gone lately.

"Your long life has come to its end, Zedra. But Cyra meant what she said — we won't hurt you or your son. This bloodrune," he tapped the page, "this is who you really are."

I huffed, trying to understand. "You're going to replace my memories? But then I'll be someone else." I sighed. "So…that's what Cyra meant. If I'm not Zedra anymore, I won't know how to bloodwrite or soulshift."

"Not just someone else. You'll be you. You'll be Nora, the young girl whose body you're in."

Of course. It never made sense why I wasn't old, like in my memories. I'd never worn a magus mask, and yet, I made myself believe I had, to justify why I wasn't a hundred years old anymore. But nothing could explain why I didn't carry Chisti's god's blood, why my blood was such a base flavor.

"You knew her?" I asked. "You'd seen her smile?"

Pashang wiped blood from his eye. "I failed her and her tribe. That's what started all this — my weakness. Tell me, Zedra, will you beg forgiveness before you die?"

I shook my head. "From who? Are there any worthy to forgive me in the first place? Who is so wonderful that their forgiveness is my salvation? Truth is, we're all stuck in a vicious circle, hacking each other to bits so we can be safe from one another. And if you're not in that circle, it's because someone else is in there, killing for you." I took in the sight of my son, sleeping in the arms of an enemy. "Aside from our children. Theirs are the only forgiveness I'll seek."

"I, too, feel it's futile to beg. Maybe I can outweigh the bad with the good, like so many killers did. I'll start with your son. We'll keep him with us. Raise him. A Seluqal hostage, he'll be — the first in a long while."

That sounded better than death, at least. But my son was to be the Padishah of the Final Hour. Uniter of the East. The shield against the Great Terror. And yet, he wasn't even the Children, nor was he a Seluqal. He was the son of some terrible angel, and perhaps a chance at life was his best hope.

"And Nora? What will you do with her?"

Pashang shrugged. "That's up to Cyra."

"It doesn't matter, does it? I'm not her. I'll be gone…finally. Thank Lat. Much better than swallowing more of this pain — the pain of a people who are long dead and can never return."

"Oh, they'll return. In the hearts of all. To separate ourselves from the Seluqal kingdoms to our north and east, we're going to make Path of the Children the faith of Alanya. Cyra's idea."

I supposed being remembered and revered was a note better than annihilation.

"Is Kato…did he survive?" Only now did I consider those I'd endangered. Men and women who had families, too, that deserved better than tears. Only now did I sip their sadness. How bitter. "And Celene?"

"Can't say about Kato. Celene's our prisoner. I wonder what the Imperator of Crucis will offer to get her back…"

"She deserves to go home." I'd failed her, spectacularly, too, and could only hope her father would give the Jotrids whatever they wanted. "And what of Kyars?"

"He lost too many men, so we're going to siege the Sand Palace. If he's smart, he'll make for Merva or Zelthuriya before we surround it. I'd wager Qandbajar is as good as ours."

"Qandbajar is only a city. You'll have to fight for the rest of Alanya. And Kyars…he'll want his son back. Me back." By starting this war, I'd ended six hundred years of Seluqal rule in Qandbajar. And if Pashang's words were to be believed, I'd restored the Path of the Children as *the* path. How strange to lose it all and still win something.

"Of course he'll want you two back. The perfect bait." Pashang stretched and yawned. "The war is just beginning. I should thank you for starting it. To be true, I kind of like you, Zedra. A shame you'll be gone. Nora isn't nearly as interesting, I'm afraid."

That was some praise. "Do me another favor…" the shame choked me, and now I finally spilled my tears. "Don't tell my son about me. Don't let him believe his mother was so wretched. If Nora is the boring girl you claim, she'll be a better mother than I ever could."

"Come now, I would've loved to have you as a mother." Pashang chuckled. "But you're right — I think it best if everyone forgot you." He held the book open to the bloody page. "And I think it's about time to say your prayers."

So I would die as Zedra, a proud daughter of Chisti. But I wasn't her, was I? I'd warred for my blood, though I didn't have that blood, and neither did my son. The real Zedra, her soul must've been in Barzakh. I was just a shadow. A mirage.

And it'd all been for nothing. Nothing but the machinations of an evil angel who wanted to curse the land.

I kissed my sleeping son on the forehead. "Goodbye, Seluq."

I took a deep breath — my final one as Zedra — held out my finger, and touched the rune.

EPILOGUE
CYRA

THE PALACE WAS EMPTY BY THE TIME WE ARRIVED. KYARS HAD ENOUGH time, it seemed, to load the treasury and flee the city, leaving us with a precarious hold. But Qandbajar, my home, was the real treasure.

Those first nights in the Sand Palace were difficult, and not merely because of my screaming bones. Lying alone on silk sheets, the new moon unseen through the window, I thought about what I'd done, ceaselessly, and could hardly sleep or eat.

Was Lat really dead? Whose hand had crushed her? Was that what Marot wanted all along? No, not Marot — whomever Marot was serving.

"*It's not a game when you're the pawn being sacrificed,*" Marot had said when we confronted him in Basil's Cathedral. "*I'm going to suffer for my failure, but not alone,*" he'd said in the desert. But if Marot was a pawn, then what was I? What were any of us?

And why did Marot leave us two melodies when all he wanted was for us to kill Lat?

I wanted to ask Eshe, but he wasn't talking to me. When we

returned to Qandbajar, he left the palace, though I didn't know to where. With my injured back, I couldn't exactly walk around searching for him but later heard he was at his house in the Glass District. I requested he come to the palace, but he didn't acquiesce, so I took an escort and traveled to his apartment.

I saw him in the window, but he wouldn't open the door. I begged and begged, cried and cried, told him how much I loved him, but still he wouldn't face me. The Jotrids offered to break the door down, but if he didn't want to see me, then I wouldn't force him.

He'd said one final thing to me on the ride from the bloody desert to Qandbajar. He said I'd *"cursed the land"* and that in ten years, the blood plague would *"spread throughout Alanya"* just like it had in Himyar. It was my fault for not heeding him, for not accepting defeat, for not dying when we were supposed to.

In the end, it seemed I'd been used. Zedra had been used. Even Marot had been used...by whom, or what, I didn't know. Marot had mentioned his *father* and *grandmother*...but also that they weren't looking our way, yet. So who was his taskmaster, then? Could it be...the Dreamer?

And what of the Blood Star? The Morning Star? What were they? How had they become one and the same? Why had Marot taught us how to use them for sorcery? Just what was going on in the sky, so high above, that we were less than ants?

Too many questions, and no answers, whatsoever.

A week later, the Sylgiz arrived. My tribe. They filled the landscape outside the city, as they'd done when this ordeal began. We needed them — the Jotrids couldn't conquer Alanya on their own, with enemies in every direction. And so, after a tough negotiation, all of us sitting in a circle on the floor in the great hall, their new khagan, Gokberk — whom I hated because he once stomped on a puppy's neck, when we were children — finally agreed to an alliance after we promised him all the river-fed land east of Dorud, though we hadn't conquered it yet. Pashang told me later he would have Gokberk strangled, just in case, once things settled down.

To seal the alliance, Pashang and I married. It wasn't the ceremony a girl my age dreams about, but it resulted in something better. No one sat the throne, and it was agreed that a council of three Sylgiz and three Jotrids would make decisions.

Everyone quickly realized that a deadlocked council wasn't much good, so we decided I would be the tiebreaker. That gave me more power than I'd hoped for, but to be true, it all seemed so hollow.

Because, like last time, Mother wasn't among the Sylgiz who came. Cihan had said she was near death, though I never asked, and no one told me whether she still breathed. Perhaps I couldn't bear the pain of knowing I was truly, fully alone. What would she think of me, anyway? Would she be proud of her starwriter daughter with the bulging black eye, or horrified at what I'd done to win?

The conversion of the Jotrids was the other bedrock of our alliance. The same day as our marriage, a Silklander scholar named Wafiq, who wore the high felt hat and metal clasp of the Philosophers, presented himself to the council. He claimed to have memorized all the books of recorded sayings of the Twelve Chiefs of the Children — scores of tomes, each hundreds of pages, kept on the top floor of the Tower. Books that had been forbidden since the time of the saint-kings, that only the Philosophers had preserved, as they did all knowledge. He would revive the Path, he claimed, arguing that because the Sylgiz had no written texts, they weren't following the Path of the Children properly, despite the earnestness with which they cursed the saints. And so, the leaders of *both* tribes testified to the Faith — to worship only Lat through the intercession of the Children, alone.

And then the Sylgiz, overtaken by a crazed fanaticism, ripped the bodies of the saints from the shrines, burned them in a bonfire at the city center, threw them in a ditch, and covered them in the dung of their horses and herd animals.

It started a fight. Many Jotrids who couldn't stomach it, as well as tens of thousands of city folk, rioted and arrayed against them to defend the path they'd adhered to all their lives. The council of seven convened in the great hall to decide what to do, splitting down the middle — three Sylgiz wanting to impose the Path of the Children, and three Jotrids, including Pashang, desiring toleration of both paths.

I really considered both arguments. Thought about it perhaps more than I'd ever considered anything. The Seluqals remained the champions of the Path of the Saints, and unless we broke from their past, we would stay in their shadow. Though followers of the Path of the Children were few, they were most numerous in Merva, where Kyars was heading, and if Zedra had taught me anything, it was that they deserved justice for all they'd suffered.

So I broke the tie. We fired upon the rioters and the rebellious Jotrids, killing hundreds, but also ending the riots and sending a clear message: the Path of the Children was the only path in the new Alanya.

What would Khizr Khaz, who I assumed had departed either with Kyars or as his prisoner, think of me, now? What would Eshe? Kevah? Ozar? Hadrith? Mirima? And yet, if there was one thing I'd learned from this whole ordeal, it was that live or die, you had to choose a side. You had to make enemies. And so we continued to, from there on.

But it was all so hollow.

THE NIGHT after we put down the riots, I visited Nora and her son. We renamed him Kazin after the Twelfth Chief of the Children, Zedra's great-grandson. Pashang had insisted we keep Nora close because she could speak and read every language. I also wondered if she could still bloodwrite and soulshift, but now wasn't the time to test that.

Poor girl was still in grief — to her, the deaths of her family and tribe had just happened. She sat on her bed and stared at the ceiling while her son cried in his crib. Of course, she couldn't remember ever becoming a mother, either. But Pashang had told me she'd helped raise her sisters, one of whom was still alive, somewhere. I'd instructed some clerks to find out where the slavers had sold her, perchance we could reunite them.

Celene wheeled me to the base of Nora's bed and went to quiet the baby. I could hardly believe this girl wasn't Zedra. Those dark, marble eyes seemed less intense, and she kept her curly hair to the back rather than the sides. Still, something about her…one day, she went into the garden and gathered a fistful of red tulips, which Zedra always loved. I also saw her twirl, the way Zedra would when happy. She even liked the ice bath.

"Is it supper time?" she asked. Her accent was as slanted as mine when I first arrived in the harem, whereas Zedra spoke Paramic like she'd invented it.

"It's always supper time if you want it to be," I said with a smile.

But Nora only squirmed. Seemed I intimidated her.

"Can I go in the garden?"

"Of course. I'll call your escort." I had ten Jotrids guarding her at all times. I assumed intrigues would soon target her and her son, and so had to keep vigilant.

Before she left the room, I took her hand and clasped it. By Lat, we shared the exact hand size. I'd not held Zedra's hand before, so never noticed. I recalled the day I discovered the blood handprint in the steam chamber, which happened to fit me perfectly. How far I'd come from that crying girl, who could hardly stomach Hadrith's intrigues, let alone those of an angel.

• • •

THE NEXT DAY, Pashang and Gokberk and I gathered in one of the smaller, more intimate meeting rooms to discuss our missive to the Imperator of Crucis.

"Are we going to ally with heathens?" Gokberk said. Half his face was a scar, starting from where a bear had pulled off his ear. "To kill heretics?"

Pashang had taken to the palace's rose wine and so always clutched a goblet, though he never seemed drunk. "Heretics. Heathens. Your vocabulary is like a four-year-old, Gokberk…"

In the end, we requested Crucian guns, bombards, and engineers in exchange for Celene. When I told her about it, she shrugged and said, "You can try to send me home, but the Archangel has decreed I die here, in the east, in your service."

How nice to have my very own sycophant. But if given the choice, I knew she would go home. Once we'd forged an agreement with the Imperator, she'd have to.

Speaking of sycophants: I won't lie, I found Wafiq strange. He had those almond-shaped Silklander eyes, a patchy beard, and the most scholarly demeanor. He was second only to Grand Philosopher Litani, it seemed, and so knew much. Too much. People who know things tend to be indispensable, and he made himself so at our gatherings.

He would hold daily lectures about the true Path of the Children, filling the room with those who sought to be missionaries, or *Lightgivers*, as he liked to call them.

"The Padishah of the Final Hour is coming," he would say. "We will prepare for his arrival, as best we know how — by being righteous Latians. By honing all we do toward one purpose — the Faith. But our weapons are honed by knowledge, and so seek knowledge, even if you must travel to the Silklands…"

I wondered if, one day, we'd have to strangle him too, like we'd do for Gokberk. For now, his preaching helped bring purpose to two tribes that hated each other. If only Wafiq knew Lat was likely dead, what would he say, then?

. . .

AN UNEXPECTED VISITOR graced the great hall as our council took audience the next morning: Ruhi, clad in her black, all-covering veil. We'd sent the Disciples a missive days ago — the Archers of the Eye had vacated the city, so it traveled by horse — demanding they recognize our authority, renounce the Path of the Saints, and embrace the Path of the Children.

"We are here to give reply to your message," Ruhi said, standing with four other Disciples, all whom I recognized from that humiliating interrogation in Zelthuriya. "The Disciples of Chisti consider this palace stolen, and its current occupiers thieves. We encourage you to vacate, turn back to the straight path, and submit to justice, in the sight of Lat and her saints."

Not unexpected. To my right and left, beneath the golden divan, sat the Council of Seven, as we now officially called ourselves. All grumbled at Ruhi's words, whereas I smiled.

"Thank you for your answer," I said. I recalled Wafiq's lectures. "We hone all we do toward one purpose — the Faith. Our weapons are knowledge. Holy Zelthuriya was once the seat of learning, where Chisti and his Children taught mankind righteousness, truthfulness, and godliness." I wheeled myself forward, a few arm spans from Ruhi. "Tell the Disciples that the light of the Children will shine there, once more, very soon."

Of course, we couldn't hold Alanya without Zelthuriya. The Disciples wouldn't give it up without a battle, one we'd have to begin planning.

Ruhi shook her head. "I knew you were a rotten date. But I didn't expect...*this*. Truly, Cyra, turn back. The straight path is always there. It's never too late."

I spread my arms out. "This is the straight path. The only straight path. Best you get on it before it's too late."

That night, Pashang bedded me. Finally. He had to be gentle because my bones had barely healed. It hurt at first, but it was quite nice by the end. Afterward, we sat on the balcony and took reports from a Jotrid scout — apples, wine, and a midnight breeze our comforts.

"Kyars' army makes its way to Merva. The magus, Kevah, and his lady are among them, as well as a third companion known to be a Crucian spy. Khizr Khaz, however, was not sighted there, and neither was gholam commander Kato."

So that was where they'd gone. I assumed Kevah would return to Zelthuriya, but it seemed he had some other plan. Sheikh Khizr might be in the holy city, though. Kato, I could only hope, was a puddle of blood in the desert.

Pashang downed his rose wine, then refilled his goblet. "Mansur's children...one is a true...true man in my own image. He won't let Kyars just walk into Merva, especially after what he did to his father."

The thought of someone else squashing Kyars for us seemed too good to be true. "But if they do join their hosts, and if Barkam marches on us, too..." I spilled my wine on the floor.

"That's precious treasure, don't waste it!" Pashang said, snapping his fingers at a eunuch to clean my spill. "Let's do the clever thing. We'll send spies into both camps, light some fires, make them think they're attacking each other. I don't think it'll be so hard."

"What about Zelthuriya? Should we not focus on that? Can you imagine how stunned the world would be if we took the center of the Faith?"

"Stunned enough for all the Latian kingdoms to unite against us?"

We planned and plotted until I fell into a wine stupor.

THE NEXT NIGHT, he finally came to see me. Eshe. Seemed I'd sent the message that without his guidance, I was doomed to inflict the horrors he'd warned about.

But I was wrong. That wasn't why he'd come.

Celene wheeled me into the garden, then left us alone. A waning crescent hung in the sky, milky and bright. Fireflies fluttered about — not the green ones. Heavy dew moistened the air and glowed on the buds of red tulips.

"I made a mistake," he said, "that day when I risked my life to carry you to Zelthuriya. I should have let you die. If only I'd known."

Hearing those words, I cried for the first time in days. "I don't regret saving you, and I never will."

He'd become...gaunt. Had he been eating? The bags under his eyes made clear he hadn't been sleeping, either. But in that, we were alike.

"You chose, Cyra, but you chose wrong. And now everyone has to suffer." He shook his head, as if shaking off his rage. "No, *I* chose wrong. It was my test, and I let my feelings for you poison me."

Was I really so evil? But I never wanted this. Fate had thrust it upon me, cruelly. "I'm sorry," I said, as if I were apologizing for spilling wine.

"I came to tell you that I'll be devoting my time to stopping the blood plague. Stopping its spread, so it doesn't engulf our country like it did to Himyar. Regardless of who rules, that's something no one wants."

Hopeful words. So, he wasn't shunning me entirely. He needed me. "Of course, Eshe. That's what I want, too. I'll support you in every way I can."

He snickered and smiled, the saddest smile I'd ever seen. Tears streamed into his beard. "You think you can sin and then just be forgiven because you're sorry? Have you asked each and every person you made suffer, and each of their families, for forgiveness, too? You think you can sin and be forgiven without justice? There's no forgiveness for what you've done, for what you're doing, to this country, every day."

But truly, was I so different from Tamaz? Unlike him, I wasn't hiding behind the Jotrids, letting them *soak the blood so my floor could sparkle.* Didn't Eshe see that at least I wasn't a hypocrite?

A gust rustled the palms and added a chill to my tongue. "The truth is, Eshe…the thing is you never asked Ruhi for forgiveness, either. Because you believed you served the greater good, despite the suffering you caused her. But the truth is, if you don't value a single human life, you don't value any of them. And I did what I had to do. I was given an awful choice, but at least I made it. I didn't leave it to someone else. I'm the one soaking in blood, bearing the sins, because that's what it takes to rule Alanya."

Eshe turned his back, as if too disgusted to look at me. "Justify it, like all the others, then. I never claimed I was a good person, but I hoped you were. That's why it hurts so much."

"I never claimed that, either. I'm sorry I didn't listen when you tried to steer me right…but if I had to choose, I'd do it again. I'm done trying to walk the straight path. I'm done trying to be good."

"I couldn't steer you right…because I don't know right in the first place. I was relieved when you saved us. I was only too happy to keep breathing, at the cost of everything. The truth is, I hate what I am, and I hate that you're as lost as me."

"Don't you see, Eshe? We all are. The blind can't lead the blind!"

At that, he walked away, leaving me alone amid the red tulips and fireflies.

CELENE WHEELED me to my room, to the balcony with its soothing breeze. I looked upon Qandbajar — how peaceful it finally seemed. And yet…how hollow. This wasn't how home was supposed to feel. This wasn't a place of hope. No more Eshe, Zedra, Kyars, Tamaz, Ozar, Mirima, Sambal, Vera, Hadrith. They'd been replaced by strange names: Pashang, Wafiq, Gokberk, Nora, Celene. Was my home merely a city named Qandbajar? An ordered pile of mud, brick, and stone? Or was it the familiar names that made it home?

Had I come all this way, fought all these battles, only to realize I could never go back? Back to that time and place, where our cares weighed little, and the stars were merely lights for the night? Was my home gone forever, and would I forever long for it?

Everything had changed, was changing, and would change. A new Alanya, a new path, a new place at the center of the world. This was what it had been for. Perhaps hope was the home I could build atop the one I'd destroyed.

WANT MORE?

Kevah faces off against Cyra in Elder Epoch (Gunmetal Gods Book 3)! Get it at Books2Read.com/EE

WANT MORE?

Get *Death Rider*, a prequel novella to Gunmetal Gods, for FREE by joining
my mailing list at ZamilAkhtar.com!

THANK YOU. PLEASE READ!

So, how're you feeling? What did you think?

If you enjoyed yourself, please leave a review on Amazon for Conqueror's Blood and Gunmetal Gods as well. **Please.** There are thousands of books published everyday, and this one needs all the help it can get to rise to the top. Even just clicking the star rating is hugely helpful. Your review could help launch this novel into the heavens and beyond. And that means I get to write more books in this series.

I really can't overstate the importance of every reader leaving a review. I'm counting on you!

The Gunmetal Gods Saga grew out of my desire to create a Middle Eastern fantasy world that was as magical and deep as the best in fantasy. To me, this series is a love letter to Middle Eastern mythology and history, and an expression of the dark depths that this region that I call home has often found itself in.

Thank you for letting me tell my story. It means everything to me.

All the love,

Zamil

FOLLOW ME!

I'd love to see you around, so please follow me at the links below. I'd REALLY love to see you on my Patreon, where I post exclusive short stories. Support me and help me write more books!

Redditors, join my subreddit. It's my most active platform!

Patreon: https://patreon.com/zamakhtar

Reddit: https://www.reddit.com/r/zamakhtar/

Facebook: https://facebook.com/zamakhtar1/

Twitter: https://twitter.com/zamakhtar

Instagram: https://www.instagram.com/zamilakhtarauthor/

QUICK GLOSSARY

Ahriyya
A dark god, scorned in the Latian faith

Alanyans
Denizens of the Kingdom of Alanya

Archers of the Eye
An Ethosian order that relays messages in Alanya, originally from
Labash

Baladict / Barzakh
Believed to be where souls go immediately after death

Children
The descendants of Father Chisti. Revered by those on the Path of
the Children.

Crucians
Denizens of the Holy Empire of Crucis

Disciples of Chisti
A saintly order responsible for protecting Zelthuriya, the Latian
holy city

Ejazi
Denizens of Ejaz, an island kingdom south of Sirm

Ethosians
Worshippers of the Archangel

Excubitors
Loyal guardsmen of the Imperator of Crucis

Fanaa
Paramic word meaning "annihilation" of identity and desire

Gholam
Loyal slave soldiers of the Shah of Alanya

Himyarites
Denizens of the Sultanate of Himyar, south of Alanya

Janissaries
Loyal slave soldiers of the Shah of Sirm

Jinn
An invisible spirit said to be the source of magic

Jotrids
An Endless Waste tribe that is a Seluqal client

Kashanese
Denizens of the Kingdom of Kashan

Khazis
Mystical warriors of the Latian faith

Labashites
Denizens of the Kingdom of Labash, south of Alanya

Latians
Worshippers of the goddess Lat

Lidya
The eastern continent, home to Sirm, Alanya, and Kashan

Majlis
A parliament of viziers without binding power

Padishah
Ruler of all three Seluqal kingdoms

Paramic
Liturgical language of the Latian faith and common tongue of the
Kingdom of Alanya

Pasgardians
Denizens of Pasgard, a territory of Crucis

Philosophers
An order of scientists that operate from the Tower of Wisdom in
Qandbajar

Rubadi
A clan of nomadic horse warriors, related to the zabadar

Ruh
Paramic word for soul or spirit

Ruthenians
Denizens of Ruthenia, a country north of Crucis

Saint-Kings
Saint Chisti's successors and rulers of Alanya prior to the Seluqal House. Revered by those on the Path of the Saints.

Sargosans
Denizens of Sargosa, a client kingdom of Crucis in the west of Yuna

Seluqal
The royal house of Sirm, Alanya, and Kashan

Silklanders
Denizens of the Silk Empire

Simurgh
A giant bird from myth

Sirmians
Denizens of the Kingdom of Sirm

Sylgiz
An Endless Waste tribe that revere the Children

Thamesians
Denizens of Thames, a country north of Crucis

Yam Sup Sea
An inlet of the Kashanese Sea in Himyar

Yuna
The western continent, home to Crucis

Vogras
A mountainous region northeast of Alanya, from where descends
the Vogras River

Zabadar
Horse warriors that live in the plains of Sirm

REVIEW THIS BOOK, OR SAY BYE-BYE TO YOUR LOVELY SHOES!

www.ingramcontent.com/pod-product-compliance
Lightning Source LLC
Chambersburg PA
CBHW010838190726
48286CB00012BA/2897